I AM CRYING
ALL INSIDE

I AM CRYING ALL INSIDE

ALL INSIDE

AND OTHER STORIES

The Complete Short Fiction
of Clifford D. Simak,
Volume One

OPEN ROAD

INTEGRATED MEDIA

NEW YORK

"Installment Plan" © 1958 by Galaxy Publishing Corp. © 1986 by Clifford D. Simak. Originally published in *Galaxy Magazine*, v. 17, no. 3, Feb., 1959. Reprinted by permission of the Estate of Clifford D. Simak.

"I Had No Head and My Eyes Were Floating Way Up in the Air" © 2015 by the Estate of Clifford D. Simak. Published by permission of the Estate of Clifford D. Simak.

"Small Deer" © 1965 by Galaxy Publishing Corp. © 1993 by the Estate of Clifford D. Simak. Originally published in *Galaxy Magazine*, v. 24, no. 1, Oct., 1965. Reprinted by permission of the Estate of Clifford D. Simak.

"Ogre" © 1943 by Street & Smith Publications, Inc. © 1971 by Clifford D. Simak. Originally published in *Astounding Science Fiction*, v. 32, no. 5, January, 1944. Reprinted by permission of the Estate of Clifford D. Simak.

"Gleaners" © 1959 by Digest Productions Corp. © 1987 by Clifford D. Simak. Originally published in *If*, v. 10, no. 1, March, 1960. Reprinted by permission of the Estate of Clifford D. Simak.

"Madness from Mars" © 1939 by Better Publications, Inc. © 1967 by Clifford D. Simak. Originally published in *Thrilling Wonder Stories*, v. 13, no. 2, April, 1939. Reprinted by permission of the Estate of Clifford D. Simak.

"Gunsmoke Interlude" © 1952 by Popular Publications, Inc. © 1980 by Clifford D. Simak. Originally published in *10 Story Western Magazine*, v. 46, no. 3, October, 1952. Reprinted by permission of the Estate of Clifford D. Simak.

"I Am Crying All Inside" © 1969 by Universal Publishing & Distributing Corp. © 1997 by the Estate of Clifford D. Simak. Originally published in *Galaxy Science Fiction*, v. 28, no. 6, August, 1969. Reprinted by permission of the Estate of Clifford D. Simak.

"The Call from Beyond" © 1950 by Fictioneers, Inc. © 1978 by Clifford D. Simak. Originally published in *Super Science Stories*, v. 6, no. 4, May, 1950. Reprinted by permission of the Estate of Clifford D. Simak.

"All the Traps of Earth" © 1960 by Mercury Press, Inc. © 1988 by the Estate of Clifford D. Simak. Originally published in *The Magazine of Fantasy & Science Fiction*, v. 18, no. 3, March, 1960. Reprinted by permission of the Estate of Clifford D. Simak.

Cover design by Jason Gabbert

978-1-5040-1267-6

Published in 2015 by Open Road Integrated Media, Inc.
345 Hudson Street
New York, NY 10014
www.openroadmedia.com

CONTENTS

CLIFFORD D. SIMAK:
GRAND MASTER INDEED!

---

*"Music that had the whisper of rockets and the quietness of the void
and the somber arches of eternal night."*
—Clifford D. Simak in "The Call from Beyond"

You are holding, either in your hands or in your circuits, the first volume of a projected series of fourteen collections that will, in the end, encompass every piece of professionally published short fiction known to the author's estate to have been written by one of the giants of science fiction, Clifford D. Simak. In addition, you will find here a Simak story that has never before been published: a piece of fiction, written for Harlan Ellison, that was intended for inclusion in the third volume of Ellison's three-part Dangerous Visions anthology, which was to have been entitled *The Last Dangerous Visions*™. Alas, that third volume has never been published. But the Simak Estate, and this editor personally, offer thanks to Mr. Ellison for his generosity in releasing that story to allow for its inclusion in this volume.

When the Science Fiction Writers of America, in 1977, named Clifford Donald Simak the third person to receive its Grand Master award, he had been writing science fiction for well over four decades—and while the award certainly reflected the esteem in which the honoree was held by his fellow writers, it also reflected their respect for, and appreciation of, the place his writings occupied in the history and development of science fiction.

It's not known exactly when Cliff Simak began writing science fiction. Born in 1904, he spent his youth in deeply rural southwestern Wisconsin, where he read stories by such writers as Jules Verne, Edgar Rice Burroughs, and H. G. Wells—but it was not until 1927 (just about the time he moved to Madison, Wisconsin, in order to take some journalism courses) that he chanced upon a copy of *Amazing Stories*. Perhaps it was simply that being in the city, rather than on farms or in small towns, put him in a place where such magazines were available to be discovered; but at any rate, he became a regular reader of science fiction magazines, and soon thereafter he himself began writing—and in the end, the period between his first and last fiction publications would span about fifty-five years.

In 1929 Cliff, newly married, left college to take advantage of an opportunity to work in journalism. With his new bride, Kay, he moved to Michigan to work on the *Iron River Reporter*. He quickly moved up to having his own column, (entitled "Driftwood"), and within a few years, he was the paper's editor.

It's hard to know just when Cliff started writing fiction. Although he kept a series of journals in which he recorded some of his submissions and sales (and occasionally other events, such as the purchase of a supply of firewood), he was sporadic at best in his data entry, and it's probable that some of those journals, like some of his stories, did not survive a lifestyle that was, for a long period, extraordinarily itinerant. A journal entry shows that he had already written and submitted at least one story in 1930, and during the following year, he sold at least six stories.

Most Simak fans have heard that Cliff's first sale was a story called "The Cubes of Ganymede," which was apparently accepted by *Amazing Stories* and held for several years before being returned with a note indicating that it no longer met the magazine's needs. Cliff, who by then had sold a number of other stories, apparently did not attempt to resubmit "Cubes" anywhere else, and at some unknown time thereafter it vanished from the author's files. (Cliff would later say that "Cubes" was "fairly bad.")

But what most Simak fans do not realize is that he wrote an even earlier tale, one that eventually did reach publication. Cliff's journals show that he actually wrote "Mutiny on Mercury" before writing either "The Cubes of Ganymede" or "The World of the Red Sun." "Mutiny" would be Cliff's first known submission, but because it was initially rejected and "Cubes" was held up, "Red Sun" became his first fiction publication. ("Mutiny" would sell a short time later.)

Of particular interest is the fact that "Red Sun," Cliff's very first published work of fiction, was listed on the cover of the issue of *Wonder Stories* in which it appeared. And as with the other authors featured in the issue, there was a line drawing of Simak, likely done by the legendary Frank R. Paul, as well as a brief introduction to the young author, which may have been written by the magazine's editor in chief, the even more legendary Hugo Gernsback. One can only speculate on how exciting this must have been for a beginning author.

Over the next two decades, Clifford D. Simak would continue writing science fiction at short length but would also try his hand at other genres, including weird fantasy, Westerns, war stories, mysteries—and there were a few stories that we cannot now characterize, since they have vanished, leaving us with only their names to go by. He wrote some nonfiction, too, including "outdoor" sorts of stories such as "In the Wisconsin Bush"—but none of these, so far as we know, were published, and none survive.

Although Cliff seems to have begun his fiction career in science fiction—no surprise, considering his early interest in the field—he nonetheless had a Western rejected in 1933. Westerns were popular in the early part of the twentieth century, and it's likely that Cliff, having grown up in a very rural area, was exposed to them early and often. And so it was that while he continued to write science fiction (including the beginning stories of the *City* cycle) before and during World War II, he also began to sell Westerns and war stories. It is worth noting that, true to his inclinations to avoid the cliché, none of Cliff's fourteen published Westerns were of the stereotypical cowboy-and-Indian sort. But with the exception of one Western, likely written earlier, all of his fiction published after 1949 would be in the science fiction and fantasy field.

Also in the fifties, Cliff began moving into the writing of novels (his only prior novel, *Cosmic Engineers*, had been written specifically for magazine serialization at the request of John W. Campbell Jr.), but he would always keep his hand in the short-story field. And it was during this period that he began to win awards for his fiction— awards that had not even existed in his first two decades in writing.

In 1953 Cliff was awarded the International Fantasy Award for his book *City*, which was not actually a novel but a compilation of a series of related stories, with interstitial connecting materials. When the Hugo Award was created, he began winning some of those (for "The Big Front Yard" in 1959, *Way Station* in 1964, and "The Grotto of the Dancing Deer" in 1981)—and when the Nebulas were invented, he won one of those (for "Grotto" in 1981 again). His novel *A Heritage of Stars* won the Jupiter Award for Best Novel in 1978; and just before his death, he was one of the three inaugural winners of the Horror Writers' Association's Bram Stoker Award for Lifetime Achievement.

When Clifford D. Simak won that last Hugo and that Nebula (for "Grotto of the Dancing Deer"), he had been writing fiction for more than fifty years.

One result of all this is that Clifford D. Simak became, and will likely remain, the only person ever to have won a Hugo, a Nebula, and an International Fantasy Award. Probably this is a somewhat unfair observation, since the International Fantasy Award, based in England, lasted less than ten years before becoming defunct, but in its day it developed an unmatched record of recognizing future classic fiction in the fields of fantasy and science fiction: Stewart's

Earth Abides, Tolkien's *Lord of the Rings*, Sturgeon's *More Than Human*, Collier's *Fancies and Goodnights*, and Pangborn's *A Mirror for Observers*, for example.

But if a science fiction writer's career is to be measured by his or her list of awards, it should be kept in mind that Cliff Simak had been a published writer for nearly two decades before any of those awards was created—and who is to say how many Hugos or Nebulas he might have won if any of them had been in existence when he was writing such stories as "Tools," "Huddling Place," "Desertion," or "Earth for Inspiration."

David W. Wixon

INSTALLMENT PLAN

This story originally appeared in the February 1959 issue of Galaxy
Magazine, *but it was an effort to get it there. A note in Cliff's journal
says that he "finished work on 'Installment Plan' and [was] greatly dis-
satisfied"—but he sent it to the magazine's editor, Horace Gold, anyway.
Gold sent it back for revisions, but he also suggested that Cliff make a
series of it and pledged himself to buy the series. Cliff did revise the
story, and then started plotting a second "robot team" story—at which
point Gold returned "Installment Plan" for more revisions, which Cliff
provided within a week. But Cliff's notes give no hint that he ever again
thought of returning to the second tale.*

*I like this story quite a lot, and it puzzles me that Cliff apparently
did not . . . but then, he was not one to indulge in sequels.*

—dww

I

The mishap came at dusk, as the last floater was settling down above
the cargo dump, the eight small motors flickering bluely in the twilight.

One instant it was floating level, a thousand feet above the
ground, descending gently, with its cargo stacked upon it and the

riding robots perched atop the cargo. The next instant it tilted as first one motor failed and then a second one. The load of cargo spilled and the riding robots with it. The floater, unbalanced, became a screaming wheel, spinning crazily, that whipped in a tightening, raging spiral down upon the base.

Steve Sheridan tumbled from the pile of crates stacked outside his tent. A hundred yards away, the cargo hit with a thundering crash that could be heard and felt above the screaming of the floater. The crates and boxes came apart and the crushed and twisted merchandise spread into a broken mound.

Sheridan dived for the open tent flaps and, as he did, the floater hit, slicing into the radio shack, which had been set up less than an hour before. It tore a massive hole into the ground, half burying itself, throwing up a barrage of sand and gravel that bulleted across the area, drumming like a storm of sleet against the tent.

A pebble grazed Sheridan's forehead and he felt the blast of sand against his cheek. Then he was inside the tent and scrambling for the transmog chest that stood beside the desk.

"Hezekiah!" he bawled. "Hezekiah, where are you!"

He fumbled his ring of keys and found the right one and got it in the lock. He twisted and the lid of the chest snapped open.

Outside, he could hear the pounding of running robot feet.

He thrust back the cover of the chest and began lifting out the compartments in which the transmogs were racked.

"Hezekiah!" he shouted.

For Hezekiah was the one who knew where all the transmogs were; he could lay his hands upon any one of them that might be needed without having to hunt for it.

Behind Sheridan, the canvas rustled and Hezekiah came in with a rush. He brushed Sheridan to one side.

"Here, let me, sir," he said.

"We'll need some roboticists," said Sheridan. "Those boys must be smashed up fairly bad."

"Here they are. You better handle them, sir. You do it better than any one of us."

Sheridan took the three transmogs and dropped them in the pocket of his jacket.

"I'm sorry there are no more, sir," Hezekiah said. "That is all we have."

"These will have to do," said Sheridan. "How about the radio shack? Was anyone in there?"

"I understand that it was quite empty. Silas had just stepped out of it. He was very lucky, sir."

"Yes, indeed," agreed Sheridan.

He ducked out of the tent and ran toward the mound of broken crates and boxes. Robots were swarming over it, digging frantically. As he ran, he saw them stoop and lift free a mass of tangled metal. They hauled it from the pile and carried it out and laid it on the ground and stood there looking at it.

Sheridan came up to the group that stood around the mass of metal.

"Abe," he panted, "did you get out both of them?"

Abraham turned around. "Not yet, Steve. Max is still in there."

Sheridan pushed his way through the crowd and dropped on his knees beside the mangled robot. The midsection, he saw, was so deeply dented that the front almost touched the back. The legs were limp and the arms were canted and locked at a crazy angle. The head was twisted and the crystal eyes were vacant.

"Lem," he whispered. "Lemuel, can you hear me?"

"No, he can't," said Abraham. "He's really busted up."

"I have roboticists in my pocket." Sheridan got to his feet. "Three of them. Who wants a go at it? It'll have to be fast work."

"Count me in," Abraham said, "and Ebenezer there and . . ."

"Me, too," volunteered Joshua.

"We'll need tools," said Abraham. "We can't do a thing unless we have some tools."

"Here are the tools," Hezekiah called out, coming on the trot. "I knew you would need them."

"And light," said Joshua. "It's getting pretty dark, and from the looks of it, we'll be tinkering with his brain."

"We'll have to get him up someplace," declared Abraham, "so we can work on him. We can't with him lying on the ground."

"You can use the conference table," Sheridan suggested.

"Hey, some of you guys," yelled Abraham, "get Lem over there on the conference table."

"We're digging here for Max," Gideon yelled back. "Do it yourself."

"We can't," bawled Abraham. "Steve is fixing to get our transmogs changed . . ."

"Sit down," ordered Sheridan. "I can't reach you standing up. And has someone got a light?"

"I have one, sir," said Hezekiah, at his elbow. He held out a flash.

"Turn it on those guys so I can get the transmogs in."

Three robots came stamping over and picked up the damaged Lemuel. They lugged him off toward the conference table.

In the light of the flash, Sheridan got out his keys, shuffled swiftly through them and found the one he wanted.

"Hold that light steady. I can't do this in the dark."

"Once you did," said Ebenezer. "Don't you remember, Steve? Out on Galanova. Except you couldn't see the labels and you got a missionary one into Ulysses when you thought you had a woodsman and he started preaching. Boy, was that a night!"

"Shut up," said Sheridan, "and hold still. How do you expect me to get these into you if you keep wiggling?"

He opened the almost invisible plate in the back of Ebenezer's skull and slid it quickly down, reached inside and found the spacehand transmog. With a quick twist, he jerked it out and dropped it in his pocket, then popped in the roboticist transmog, clicked it into place and drove it home. Then he shoved up the brain plate and heard it lock with a tiny click.

Swiftly he moved along. He had switched the transmogs in the other two almost as soon as Ebenezer had regained his feet and picked up the kit of tools.

"Come on, men," said Ebenezer. "We have work to do on Lem."

The three went striding off.

Sheridan looked around. Hezekiah and his light had disappeared, galloping off somewhere, more than likely, to see to something else.

The robots still were digging into the heap of merchandise. He ran around the pile to help them. He began pulling stuff from the pile and throwing it aside.

Beside him, Gideon asked: "What did you run into, Steve?"

"Huh?"

"Your face is bloody."

Sheridan put up his hand. His face was wet and sticky. "A piece of gravel must have hit me."

"Better have Hezekiah fix it."

"After Max is out," said Sheridan, going back to work.

They found Maximilian fifteen minutes later, at the bottom of the heap. His body was a total wreck, but he still could talk.

"It sure took you guys long enough," he said.

"Ah, dry up," Reuben said. "I think you engineered this so you could get a new body."

They hauled him out and skidded him along the ground. Bits of broken arms and legs kept dropping off him. They plunked him on the ground and ran toward the radio shack.

Maximilian squalled after them: "Hey, come back! You can't just dump me here!"

Sheridan squatted down beside him. "Take it easy, Max. The floater hit the radio shack and there's trouble over there."

"Lemuel? How is Lemuel?"

"Not too good. The boys are working on him."

"I don't know what happened, Steve. We were going all right and all at once the floater bucked us off."

"Two of the motors failed," said Sheridan. "Just why, we'll probably never know, now that the floater's smashed. You sure you feel all right?"

"Positive. But don't let the fellows fool around. It would be just like them to hold out on a body. Just for laughs. Don't let them."

"You'll have one as soon as we can manage. I imagine Hezekiah is out running down spare bodies."

"It does beat all," said Maximilian. "Here we had all the cargo down—a billion dollars' worth of cargo and we hadn't broken—"

"That's the way it is, Max. You can't beat the averages."

Maximilian chuckled. "You human guys," he said. "You always figure averages and have hunches and . . ."

Gideon came running out of the darkness. "Steve, we got to get those floater motors stopped. They're running wild. One of them might blow."

"But I thought you fellows—"

"Steve, it's more than a spacehand job. It needs a nuclear technician."

"Come with me."

"Hey!" yelled Maximilian.

"I'll be back," said Sheridan.

At the tent, there was no sign of Hezekiah. Sheridan dug wildly through the transmog chest. He finally located a nuclear technician transmog.

"I guess you're elected," he said to Gideon.

"Okay," the robot said. "But make it fast. One of those motors can blow and soak the entire area with radiation. It wouldn't bother us much, but it would be tough on you."

Sheridan clicked out the spacehand transmog, shoved the other in.

"Be seeing you," said Gideon, dashing from the tent.

Sheridan stood staring at the scattered transmogs.

Hezekiah will give me hell, he thought.

Napoleon walked into the tent. He had his white apron tucked into the belt. His white cook's hat was canted on his head.

"Steve," he asked, "how would you like a cold supper for tonight?"

"I guess it would be all right."

"That floater didn't only hit the shack. It also flattened the stove."

"A cold supper is fine. Will you do something for me?"

"What is it?"

"Max is out there, scared and busted up and lonely. He'll feel better in the tent."

Napoleon went out, grumbling: "Me, a chef, lugging a guy . . ."

Sheridan began picking up the transmogs, trying to get them racked back in order once again.

Hezekiah returned. He helped pick up the transmogs, began rearranging them.

"Lemuel will be all right, sir," he assured Sheridan. "His nervous system was all tangled up and short-circuiting. They had to cut out great hunks of wiring. About all they have at the moment, sir, is a naked brain. It will take a while to get him back into a body and all hooked up correctly."

"We came out lucky, Hezekiah."

"I suppose you are right, sir. I imagine Napoleon told you about the stove."

Napoleon came in, dragging the wreckage that was Maximilian, and propped it against the desk.

"Anything else?" he asked with withering sarcasm.

"No, thank you, Nappy. That is all."

"Well," demanded Maximilian, "how about my body?"

"It will take a while," Sheridan told him. "The boys have their hands full with Lemuel. But he's going to be all right."

"That's fine," said Maximilian. "Lem is a damn good robot. It would be a shame to lose him."

"We don't lose many of you," Sheridan observed.

"No," said Maximilian. "We're plenty tough. It takes a lot to destroy us."

"Sir," Hezekiah said, "you seem to be somewhat injured. Perhaps I should call in someone and put a medic transmog in him . . ."

"It's all right," said Sheridan. "Just a scratch. If you could find some water, so I could wash my face?"

"Certainly, sir. If it is only minor damage, perhaps I can patch you up."

He went to find the water.

"That Hezekiah is a good guy, too," said Maximilian, in an expansive mood. "Some of the boys think at times that he's a sort of sissy, but he comes through in an emergency."

"I couldn't get along without Hezekiah," Sheridan answered evenly. "We humans aren't rough and tough like you. We need someone to look after us. Hezekiah's job is in the very best tradition."

"Well, what's eating you?" asked Maximilian. "I *said* he was a good guy."

Hezekiah came back with a can of water and a towel. "Here's the water, sir. Gideon said to tell you the motors are okay. They have them all shut off."

"I guess that just about buttons it all up—if they're sure of Lemuel," Sheridan said.

"Sir, they seemed very sure."

"Well, fine," said Maximilian, with robotic confidence. "Tomorrow morning we can start on the selling job."

"I imagine so," Sheridan said, standing over the can of water and taking off his jacket.

"This will be an easy one. We'll be all cleaned up and out of here in ninety days or less."

Sheridan shook his head. "No, Max. There's no such thing as an easy one."

He bent above the can and sloshed water on his face and head.

And that was true, he insisted to himself. An alien planet was an alien planet, no matter how you approached it. No matter how thorough the preliminary survey, no matter how astute the planning, there still would always be that lurking factor one could not foresee.

Maybe if a crew could stick to just one sort of job, he thought, it eventually might be possible to work out what amounted to a foolproof routine. But that was not the way it went when one worked for Central Trading.

Central Trading's interests ran to many different things. Garson IV was sales. Next time it could just as well be a diplomatic mission or a health-engineering job. A man never knew what he and his crew of robots might be in for until he was handed his assignment.

He reached for the towel.

"You remember Carver VII?" he asked Maximilian.

"Sure, Steve. But that was just hard luck. It wasn't Ebenezer's fault he made that small mistake."

"Moving the wrong mountain is not a small mistake," Sheridan observed with pointed patience.

"That one goes right back to Central," Maximilian declared, with a show of outrage. "They had the blueprints labeled wrong . . ."

"Now let's hold it down," Sheridan advised. "It is past and done with. There's no sense in getting all riled up."

"Maybe so," said Maximilian, "but it burns me. Here we go and make ourselves a record no other team can touch. Then Central pulls this boner and pins the blame on us. I tell you, Central's got too big and clumsy."

And smug as well, thought Sheridan, but he didn't say it. Too big and too complacent in a lot of ways. Take this very planet, for example. Central should have sent a trading team out here many years ago, but instead had fumed and fussed around, had connived and schemed; they had appointed committees to delve into the situation and there had been occasional mention of it at the meetings of the board, but there had been nothing done until the matter had ground its way through the full and awesome maze of very proper channels.

A little competition, Sheridan told himself, was the very thing that Central needed most. Maybe, if there were another outfit out to get the business, Central Trading might finally rouse itself off its big, fat dignity, he was thinking when Napoleon came clumping in and banged a plate and glass and bottle down upon the table. The plate was piled with cold cuts and sliced vegetables; the bottle contained beer.

Sheridan looked surprised. "I didn't know we had beer."

"Neither did I," said Napoleon, "but I looked and there it was. Steve, it's getting so you never know what is going on."

Sheridan tossed away the towel and sat down at the desk. He poured a glass of beer.

"I'd offer you some of this," he told Maximilian, "except I know it would rust your guts."

Napoleon guffawed.

"Right as of this moment," Maximilian said, "I haven't any guts to speak of. Most of them's dropped out."

Abraham came tramping briskly in. "I hear you have Max hidden out some place."

"Right here, Abe," called Maximilian eagerly.

"You certainly are a mess," said Abraham. "Here we were going fine until you two clowns gummed up the works."

"How is Lemuel?" asked Sheridan.

"He's all right," said Abraham. "The other two are working on him and they don't really need me. So I came hunting Max." He said to Napoleon, "Here, grab hold and help me get him to the table. We have good light out there."

Grumbling, Napoleon lent a hand. "I've lugged him around half the night," he complained. "Let's not bother with him. Let's just toss him on the scrap heap."

"It would serve him right," Abraham agreed, with pretended wrath.

The two went out, carrying Maximilian between them. He still was dropping parts.

Hezekiah finished with the transmog chest, arranging all the transmogs neatly in their place. He closed the lid with some satisfaction.

"Now that we're alone," he said, "let me see your face."

Sheridan grunted at him through a mouth stuffed full of food.

Hezekiah looked him over. "Just a scratch on the forehead, but the left side of your face, sir, looks as if someone had sandpapered it. You are sure you don't want to transmog someone? A doctor should have a look at it."

"Just leave it as it is," said Sheridan. "It will be all right."

Gideon stuck his head between the tent flaps. "Hezekiah, Abe is raising hell about the body you found for Max. He says it's an old, rebuilt job. Have you got another one?"

"I can look and see," said Hezekiah. "It was sort of dark. There are several more. We can look them over."

He left with Gideon, and Sheridan was alone.

He went on eating, mentally checking through the happenings of the evening.

It had been hard luck, of course, but it could have been far worse. One had to expect accidents and headaches every now and then. After all, they had been downright lucky. Except for some lost time and a floater load of cargo, they had come out unscathed.

All in all, he assured himself, they'd made a good beginning. The cargo sled and ship were swinging in tight orbits, the cargo had been ferried down and on this small peninsula, jutting out into the lake, they had as much security as one might reasonably expect on any alien planet.

The Garsonians, of course, were not belligerent, but even so one could never afford to skip security.

He finished eating and pushed the plate aside. He pulled a portfolio out of a stack of maps and paperwork lying on the desk. Slowly he untied the tapes and slid the contents out. For the hundredth time, at least, he started going through the summary of reports brought back to Central Trading by the first two expeditions.

Man first had come to the planet more than twenty years ago to make a preliminary check, bringing back field notes, photographs and samples. It had been mere routine; there had been no thorough or extensive survey. There had been no great hope nor expectation; it had been simply another job to do. Many planets were similarly spot-checked, and in nineteen out of twenty of them, nothing ever came of it.

But something very definite had come of it in the case of Garson IV.

The something was a tuber that appeared quite ordinary, pretty much, in fact, like an undersize, shriveled-up potato. Brought back by the survey among other odds and ends picked up on the planet, it had in its own good time been given routine examination and analysis by the products laboratory—with startling results.

From the *podar,* the tuber's native designation, had been derived a drug which had been given a long and agonizing name and had turned out to be the almost perfect tranquilizer. It appeared to have no untoward side-effects; it was not lethal if taken in too enthusiastic dosage; it was slightly habit-forming, a most attractive feature for all who might be concerned with the sale of it.

To a race vitally concerned with an increasing array of disorders traceable to tension, such a drug was a boon, indeed. For years, a search for such a tranquilizer had been carried on in the laboratories and here it suddenly was, a gift from a new-found planet.

Within an astonishingly short time, considering the deliberation with which Central Trading usually operated, a second expedition had been sent out to Garson IV, with the robotic team heavily transmogged as trade experts, psychologists and diplomatic functionaries. For two years the team had worked, with generally satisfactory results. When they had blasted off for Earth, they carried a cargo of the *podars,* a mass of meticulously gathered data and a trade agreement under which the Garsonians agreed to produce and store the *podars* against the day when another team should arrive to barter for them.

And that, thought Sheridan, is us.

And it was all right, of course, except that they were late by fifteen years.

For Central Trading, after many conferences, had decided to grow the *podar* on Earth. This, the economists had pointed out, would be far cheaper than making the long and expensive trips that would be necessary to import them from a distant planet. That it might leave the Garsonians holding the bag insofar as the trade agreement was concerned seemed not to have occurred to anyone at all. Although, considering the nature of the Garsonians, they probably had not been put out too greatly.

For the Garsonians were a shiftless tribe at best and it had been with some initial difficulty that the second team had been able to explain to them the mechanics and desirability of interstellar trade. Although, in fairness, it might be said of them that, once they understood it, they had been able to develop a creditable amount of eagerness to do business.

Podars had taken to the soil of Earth with commendable adaptiveness. They had grown bigger and better than they'd ever grown on their native planet. This was not surprising when one took into account the slap-dash brand of agriculture practiced by the Garsonians.

Using the tubers brought back by the second expedition for the initial crop, it required several years of growing before a sufficient supply of seed *podars* were harvested to justify commercial growing.

But finally that had come about and the first limited supply of the wonder drug had been processed and put on sale with wide advertising fanfare and an accompanying high price.

And all seemed well, indeed.

Once again the farmers of the Earth had gained a new cash crop from an alien planet. Finally Man had the tranquillizer which he'd sought for years.

But as the years went by, some of the enthusiasm dimmed. For the drug made from the *podars* appeared to lose its potency. Either it had not been as good as first believed or there was some factor lacking in its cultivation on Earth.

The laboratories worked feverishly on the problem. The *podars* were planted in experimental plots on other planets in the hope that the soil or air or general characteristics there might supply the needed element—if missing element it were.

And Central Trading, in its ponderous, bureaucratic fashion, began preliminary plans for importation of the tubers, remembering belatedly, perhaps, the trade agreement signed many years before. But the plans were not pushed too rapidly, for any day, it was believed, the answer might be found that would save the crop for Earth.

But when the answer came, it ruled out Earth entirely; it ruled out, in fact, every place but the *podar's* native planet. For, the laboratories found, the continued potency of the drug relied to a large extent upon the chemical reaction of a protozoan which the *podar* plants nourished in their roots. And the protozoan flourished, apparently, on Garson IV alone.

So finally, after more than fifteen years, the third expedition had started out for Garson IV. And had landed and brought the cargo down and now was ready, in the morning, to start trading for the *podars*.

Sheridan flipped idly through the sheets from the portfolio. There was, he thought, actually no need to look at all the data once again. He knew it all by heart.

• • •

The canvas rustled and Hezekiah stepped into the tent.

Sheridan looked up. "Good," he said, "you're back. Did you get Max fixed up?"

"We found a body, sir, that proved acceptable."

Sheridan pushed the pile of reports aside. "Hezekiah, what are your impressions?"

"Of the planet, sir?"

"Precisely."

"Well, it's those barns, sir. You saw them, sir, when we were coming down. I believe I mentioned them to you."

Sheridan nodded. "The second expedition taught the natives how to build them. To store the *podars* in."

"All of them painted red," the robot said. "Just like the barns we have on Christmas cards."

"And what's wrong with that?"

"They look a little weird, sir."

Sheridan laughed. "Weird or not, those barns will be the making of us. They must be crammed with *podars.* For fifteen years, the natives have been piling up their *podars,* more than likely wondering when we'd come to trade . . ."

"There were all those tiny villages," Hezekiah said, "and those big red barns in the village square. It looked, if you will pardon the observation, sir, like a combination of New England and Lower Slobbovia."

"Well, not quite Lower Slobbovia. Our Garsonian friends are not as bad as that. They may be somewhat shiftless and considerably scatterbrained, but they keep their villages neat and their houses spic and span."

He pulled a photograph from a pile of data records. "Here, take a look at this."

The photograph showed a village street, neat and orderly and quiet, with its rows of well-kept houses huddled underneath the shade trees. There were rows of gay flowers running along the roadway and there were people—little, happy, gnomelike people—walking in the road.

Hezekiah picked it up. "I will admit, sir, that they look fairly happy. Although, perhaps, not very smart."

Sheridan got to his feet. "I think I'll go out and check around and see how things are going."

"Everything is all right, sir," said Hezekiah. "The boys have the wreckage cleared up. I'm sorry to have to tell you, sir, that not much of the cargo could be saved."

"From the looks of it, I'm surprised we could salvage any of it."

"Don't stay out too long," Hezekiah warned him. "You'll need a good night's sleep. Tomorrow will be a busy day and you'll be out at the crack of dawn."

"I'll be right back," Sheridan promised and ducked out of the tent.

Batteries of camp lights had been erected and now held back the blackness of the night. The sound of hammering came from the chewed-up area where the floater had come down. There was no sign of the floater now and a gang of spacehand robots were busily going about the building of another radio shack. Another gang was erecting a pavilion tent above the conference table, where Abraham and his fellow roboticists still worked on Lemuel and Maximilian. And in front of the cook shack, Napoleon and Gideon were squatted down, busily shooting craps.

Sheridan saw that Napoleon had set up his outdoors stove again.

He walked over to them and they turned their heads and greeted him, then went back to their game.

Sheridan watched them for a while and then walked slowly on.

He shook his head in some bewilderment—a continuing bewilderment over this robotic fascination with all the games of chance. It was, he supposed, just one of the many things that a human being—any human being—would never understand.

For gambling seemed entirely pointless from a robotic point of view. They had no property, no money, no possessions. They had no need of any and they had no wish for any—and yet they gambled madly.

It might be, he told himself, no more than an aping of their fellow humans. By his very nature, a robot was barred effectively from participating in most of the human vices. But gambling was something that he could do as easily and perhaps more efficiently than any human could.

But what in the world, he wondered, did they get out of it? No gain, no profit, for there were no such things as gain or profit so far as a robot was concerned. Excitement, perhaps? An outlet for aggressiveness?

Or did they keep a phantom score within their mind—mentally chalking up their gains and loss—and did a heavy winner at a game of chance win a certain prestige that was not visible to Man, that might, in fact, be carefully hidden from a man?

A man, he thought, could never know his robots in their entirety and that might be as well—it would be an unfair act to strip the final shreds of individuality from a robot.

For if the robots owed much to Man—their conception and their manufacture and their life—by the same token Man owed as much, or even more, to robots.

Without the robots, Man could not have gone as far or fast, or as effectively, out into the Galaxy. Sheer lack of transportation for skilled manpower alone would have held his progress to a crawl.

But with the robots there was no shipping problem.

And with the transmogs there was likewise no shortage of the kind of brains and skills and techniques—as there would otherwise have been—necessary to cope with the many problems found on the far-flung planets.

He came to the edge of the camp area and stood, with the lights behind him, facing out into the dark from which came the sound of running waves and the faint moaning of the wind.

He tilted back his head and stared up at the sky and marveled once again, as he had marveled many other times on many other planets, at the sheer, devastating loneliness and alienness of unfamiliar stars.

Man pinned his orientation to such fragile things, he thought— to the way the stars were grouped, to how a flower might smell, to the color of a sunset.

But this, of course, was not entirely unfamiliar ground. Two human expeditions already had touched down.

And now the third had come, bringing with it a cargo sled piled high with merchandise.

He swung around, away from the lake, and squinted at the area just beyond the camp and there the cargo was, piled in heaps and snugged down with tough plastic covers from which the starlight glinted. It lay upon the alien soil like a herd of hump-backed monsters bedded for the night.

There was no ship built that could handle that much cargo— no ship that could carry more than a dribble of the merchandise needed for interstellar trade.

For that purpose, there was the cargo sled.

The sled, set in an orbit around the planet of its origin, was loaded by a fleet of floaters, shuttling back and forth. Loaded, the sled was manned by robots and given the start on its long journey by the expedition ship. By the dint of the engines on the sled itself and the power of the expedition ship, the speed built up and up.

There was a tricky point when one reached the speed of light, but after that it became somewhat easier—although, for interstellar travel, there was need of speed many times in excess of the speed of light.

And so the sled sped on, following close behind the expedition ship, which served as a pilot craft through that strange gray area where space and time were twisted into something other than normal space and time.

Without robots, the cargo sleds would have been impossible; no human crew could ride a cargo ship and maintain the continuous routine of inspection that was necessary.

Sheridan swung back toward the lake again and wondered if he could actually see the curling whiteness of the waves or if it were sheer imagination. The wind was moaning softly and the stranger stars were there, and out beyond the waters the natives huddled in their villages with the big red barns looming in the starlit village squares.

II

In the morning, the robots gathered around the conference table beneath the gay pavilion tent and Sheridan and Hezekiah lugged out the metal transmog boxes labeled SPECIAL—GARSON IV.

"Now I think," said Sheridan, "that we can get down to business, if you gentlemen will pay attention to me." He opened one of the transmog boxes. "In here, we have some transmogs tailor-made for the job that we're to do. Because we had prior knowledge of this planet, it was possible to fabricate this special set. So on this job we won't start from scratch, as we are often forced to do . . ."

"Cut out the speeches, Steve," yelled Reuben, "and let's get started with this business."

"Let him talk," said Abraham. "He certainly has the right to, just like any one of us."

"Thank you, Abe," Sheridan said.

"Go ahead," said Gideon. "Rube's just discharging excess voltage."

"These transmogs are basically sales transmogs, of course. They will provide you with the personality and all the techniques of a salesman. But, in addition to that, they contain as well all the data pertaining to the situation here and the language of the natives, plus a mass of planetary facts."

He unlocked another of the boxes and flipped back the lid.

"Shall we get on with it?" he asked.

"Let's get going," demanded Reuben. "I'm tired of this space-hand transmog."

Sheridan made the rounds, with Hezekiah carrying the boxes for him.

Back at his starting point, he shoved aside the boxes, filled now with spacehand and other assorted transmogs. He faced the crew of salesmen.

"How do they feel?" he asked.

"They feel okay," said Lemuel. "You know, Steve, I never realized until now how dumb a spacehand is."

"Pay no attention to him," Abraham said, disgusted. "He always makes that crack."

Maximilian said soberly: "It shouldn't be too bad. These people have been acclimated to the idea of doing business with us. There should be no initial sales resistance. In fact, they may be anxious to start trading."

"Another thing," Douglas pointed out. "We have the kind of merchandise they've evinced interest in. We won't have to waste our time in extensive surveys to find out what they want."

"The market pattern seems to be a simple one," said Abraham judiciously. "There should be no complications. The principal thing, it would appear, is the setting of a proper rate of exchange—how many *podars* they must expect to pay for a shovel or a hoe or other items that we have."

"That will have to come," said Sheridan, "by a process of trial and error."

"We'll have to bargain hard," Lemuel said, "in order to establish a fictitious retail price, then let them have it wholesale. There are many times when that works effectively."

Abraham rose from his chair. "Let's get on with it. I suppose, Steve, that you will stay in camp."

Sheridan nodded. "I'll stay by the radio. I'll expect reports as soon as you can send them."

The robots got on with it. They scrubbed and polished one another until they fairly glittered. They brought out fancy dress hardware and secured it to themselves with magnetic clamps. There were colorful sashes and glistening rows of medals and large chunks of jewelry not entirely in the best of taste, but designed to impress the natives.

They got out their floaters and loaded up with samples from the cargo dump. Sheridan spread out a map and assigned each one a village. They checked their radios. They made sure they had their order boards.

By noon, they all were off.

Sheridan went back to the tent and sat down in his camp chair. He stared down the shelving beach to the lake, sparkling in the light of the noon-high sun.

Napoleon brought his lunch and hunkered down to talk, gathering his white cook's apron carefully in his lap so it would not touch the ground. He pushed his tall white cap to a rakish angle.

"How you got it figured, Steve?"

"You can never figure one beforehand," Sheridan told him. "The boys are all set for an easy time and I hope they have it. But this is an alien planet and I never bet on aliens."

"You look for any trouble?"

"I don't look for anything. I just sit and wait and hope feebly for the best. Once the reports start coming in . . ."

"If you worry so much, why not go out yourself?"

Sheridan shook his head. "Look at it this way, Nappy. I am not a salesman and this crew is. There'd be no sense in my going out. I'm not trained for it."

And, he thought, the fact of the matter was that he was not trained for anything. He was not a salesman and he was not a spacehand; he was not any of the things that the robots were or could be.

He was just a human, period, a necessary cog in a team of robots.

There was a law that said no robot or no group of robots could be assigned a task without human supervision, but that was not the whole of it. It was, rather, something innate in the robot makeup, not built into them, but something that was there and always might be there—the ever-present link between the robot and his human.

Sent out alone, a robot team would blunder and bog down, would in the end become unstuck entirely—would wind up worse than useless. With a human accompanying them, there was almost no end to their initiative and their capability.

It might, he thought, be their need of leadership, although in very truth the human member of the team sometimes showed little of that. It might be the necessity for some symbol of authority and yet, aside from their respect and consideration for their human, the robots actually bowed to no authority.

It was something deeper, Sheridan told himself, than mere leadership or mere authority. It was comparable to the affection and rapport which existed as an undying bond between a man and dog and yet it had no tinge of the god-worship associated with the dog.

He said to Napoleon: "How about yourself? Don't you ever hanker to go out? If you'd just say the word, you could."

"I like to cook," Napoleon stated. He dug at the ground with a metal finger. "I guess, Steve, you could say I'm pretty much an old retainer."

"A transmog would take care of that in a hurry."

"And then who'd cook for you? You know you're a lousy cook."

Sheridan ate his lunch and sat in his chair, staring at the lake, waiting for the first reports on the radio.

The job at last was started. All that had gone before—the loading of the cargo, the long haul out through space, the establishing of the orbits and the unshipping of the cargo—had been no more than preliminary to this very moment.

The job was finally started, but it was far from done. There would be months of work. There would be many problems and a thousand headaches. But they'd get it done, he told himself with a sure pride. There was nothing, absolutely nothing, that could stump this gang of his.

Late in the afternoon, Hezekiah came with the word: "Abraham is calling, sir. It seems that there is trouble."

Sheridan leaped to his feet and ran to the shack. He pulled up a chair and reached for the headset. "That you, Abe? How is it going, boy?"

"Badly, Steve," said Abraham. "They aren't interested in doing business. They want the stuff, all right. You can see the way they look at it. But they aren't buying. You know what I think? I don't believe they have anything to trade."

"That's ridiculous, Abe! They've been growing *podars* all these years. The barns are crammed with them."

"Their barn is all nailed up," said Abraham. "They have bars across the doors and the windows boarded. When I tried to walk up to it, they acted sort of ugly."

"I'll be right out," decided Sheridan. "I want to look this over." He stood up and walked out of the shack. "Hezekiah, get the flier started. We're going out and have a talk with Abe. Nappy, you mind the radio. Call me at Abe's village if anything goes wrong."

"I'll stay right here beside it," Napoleon promised him.

Hezekiah brought the flier down in the village square, landing it beside the floater, still loaded with its merchandise.

Abraham strode over to them as soon as they were down. "I'm glad you came, Steve. They want me out of here. They don't want us around."

Sheridan climbed from the flier and stood stiffly in the square. There was a sense of wrongness—a wrongness with the village and the people—something wrong and different.

There were a lot of natives standing around the square, lounging in the doorways and leaning against the trees. There was a group of them before the barred door of the massive barn that stood in the center of the square, as if they might be a guard assigned to protect the barn.

"When I first came down," said Abraham, "they crowded around the floater and stood looking at the stuff and you could see they could hardly keep their hands off it. I tried to talk to them, but they wouldn't talk too much, except to say that they were poor. Now all they do is just stand off and glare."

The barn was a monumental structure when gauged against the tiny houses of the village. It stood up foursquare and solid and entirely without ornament and it was an alien thing—alien of Earth. For, Sheridan realized, it was the same kind of barn that he had seen on the backwoods farms of Earth—the great hip-roof, the huge barn door, the ramp up to the door, and even the louvered cupola that rode astride the ridge-pole.

The man and the two robots stood in a pool of hostile silence and the lounging natives kept on staring at them and there was something decidedly wrong.

Sheridan turned slowly and glanced around the square and suddenly he knew what the wrongness was.

The place was shabby; it approached the downright squalid. The houses were neglected and no longer neat and the streets were littered. And the people were a piece with all the rest of it.

"Sir," said Hezekiah, "they are a sorry lot."

And they were all of that.

There was something in their faces that had a look of haunting and their shoulders stooped and there was fatigue upon them.

"I can't understand it," said the puzzled Abraham. "The data says they were a happy-go-lucky bunch, but look at them out there. Could the data have been wrong?"

"No, Abe. It's the people who have changed."

For there was no chance that the data could be wrong. It had been compiled by a competent team, one of the very best, and headed by a human who had long years of experience on many alien planets. The team had spent two years on Garson IV and had made it very much its business to know this race inside out.

Something had happened to the people. They had somehow lost their gaiety and pride. They had let the houses go uncared for. They had allowed themselves to become a race of ragamuffins.

"You guys stay here," Sheridan said.

"You can't do it, sir," said Hezekiah in alarm.

"Watch yourself," warned Abraham.

Sheridan walked toward the barn. The group before it did not stir. He stopped six feet away.

Close up, they looked more gnomelike than they had appeared in the pictures brought back by the survey team. Little wizened gnomes, they were, but not happy gnomes at all. They were seedy-looking and there was resentment in them and perhaps a dash of hatred. They had a hangdog look and there were some among them who shuffled in discomfiture.

"I see you don't remember us," said Sheridan conversationally. "We were away too long, much longer than we had thought to be."

He was having, he feared, some trouble with the language. It was, in fact, not the easiest language in the Galaxy to handle. For a fleeting moment, he wished that there were some sort of transmog that could be slipped into the human brain. It would make moments like this so much easier.

"We remember you," said one of them in a sullen voice.

"That's wonderful," said Sheridan with forced enthusiasm. "Are you speaker for this village?"

Speaker because there was no leader, no chief—no government at all beyond a loose, haphazard talking over what daily problems they had, around the local equivalent of the general store, and occasional formless town meetings to decide what to do in their rare crises, but no officials to enforce the decisions.

"I can speak for them," the native said somewhat evasively. He shuffled slowly forward. "There were others like you who came many years ago."

"You were friends to them."

"We are friends to all."

"But special friends to them. To them you made the promise that you would keep the *podars.*"

"Too long to keep the *podars.* The *podars* rot away."

"You had the barn to store them in."

"One *podar* rots. Soon there are two *podars* rotten. And then a hundred *podars* rotten. The barn is no good to keep them. No place is any good to keep them."

"But we—those others showed you what to do. You go through the *podars* and throw away the rotten ones. That way you keep the other *podars* good."

The native shrugged. "Too hard to do. Takes too long."

"But not all the *podars* rotted. Surely you have some left."

The creature spread his hands. "We have bad seasons, friend. Too little rain, too much. It never comes out right. Our crop is always bad."

"But we have brought things to trade you for the *podars.* Many things you need. We had great trouble bringing them. We came from far away. It took us long to come."

"Too bad," the native said. "No *podars.* As you can see, we are very poor."

"But where have all the *podars* gone?"

"We," the man said stubbornly, "don't grow *podars* any more. We changed the *podars* into another crop. Too much bad luck with *podars.*"

"But those plants out in the fields?"

"We do not call them *podars.*"

"It doesn't matter what you call them. Are they *podars* or are they not?"

"We do not grow the *podars.*"

• • •

Sheridan turned on his heel and walked back to the robots. "No soap," he said. "Something's happened here. They gave me a poor-mouth story and finally, as a clincher, said they don't grow *podars* any more."

"But there are fields of *podars,*" declared Abraham. "If the data's right, they've actually increased their acreage. I checked as I was coming in. They're growing more right now than they ever grew before."

"I know," said Sheridan. "It makes no sense at all. Hezekiah, maybe you should give base a call and find what's going on."

"One thing," Abraham pointed out. "What about this trade agreement that we have with them? Has it any force?"

Sheridan shook his head. "I don't know. Maybe we can wave it in their faces, just to see what happens. It might serve as a sort of psychological wedge a little later on, once we get them softened up a bit."

"*If* we get them softened up."

"This is our first day and this is only one village."

"You don't think we could use the agreement as a club?"

"Look, Abe, I'm not a lawyer, and we don't have a lawyer trans-mog along with us for a damned good reason—there isn't any legal setup whatever on this planet. But let's say we could haul them into a galactic court. Who signed for the planet? Some natives we picked as its representatives, not the natives themselves; their signing couldn't bind anything or anybody. The whole business of drawing up a contract was nothing but an impressive ceremony without any legal basis—it was just meant to awe the natives into doing business with us."

"But the second expedition must have figured it would work."

"Well, sure. The Garsonians have a considerable sense of moral-ity—individually and as families. Can we make that sense of moral-ity extend to bigger groups? That's our problem."

"That means we have to figure out an angle," said Abraham. "At least for this one village."

"If it's just this village," declared Sheridan, "we can let them sit and wait. We can get along without it."

But it wasn't just one village. It was all the rest of them, as well. Hezekiah brought the news.

"Napoleon says everyone is having trouble," he announced. "No one sold a thing. From what he said, it's just like this all over."

"We better call in all the boys," said Sheridan. "This is a situation that needs some talking over. We'll have to plan a course of action. We can't go flying off at a dozen different angles."

"And we'd better pull up a hill of *podars,*" Abraham suggested, "and see if they are *podars* or something else."

III

Sheridan inserted a chemist transmog into Ebenezer's brain case and Ebenezer ran off an analysis.

He reported to the sales conference seated around the table.

"There's just one difference," he said, "The *podars* that I analyzed ran a higher percentage of calenthropodensia—that's the drug used as a tranquilizer—than the *podars* that were brought in by the first and second expeditions. The factor is roughly ten per cent, although that might vary from one field to another, depending upon weather and soil conditions—I would suspect especially soil conditions."

"Then they lied," said Abraham, "when they said they weren't growing *podars.*"

"By their own standards," observed Silas, "they might not have lied to us. You can't always spell out alien ethics—satisfactorily, that is—from the purely human viewpoint. Ebenezer says that the composition of the tuber has changed to some extent. Perhaps due to better cultivation, perhaps to better seed or to an abundance of rainfall or a heavier concentration of the protozoan in the soil—or maybe because of something the natives did deliberately to make it shift . . ."

"Si," said Gideon, "I don't see what you are getting at."

"Simply this. If they knew of the shift or change, it might have given them an excuse to change the *podar* name. Or their language or their rules of grammar might have demanded that they change it. Or they may have applied some verbal mumbo-jumbo so they would have an out. And it might even have been a matter of superstition. The native told Steve at the village that they'd had bad luck with *podars*. So perhaps they operated under the premise that if they changed the name, they likewise changed the luck."

"And this is ethical?"

"To them, it might be. You fellows have been around enough to know that the rest of the Galaxy seldom operates on what we view as logic or ethics."

"But I don't see," said Gideon, "why they'd want to change the name unless it was for the specific purpose of not trading with us— so they could tell us they weren't growing *podars.*"

"I think that is exactly why they changed the name," Maximilian said. "It's all a piece with those nailed-up barns. They knew we had arrived. They could hardly have escaped knowing. We had clouds of floaters going up and down and they must have seen them."

"Back at that village," said Sheridan, "I had the distinct impression that they had some reluctance telling us they weren't growing *podars*. They had left it to the last, as if it were a final clincher they'd hoped they wouldn't have to use, a desperate, last-ditch argument when all the other excuses failed to do the trick and—"

"They're just trying to jack up the price," Lemuel interrupted in a flat tone.

Maximilian shook his head. "I don't think so. There was no price set to start with. How can you jack it up when you don't know what it is?"

"Whether there was a price or not," said Lemuel testily, "they still could create a situation where they could hold us up."

"There is another factor that might be to our advantage," Maximilian said. "If they changed the name so they'd have an excuse not to trade with us, that argues that the whole village feels a moral obligation and has to justify its refusal."

"You mean by that," said Sheridan, "that we can reason with them. Well, perhaps we can. I think at least we'll try."

"There's too much wrong," Douglas put in. "Too many things have changed. The new name for the *podars* and the nailed-up barns and the shabbiness of the villages and the people. The whole planet's gone to pot. It seems to me our job—the first job we do—is to find what happened here. Once we find that out, maybe we'd have a chance of selling."

"I'd like to see the inside of those barns," said Joshua. "What have they got in there? Do you think there's any chance we might somehow get a look?"

"Nothing short of force," Abraham told him. "I have a hunch that while we're around, they'll guard them night and day."

"Force is out," said Sheridan. "All of you know what would happen to us if we used force short of self-defense against an alien people. The entire team would have its license taken away. You guys would spend the rest of your lives scrubbing out headquarters."

"Maybe we could just sneak around. Do some slick detective work."

"That's an idea, Josh," Sheridan said. "Hezekiah, do you know if we have some detective transmogs?"

"Not that I know of, sir. I have never heard of any team using them."

"Just as well," Abraham observed. "We'd have a hard time disguising ourselves."

"If we had a volunteer," Lemuel said with some enthusiasm, "we could redesign him . . ."

"It would seem to me," said Silas, "that what we have to do is figure out all the different approaches that are possible. Then we can try each approach on a separate village till we latch onto one that works."

"Which presupposes," Maximilian pointed out, "that each village will react the same."

Silas said: "I would assume they would. After all, the culture is the same and their communications must be primitive. No village would know what was happening in another village until some little time had passed, which makes each village a perfectly isolated guinea pig for our little tests."

"Si, I think you're right," said Sheridan. "Somehow or other we have to find a way to break their sales resistance. I don't care what kind of prices we have to pay for the *podars* at the moment. I'd be willing to let them skin us alive to start with. Once we have them buying, we can squeeze down the price and come out even in the end. After all, the main thing is to get that cargo sled of ours loaded down with all the *podars* it can carry."

"All right," said Abraham. "Let's get to work."

They got to work. They spent the whole day at it. They mapped out the various sales approaches. They picked the villages where each one would be tried. Sheridan divided the robots into teams and assigned a team to each project. They worked out every detail. They left not a thing to chance.

Sheridan sat down to his supper table with the feeling that they had it made—if one of the approaches didn't work, another surely would. The trouble was that, as he saw it, they had done no planning. They had been so sure that this was an easy one that they had plunged ahead into straight selling without any thought upon the matter.

In the morning, the robots went out, full of confidence.

Abraham's crew had been assigned to a house-to-house campaign and they worked hard and conscientiously. They didn't miss a single house in the entire village. At every house, the answer had been no. Sometimes it was a firm but simple no; sometimes it was a door slammed in the face; at other times, it was a plea of poverty.

One thing was plain: Individual Garsonians could be cracked no more readily than Garsonians en masse.

Gideon and his crew tried the sample racket—handing out gift samples door to door with the understanding they would be back again to display their wares. The Garsonian householders weren't having any. They refused to take the samples.

Lemuel headed up the lottery project. A lottery, its proponents argued, appealed to basic greed. And this lottery had been rigged to carry maximum appeal. The price was as low as it could be set—one *podar* for a ticket. The list of prizes offered was just this side of fabulous. But the Garsonians, as it appeared, were not a greedy people. Not a ticket was sold.

And the funny thing about it—the unreasonable, maddening, impossible thing about it—was that the Garsonians seemed tempted.

"You could see them fighting it," Abraham reported at the conference that night. "You could see they wanted something we had for sale, but they'd steel themselves against it and they never weakened."

"We may have them on the very edge," said Lemuel. "Maybe just a little push is all it will take. Do you suppose we could start a whispering campaign? Maybe we could get it rumored that some other villages are buying right and left. That should weaken the resistance."

But Ebenezer was doubtful. "We have to dig down to causes. We have to find out what is behind this buyers' strike. It may be a very simple thing, if we only knew . . ."

Ebenezer took out a team to a distant village. They hauled along with them a pre-fabricated supermarket, which they set up in the village square. They racked their wares attractively. They loaded the place with glamor and excitement. They installed loud-speakers all over town to bellow out their bargains.

Abraham and Gideon headed up two talking-billboard crews.

They ranged far and wide, setting up their billboards splashed with attractive color, and installing propaganda tapes.

Sheridan had transmogged Oliver and Silas into semantics experts and they had engineered the tapes—a careful, skillful job. They did not bear down too blatantly on the commercial angle, although it certainly was there. The tapes were cuddly in spots and candid in others. At all times, they rang with deep sincerity. They sang the praises of the Garsonians for the decent, upstanding folks they were; they preached pithy homilies on honesty and fairness and the keeping of contracts; they presented the visitors as a sort of cross between public benefactors and addle-pated nitwits who could easily be outsmarted.

The tapes ran day and night. They pelted the defenseless Garsonians with a smooth, sleek advertising—and the effects should have been devastating, since the Garsonians were entirely unfamiliar with any kind of advertising.

Lemuel stayed behind at base and tramped up and down the beach, with his hands clenched behind his back, thinking furiously. At times he stopped his pacing long enough to scribble frantic notes, jotting down ideas.

Lemuel was trying to arrive at some adaptation of an old sales gag that he felt sure would work if he could only get it figured out—the ancient I-am-working-my-way-through-college wheeze.

Joshua and Thaddeus came to Sheridan for a pair of playwright transmogs. Sheridan said they had none, but Hezekiah, forever optimistic, ferreted into the bottom of the transmog chest. He came up with one transmog labeled auctioneer and another public speaker. They were the closest he could find.

Disgusted, the two rejected them and retired into seclusion, working desperately and as best they could on a medicine show routine.

For example, how did one write jokes for an alien people? What would they regard as funny? The off-color joke—oh, very fine, except that one would have to know in some detail the sexual life of the people it was aimed at. The mother-in-law joke—once again one would have to know; there were a lot of places where mothers-in-law were held in high regard, and other places where it was bad taste to even mention them. The dialect routine, of course, was strictly out, as it well deserved to be. Also, so far as the Garsonians were concerned, was the business slicker joke. The Garsonians were no commercial people; such a joke would sail clear above their heads.

But Joshua and Thaddeus, for all of that, were relatively undaunted. They requisitioned the files of data from Sheridan and spent hours poring over them, analyzing the various aspects of Garsonian life that might be safely written into their material. They made piles of notes. They drafted intricate charts showing relationships of Garsonian words and the maze of native social life. They wrote and rewrote and revised and polished. Eventually, they hammered out their script.

"There's nothing like a show," Joshua told Sheridan with conviction, "to loosen up a people. You get them feeling good and they lose their inhibitions. Besides, you have made them become somewhat indebted to you. You have entertained them and naturally they must feel the need to reciprocate."

"I hope it works," said Sheridan, somewhat doubtful and discouraged.

For nothing else was working.

In the distant village, the Garsonians had unbent sufficiently to visit the supermarket—to visit, not to buy. It almost seemed as if to them the market was some great museum or showplace. They would file down the aisles and goggle at the merchandise and at times reach out and touch it, but they didn't buy. They were, in fact, insulted if one suggested perhaps they'd like to buy.

In the other villages, the billboards had at first attracted wide attention. Crowds had gathered around them and had listened by the hour. But the novelty had worn off by now and they paid the tapes very little attention. And they still continued to ignore the robots. Even more pointedly, they ignored or rebuffed all attempts to sell.

It was disheartening.

Lemuel gave up his pacing and threw away his notes. He admitted he was licked. There was no way, on Garson IV, to adapt the idea of the college salesman.

Baldwin headed up a team that tried to get the whisper campaign started. The natives flatly disbelieved that any other village would go out and buy.

There remained the medicine show and Joshua and Thaddeus had a troupe rehearsing. The project was somewhat hampered by the fact that even Hezekiah could not dig up any actor transmogs, but, even so, they were doing well.

Despite the failure of everything they had tried, the robots kept going out to the villages, kept plugging away, kept on trying to sell, hoping that one day they would get a clue, a hint, an indication that might help them break the shell of reserve and obstinacy set up by the natives.

One day Gideon, out alone, radioed to base.

"There's something out here underneath a tree that you should take a look at," he told Sheridan.

"Something?"

"A different kind of being. It looks intelligent."

"A Garsonian?"

"Humanoid, all right, but it's no Garsonian."

"I'll be right out," said Sheridan. "You stay there so you can point it out to me."

"It has probably seen me," Gideon said, "but I did not approach it. I thought you might like first whack at it yourself."

As Gideon had said, the creature was sitting underneath a tree. It had a glittering cloth spread out and an ornate jug set out and was taking things out of a receptacle that probably was a hamper.

It was more attractively humanoid than the Garsonians. Its features were finely chiseled and its body had a look of lithe ranginess. It was dressed in the richest fabrics and was all decked out with jewels. It had a decided social air about it.

"Hello, friend," Sheridan said in Garsonian.

The creature seemed to understand him, but it smiled in a superior manner and seemed not to be too happy at Sheridan's intrusion.

"Perhaps," it finally said, "you have the time to sit down for a while."

Which, the way that it was put, was a plain and simple invitation for Sheridan to say no, he was sorry, but he hadn't and he must be getting on.

"Why, certainly," said Sheridan. "Thank you very much."

He sat down and watched the creature continue to extract things from the hamper.

"It's slightly difficult," the creature told him, "for us to communicate in this barbaric language. But I suppose it's the best we can do. You do not happen to know Ballic, do you?"

"I'm sorry," said Sheridan. "I've never heard of it."

"I had thought you might. It is widely used."

"We can get along," said Sheridan quietly, "with the language native to this planet."

"Oh, certainly," agreed the creature. "I presume I'm not trespassing. If I am, of course—"

"Not at all. I'm glad to find you here."

"I would offer you some food, but I hesitate to do so. Your metabolism undoubtedly is not the same as mine. It should pain me to poison you."

Sheridan nodded to indicate his gratitude. The food indeed was tempting. All of it was packaged attractively and some of it looked so delectable that it set the mouth to watering.

"I often come here for . . ." The creature hunted for the Garsonian word and there wasn't any.

Sheridan tried to help him out. "I think in my language I would call it picnic."

"An eating-out-of-doors," the stranger said. "That is the nearest I can come in the language of our hosts."

"We have the same idea."

The creature brightened up considerably at this evidence of mutual understanding. "I think, my friend, that we have much in common. Perhaps I could leave some of this food with you and you could analyze it. Then the next time I come, you could join me."

Sheridan shook his head. "I doubt I'll stay much longer."

"Oh," the stranger said, and he seemed pleased at it. "So you're a transitory being, too. Wings passing in the night. One hears a rustle and then the sound is gone forever."

"A most poetic thought," said Sheridan, "and a most descriptive one."

"Although," the creature said, "I come here fairly often. I've grown to love this planet. It is such a fine spot for an eating-out-of-doors. So restful and simple and unhurried. It is not cluttered up with activity and the people are so genuine, albeit somewhat dirty and very, very stupid. But I find it in my heart to love them for their lack of sophistication and their closeness to the soil and the clear-eyed view of life and their uncomplicated living of that life."

He halted his talk and cocked an eye at Sheridan.

"Don't you find it so, my friend?"

"Yes, of course I do," agreed Sheridan, rather hurriedly.

"There are so few places in the Galaxy," mourned the stranger, "where one can be alone in comfort. Oh, I do not mean alone entirely, or even physically. But an aloneness in the sense that there is space to live, that one is not pushed about by boundless, blind ambitions or smothered by the impact of other personalities. There are, of course, the lonely planets which are lonely only by the virtue of their being impossible for one to exist upon. These we must rule out."

He ate a little, daintily, and in a mincing manner. But he took a healthy snort from the ornate jug.

"This is excellent," said the creature, holding out the jug. "Are you sure you do not want to chance it?"

"I think I'd better not."

"I suppose it's wise of you," the stranger admitted. "Life is not a thing that a person parts from without due consideration."

He had another drink, then put the jug down in his lap and sat there fondling it.

"Not that I am one," he said, "to extoll the virtue of living above all other things. Surely there must be other facets of the universal pattern that have as much to offer . . ."

They spent a pleasant afternoon together.

When Sheridan went back to the flier, the creature had finished off the jug and was sprawled, happily pickled, among the litter of the picnic.

IV

Grasping at straws, Sheridan tried to fit the picnicking alien into the pattern, but there was no place where he'd fit.

Perhaps, after all, he was no more than what he seemed—a flitting dilettante with a passion for a lonely eating-out-of-doors and an addiction to the bottle.

Yet he knew the native language and he had said he came here often and that in itself was more than merely strange. With apparently the entire Galaxy in which to flit around, why should he gravitate to Garson IV, which, to the human eye, at least, was a most unprepossessing planet?

And another thing—how had he gotten here?

"Gideon," asked Sheridan, "did you see, by any chance, any sort of conveyance parked nearby that our friend could have traveled in?"

Gideon shook his head. "Now that you mention it, I am sure there wasn't. I would have noticed it."

"Has it occurred to you, sir," inquired Hezekiah, "that he may have mastered the ability of teleportation? It is not impossible. There was that race out on Pilico . . ."

"That's right," said Sheridan, "but the Pilicoans were good for no more than a mile or so at a time. You remember how they went popping along, like a jack rabbit making mile-long jumps, but making them so fast that you couldn't see him jump. This gent must have covered light-years. He asked me about a language that I never heard of. Indicated that it is widely spoken in at least some parts of the Galaxy."

"You are worrying yourself unduly, sir," cautioned Hezekiah. "We have more important things than this galivanting alien to trouble ourselves about."

"You're right," said Sheridan. "If we don't get this cargo moving, it will be my neck."

But he couldn't shake entirely the memory of the afternoon.

He went back, in his mind, through the long and idle chatter and found, to his amazement, that it had been completely idle. So far as he could recall, the creature had told him nothing of itself. For three solid hours or more, it had talked almost continuously and in all that time had somehow managed to say exactly nothing.

That evening, when he brought the supper, Napoleon squatted down beside the chair, gathering his spotless apron neatly in his lap.

"We are in a bad way, aren't we?" he asked.

"Yes, I suppose you could say we are."

"What will we do, Steve, if we can't move the stuff at all—if we can't get any *podars*?"

"Nappy," said Sheridan, "I've been trying very hard not to think of it."

But now that Napoleon had brought it up, he could well imagine the reaction of Central Trading if he should have to haul a billion-dollar cargo back intact. He could imagine, a bit more vividly, what might be said to him if he simply left it here and went back home without it.

No matter how he did it, he had to sell the cargo!

If he didn't, his career was in a sling.

Although there was more, he realized, than just his career at stake. The whole human race was involved.

There was a real and pressing need for the tranquilizer made from *podar* tubers. A search for such a drug had started centuries before and the need of it was underlined by the fact that through all those centuries the search had never faltered. It was something that Man needed badly—that Man, in fact, had needed badly since the very moment he'd become something more than animal.

And here, on this very planet, was the answer to that terrible human need—an answer denied and blocked by the stubbornness of a shiftless, dirty, backward people.

"If we only had this planet," he said, speaking more to himself than to Napoleon, "if we could only take it over, we could grow all the *podars* that we needed. We'd make it one big field and we'd grow a thousand times more *podars* than these natives ever grew."

"But we can't," Napoleon said. "It is against the law."

"Yes, Nappy, you are right. Very much against the law."

For the Garsonians were intelligent—not startlingly so, but intelligent, at least, within the meaning of the law.

And you could do nothing that even hinted of force against an intelligent race. You couldn't even buy or lease their land, for the law would rule that in buying one would be dispossessing them of the inalienable rights of all alien intelligences.

You could work with them and teach them—that was very laudable. But the Garsonians were almost unteachable. You could barter with them if you were very careful that you did not cheat them too outrageously. But the Garsonians refused to barter.

"I don't know what we'll do," Sheridan told Napoleon. "How are we going to find a way?"

"I have a sort of suggestion. If we could introduce these natives to the intricacies of dice, we might finally get somewhere. We robots, as you probably know, are very good at it."

Sheridan choked on his coffee. He slowly and with great care set the cup down.

"Ordinarily," he told Napoleon solemnly, "I would frown upon such tactics. But with the situation as it stands, why don't you get some of the boys together and have a try at it?"

"Glad to do it, Steve."

"And . . . uh, Nappy . . ."

"Yes, Steve?"

"I presume you'd pick the best crap-shooters in the bunch."

"Naturally," said Napoleon, getting up and smoothing his apron.

Joshua and Thaddeus took their troupe to a distant village in entirely virgin territory, untouched by any of the earlier selling efforts, and put on the medicine show.

It was an unparalleled success. The natives rolled upon the ground, clutching at their bellies, helpless with laughter. They howled and gasped and wiped their streaming eyes. They pounded one another on the back in appreciation of the jokes. They'd never seen anything like it in all their lives—there had never been anything like it on all of Garson IV.

And while they were weak with merriment, while they were still well-pleased, at the exact psychological moment when all their inhibitions should be down and all stubbornness and hostility be stilled, Joshua made the sales pitch.

The laughter stopped. The merriment went away. The audience simply stood and stared.

The troupe packed up and came trailing home, deep in despondency.

Sheridan sat in his tent and faced the bleak prospect. Outside the tent, the base was still as death. There was no happy talk or singing and no passing laughter. There was no neighborly tramping back and forth.

"Six weeks," Sheridan said bitterly to Hezekiah. "Six weeks and not a sale. We've done everything we can and we've not come even close."

He clenched his fist and hit the desk. "If we could only find what the trouble is! They want our merchandise and still they refuse to buy. What is the holdup, Hezekiah? Can you think of anything?"

Hezekiah shook his head. "Nothing, sir. I'm stumped. We all are."

"They'll crucify me back at Central," Sheridan declared. "They'll nail me up and keep me as a horrible example for the next ten thousand years. There've been failures before, but none like this."

"I hesitate to say this, sir," said Hezekiah, "but we could take it on the lam. Maybe that's the answer. The boys would go along. Theoretically they're loyal to Central, but deep down at the bottom of it, it's you they're really loyal to. We could load up the cargo and that would give us capital and we'd have a good head start . . ."

"No," Sheridan said firmly. "We'll try a little longer and we may solve the situation. If not, I face the music."

He scraped his hand across his jaw.

"Maybe," he said, "Nappy and his crap-shooters can turn the trick for us. It's fantastic, sure, but stranger things have happened."

Napoleon and his pals came back, sheepish and depressed.

"They beat the pants off us," the cook told Sheridan in awe. "Those boys are really naturals. But when we tried to pay our bets, they wouldn't take our stuff!"

"We have to try to arrange a powwow," said Sheridan, "and talk it out with them, although I hold little hope for it. Do you think, Napoleon, if we came clean and told them what a spot we're in, it would make a difference?"

"No, I don't," Napoleon said.

"If they only had a government," observed Ebenezer, who had been a member of Napoleon's gambling team, "we might get somewhere with a powwow. Then you could talk with someone who represented the entire population. But this way you'll have to talk with each village separately and that will take forever."

"We can't help it, Eb," said Sheridan. "It's all we have left."

But before any powwow could be arranged, the *podar* harvest started. The natives toiled like beavers in the fields, digging up the tubers, stacking them to dry, packing them in carts and hauling them to the barns by sheer manpower, for the Garsonians had no draft animals.

They dug them up and hauled them to the barns, the very barns where they'd sworn that they had no *podars*.

But that was not to wonder at when one stopped to think of it, for the natives had also sworn that they grew no *podars*.

They did not open the big barn doors, as one would have normally expected them to do. They simply opened a tiny, man-size door set into the bigger door and took the *podars* in that way. And when any of the Earth party hove in sight, they quickly stationed a heavy guard around the entire square.

"We'd better let them be," Abraham advised Sheridan. "If we try to push them, we may have trouble in our lap."

So the robots pulled back to the base and waited for the harvest to end. Finally it was finished and Sheridan counseled lying low for a few days more to give the Garsonians a chance to settle back to their normal routine.

Then they went out again and this time Sheridan rode along, on one of the floaters with Abraham and Gideon.

The first village they came to lay quiet and lazy in the sun. There was not a creature stirring.

Abraham brought the floater down into the square and the three stepped off.

The square was empty and the place was silent—a deep and deathly silence.

Sheridan felt the skin crawling up his back, for there was a stealthy, unnatural menace in the noiseless emptiness.

"They may be laying for us," suggested Gideon.

"I don't think so," said Abraham. "Basically they are peaceful."

They moved cautiously across the square and walked slowly down a street that opened from the square.

And still there was no living thing in sight.

And stranger still—the doors of some of the houses stood open to the weather and the windows seemed to watch them out of blind eyes, with the colorful crude curtains gone.

"Perhaps," Gideon suggested, "they may have gone away to some harvest festival or something of that nature."

"They wouldn't leave their doors wide open, even for a day," declared Abraham. "I've lived with them for weeks and I've studied them. I know what they would do. They'd have closed the doors very carefully and tried them to be sure that they were closed."

"But maybe the wind . . ."

"Not a chance," insisted Abraham. "One door, possibly. But I see four of them from here."

"Someone has to take a look," said Sheridan. "It might as well be me."

He turned in at a gate where one of the doors stood open and went slowly up the path. He halted at the threshold and peered in. The room beyond was empty. He stepped into the house and went from room to room and all the rooms were empty—not simply of the natives, but of everything. There was no furniture and the utensils and the tools were gone from hooks and racks. There was no scrap of clothing. There was nothing left behind. The house was dead and bare and empty, a shabby and abandoned thing discarded by its people.

He felt a sense of guilt creep into his soul. What if we drove them off? What if we hounded them until they'd rather flee than face us?

But that was ridiculous, he told himself. There must be some other reason for this incredibly complete mass exodus.

He went back down the walk. Abraham and Gideon went into other houses. All of them were empty.

"It may be this village only," suggested Gideon. "The rest may be quite normal."

But Gideon was wrong.

Back at the floater, they got in touch with base.

"I can't understand it," said Hezekiah, "I've had the same report from four other teams. I was about to call you, sir."

"You'd better get out every floater that you can," said Sheridan. "Check all the villages around. And keep a lookout for the people. They may be somewhere in the country. There's a possibility they're at a harvest festival."

"If they're at a festival, sir," asked Hezekiah, "why did they take their belongings? You don't take along your furniture when you attend a festival."

"I know," said Sheridan. "You put your finger on it. Get the boys out, will you?'

"There's just the possibility," Gideon offered, "that they are changing villages. Maybe there's a tribal law that says they have to build a new village every so often. It might have its roots in an ancient sanitation law that the camp must be moved at stated intervals."

"It could be that," Sheridan said wearily. "We'll have to wait and see."

Abraham thumbed a fist toward the barn.

Sheridan hesitated, then threw caution to the winds.

"Go ahead," he said.

Gideon stalked up the ramp and reached the door. He put out a hand and grasped one of the planks nailed across the door. He wrenched and there was an anguished shriek of tortured nails ripping from the wood and the board came free. Another plank came off and then another one and Gideon put his shoulder to the door and half of it swung open.

Inside, in the dimness of the barn, was the dull, massive shine of metal—a vast machine sitting on the driveway floor.

Sheridan stiffened with a cold, hollow sense of terror.

It was wrong, he thought. There could be no machine.

The Garsonians had no business having a machine. Their culture was entirely non-mechanical. The best they had achieved so far had been the hoe and wheel, and even yet they had not been able to put the hoe and wheel together to make themselves a plow.

They had had no machine when the second expedition left some fifteen years ago, and in those fifteen years they could not have spanned the gap. In those fifteen years, from all surface indications, they had not advanced an inch.

And yet the machine stood in the driveway of the barn.

It was a fair-sized cylinder, set on end and with a door in one side of it. The upper end of it terminated in a dome-shaped cap. Except for the door, it resembled very much a huge and snub-nosed bullet.

Interference, thought Sheridan. There had been someone here between the time the second expedition left and the third one had arrived.

"Gideon," he said.

"What is it, Steve?"

"Go back to base and bring the transmog chest. Tell Hezekiah to get my tent and all the other stuff over here as soon as he is able. Call some of the boys off reconnaissance. We have work to do."

There had been someone here, he thought—and most certainly there had. A very urbane creature who sat beneath a tree beside a spread-out picnic cloth, swigging at his jug and talking for three solid hours without saying anything at all!

V

The messenger from Central Trading brought his small ship down to one side of the village square, not far from where Sheridan's tent was pitched. He slid back the visi-dome and climbed out of his seat.

He stood for a moment, shining in the sun, during which be straightened his SPECIAL COURIER badge, which had become askew upon his metal chest. Then he walked deliberately toward the barn, heading for Sheridan, who sat upon the ramp.

"You are Sheridan?" he asked.

Sheridan nodded, looking him over. He was a splendid thing.

"I had trouble finding you. Your base seems to be deserted."

"We ran into some difficulty," Sheridan said quietly.

"Not too serious, I trust. I see your cargo is untouched."

"Let me put it this way—we haven't been bored."

"I see," the robot said, disappointed that an explanation was not immediately forthcoming. "My name is Tobias and I have a message for you."

"I'm listening."

Sometimes, Sheridan told himself, these headquarters robots needed taking down a peg or two.

"It is a verbal message. I can assure you that I am thoroughly briefed. I can answer any questions you may wish to ask."

"Please," said Sheridan. "The message first."

"Central Trading wishes to inform you that they have been offered the drug calenthropodensia in virtually unlimited supply by a firm which describes itself as Galactic Enterprises. We would like to know if you can shed any light upon the matter."

"Galactic Enterprises," said Sheridan. "I've never heard of them."

"Neither has Central Trading. I don't mind telling you that we're considerably upset."

"I should imagine you would be."

Tobias squared his shoulders. "I have been instructed to point out to you that you were sent to Garson IV to obtain a cargo of *podars,* from which this drug is made, and that the assignment, in view of the preliminary work already done upon the planet, should not have been so difficult that—"

"Now, now," cautioned Sheridan. "Let us keep our shirts on. If it will quiet your conscience any, you may consider for the record that I have accepted the bawling out you're supposed to give me."

"But you—"

"I assume," said Sheridan, "that Galactic Enterprises is quoting a good stiff price on this drug of theirs."

"It's highway robbery. What Central Trading has sent me to find out—"

"Is whether I am going to bring in a cargo of *podars*. At the moment, I can't tell you."

"But I must take back my report!"

"Not right now, you aren't. I won't be able to make a report to you for several days at least. You'll have to wait."

"But my instructions are—"

"Suit yourself," Sheridan said sharply. "Wait for it or go back without it. I don't give a damn which you do."

He got up from the ramp and walked into the barn.

The robots, he saw, had finally pried or otherwise dislodged the cap from the big machine and had it on the side on the driveway floor, tilted to reveal the innards of it.

"Steve," said Abraham bitterly, "take a look at it."

Sheridan took a look. The inside of the cap was a mass of fused metal.

"There were some working parts in there," said Gideon, "but they have been destroyed."

Sheridan scratched his head. "Deliberately? A self-destruction relay?"

Abraham nodded. "They apparently were all finished with it. If we hadn't been here, I suppose they would have carted this machine and the rest of them back home, wherever that may be. But they couldn't take a chance of one of them falling in our hands. So they pressed the button or whatever they had to do and the entire works went pouf."

"But there are other machines. Apparently one in every barn."

"Probably just the same as this," said Lemuel, rising from his knees beside the cap.

"What's your guess?" asked Sheridan.

"A matter transference machine, a teleporter, whatever you want to call it," Abraham told him. "Not deduced, of course, from anything in the machine itself, but from the circumstances. Look at this barn. There's not a *podar* in it. Those *podars* went somewhere. This picnicking friend of yours –"

"They call themselves," said Sheridan, "Galactic Enterprises. A messenger just arrived. He says they offered Central Trading a deal on the *podar* drug."

"And now Central Trading," Abraham supplied, "enormously embarrassed and financially outraged, will pin the blame on us because we've delivered not a *podar.*"

"I have no doubt of it," said Sheridan. "It all depends upon whether or not we can locate these native friends of ours."

"I would think that most unlikely," Gideon said. "Our reconnaissance showed all the villages empty throughout the entire planet. Do you suppose they might have left in these machines? If they'd transport *podars,* they'd probably transport people."

"Perhaps," said Lemuel, making a feeble joke, "everything that begins with the letter p."

"What are the chances of finding how they work?" asked Sheridan. "This is something that Central could make a lot of use of."

Abraham shook his head. "I can't tell you, Steve. Out of all these machines on the planet, which amounts to one in every barn, there is a certain mathematical chance that we might find one that was not destroyed."

"But even if we did," said Gideon, "there is an excellent chance that it would immediately destroy itself if we tried to tamper with it."

"And if we don't find one that is not destroyed?"

"There is a chance," Lemuel admitted. "All of them would not destroy themselves to the same degree, of course. Nor would the pattern of destruction always be the same. From, say, a thousand of them, you might be able to work out a good idea of what kind of machinery there was in the cone."

"And say we could find out what kind of machinery was there?"

"That's a hard one to answer, Steve," Abraham said. "Even if we had one complete and functioning, I honestly don't know if we could ferret out the principle to the point where we could duplicate it. You must remember that at no time has the human race come even close to something of this nature."

It made a withering sort of sense to Sheridan. Seeing a totally unfamiliar device work, even having it blueprinted in exact detail, would convey nothing whatever if the theoretical basis was missing. It was, completely, and there was a great deal less available here than a blueprint or even working model.

"They used those machines to transport the *podars*," he said, "and possibly to transport the people. And if that is true, it must be the people went voluntarily—we'd have known if there was force involved. Abe, can you tell me: Why would the people go?"

"I wouldn't know," said Abraham. "All I have now is a physicist transmog. Give me one on sociology and I'll wrestle with the problem."

There was a shout outside the barn and they whirled toward the door. Ebenezer was coming up the ramp and in his arms he carried a tiny, dangling form.

"It's one of them," gasped Gideon. "It's a native, sure enough!"

Ebenezer knelt and placed the little native tenderly on the floor. "I found him in the field. He was lying in a ditch. I'm afraid he's done for."

Sheridan stepped forward and bent above the native. It was an old man—any one of the thousands of old men he'd seen in the villages. The same leathery old face with the wind and weather wrinkles in it, the same shaggy brows shielding deep-sunk eyes, the same scraggly crop of whiskers, the same sense of forgotten shiftlessness and driven stubbornness.

"Left behind," said Ebenezer. "Left behind when all the others went. He must have fallen sick out in the field . . ."

"Get my canteen," Sheridan said. "It's hanging by the door."

The oldster opened his eyes and glanced around the circle of faces that stared down at him. He rubbed a hand across his face, leaving streaks of dirt.

"I fell," he mumbled. "I remember falling. I fell into a ditch."

"Here's the water, Steve," said Abraham.

Sheridan took it, lifted the old man and held him half upright against his chest. He tilted the canteen to the native's lips. The oldster drank unneatly, gulping at the water. Some of it spilled, splashing down his whiskers to drip onto his belly.

Sheridan took the canteen away.

"Thank you," the native said and, Sheridan reflected, that was the first civil word to come their way from any of the natives.

The native rubbed his face again with a dirty claw. "The people all are gone?"

"All gone," said Sheridan.

"Too late," the old man said. "I would have made it if I hadn't fallen down. Perhaps they hunted for me . . ." His voice trailed off into nothingness.

"If you don't mind, sir," suggested Hezekiah, "I'll get a medic transmog."

"Perhaps you should," said Sheridan. "Although I doubt it'll do much good. He should have died days ago out there in the field."

"Steve," said Gideon, speaking softly, "a human doctor isn't too much use treating alien people. In time, if we had the time, we could find out about this fellow—something about his body chemistry and his metabolism. Then we could doctor him."

"That's right, Steve," Abraham said.

Sheridan shrugged. "All right then, Hezekiah. Forget about the transmog."

He laid the old man back on the floor again and got up off his knees.

He sat on his heels and rocked slowly back and forth.

"Perhaps," he said to the native, "you'll answer one question. Where did all your people go?"

"In there," the native said, raising a feeble arm to point at the machine. "In there, and then they went away just as the harvest we gathered did."

Sheridan stayed squatting on the floor beside the stricken native.

Reuben brought in an armload of grass and wadded it beneath the native's head as a sort of pillow.

So the Garsonians had really gone away, Sheridan told himself, had up and left the planet. Had left it, using the machines that had been used to make delivery of the *podars*. And if Galactic Enterprises had machines like that, then they (whoever, wherever they might be) had a tremendous edge on Central Trading. For Central Trading's lumbering cargo sleds, snaking their laborious way across the light-years, could offer only feeble competition to machines like those.

He had thought, be remembered, the first day they had landed, that a little competition was exactly what Central Trading needed. And here was that competition—a competition that had not a hint of ethics. A competition that sneaked in behind Central Trading's back and grabbed the market that Central Trading needed—the market that Central could have cinched if it had not fooled around, if it had not been so sly and cynical about adapting the *podar* crop to Earth.

Just where and how, he wondered, had Galactic Enterprises found out about the *podars* and the importance of the drug? Under what circumstances had they learned the exact time limit during which they could operate in the *podar* market without Central interference? And had they, perhaps, been slightly optimistic in regard to that time limit and gotten caught in a situation where they had been forced to destroy all those beautiful machines?

Sheridan chuckled quietly to himself. That destruction must have hurt them!

It wasn't hard, however, to imagine a hundred or a thousand ways in which they might have learned about the *podar* situation, for they were a charming people and really quite disarming. He would not be surprised if some of them might be operating secretly inside of Central Trading.

The native stirred. He reached out a skinny hand and tugged at the sleeve of Sheridan's jacket.

"Yes, what is it, friend?"

"You will stay with me?" the native begged. "These others here, they are not the same as you and I."

"I will stay with you," Sheridan promised.

"I think we'd better go," said Gideon. "Maybe we disturb him."

The robots walked quietly from the barn and left the two alone.

Reaching out, Sheridan put a hand on the native's brow. The flesh was clammy cold.

"Old friend," he said, "I think perhaps you owe me something."

The old man shook his head, rolling it slowly back and forth upon the pillow. And the fierce light of stubbornness and a certain slyness came into his eyes.

"We don't owe you," he said. "We owed the other ones."

And that, of course, hadn't been what Sheridan had meant.

But there they lay—the words that told the story, the solution to the puzzle that was Garson IV.

"That was why you wouldn't trade with us," said Sheridan, talking to himself rather than to the old native on the floor. "You were so deep in debt to these other people that you needed all the *podars* to pay off what you owed them?"

And that must have been the way it was. Now that he thought back on it, that supplied the one logical explanation for everything that happened. The reaction of the natives, the almost desperate sales resistance was exactly the kind of thing one would expect from people in debt up to their ears.

That was the reason, too, the houses bad been so neglected and the clothes had been in rags. It accounted for the change from the happy-go-lucky shiftlessness to the beaten and defeated and driven attitude. So pushed, so hounded, so fearful that they could not meet the payments on the debt that they strained their every resource, drove themselves to ever harder work, squeezing from the soil every *podar* they could grow.

"That was it?" he demanded sharply. "That was the way it was?"

The native nodded with reluctance.

"They came along and offered such a bargain that you could not turn it down. For the machines, perhaps? For the machines to send you to other places?"

The native shook his head. "No, not the machines. We put the *podars* in the machines and the *podars* went away. That was how we paid."

"You were paying all these years?"

"That is right," the native said. Then he added, with a flash of pride: "But now we're all paid up."

"That is fine," said Sheridan. "It is good for a man to pay his debts."

"They took three years off the payments," said the native eagerly. "Was that not good of them?"

"I'm sure it was," said Sheridan, with some bitterness.

He squatted patiently on the floor, listening to the faint whisper of a wind blowing in the loft and the rasping breath of the dying native.

"But then your people used the machines to go away. Can't you tell me why?"

A racking cough shook the old man and his breath came in gasping sobs.

Sheridan felt a sense of shame in what he had to do. I should let him die in peace, he thought. I should not badger him. I should let him go in whatever dignity he can—not pushed and questioned to the final breath he draws.

But there was that last answer—the one Sheridan had to have.

Sheridan said gently: "But tell me, friend, what did you bargain for? What was it that you bought?"

He wondered if the native heard. There was no indication that he had.

"What did you buy?" Sheridan insisted.

"A planet," said the native.

"But you had a planet!"

"This one was different," the native told him in a feeble whisper. "This was a planet of immortality. Anyone who went there would never, never die."

Sheridan squatted stiffly in shocked and outraged silence.

And from the silence came a whisper—a whisper still of faith and belief and pity that would haunt the human all his life.

"That was what I lost," the whisper said. "That was what I lost . . ."

Sheridan opened his hands and closed them, strangling the perfect throat and the winning smile, shutting off the cultured flow of words.

If I had him now, he thought, if I only had him now!

He remembered the spread-out picnic cloth and the ornate jug and the appetizing food, the smooth, slick gab and the assurance of the creature. And even the methodical business of getting very drunk so that their meeting could end without unpleasant questions or undue suspicion.

And the superior way in which he'd asked if the human might know Ballic, all the time, more than likely, being able to speak English himself.

So Central Trading finally had its competition. From this moment, Central Trading would be fighting with its back against the wall. For these jokers in Galactic Enterprises played dirty and for keeps.

The Garsonians had been naive fools, of course, but that was no true measure of Galactic Enterprises. They undoubtedly would select different kinds of bait for different kinds of fish, but the old never-never business of immortality might be deadly bait for even the most sophisticated if appropriately presented.

An utter lack of ethics and the transference machines were the trumps Galactic held.

What had really happened, he wondered, to all the people who had lived on this planet? Where had they really gone when they followed the *podars* into those machines?

Could the Galactic boys, by chance, have ferreted out a place where there would be a market for several million slaves?

Or had they simply planned to get the Garsonians out of the way as an effective means of cutting off the *podar* supply for Central Trading, thus insuring a ready and profitable sale for their supply of drugs?

Or had they lured the Garsonians away so they themselves could take over the planet?

And if that was the case—perhaps in *any* case—Galactic Enterprises definitely had lost this first encounter. Maybe, Sheridan told himself, they are really not so hot.

They gave us exactly what we need, he realized with a pleased jolt. They did us a favor!

Old blundering, pompous Central Trading had won the first round, after all.

He got to his feet and headed for the door. He hesitated and turned back to the native.

"Maybe, friend," he said, "you were the lucky one."

The native did not hear him.

Gideon was waiting at the door.

"How is he?" he asked.

"He's dead," Sheridan said. "I wonder if you'd arrange for burial."

"Of course," said Gideon. "You'll let me see the data. I'll have to bone up on the proper rites."

"But first do something else for me."

"Name it, Steve."

"You know this Tobias, the messenger that Central Trading sent? Find him and see that he doesn't leave."

Gideon grinned. "You may rest assured."

"Thank you," said Sheridan.

On his way to the tent, he passed the courier's ship. It was, he noted, a job that was built for speed—little more than an instrument board and seat tacked onto a powerful engine.

In a ship like that, he thought, a pilot could really make some time.

Almost to the tent, he met Hezekiah.

"Come along with me," he said. "I have a job for you."

Inside the tent, he sat down in his chair and reached for a sheet of paper.

"Hezekiah," he said, "dig into that chest. Find the finest diplomatic transmog that we have."

"I know just where it is, sir," said Hezekiah, pawing through the chest.

He came out with the transmog and laid it on the desk.

"Hezekiah," said Sheridan, "listen to me carefully. Remember every word I say."

"Sir," replied Hezekiah, a little huffily, "I always listen carefully."

"I know you do. I have perfect faith and trust in you. That is why I'm sending you to Central."

"To Central, sir! You must be joking, surely. You know I cannot go. Sir, who would look after you? Who would see that you—"

"I can get along all right. You'll be coming back. And I'll still have Napoleon."

"But I don't want to go, sir!"

"Hezekiah, I must have someone I can trust. We'll put that transmog in you and—"

"But it will take me weeks, sir!"

"Not with the courier ship. You're going back instead of the courier. I'll write an authorization for you to represent me. It'll be as if I were there myself."

"But there is Abraham. Or Gideon. Or you could send any of the others . . ."

"It's you, Hezekiah. You are my oldest friend."

"Sir," said Hezekiah, straightening to attention, "what do you wish me to do?"

"You're to tell Central that Garson IV is now uninhabited. You're to say that such being the case, I'm possessing it formally in the name of Central Trading. Tell them I'll need reinforcements immediately because there is a possibility that Galactic Enterprises may try to take it from us. They're to send out one sled loaded with robots as an initial occupying and colonizing force, and another sledload of agricultural implements so we can start our farming. And every last *podar* that they have, for seed. And, Hezekiah . . ."

"Yes, sir?"

"That sledload of robots. They'd better be deactivated and knocked down. That way they can pile on more of them. We can assemble them here."

Hezekiah repressed a shudder. "I will tell them, sir."

"I am sorry, Hezekiah."

"It is quite all right, sir."

Sheridan finished writing out the authorization. "Tell Central Trading," he said, "that in time we'll turn this entire planet into one vast *podar* field. But they must not waste a minute. No committee sessions, no meetings of the board, no dawdling around. Keep right on their tail every blessed second."

"I will not let them rest, sir," Hezekiah assured him.

VI

The courier ship had disappeared from sight. Try as he might, Sheridan could catch no further glimpse of it.

Good old Hezekiah, he thought, he'll do the job. Central Trading will be wondering for weeks exactly what it was that hit them.

He tilted his head forward and rubbed his aching neck.

He said to Gideon and Ebenezer: "You can get up off him now."

The two arose, grinning, from the prostrate form of Tobias. Tobias got up, outraged. "You'll hear of this," he said to Sheridan.

"Yes, I know," said Sheridan. "You hate my guts."

Abraham stepped forward, "What is next?" he asked.

"Well," Sheridan said, "I think we should all turn gleaners."

"Gleaners?"

"There are bound to be some *podars* that the natives missed. We'll need every one we can find for seed."

"But we're all physicists and mechanical engineers and chemists and other things like that. Surely you would not expect such distinguished specialists—"

"I think I can remedy that," said Sheridan. "I imagine we still can find those spacehand transmogs. They should serve until Central sends us some farmer units."

Tobias stepped forward and ranged himself alongside of Abraham. "As long as I must remain here, I demand to be of use. It's not in a robot's nature just to loaf around."

Sheridan slapped his hand against his jacket pocket, felt the bulge of the transmog he'd taken out of Hezekiah.

"I think," he told Tobias, "I have just the thing for you."

I HAD NO HEAD AND
MY EYES WERE FLOATING WAY
UP IN THE AIR

Created for inclusion in The Last Dangerous Visions ™, *which was to have been the final entry in Harlan Ellison's acclaimed series of original anthologies, this story has never actually seen print until now because the anthology has never been published.*

This story, as is often the case with Simak stories, provides new takes on themes Cliff touched on elsewhere, but I keep thinking that it's a story about life after life.

And it's sad, for the line "You were so badly made" has more than a single meaning.

—dww

He had been Charlie Tierney, but was no longer. He had been a man, but was no longer. Now he was something else, something cobbled together. Now he had no head, had no arms, and his eyes were floating on stalks above his awakening body.

When he had been Charlie Tierney there had been only two really important things to know about him: he was venal, and he was alone. Venal to the point of it being a sickness, a poison that infected his every act. Alone, through years as a child, years as a man, years in space. So alone he could never learn that his ability to be bought was an illness.

Now he was more alone than he had ever been . . . and he was no longer venal. Venality was a human quality, and he was no longer human. Alone, because he was the only one like himself in the universe.

Tierney sat drinking sunlight, and he remembered.

I had it made.

After years of fumbling around, after years of chewing stardust, of hope that never quite came off, of finally giving up the hope—here finally I was, walking down a hill, walking on a planet that I owned, with the pre-emption signals planted and all that needed to be done the filing of the claim. A planet that was worth the claiming—not one of those methane worlds, not carbon dioxide, not soup, but air that a man could breathe, and something to walk on besides rock, a world with vegetation and running water and not too great a sea surface and, what was best of all, a working force of natives who had just enough intelligence, if handled right, to exploit such a planet for you. They didn't know it yet, but I had plans for them. It might take a bit of doing to get them into harness, but I was just the man who knew how to do it.

I was a little drunk, I guess. Christ, I had a right to be. After squatting on that hilltop with those crummy natives, lapping up the stuff, I should have been out cold. But I had soaked up too much alcoholic poison—and some that weren't alcoholic—at too many grimy way stations all through space, to cave in from drinking stuff that wasn't fit to drink. In my day, I'd drunk a lot of booze that wasn't fit to drink. Come in from a long, hard run with nothing found and headaches all the way and you'll drink anything at all just so it gives forgetfulness.

There always had been a lot of forgetting to be done. But that was over now. In just a while from now I'd be wading up to my knees through cash.

The luckiest part of it was those stupid natives. And that was just the way it should be. Hell, I told myself, they wouldn't even know the difference. They might even like it. They would love working out their guts for me. I had them all psyched out. I knew what made them tick.

It had taken a lot of patience and a lot of observation and more work than I liked to think about, but I finally had them pegged. They had a culture, if you could call it that. They had a feeble kind of intelligence, enough intelligence so that you could tell them to put their backs into it and they'd put their backs into it. Before I was through with them they'd think I was the best friend they had and they'd bust their silly guts for me. They had been the ones who had asked me to the hilltop for a little get-together. They had supplied the food, which I had barely been able to gag down, and the likker, which had been a little easier to gag down, and we'd talked after a fashion—good, solid, friendly talk.

I had the little creeps in the hollow of my hand.

They were crazy-looking things, but for that matter all aliens are crazy-looking things.

They stood four feet or so in height and looked something like a lobster, or at least like something that far back in its evolutionary line had been something like a lobster. As if the crustacea, instead of striking out, had developed as the primates had developed on the Earth. They had been modified considerably from the ancestral lobster, but the resemblance was still there. They lived in burrows and there were big villages of these burrows everywhere I went. There were a lot of them and that suited me just fine. It takes a big labor force to milk a planet. If you had to import that kind of labor or bring in machines the overhead would kill you.

So I was walking down the hillside, perhaps not too steadily, but I was feeling fine. I could see the spaceship in the bright moonlight, just across the valley, and in the morning I'd take off and file the claim and see some people that I knew and then I'd be in business. No more tearing around in uncharted space to find that one particular planet, no more begging grubstakes to go out on another hunt, no more stinking fleabags in little planetary outposts, no more rotgut liquor, no more frowsy whores. From here on out I'd have the best there was. I'd made the kind of strike every planet hunter dreams about. I had struck it rich. Oh, it was sweet all right—an absolutely virgin planet with all sorts of riches and a gang of stupid natives to work for me.

I came to the rockslide and I could have walked around it and in a more sober moment I suppose I would have done just that. But I wasn't sober. I was drunk on alien booze and on happiness, if happiness is finding what you've hunted all your life.

I saw that I could save some time by crossing the rockslide and it didn't look too bad. Just a sheet of rubble where, in ages past, a cliff near the top of the hill had shed part of its face, sending down a fan of rock and boulders. A number of boulders were embedded in the slide and others, I saw, had simply slid off the cliff face and not rolled down the hill, remaining poised where they had fallen. I remember thinking, as I started across the slide, that it would not take too much to send them plunging down the slope. But they had been there, safely anchored, for many unknown years, and, anyhow, I was somewhat fuddled.

So I started across the slide and the walking was rougher than I'd expected it to be, but I was being careful so as not to fall and break my neck and I was getting along all right. I had to watch where I put my feet and was going slow and wasn't paying too much attention to anything that might be happening.

A sudden grinding sound from somewhere above me jerked me around and a stone rolled underneath one foot and threw me to my knees. I saw the boulders coming down the slope straight at me. They came slow at first, slow and deliberate, seeming to topple rather than to roll. I yelled. I don't remember what I yelled. I just yelled. I knew I didn't have the time to get away, but I tried. I tried to get to my feet and had almost made it when another stone shifted underneath a foot and threw me down again. The boulders were much closer now, gathering speed, bounding high into the air when they struck other boulders in their paths, and the rest of the slide above me, jarred by the rolling boulders, was moving down on top of me, as if the rock and rubble had somehow come alive.

Before the first of the boulders reached me I seemed to see little shadowy figures running frantically along the base of the cliff and I thought, "Those God damned lobsters!"

Then the boulders reached me and I put out my hands to stop them, just as if there might have been a chance of stopping them; and I was still yelling.

The boulders hit and killed me. They smashed my flesh and bone. They busted in my rib cage and they cracked my skull. They smashed and rolled me flat. The blood went spraying out and stained the stones. The bladder broke, the intestines ruptured.

But there was, after a time, it seemed, a part of me that wasn't killed. In the darkness of no-seeing I knew I had been killed. But there was this part of me that still hung onto knowing with bleeding fingernails.

I don't believe I thought at first. I existed, that was all. In darkness, in emptiness, in nothingness; I was there, not dead. Or at least not entirely dead. I'd forgotten everything I had ever known. I began from scratch. No better than a worm. I tried to take it easy, but there was no such thing as easy. For no reason, I was frantic. Frantic without purpose. Just frantic to exist, to continue hanging on with bloody fingernails. A frantic worm, without knowing, with no reason.

After a time the tension eased a little and I thought. Not simple thoughts, but convoluted and intricate, going on and on, reaching for a simple answer, but going through a maze of mental contortions that were worse than hanging on to existence with no more than fingernails. The terrible thing about it was that I, or the existence that was I, for there was as yet no I, did not even know the problem to which it sought an answer.

Wonder came to replace the thinking, a quiet, hard, chilling wonder that stretched out flat and thin. And the wonder asked: Is this afterlife? Is there really afterlife? Is this what happens when one dies? Hoping it was not, frantic it was not, despairing at the prospect of an eternal, groping afterlife, so flat and thin and dark. Wonder went on forever and forever—not thinking, not reasoning, not speculating, just a wonder that filled the little being that existed, a hopeless, helpless wonder that grew no less or greater, but stretched, unmarked, toward eternity.

Then the wonder went and the darkness went. There was light again and knowing, not only the knowing of the present, but of the past as well. As if something had snapped a switch or pushed a button. As if I'd been turned on.

I had been human once (and I knew what human was), but I was no longer. I knew it from the instant that unseen operator snapped the switch. It wasn't hard to know. I hadn't any head and my eyes were floating way up in the air and they were funny eyes. They didn't look just one way; they looked all the way around and saw everything. Somewhere between my eyes and me were hearing and taste and smell and a lot of other senses I'd never had before—a heat sense, a magnetic indicator, a sniffer-out of life.

I sniffed out a lot of life—big life—and it was moving fast and I saw it was the lobsters, moving very fast to dive down into their burrows. They must have dived down like scared rabbits, for in an instant I lost all sense of them, the sense of them shielded out by many feet of ground. But to replace them was a great deal of other life, a thousand different kinds of life, perhaps more than a thousand different kinds of life and I knew that deep inside my brain all these different life forms—all the plants and grasses, all the insects (or this planet's equivalent of insects), all the viruses and bacteria— were being filed away most neatly, to be pulled out and identified if there ever should be need.

My brain, I knew, was somewhere in my guts. It had to be, I knew, for I hadn't any head. It was no proper place for a brain to be, but I had no more than thought that than I knew that it was the right place, down where it was protected and not sticking up into the air where anything or anyone at all could take a swipe at it.

I hadn't any head and my brain was somewhere in the middle of me and my body was an oval, sort of like an egg, and it was armor-plated. Legs—I had a hundred legs, tiny things like caterpillar legs. I figured out, as well, that my eyes weren't floating in the air, but were at the ends of two flexible stalks, which I guess you'd call antennae. And those antennae were more than just stalks to hold up my eyes. They were ears as well, more sensitive than my human ears had been, and taste and smell, heat sense, life sense, magnetic sense and other things which had not come clear as yet.

Just knowing all I had parked away in those two antennae gave me a queasy feeling, but there seemed really nothing bad about it, nothing that I couldn't handle. With all the extra senses, I thought, I'd sure be hard to catch. Even feeling a little proud, perhaps, at how well equipped I was.

I saw that I was on a hilltop, the very hilltop I'd sat upon with the lobsters lapping up the booze. How long ago I might have been there, there was no way of knowing. The ashes of the fire were still there, the fire that they had kindled, proudly, with a fire-drill, and I had let them kindle it, never letting on that I could have lit the fire with a thumb-stroke on my lighter. Even managing, if I remembered rightly, to look a little envious at the ease with which they handled fire. The campfire was old, however, with the prints of pattering raindrops imprinted on the ash.

The ship was just across the valley and in a little while I'd go over to it and take off. I'd file my claim and make arrangements to put the planet on a paying basis. Everything was all right, except that I wasn't human, and there upon that hilltop I began to miss my humanness. It's a funny thing; you don't ever stop to think what human is until you haven't got it.

I was slightly scared, I suppose, at not being human; perhaps more than a little scared at all the junk I had that made me not be human. With a little effort I still could make myself feel human in my mind, although I knew damn well I wasn't. And I got lonesome, just like that, for the spaceship squatting over there across the valley. Once I got inside it, I told myself, I would finally be safe.

But safe from what, I wondered. I had been dead, but now I wasn't dead. It seemed to me I should be happy, but I couldn't seem to be.

One of the lobsters stuck his head out of a burrow. I saw him and I heard him and I sensed his lifeness and his temperature. I thought that he would know.

"What is going on?" I asked him. "What has happened to me?"

"There was nothing else to do," he told me. "We feel so sorry for you. There was so much wrong with you. We did the best we could, but you were so badly made."

"Badly made!" I yelled and started for him and he went down the burrow so fast that even with all my sensory equipment I never saw him go.

Two things hit me hard.

I had talked to him and he'd answered and we'd understood each other and that night by the campfire we had barely passed the grunt-and-gesture stage.

And if I'd heard him right, it had been the lobsters that had put me back together, that had made me what I was. It was all insane, of course. How could those crummy lobsters do a thing like that? They lived in burrows and they used a fire-drill to build themselves a campfire and they didn't even know how to make decent booze. It made no sense that a pack of lobsters living like a herd of wood-chucks could have patched me back together.

But apparently they had; they were the only ones around. But if they had—and, again, they must have—they could have put me back into my former shape. It they were able to make me the kind of thing I was, they could have made me human. They must have used a lot of bio-engineering to fix me up at all, working with com-pletely flexible culture tissues and a lot of other stuff of which I had no idea. If they had that kind of stuff to work with, the little creeps could have made me human.

I wondered if they'd played some sort of joke on me, and if, by God, they had, they would pay for it. When I got back I'd work their stupid tails off; I'd show them who was playing jokes.

They had dug me out and patched me up and I was still alive. There must not have been much left of me the way those boulders socked me. Perhaps they had no more than a hunk of brain to build on. It must have been a job to make anything of me. I suppose I should have been grateful to them, but I wasn't able to work up much gratitude.

They had loused me up for sure. No matter how human I might feel or even act, to the eye I wasn't human. Out in the galaxy I'd not be accepted as a human. By certain people, perhaps, and intellectually, but to most human beings I'd be nothing but a freak.

I'd get along, of course. With a planet such as this, one couldn't help but get along. With the kind of bankroll I'd have I'd get along all right.

When I started for the ship I was afraid those caterpillar legs of mine might slow me down, but they didn't. I went skimming along faster than I would have walked and over uneven ground I ordinarily would have walked around. I thought at first I might have to concentrate to make all those legs track in line, but I went along as if I'd been walking caterpillar-fashion all my life.

The eyes were something, too. I could see all around me and up into the sky as well. I realized that, as a primate, I had been looking down a tunnel, blind by more than half. And I realized, too, that as a primate I would have been confused and disoriented by this total vision, but as I was made it wasn't. Not only my body had been changed, but my sensory centers as well.

Total vision wasn't all of it, of course. There were many other sensory centers located in the eyestalks, some of which I had figured out, but a lot of others that still had me puzzled and a bit confused; they were picking up information to which my human senses had been blind—the kind of stuff I'd never known about and couldn't put a name to. The really curious thing about it was that none of these new senses were particularly emphasized—they seemed very natural. They were feeding into me an integrated awareness of all the forces and conditions that surrounded me. I had a total and absolute awareness of my physical environment.

I reached the spaceship and I didn't bother with the ladder. I just upended myself and went scooting up the side of that slick metal without a single thought. There were sucking discs in the pads of the caterpillar legs and I hadn't known about them until it came time to use them. I wondered how many other abilities I wouldn't know about until there was need of them.

I hadn't bothered to lock the hatch cover when I'd left, because there was nothing on the planet that could get into the ship, and now, finally at the hatch, I was glad I hadn't: if I had, the key would now be lost, buried somewhere in the rock slide.

All I had to do was push and the cover of the hatch would open. So I went to put out an arm to push and absolutely nothing happened. I didn't have arms.

I hung there, sick and cold.

And in that moment of shock, in the sick and cold, not only the lack of arms and hands, but all the rest of it, all the impact of what had happened and what I had become hit me in the face, except I hadn't any face. My entrails shriveled up. My marrow turned to water. The bitter taste of bile surged up inside of me.

I huddled close against the hard metal of the ship, clinging to it as the last thing of any meaning in my life. A cold wind out of nowhere was blowing through and through me, moaning as it blew. This was it, I thought. There wasn't anything more pitiful than a being without manipulatory organs and, even in my present mental state, pity was something I could get along without.

Thinking about the pity made me sore, I guess, the idea that anything, anything at all, would feel sorry for me. Pity was the one thing that I couldn't stomach.

Those crummy lobsters, I thought, the stupid bunglers, the stinking yokels! To give me better senses and better feet and a better body and then forget the arms! How could they expect me to do anything without arms?

And, hanging there, still sick, still cold, but feeling an edge of anger now, I knew there had been no mistake. They weren't bunglers and they weren't yokels. They were miles ahead of me. They'd left off the arms on purpose so I could do nothing. They had crippled me and tied me to the planet. They'd upset all my plans. I could never get away and I'd never tell anyone about this planet and they could go on living out their stupid lives inside their filthy burrows.

They'd upset my plans and that must have meant they had known, or guessed, my plans. They had me figured out to the fraction of a millimeter. While I had been psyching them, they'd been psyching me. They knew exactly what I was and what I'd meant to do and, when the time had come, they had known exactly what to do about me.

The rolling boulders had been no accident. I remembered, now that I thought about it, the shadowy figures running along the cliff's base when the rocks had begun to move.

They had killed me, and much as I might resent it, I could understand the killing. What I couldn't understand was why they didn't let it go at that. They had solved their problem with my death; why did they bother to dig into the rubble to get a piece of brain so they could resurrect me?

As I thought about all the implications of it, rage built up in me. They had not let well enough alone, they'd not been satisfied; they'd made a plaything out of me—a toy, a bauble in which they could find amusement, but if I knew them, amusement from afar, at a distance where there'd be no danger to them. Although what in hell I could do to them, without any arms, was more than I could imagine.

But I wasn't going to let them get away with it, by God!

I'd get into the spaceship somehow and take off and somewhere I would find a human or some other thing that had arms or the equivalent of arms and I'd make a deal with them and those stinking lobsters would finish up working out their hearts for me.

I bent an eyestalk down and tried to push against the cover, but the stalk had little power. So I doubled it over and pushed with it again and the cover barely moved—but it did move. I kept on pushing and the cover swung slowly inward and finally stood open. Who needed arms, I thought triumphantly. If I could use an eyestalk to open the hatch, I could practice with the stalks until I could use them to operate the ship.

You clowns out there, I said, better start right now to dig those burrows deeper because, so help me, I'm coming back to get you. There couldn't no one do what they'd done to me and get away with it.

I moved over a bit to get into the hatch and I found there was no way to get into the hatch. I was just a bit too big. Not very much, just a bit too big. I pushed and shoved. I twisted and turned every way I could. No matter what I did, the body was too big.

Planned, I thought. They never missed a lick. They hadn't overlooked a thing. They'd made me without arms and had the hatch all measured and made me just too big—not too much too big, but just a shade too big. They had led me on and now they were rolling in their burrows laughing and the day would come when I'd make them smart for that.

But that was an empty thought and I knew it was. There was no way that I could make them smart.

I wasn't going anywhere and I wasn't doing anything. I wasn't going to get into the ship and if I couldn't get into the ship, I wouldn't leave the planet. I hadn't any arms and I hadn't any head and since I didn't have a head, I hadn't any mouth. Without a mouth, how was a man to eat? Had they condemned me not only to being trapped upon this planet, but dying of starvation?

I climbed down to the ground, so shaken with fear and anger

that I was extra careful in my climbing down for fear that I might slip and fall.

Once down I crouched beside the ship and tried to lay it all out in a row so I could have a look at it.

I wasn't human any more. Still human in my mind, of course, but certainly not in body. I was trapped upon the planet and would not be going back to the human race again. And even if I could, there'd be a lot of things I couldn't do. I'd never take a babe to bed again. I'd never eat a steak. I'd never have a drink. And my own people would either laugh at me or be scared of me and I couldn't quite make out which would be the worse.

It seemed incredible, on the face of it, that the lobsters would be able to do a thing like this. It didn't quite make sense that a tribe of prairie dogs that looked like something you'd expect upon your dinner plate could take a piece of brain and from it construct a new and living being. There was about them nothing that suggested such ability and knowledge, no trappings to indicate they were other than what they appeared to be, a species of creatures that had developed some intelligence, but had made no great cultural advances.

But appearances were wrong; there was no doubt of that. They had a culture and an ability and knowledge—far more of both of them than my psych testing had even hinted at. And that, of course, would be the way with a race like them. I hadn't based my conclusions upon fact, but on data they had fed me.

If they had this kind of culture, why were they hiding it? Why live in burrows? Why use a drill to start a fire? Why not a city? Why not a road? Why couldn't the crummy little stinkers at least act civilized?

The answer wasn't hard to find. If you act civilized, you stick out like a bandaged thumb. But if you lay doggo and act stupid, you got the edge. Anything that comes along will underestimate you and then you are in a good position to let them have it, right between the eyes. Maybe I hadn't been the first planet hunter to show up. Maybe there had been other planet hunters in the past.

Maybe through the years these vicious little lobsters had figured out exactly how to deal with them.

Although what I couldn't figure out was why they didn't do it simple. Why all the fancy frills? When they killed a planet hunter why not let it go at that? Why did they have to bring him back to life and play silly games with him?

I crouched on the ground and looked across the land and it was as good, or better, than I had thought it was. There were forests along the streams that would provide good timber and back from the watercourses great stretches of rich and level land that could be used for farming. In those hills beyond lay silver ore—and how in the hell could I be so sure there was silver there?

It shook me up to know. I shouldn't have known. I might guess there were minerals in the hills, but there was no way to know exactly where they were or what kind they'd be. But I did know—not guessing, not hoping, but *knowing*. It was my new body that knew, of course, employing some as yet unrealized sensor that was planted in it. More than likely later on, when it really got to working, I could look at any stretch of land and know precisely what was in it. It was all wonderful, of course, but without any arms and no way to get off the planet, it was a total loss. That was the way they worked it, that was how they got their laughs. They held out a piece of candy and when baby reached for it, they slashed off his grasping paws.

The sun felt warm on my body and I didn't want to move. I should be up and doing, although I could not think, for the life of me, of a thing I should be doing. Doing, for the moment, was at an end for me. In a little while, perhaps, I might be able to figure out a thing or two to do. In the meantime I'd simply sit here and eat up some more sunlight.

That's the way I knew. It came sneaking in upon me—all these new-fashioned abilities, all the fancy senses, all the newfound knowledge. I was eating sunlight. I didn't need a mouth. I simply fed on the energy of sunlight. I thought about this eating, this soaking up of sunlight and I knew, as I thought about it, that it need not be sunlight, although sunlight was the easiest. But if necessary I could reach out and grab energy from anything at all. I could suck up the energy in a stream of water. I could drain it from a tree or rob a blade of grass. I could extract it from the soil.

Simple and efficient, and as close to foolproof as a body could be made. The dirty little creep, sticking his head out of the burrow, had said my human body had been badly made. And, of course, it had. It had not been engineered. It had simply grown evolutionally, through millennia, doing the best it could with the little that it had.

I felt the sunlight on me and I soaked it up and I knew about the sunlight, how it came about—the proton-proton reactions that brought about the rapid shuffling of subatomic particles from one form to another, releasing in the process the flood of energy which poured out from the star. I'd known all this before, of course, in my human form. But I had learned it once and then had never thought of it again. This was different. This was not a matter of simple learning, of an intellectual knowledge. Now I felt it, saw it, sensed it. I could, without half trying, imagine myself a hydrogen nucleus within that place of energy and pressure. I could hear the hissing of the gamma rays, glimpse the giddy flight of new-born neutrinos. And I knew it was not the star alone—I could probe, as well, into the secret of a plant, seek out the microbes and other tiny life forms that swarmed deep within the soil, trace the processes by which a geologic formation had come into being. Not only knowing, but being one with any of it, sharing with it, understanding far better than it (whatever it might be) could understand itself.

I was cold with a coldness that sunlight could not warm. My mind was frozen hard.

I wasn't human any more at all. I wasn't thinking human. My mind and thinking, my senses and my viewpoints had been tinkered with. I had been edited and only now was the editing beginning to take effect. It was not only my body, it was all of me. I was turning into something I didn't want to be, that no human would ever want to be.

This thinking of the proton-proton business was all damn foolishness. There were more important things I should be thinking, of a plan to force my way into the ship, of how to cash in on this planet. There was a mint to be made out of this planet, more money than I could ever spend. But now, I thought, what did I need the money for? Certainly not for drink or food or clothes or women—and I wondered a bit about that woman business. I was, I suspected, the only thing of my kind existing in the galaxy and what about the reproductive process? Would there be just the one of me and not be any more? Or could I be bisexual and bear or spawn or hatch others of my kind? Or could I be immortal? Was there such a thing as death for me? Was there, perhaps, no need of reproduction? Was there just the one of me and no need of any more? No room for any more?

If that should be the case, why all this worry over money? And, thinking that, I didn't seem to care as much about the money as I had at one time.

That was the hell of it—the human hell of it. I didn't care. Not about the money, nor the lobsters nor what they'd done to me, nor about the humanity I'd lost. Perhaps that was the way I had been engineered, maybe it was the only way I could survive, the shape that I was in.

I fought against the great uncaring with all the bitterness I had. So you did it, I said to those lousy lobsters. So you pulled it off. You scratched one human who could have been a threat, who would have exploited you down to skin and bones. And you built a model of a new experimental life form you'd been aching to try out, but didn't have the guts to try on one of your own people. You had to wait until someone else showed up. And now you'll watch me all the time to see how I'm doing, to figure out the bugs and miscalculations, so that sometime in the future you can build a better one.

I hadn't known of it before but there it was, naked, in my mind, as naturally in my mind as if I'd always known it, as if from the very beginning I had known I was no more than an experimental model.

They'd taken away my humanity and added a great uncaring, and that uncaring had been the gadget they had thought would be the final factor. But there was some stubbornness still left in me from the almost-vanished humanity of which they'd tried to rob me, so sneakily and smoothly that I never would suspect that it was gone until it was too late to do anything to save it.

Frantically, with panic rising in me, I went hunting down inside myself, scrabbling like a dog digging out a gopher, seeking for any fragment of humanity that might be left to me. Down into the dark, sniffing out the secret places where a fragmented piece of humanity might hide.

And I found it! A nasty piece of me hiding deep and dark, and yet a piece of me that was quite familiar, that I was well acquainted with, that in other times I had hugged close against me for the vicious comfort it had given me.

I found hatred.

It was tough and hard to kill. It resisted routing out. It still clung tenaciously.

As I clasped it hard inside my mind and hugged it close against me, as an old friend, an ancient weapon, I wondered vaguely if the reason it had been left was that the race of lobsters had no concept of hatred, that it might be something of which they were unaware, that what they had done to me might have been done for many reasons, but that hatred of me for what I meant to do to them was not one of the reasons.

That made me one up on them, I thought fiercely as I clutched the hatred at the core of me. It gave me an advantage they would never guess. With hatred to bolster and sustain me, I could hope and wait and plan and the time would never seem too long if revenge could be at the end of it.

They'd taken away my body, my motives, almost all my human-ity. They had tinkered with my thinking and my values and my viewpoints. They had taken me; they had taken me but good. They had outfoxed me on every point but one and on that one point they had, unknowingly, outfoxed themselves as badly. Maybe they had seen that little piece of hatred as no more than a minor biochemical imperfection. After all, as the lobster had pointed out, I had been badly made. But in mistaking it, or neglecting it, they had fouled up their project. With a piece of hatred still left in him, a man would never utterly lose his hold upon humanity. What a wondrous thing it is to be a hating creature!

I held the hatred and could feel it turning cold—and cold hatred is the best of all. I know. It drives you, it never lets you be, it keeps on nagging you. Hot hatred flashes up and is over in a moment, but cold hatred lies there, at the heart and gut of you, and you know it all the time. It niggles at your brain and it clenches up your fists even when there is no one there to hit.

But I hadn't any fists, I thought, I hadn't any arms. I was just an armor-plated oval with silly caterpillar legs and eyestalks sticking up into the air.

Then, on schedule, as if there might be some sort of biological computer tucked away inside me, feeding in the data that was *me,* feeding it in slowly so I wouldn't be overwhelmed by a rush of data, not overloading me, I knew about the arms.

I didn't have them yet and I wouldn't have them for a while. But they were there and growing underneath my shell, waiting to be freed. I would have to moult before I had the arms. It wasn't only arms. There were other things as well—other appendages, other budding senses, other extensions of new abilities, all of them only dimly sensed, fogged in the mist of things-to-come. But the arms I knew about because arms were not new to me. I had had arms before and I knew about them. These other things I didn't know about, but in time I would. Marvelous additional adjuncts to the performance of a life form's full abilities, planned most carefully by the lobsters, to be tried out in an experimental model before the lobsters made such bodies for themselves.

They had planned long and hard. They had figured out the angles and then had engineered them. They were aiming at an ideal body. And I would take all that planning and all the engineering and all their dirty scheming and I'd shove it down their throats. As soon as I had arms and all those other appendages and senses and God knows what, I'd cram it down their throats.

I couldn't go back to the human race, nor to women, nor to money, nor to food and drink. But I didn't need them any more. I had never needed them—really needed them. The one thing I did need I had, the one last thing that was left to me. It seemed sheer cosmic justice that the one thing that I needed was the one thing I had left—the capacity to get even with the ones who'd done me dirt, to cram it down their throats, to make them mourn the day that saw their spawning.

I was different and I would be more different still. I would, in the end, be human in only one regard. And the important thing, the most important thing of all, was that in this one regard my one remnant of humanity was stronger than all the rest of it. It had come from the bowels of time. It came from that never-dated day when a certain little primate, with a new-found cunning that was stronger than the jungle's tooth-and-claw, remembered an anger that should have been over in a moment and had waited for a chance to act upon that remembered anger, nursing that cooling anger as a comfort and a prop to dignity, changing it from anger into hatred. Long before anything that could have been called Australopithecine walked the earth, the concept of revenge had been forged and in those millennia it had served the vicious little strain of primates well. It had made them the most deadly creatures that had ever come to life.

It would serve me well, I told myself. I would make it serve me well. It would give me purpose and a certain kind of dignity and self-respect.

A figure came to mind, another piece of information spewed into me from the biochemical computer. A thousand years, it said. A thousand years to moult. A thousand years to wait.

A long time. Ten centuries. Thirty human generations. Empires rose and fell in a thousand years. Were forgotten in another thousand. A thousand years would give me time to think and plan, to harden the coldness of the hatred, to realize and examine the new abilities and capacities that would evolve with moulting.

It called for planning. No simple, easy revenge. No mere physical torture, no killing. By the time I got through with them death would be the height of kindness, physical torture a mere inconvenience. Nor would it merely be an exploitation of them to harvest the resources of the planet. It was the worst day they'd ever known when they had taken from me the need (or desire) for those resources. If I still held that need, normal human greed might have stayed my hand. But now, nothing would stay my hand.

I had them, I thought. Thinking coldly and with calculation. With no anger. With no urgency. With no mercy in me. Mercy was a human trait made to balance revenge and now the balance had been wiped out and I had only hatred left.

How it might be done I did not know. I would not know until I had explored to the limit the capacity of the abilities that waited upon moulting. But I knew this: they would live out their lives in ever-mounting terror; they would seek for hiding places and there'd be no hiding places; each day they would face new horrors and their nerves would strain and their brains would turn to water, then congeal again to face another fear. They would be allowed, at times, a slender hope so the agony would be the greater when the tiny hope had failed. They would run in the hopeless circles of their panic, they would squeal with an insanity which would never reach the point where it might offer refuge, and while they might pray for surcease, I would most tenderly see that they stayed alive and capable of fear. Not just a few of them, but all of them, every stinking soul of them. And I would keep it up, I would never tire. I would never have enough, I would feed upon my hatred of them. It would be the breath of life to me. It would be my only purpose, taking the place of all the other purposes they had taken from me. It was the one last shred of humanity I had left and I would never let it go.

I hugged the hatred and thought of a thousand years. A long, long time. Empires totter, technologies change, religions shift their forms, social mores undergo revisions, ideas blossom and have their day and die, stars slide down just a little toward stellar death, light travels a hundredth of the way across the galaxy. So long a span of time that the mind of man quails before the prospect of it.

But not me. I do not quail before a thousand years.

I can use those thousand years. I can study the lobsters and see what makes them tick. I can learn their purposes, their philosophies, their dreams—learning all the things to strip away from them, giving them instead the things they fear and loathe and sicken at the sight and feel of.

I'll enjoy it, every minute of it.

I am in no hurry.

I can wait.

The alien wind blows cool and sweet around Charlie Tierney as he sits drinking sunlight. He remembers and remembers, playing it over and over in his mind: a mind growing more acute every moment. He clings to the last vestige of his humanity, the greatest gift handed down to him from his ape ancestors: a desire for killing, torturing, never-ending revenge. He sits and is content in his hatred. It will sustain him.

It will keep him in check, as no bonds or fetters ever could.

The lobster creatures in their burrows understood that from the moment they rebuilt him. Necessary, yes, very necessary for Charlie Tierney to stay the thousand years, to evolve through those thousand years so they could evaluate the viability of what they had created, for their own purposes. But without something to distract him, with only the helplessness and despair of knowing he would never again be human, Charlie Tierney might have destroyed himself. And that they could not permit. The experiment had to run its course.

They had left him a distraction, something useless he could hold close to placate him while the evolutionary experiment ran its course. A thousand-year toy for an alert laboratory animal.

Charlie Tierney holds close the hatred, examines with pathological attention the concept of revenge. He can wait. He has a thousand years to grow until he can wreak revenge on the damned lobster things.

What he does not know is that even before he came to them, the lobster creatures had learned all there was to know about waiting. They had waited for a Charlie Tierney, and now they could wait for the results of the experiment.

And they had no need of thousand-year toys.

SMALL DEER

Originally published in the October 1965 issue of Galaxy Science Fiction, *which by then had long supplanted* Astounding *as Cliff Simak's main market, this story is one of those that really stuck in my youthful memory. That was because it scared the hell out of me . . . !*

—*dww*

Willow Bend,
Wisconsin
June 23, 1966

Dr. Wyman Jackson,
Wyalusing College,
Muscoda, Wisconsin

My dear Dr. Jackson:

I am writing to you because I don't know who else to write to and there is something I have to tell someone who can understand. I know your name because I read your book, 'Cretaceous Dinosaurs,' not once, but many times. I tried to get Dennis to read it, too, but I guess he never did. All Dennis was interested in were the mathematics of his time concept—not the time machine itself. Besides, Dennis doesn't read too well. It is a chore for him.

Maybe I should tell you, to start with, that my name is Alton James. I live with my widowed mother and I run a fix-it shop. I fix bicycles and lawn mowers and radios and television sets—I fix anything that is brought to me. I'm not much good at anything else, but I do seem to have the knack of seeing how things go together and understanding how they work and seeing what is wrong with them when they aren't working. I never had no training of any sort, but I just seem to have a natural bent for getting along with mechanical contraptions.

Dennis is my friend and I'll admit right off that he is a strange one. He doesn't know from nothing about anything, but he's nuts on mathematics. People in town make fun of him because he is so strange and Ma gives me hell at times for having anything to do with him. She says he's the next best thing to a village idiot. I guess a lot of people think the way that Ma does, but it is not entirely true, for he does know his math.

I don't know how he knows it. He didn't learn it at school and that's for sure. When he got to be 17 and hadn't got no farther than eighth grade, the school just sort of dropped him. He didn't really get to eighth grade honest; the teachers after a while got tired of seeing him on one grade and passed him to the next. There was talk, off and on, of sending him to some special school, but it never got nowhere.

And don't ask me what kind of mathematics he knew. I tried to read up on math once because I had the feeling, after seeing some of the funny marks that Dennis put on paper, that maybe he knew more about it than anyone else in the world. And I still think that he does—or that maybe he's invented an entirely new kind of math. For in the books I looked through I never did find any of the symbols that Dennis put on paper. Maybe Dennis used symbols he made up, inventing them as he went along, because no one had ever told him what the regular mathematicians used. But I don't think that's it—I'm inclined to lean to the idea Dennis came up with a new brand of math, entirely.

There were times I tried to talk with Dennis about this math of his and each time he was surprised that I didn't know it, too. I guess he thought most people knew about it. He said that it was simple, that it was plain as day. It was the way things worked, he said.

I suppose you'll want to ask how come I understood his equations well enough to make the time machine. The answer is I didn't. I suppose that Dennis and I are alike in a lot of ways, but in different ways. I know how to make contraptions work (without knowing any of the theory) and Dennis sees the entire universe as something operating mechanically (and him scarcely able to read a page of simple type).

And another thing. My family and Dennis's family live in the same end of town and from the time we were toddlers, Dennis and I played together. Later on, we just kept on together. We didn't have a choice. For some reason or other, none of the kids would play with us. Unless we wanted to play alone, we had to play together. I guess we got so, through the years, that we understood each other.

I don't suppose there'd have been any time machine if I hadn't been so interested in paleontology. Not that I knew anything about it; I was just interested. From the time I was a kid I read everything I could lay my hands on about dinosaurs and saber-tooths and such. Later on I went fossil hunting in the hills, but I never found nothing really big. Mostly I found brachiopods. There are great beds of them in the Platteville limestone. And lots of times I'd stand in the street and look up at the river bluffs above the town and try to imagine what it had been like a million years ago, or a hundred million. When I first read in a story about a time machine, I remember thinking how I'd like to have one. I guess that at one time I thought a little about making one, but then realized I couldn't.

Dennis had a habit of coming to my shop and talking, but most of the time talking to himself rather than to me. I don't remember exactly how it started, but after a while I realized that he had stopped talking about anything but time. One day he told me he had been able to figure out everything but time, and now it seemed he was getting that down in black and white, like all the rest of it.

Mostly I didn't pay too much attention to what he said, for a lot of it didn't make much sense. But after he'd talked, incessantly, for a week or two, on time, I began to pay attention. But don't expect me to tell you what he said or make any sense of it, for there's no way that I can. To understand what Dennis said and meant, you'd have to live with him, like I did, for twenty years or more. It's not so much understanding what Dennis says as understanding Dennis.

I don't think we actually made any real decision to build a time machine, it just sort of grew on us. All at once we found that we were making one.

We took our time. We had to take our time, for we went back a lot and did things over, almost from the start. It took weeks to get some of the proper effects—at least, that's what Dennis called them. Me, I didn't know anything about effects. All that I knew was that Dennis wanted to make something work a certain way and I tried to make it work that way. Sometimes, even when it worked the way he wanted it, it turned out to be wrong. So we'd start all over.

But finally we had a working model of it and took it out on a big bald bluff, several miles up the river, where no one ever went. I rigged up a timer to a switch that would turn it on, then after two minutes would reverse the field and send it home again.

We mounted a movie camera inside the frame that carried the machine, and we set the camera going, then threw the timer switch.

I had my doubts that it would work, but it did. It went away and stayed for two minutes, then came back again.

When we developed the camera film, we knew without any question the camera had traveled back in time. At first there were pictures of ourselves standing there and waiting. Then there was a little blur, no more than a flicker across a half a dozen frames, and the next frames showed a mastodon walking straight into the camera. A fraction of a second later his trunk jerked up and his ears flared out as he wheeled around with clumsy haste and galloped down the ridge.

Every now and then he'd swing his head around to take a look behind him. I imagine that our time machine, blossoming suddenly out of the ground in front of him, scared him out of seven years of growth.

We were lucky, that was all. We could have sent that camera back another thousand times, perhaps, and never caught a mastodon— probably never caught a thing. Although we would have known it had moved in time, for the landscape had been different, although not a great deal different, but from the landscape we could not have told if it had gone back a hundred or a thousand years. When we saw the mastodon, however, we knew we'd sent the camera back 10,000 years at least.

I won't bore you with how we worked out a lot of problems on our second model, or how Dennis managed to work out a time-meter that we could calibrate to send the machine a specific distance into time. Because all this is not important. What is important is what I found when I went into time.

I've already told you I'd read your book about Cretaceous dino-saurs and I liked the entire book, but that final chapter about the extinction of the dinosaurs is the one that really got me. Many a time I'd lie awake at night thinking about all the theories you wrote about and trying to figure out in my own mind how it really was.

So when it was time to get into that machine and go, I knew where I would be headed.

Dennis gave me no argument. He didn't even want to go. He didn't care no more. He never was really interested in the time machine. All he wanted was to prove out his math. Once the machine did that, he was through with it.

I worried a lot, going as far as I meant to go, about the ris-ing or subsidence of the crust. I knew that the land around Wil-low Bend had been stable for millions of years. Sometime during the Cretaceous a sea had crept into the interior of the continent, but had stopped short of Wisconsin and, so far as geologists could determine, there had been no disturbances in the state. But I still felt uneasy about it. I didn't want to come out into the Late Cretaceous with the machine buried under a dozen feet of rock or, maybe, hanging a dozen feet up in the air.

So I got some heavy steel pipes and sunk them six feet into the rock on the bald bluff top we had used the first time, with about ten feet of their length extending in the air. I mounted the time frame on top of them and rigged up a ladder to get in and out of it and tied the pipes into the time field. One morning I packed a lunch and filled a canteen with water. I dug the old binoculars that had been my father's out of the attic and debated whether I should take along a gun. All I had was a shotgun and I decided not to take it. If I'd had a rifle, there'd been no question of my taking it, but I didn't have one. I could have borrowed one, but I didn't want to. I'd kept pretty quiet about what I was doing and I didn't want to start any gossip in the village.

I went up to the bluff top and climbed up to the frame and set the time-meter to 63-1/2 million years into the past and then I turned her on. I didn't make any ceremony out of it. I just turned her on and went.

I told you about the little blur in the movie film and that's the best way, I suppose, to tell you how it was. There was this little blur, like a flickering twilight. Then it was sunlight once again and I was on the bluff top, looking out across the valley.

Except it wasn't a bluff top any longer, but only a high hill. And the valley was not the rugged, tree-choked, deeply cut valley I had always known, but a great green plain, a wide and shallow valley with a wide and sluggish river flowing at the far side of it. Far to the west I could see a shimmer in the sunlight, a large lake or sea. But a sea, I thought, shouldn't be this far east. But there it was, either a great lake or a sea—I never did determine which.

And there was something else as well. I looked down to the ground and it was only three feet under me. Was I ever glad I had used those pipes!

Looking out across the valley, I could see moving things, but they were so far away that I could not make them out. So I picked up the binoculars and jumped down to the ground and walked across the hilltop until the ground began to slope away.

I sat down and put the binoculars to my eyes and worked across the valley with them.

There were dinosaurs out there, a whole lot more of them than I had expected. They were in herds and they were traveling. You'd expect that out of any dozen herds of them, some of them would be feeding, but none of them was. All of them were moving and it seemed to me there was a nervousness in the way they moved. Although, I told myself, that might be the way it was with dinosaurs.

They all were a long way off, even with the glasses, but I could make out some of them. There were several groups of duckbills, waddling along and making funny jerky movements with their heads. I spotted a couple of small herds of thescelosaurs, pacing along, with their bodies tilted forward. Here and there were small groups of triceratops. But strangest of all was a large herd of brontosaurs, ambling nervously and gingerly along, as if their feet might hurt. And it struck me strange, for they were a long way from water and from what I'd read in your book, and in other books, it didn't seem too likely they ever wandered too far away from water.

And there were a lot of other things that didn't look too much like the pictures I had seen in books.

The whole business had a funny feel about it. Could it be, I wondered, that I had stumbled on some great migration, with all the dinosaurs heading out for some place else?

I got so interested in watching that I was downright careless and it was foolish of me. I was in another world and there could have been all sorts of dangers and I should have been watching out for them, but I was just sitting there, flat upon my backside, as if I were at home.

Suddenly there was a pounding, as if someone had turned loose a piledriver, coming up behind me and coming very fast. I dropped the glasses and twisted around and as I did something big and tall rushed past me, no more than three feet away, so close it almost brushed me. I got just a brief impression of it as it went by—huge and gray and scaly.

Then, as it went tearing down the hill, I saw what it was and I had a cold and sinking feeling clear down in my gizzard. For I had been almost run down by the big boy of them all—Tyrannosaurus rex.

His two great legs worked like driving pistons and the light of the sun glinted off the wicked, recurved claws as his feet pumped up and down. His tail rode low and awkward, but there was no awkwardness in the way he moved. His monstrous head swung from side to side, with the great rows of teeth showing in the gaping mouth, and he left behind him a faint foul smell—I suppose from the carrion he ate. But the big surprise was that the wattles hanging underneath his throat were a brilliant iridescence—red and green and gold and purple, the color of them shifting as he swung his head.

I watched him for just a second and then I jumped up and headed for the time machine. I was more scared than I like to think about. I had, I want to testify right here, seen enough of dinosaurs for a lifetime.

But I never reached the time machine.

Up over the brow of the hill came something else. I say something else because I have no idea what it really was. Not as big as rex, but ten times worse than him.

It was long and sinuous and it had a lot of legs and it stood six feet high or so and was a sort of sickish pink. Take a caterpillar and magnify it until it's six feet tall, then give it longer legs so that it can run instead of crawl and hang a death mask dragon's head upon it and you get a faint idea. Just a faint idea.

It saw me and swung its head toward me and made an eager whimpering sound and it slid along toward me with a side-wheeling gait, like a dog when it's running out of balance and lop-sided.

I took one look at it and dug in my heels and made so sharp a turn that I lost my hat. The next thing I knew, I was pelting down the hill behind old Tyrannosaurus.

And now I saw that myself and rex were not the only things that were running down the hill. Scattered here and there along the hillside were other running creatures, most of them in small groups and herds, although there were some singles. Most of them were dinosaurs, but there were other things as well.

I'm sorry I can't tell you what they were, but at that particular moment I wasn't what you might call an astute observer. I was running for my life, as if the flames of hell were lapping at my heels.

I looked around a couple of times and that sinuous creature was still behind me. He wasn't gaining on me any, although I had the feeling that he could if he put his mind to it. Matter of fact, he didn't seem to be following me alone. He was doing a lot of weaving back and forth. He reminded me of nothing quite so much as a faithful farm dog bringing in the cattle. But even thinking this, it took me a little time to realize that was exactly what he was—an old farm dog bringing in a bunch of assorted dinosaurs and one misplaced human being. At the bottom of the hill I looked back again and now that I could see the whole slope of the hill, I saw that this was a bigger cattle drive than I had imagined. The entire hill was alive with running beasts and behind them were a half dozen of the pinkish dogs.

And I knew when I saw this that the moving herds I'd seen out on the valley floor were not migratory herds, but they were moving because they were being driven—that this was a big roundup of some sort, with all the reptiles and the dinosaurs and myself being driven to a common center.

I knew that my life depended on getting lost somehow, and being left behind. I had to find a place to hide and I had to dive into this hiding place without being seen. Only trouble was there seemed no place to hide. The valley floor was naked and nothing bigger than a mouse could have hidden there.

Ahead of me a good-size swale rose up from the level floor and I went pelting up it. I was running out of wind. My breath was getting short and I had pains throbbing in my chest and I knew I couldn't run much farther.

I reached the top of the swale and started down the reverse slope. And there, right in front of me, was a bush of some sort, three feet high or so, bristling with thorns. I was too close to it and going too fast to even try to dodge it, so I did the only thing I could—I jumped over it.

But on the other side there was no solid ground. There was, instead, a hole. I caught just a glimpse of it and tried to jerk my body to one side, and then I was falling into the hole.

It wasn't much bigger than I was. It bumped me as I fell and I picked up some bruises, then landed with a jolt. The fall knocked the breath out of me and I was doubled over, with my arms wrapped about my belly.

My breath came slowly back and the pain subsided and I was able to take a look at where I was.

The hole was some three feet in diameter and perhaps as much as seven deep. It slanted slightly toward the forefront of the slope and its sides were worn smooth. A thin trickle of dirt ran down from the edge of it, soil that I had loosened and dislodged when I had hit the hole. And about halfway up was a cluster of small rocks, the largest of them about the size of a human head, projecting more than half their width out of the wall. I thought, idly, as I looked at them, that some day they'd come loose and drop into the hole. And at the thought I squirmed around a little to one side, so that if they took a notion to fall I'd not be in the line of fire.

Looking down, I saw that I'd not fallen to the bottom of the hole, for the hole went on, deeper in the ground. I had come to rest at a point where the hole curved sharply, to angle back beneath the swale top.

I hadn't noticed it at first, I suppose because I had been too shook up, but now I became aware of a musky smell. Not an overpowering odor, but a sort of scent—faintly animal, although not quite animal.

A smooth-sided hole and a musky smell—there could be no other answer: I had fallen not into just an ordinary hole, but into a burrow of some sort. And it must be the burrow of quite an animal, I thought, to be the size it was. It would have taken something with hefty claws, indeed, to have dug this sort of burrow.

And even as I thought it, I heard the rattling and the scrabbling of something coming up the burrow, no doubt coming up to find out what was going on.

I did some scrabbling myself. I didn't waste no time. But about three feet up I slipped. I grabbed for the top of the hole, but my fingers slid through the sandy soil and I couldn't get a grip. I shot out my feet and stopped my slide short of the bottom of the hole. And there I was, with my back against one side of the hole and my feet braced against the other, hanging there, halfway up the burrow.

While all the time below me the scrabbling and the clicking sounds continued. The thing, whatever it might be, was getting closer, and it was coming fast.

Right in front of me was the nest of rocks sticking from the wall. I reached out and grabbed the biggest one and jerked and it came loose. It was heavier than I had figured it would be and I almost dropped it, but managed to hang on.

A snout came out of the curve in the burrow and thrust itself quickly upward in a grabbing motion. The jaws opened up and they almost filled the burrow and they were filled with sharp and wicked teeth.

I didn't think. I didn't plan. What I did was instinct. I dropped the rock between my spread-out legs straight down into that gaping maw. It was a heavy rock and it dropped four feet or so and went straight between the teeth, down into the blackness of the throat. When it hit it splashed and the jaws snapped shut and the creature backed away.

How I did it, I don't know, but I got out of the hole. I clawed and kicked against the wall and heaved my body up and rolled out of the hole onto the naked hillside.

Naked, that is, except for the bush with the inch-long thorns, the one that I'd jumped over before I fell into the burrow. It was the only cover there was and I made for the upper side of it, for by now, I figured, the big cattle drive had gone past me and if I could get the bush between myself and the valley side of the swale, I might have a chance. Otherwise, sure as hell, one of those dogs would see me and would come out to bring me in.

For while there was no question that they were dinosaur herders, they probably couldn't tell the difference between me and a dinosaur. I was alive and could run and that would qualify me.

There was always the chance, of course, that the owner of the burrow would come swarming out, and if he did I couldn't stay behind the bush. But I rather doubted he'd be coming out, not right away, at least. It would take him a while to get that stone out of his throat.

I crouched behind the bush and the sun was hot upon my back and, peering through the branches, I could see, far out on the valley floor, the great herd of milling beasts. All of them had been driven together and there they were, running in a knotted circle, while outside the circle prowled the pinkish dogs and something else as well—what appeared to be men driving tiny cars. The cars and men were all of the same color, a sort of greenish gray, and the two of them, the cars and men, seemed to be a single organism. The men didn't seem to be sitting in the cars; they looked as if they grew out of the cars, as if they and the cars were one. And while the cars went zipping along, they appeared to have no wheels. It was hard to tell, but they seemed to travel with the bottom of them flat upon the ground, like a snail would travel, and as they traveled, they rippled, as if the body of the car were some sort of flowing muscle.

I crouched there watching and now, for the first time, I had a chance to think about it, to try to figure out what was going on. I had come here, across more than sixty million years, to see some dinosaurs, and I sure was seeing them, but under what you might say were peculiar circumstances. The dinosaurs fit, all right. They looked mostly like the way they looked in books, but the dogs and car-men were something else again. They were distinctly out of place.

The dogs were pacing back and forth, sliding along in their sinuous fashion, and the car-men were zipping back and forth, and every once in a while one of the beasts would break out of the circle and the minute that it did, a half dozen dogs and a couple of car-men would race to intercept it and drive it back again.

The circle of beasts must have had, roughly, a diameter of a mile or more—a mile of milling, frightened creatures. A lot of paleontologists have wondered whether dinosaurs had any voice and I can tell you that they did. They were squealing and roaring and quacking and there were some of them that hooted—I think it was the duckbills hooting, but I can't be sure.

Then, all at once, there was another sound, a sort of fluttering roar that seemed to be coming from the sky. I looked up quickly and I saw them coming down—a dozen or so spaceships, they couldn't have been anything but spaceships. They came down rather fast and they didn't seem too big and there were tails of thin, blue flame flickering at their bases. Not the billowing clouds of flame and smoke that our rockets have, but just a thin blue flicker.

For a minute it looked like one of them would land on top of me, but then I saw that it was too far out. It missed me, matter of fact, a good two miles or so. It and the others sat down in a ring around the milling herd out in the valley.

I should have known what would happen out there. It was the simplest explanation one could think of and it was logical. I think, maybe, way deep down, I did know, but my surface mind had pushed it away because it was too matter-of-fact and too ordinary.

Thin snouts spouted from the ships and purple fire curled mistily at the muzzle of those snouts and the dinosaurs went down in a fighting, frightened, squealing mass. Thin trickles of vapor drifted upward from the snouts and out in the center of the circle lay that heap of dead and dying dinosaurs, all those thousands of dinosaurs piled in death.

It is a simple thing to tell, of course, but it was a terrible thing to see. I crouched there behind the bush, sickened at the sight, startled by the silence when all the screaming and the squealing and the hooting ceased. And shaken, too—not by what shakes me now as I write this letter, but shaken by the knowledge that something from outside could do this to the Earth.

For they were from outside. It wasn't just the spaceships, but those pinkish dogs and gray-green car men, which were not cars and men, but a single organism, were not things of Earth, could not be things of Earth.

I crept back from the bush, keeping low in hope that the bush would screen me from the things down in the valley until I reached the swale top. One of the dogs swung around and looked my way and I froze, and after a time he looked away.

Then I was over the top of the swale and heading back toward the time machine. But half way down the slope, I turned around and came back again, crawling on my belly, squirming to the hilltop to have another look.

It was a look I'll not forget.

The dogs and car-men had swarmed in upon the heap of dead dinosaurs, and some of the cars already were crawling back toward the grounded spaceships, which had let down ramps. The cars were moving slowly, for they were heavily loaded and the loads they carried were neatly butchered hams and racks of ribs.

And in the sky there was a muttering and I looked up to see yet other spaceships coming down—the little transport ships that would carry this cargo of fresh meat up to another larger ship that waited overhead.

It was then I turned and ran.

I reached the top of the hill and piled into the time machine and set it at zero and came home. I didn't even stop to hunt for the binoculars I'd dropped.

And now that I am home, I'm not going back again. I'm not going anywhere in that time machine. I'm afraid of what I might find any place I go. If Wyalusing College has any need of it, I'll give them the time machine.

But that's not why I wrote.

There is no doubt in my mind what happened to the dinosaurs, why they became extinct. They were killed off and butchered and hauled away, to some other planet, perhaps many light years distant, by a race which looked upon the Earth as a cattle range—a planet that could supply a vast amount of cheap protein.

But that, you say, happened more than sixty million years ago. This race did once exist. But in sixty million years it would almost certainly have changed its ways or drifted off in its hunting to some other sector of the galaxy, or, perhaps, have become extinct, like the dinosaurs.

But I don't think so. I don't think any of those things happened. I think they're still around. I think Earth may be only one of many planets that supply their food.

And I'll tell you why I think so. They were back on Earth again, I'm sure, some 10,000 or 11,000 years ago, when they killed off the mammoth and the mastodon, the giant bison, the great cave bear and the saber-tooth and a lot of other things. Oh, yes. I know they missed Africa. They never touched the big game there. Maybe, after wiping out the dinosaurs, they learned their lesson, and left Africa for breeding stock.

And now I come to the point of this letter, the thing that has me worried.

Today there are just a few less than three billion of us humans in the world. By the year 2000 there may be as many as six billion of us.

We're pretty small, of course, and these things went in for tonnage, for dinosaurs and mastodon and such. But there are so many of us! Small as we are, we may be getting to the point where we'll be worth their while.

OGRE

One of the earliest of many Simak stories that explore the notion of plant-based intelligence, this story, originally published in the January 1944 issue of Astounding Science Fiction, *was initially entitled "Last Concert," which gives a better hint at the point of the story than does the title under which it was ultimately released. But while there is a great deal that could be said about numerous aspects of this story, going into such detail might spoil it for you. However, I'll mention the rather unusual action Cliff took, more than a decade later, of using the concept of the "life blanket" in his later story "So Bright the Vision"—not the usual reuse of an idea or name from an older story, but a rare form of self-reference that implied credit to the older story for providing a concept in the newer one.*

—dww

The moss brought the news. Hundreds of miles the word had gossiped its way along, through many devious ways. For the moss did not grow everywhere. It grew only where the soil was sparse and niggardly, where the larger, lustier, more vicious plant things could not grow to rob it of light, or uproot it, or crowd it out, or do it other harm.

The moss told the story to Nicodemus, life blanket of Don Mackenzie, and it all came about because Mackenzie took a bath.

Mackenzie took his time in the bathroom, wallowing around in the tub and braying out a song, while Nicodemus, feeling only half a thing, moped outside the door. Without Mackenzie, Nicodemus was, in fact, even less than half of a thing. Accepted as intelligent life, Nicodemus and others of his tribe were intelligent only when they were wrapped about their humans. Their intelligence and emotions were borrowed from the things that wore them.

For the aeons before the human beings came to this twilight world, the life blankets had dragged out a humdrum existence. Occasionally one of them allied itself with a higher form of plant life, but not often. After all, such an arrangement was very little better than staying as they were.

When the humans came, however, the blankets finally clicked. Between them and the men of Earth grew up a perfect mutual agreement, a highly profitable and agreeable instance of symbiosis. Overnight, the blankets became one of the greatest single factors in galactic exploration.

For the man who wore one of them, like a cloak around his shoulders, need never worry where a meal was coming from; knew, furthermore, that he would be fed correctly, with a scientific precision that automatically counterbalanced any upset of metabolism that might be brought by alien conditions. For the curious plants had the ability to gather energy and convert it into food for the human body, had an uncanny instinct as to the exact needs of the body, extending, to a limited extent, to certain basic medical requirements.

But if the life blankets gave men food and warmth, served as a family doctor, man lent them something that was even more precious—the consciousness of life. The moment one of the plants wrapped itself around a man it became, in a sense, the double of that man. It shared his intelligence and emotions, was whisked from the dreary round of its own existence into a more exalted pseudo-life.

Nicodemus, at first moping outside the bathroom door, gradually grew peeved. He felt his thin veneer of human life slowly ebbing from him and he was filled with a baffling resentment.

Finally, feeling very put upon, he waddled out of the trading post upon his own high lonesome, flapping awkwardly along, like a sheet billowing in the breeze.

The dull brick-red sun that was Sigma Draco shone down upon a world that even at high noon appeared to be in twilight and Nicodemus' bobbling shape cast squirming, unsubstantial purple shadows upon the green and crimson ground. A rifle tree took a shot at Nicodemus but missed him by a yard at least. That tree had been off the beam for weeks. It had missed everything it shot at. Its best effort had been scaring the life out of Nellie, the bookkeeping robot that never told a lie, when it banked one of its bulletlike seeds against the steel-sheeted post.

But no one had felt very badly about that, for no one cared for Nellie. With Nellie around, no one could chisel a red cent off the company. That, incidentally, was the reason she was at the post.

But for a couple of weeks now, Nellie hadn't bothered anybody. She had taken to chumming around with Encyclopedia, who more than likely was slowly going insane trying to figure out her thoughts.

Nicodemus told the rifle tree what he thought of it, shooting at its own flesh and blood, as it were, and kept shuffling along. The tree, knowing Nicodemus for a traitor to his own, a vegetable renegade, took another shot at him, missed by two yards and gave up in disgust.

Since he had become associated with a human, Nicodemus hadn't had much to do with other denizens of the planet—even the Encyclopedia. But when he passed a bed of moss and heard it whispering and gossiping away, he tarried for a moment, figurative ear cocked to catch some juicy morsel.

That is how he heard that Alder, a minor musician out in Melody Bowl, finally had achieved a masterpiece. Nicodemus knew it might have happened weeks before, for Melody Bowl was half a world away and the news sometimes had to travel the long way round, but just the same he scampered as fast as he could hump back toward the post.

For this was news that couldn't wait. This was news Mackenzie had to know at once. He managed to kick up quite a cloud of dust coming down the home stretch and flapped triumphantly through the door, above which hung the crudely lettered sign:

GALACTIC TRADING CO.

Just what good the sign did, no one yet had figured out. The humans were the only living things on the planet that could read it.

Before the bathroom door, Nicodemus reared up and beat his fluttering self against it with tempestuous urgency.

"All right," yelled Mackenzie. "All right. I know I took too long again. Just calm yourself. I'll be right out."

Nicodemus settled down, still wriggling with the news he had to tell, heard Mackenzie swabbing out the tub.

With Nicodemus wrapped happily about him, Mackenzie strode into the office and found Nelson Harper, the factor, with his feet up on the desk, smoking his pipe and studying the ceiling.

"Howdy, lad," said the factor. He pointed at a bottle with his pipestem. "Grab yourself a snort."

Mackenzie grabbed one.

"Nicodemus has been out chewing fat with the moss," he said. "Tells me a conductor by the name of Alder has composed a symphony. Moss says it's a masterpiece."

Harper took his feet off the desk. "Never heard of this chap, Alder," he said.

"Never heard of Kadmar, either," Mackenzie reminded him, "until he produced the Red Sun symphony. Now everyone is batty over him. If Alder has anything at all, we ought to get it down. Even a mediocre piece pays out. People back on Earth are plain wacky over this tree music of ours. Like that one fellow . . . that composer—"

"Wade," Harper filled in. "J. Edgerton Wade. One of the greatest composers Earth had ever known. Quit in mortification after he heard the *Red Sun* piece. Later disappeared. No one knows where he went."

The factor nursed his pipe between his palms. "Funny thing. Came out here figuring our best trading bet would be new drugs or maybe some new kind of food. Something for the high-class restaurants to feature, charge ten bucks a plate for. Maybe even a new mineral. Like out on Eta Cassiop. But it wasn't any of those things. It was music. Symphony stuff. High-brow racket."

Mackenzie took another shot at the bottle, put it back and wiped his mouth. "I'm not so sure I like this music angle," he declared. "I don't know much about music. But it sounds funny to me, what I've heard of it. Brain-twisting stuff."

Harper grunted. "You're O.K. as long as you have plenty of serum along. If you can't take the music, just keep yourself shot full of serum. That way it can't touch you."

Mackenzie nodded. "It almost got Alexander that time, remember? Ran short of serum while he was down in the Bowl trying to dicker with the trees. Music seemed to have a hold on him. He didn't want to leave. He fought and screeched and yelled around. . . . I felt like a heel, taking him away. He never has been quite the same since then. Doctors back on Earth finally were able to get him straightened out, but warned him never to come back."

"Alexander's back again," said Harper. "Grant spotted him over at the Groombridge post. Throwing in with the Groomies, I guess. Just a yellow-bellied renegade. Going against his own race. You boys shouldn't have saved him that time. Should have let the music get him."

"What are you going to do about it?" demanded Mackenzie.

Harper shrugged his shoulders. "What can I do about it? Unless I want to declare war on the Groombridge post. And that is out. Haven't you heard it's all sweetness and light between Earth and Groombridge 34? That's the reason the two posts are stuck away from Melody Bowl. So each one of us will have a fair shot at the music. All according to some pact the two companies rigged up. Galactic's got so pure they wouldn't even like it if they knew we had a spy planted on the Groomie post."

"But they got one planted on us," declared Mackenzie. "We haven't been able to find him, of course, but we know there is one. He's out there in the woods somewhere, watching every move we make."

Harper nodded his head. "You can't trust a Groomie. The lousy little insects will stoop to anything. They don't want that music, can't use it. Probably don't even know what music is. Haven't any hearing. But they know Earth wants it, will pay any price to get it, so they are out here to beat us to it. They work through birds like Alexander. They get the stuff, Alexander peddles it."

"What if we run across Alexander, chief?"

Harper clicked his pipestem across his teeth. "Depends on circumstances. Try to hire him, maybe. Get him away from the Groomies. He's a good trader. The company would do right by him."

Mackenzie shook his head. "No soap. He hates Galactic. Something that happened years ago. He'd rather make us trouble than turn a good deal for himself."

"Maybe he's changed," suggested Harper. "Maybe you boys saving him changed his mind."

"I don't think it did," persisted Mackenzie.

The factor reached across the desk and drew a humidor in front of him, began to refill his pipe.

"Been trying to study out something else, too," he said. "Wondering what to do with the Encyclopedia. He wants to go to Earth. Seems he's found out just enough from us to whet his appetite for knowledge. Says he wants to go to Earth and study our civilization."

Mackenzie grimaced. "That baby's gone through our minds with a fine-toothed comb. He knows some of the things we've forgotten we ever knew. I guess it's just the nature of him, but it gets my wind up when I think of it."

"He's after Nellie now," said Harper. "Trying to untangle what she knows."

"It would serve him right if he found out."

"I've been trying to figure it out," said Harper. "I don't like this brain-picking of his any more than you do, but if we took him to Earth, away from his own stamping grounds, we might be able to soften him up. He certainly knows a lot about this planet that would be of value to us. He's told me a little—"

"Don't fool yourself," said Mackenzie. "He hasn't told you a thing more than he's had to tell to make you believe it wasn't a one-way deal. Whatever he has told you has no vital significance. Don't kid yourself he'll exchange information for information. That cookie's out to get everything he can get for nothing."

The factor regarded Mackenzie narrowly. "I'm not sure but I should put you in for an Earth vacation," he declared. "You're letting things upset you. You're losing your perspective. Alien planets aren't Earth, you know. You have to expect wacky things, get along with them, accept them on the basis of the logic that makes them the way they are."

"I know all that," agreed Mackenzie, "but honest, chief, this place gets in my hair at times. Trees that shoot at you, moss that talks, vines that heave thunderbolts at you—and now the Encyclopedia."

"The Encyclopedia is logical," insisted Harper. "He's a repository for knowledge. We have parallels on Earth. Men who study merely for the sake of learning, never expect to use the knowledge they amass. Derive a strange, smug satisfaction from being well informed. Combine that yearning for knowledge with a phenomenal ability to memorize and co-ordinate that knowledge and you have the Encyclopedia."

"But there must be a purpose to him," insisted Mackenzie. "There must be some reason at the back of this thirst for knowledge. Just soaking up facts doesn't add up to anything unless you use those facts."

Harper puffed stolidly at his pipe. "There may be a purpose in it, but a purpose so deep, so different, we could not recognize it. This planet is a vegetable world and a vegetable civilization. Back on earth the animals got the head start and plants never had a chance to learn or to evolve. But here it's a different story. The plants were the ones that evolved, became masters of the situation."

"If there is a purpose, we should know it," Mackenzie declared, stubbornly. "We can't afford to go blind on a thing like this. If the Encyclopedia has a game, we should know it. Is he acting on his own, a free lance? Or is he the representative of the world, a sort of prime minister, a state department? Or is he something that was left over by another civilization, a civilization that is gone? A kind of living archive of knowledge, still working at his old trade even if the need of it is gone?"

"You worry too much," Harper told him.

"We have to worry, chief. We can't afford to let anything get ahead of us. We have taken the attitude we're superior to this vegetable civilization, if you can call it a civilization, that has developed here. It's the logical attitude to take because nettles and dandelions and trees aren't anything to be afraid of back home. But what holds on Earth, doesn't hold here. We have to ask ourselves what a vegetable civilization would be like. What would it want? What would be its aspirations and how would it go about realizing them?"

"We're getting off the subject," said Harper, curtly. "You came in here to tell me about some new symphony."

Mackenzie flipped his hands. "O.K., if that's the way you feel about it."

"Maybe we better figure on grabbing up this symphony soon as we can," said Harper. "We haven't had a really good one since the *Red Sun*. And if we mess around, the Groomies will beat us to it."

"Maybe they have already," said Mackenzie.

Harper puffed complacently at his pipe. "They haven't done it yet. Grant keeps me posted on every move they make. He doesn't miss a thing that happens at the Groombridge post."

"Just the same," declared Mackenzie, "we can't go rushing off and tip our hand. The Groomie spy isn't asleep, either."

"Got any ideas?" asked the factor.

"We could take the ground car," suggested Mackenzie. "It's slower than the flier, but if we took the flier the Groomie would know there was something up. We use the car a dozen times a day. He'd think nothing of it."

Harper considered. "The idea has merit, lad. Who would you take?"

"Let me have Brad Smith," said Mackenzie. "We'll get along all right, just the two of us. He's an old-timer out here. Knows his way around."

Harper nodded. "Better take Nellie, too."

"Not on your life!" yelped Mackenzie. "What do you want to do? Get rid of her so you can make a cleaning?"

Harper wagged his grizzled head sadly. "Good idea, but it can't be did. One cent off and she's on your trail. Used to be a little graft a fellow could pick up here and there, but not any more. Not since they got these robot bookkeepers indoctrinated with truth and honesty."

"I won't take her," Mackenzie declared, flatly. "So help me, I won't. She'll spout company law all the way there and back. With the crush she has on this Encyclopedia, she'll probably want to drag him along, too. We'll have trouble enough with rifle trees and electro vines and all the other crazy vegetables without having an educated cabbage and a tin-can lawyer underfoot."

"You've got to take her," insisted Harper, mildly. "New ruling. Got to have one of the things along on every deal you make to prove you did right by the natives. Come right down to it, the ruling probably is your own fault. If you hadn't been so foxy on that *Red Sun* deal, the company never would have thought of it."

"All I did was to save the company some money," protested Mackenzie.

"You knew," Harper reminded him crisply, "that the standard price for a symphony is two bushels of fertilizer. Why did you have to chisel half a bushel on Kadmar?"

"Cripes," said Mackenzie, "Kadmar didn't know the difference. He practically kissed me for a bushel and a half."

"That's not the point," declared Harper. "The company's got the idea we got to shoot square with everything we trade with, even if it's nothing but a tree."

"I know," said Mackenzie, drily. "I've read the manual."

"Just the same," said Harper, "Nellie goes along."

He studied Mackenzie over the bowl of his pipe.

"Just to be sure you don't forget again," he said.

The man, who back on Earth had been known as J. Edgerton Wade, crouched on the low cliff that dropped away into Melody Bowl. The dull red sun was slipping toward the purple horizon and soon, Wade knew, the trees would play their regular evening concert. He hoped that once again it would be the wondrous new symphony Alder had composed. Thinking about it, he shuddered in ecstasy— shuddered again when he thought about the setting sun. The evening chill would be coming soon.

Wade had no life blanket. His food, cached back in the tiny cave in the cliff, was nearly gone. His ship, smashed in his inexpert landing on the planet almost a year before, was a rusty hulk. J. Edgerton Wade was near the end of his rope—and knew it. Strangely, he didn't care. In that year since he'd come here to the cliffs, he'd lived in a world of beauty. Evening after evening he had listened to the concerts. That was enough, he told himself. After a year of music such as that any man could afford to die.

He swept his eyes up and down the little valley that made up the Bowl, saw the trees set in orderly rows, almost as if someone had planted them. Some intelligence that may at one time, long ago, have squatted on this very cliff edge, even as he squatted now, and listened to the music.

But there was no evidence, he knew, to support such a hypothesis. No ruins of cities had been found upon this world. No evidence that any civilization, in the sense that Earth had built a civilization, ever had existed here. Nothing at all that suggested a civilized race had ever laid eyes upon this valley, had ever had a thing to do with the planning of the Bowl.

Nothing, that was, except the cryptic messages on the face of the cliff above the cave where he cached his food and slept. Scrawlings that bore no resemblance to any other writing Wade had ever seen. Perhaps, he speculated, they might have been made by other aliens who, like himself, had come to listen to the music until death had come for them.

Still crouching, Wade rocked slowly on the balls of his feet. Perhaps he should scrawl his own name there with the other scrawlings. Like one would sign a hotel register. A lonely name scratched upon the face of a lonely rock. A grave name, a brief memorial—and yet it would be the only tombstone he would ever have.

The music would be starting soon and then he would forget about the cave, about the food that was almost gone, about the rusting ship that never could carry him back to Earth again—even had he wanted to go back. And he didn't—he couldn't have gone back. The Bowl had trapped him, the music had spun a web about him. Without it, he knew, he could not live. It had become a part of him. Take it from him and he would be a shell, for it was now a part of the life force that surged within his body, part of his brain and blood, a silvery thread of meaning that ran through his thoughts and purpose.

The trees stood in quiet, orderly ranks and beside each tree was a tiny mound, podia for the conductors, and beside each mound the dark mouths of burrows. The conductors, Wade knew, were in those burrows, resting for the concert. Being animals, the conductors had to get their rest.

But the trees never needed rest. They never slept. They never tired, these gray, drab music trees, the trees that sang to the empty sky, sang of forgotten days and days that had not come, of days when Sigma Draco had been a mighty sun and of the later days when it would be a cinder circling in space. And of other things an Earthman could never know, could only sense and strain toward and wish he knew. Things that stirred strange thoughts within one's brain and choked one with alien emotion an Earthman was never meant to feel. Emotion and thought that one could not even recognize, yet emotion and thought that one yearned toward and knew never could be caught.

Technically, of course, it wasn't the trees that sang. Wade knew that, but he did not think about it often. He would rather it had been the trees alone. He seldom thought of the music other than belonging to the trees, disregarded the little entities inside the trees that really made the music, using the trees for their sounding boards. Entities? That was all he knew. Insects, perhaps, a colony of insects to each tree—or maybe even nymphs or sprites or some of the other little folk that run on skipping feet through the pages of children's fairy books. Although that was foolish, he told himself—there were no sprites.

Each insect, each sprite contributing its own small part to the orchestration, compliant to the thought-vibrations of the conductors. The conductors thought the music, held it in their brains and the things in the trees responded.

It did sound so pretty that way, Wade told himself. Thinking it out spoiled the beauty of it. Better to simply accept it and enjoy it without explanation.

Men came at times—not often—men of his own flesh and blood, men from the trading post somewhere on the planet. They came to record the music and then they went away. How anyone could go away once they had heard the music, Wade could not understand. Faintly he remembered there was a way one could immunize one's self against the music's spell, condition one's self so he could leave after he had heard it, dull his senses to a point where it could not hold him. Wade shivered at the thought. That was sacrilege. But still no worse than recording the music so Earth orchestras might play it. For what Earth orchestra could play it as he heard it here, evening after evening? If Earth music lovers only could hear it as it was played here in this ancient bowl!

When the Earthmen came, Wade always hid. It would be just like them to try to take him back with them, away from the music of the trees.

Faintly the evening breeze brought the foreign sound to him, the sound that should not have been heard there in the Bowl—the clank of steel on stone.

Rising from his squatting place, he tried to locate the origin of the sound. It came again, from the far edge of the Bowl. He shielded his eyes with a hand against the setting sun, stared across the Bowl at the moving figures.

There were three of them and one, he saw at once, was an Earthman. The other two were strange creatures that looked remotely like monster bugs, chitinous armor glinting in the last rays of Sigma Draco. Their heads, he saw, resembled grinning skulls and they wore dark harnesses, apparently for the carrying of tools or weapons.

Groombridgians! But what would Groombridgians be doing with an Earthman? The two were deadly trade rivals, were not above waging intermittent warfare when their interests collided.

Something flashed in the sun—a gleaming tool that stabbed and probed, stabbed and lifted.

J. Edgerton Wade froze in horror.

Such a thing, he told himself, simply couldn't happen!

The three across the Bowl were digging up a music tree!

The vine sneaked through the rustling sea of grass, cautious tendrils raised to keep tab on its prey, the queer, clanking thing that still rolled on unswervingly. Came on without stopping to smell out the ground ahead, without zigzagging to throw off possible attack.

Its action was puzzling; that was no way for anything to travel on this planet. For a moment a sense of doubt trilled along the length of vine, doubt of the wisdom of attacking anything that seemed so sure. But the doubt was short lived, driven out by the slavering anticipation that had sent the vicious vegetable from its lair among the grove of rifle trees. The vine trembled a little—slightly drunk with the vibration that pulsed through its tendrils.

The queer thing rumbled on and the vine tensed itself, every fiber alert for struggle. Just let it get so much as one slight grip upon the thing—

The prey came closer and for one sense-shattering moment it seemed it would be out of reach. Then it lurched slightly to one side as it struck a hump in the ground and the vine's tip reached out and grasped, secured a hold, wound itself in a maddened grip and hauled, hauled with all the might of almost a quarter mile of trailing power.

Inside the ground car, Don Mackenzie felt the machine lurch sickeningly, kicked up the power and spun the tractor on its churning treads in an effort to break loose.

Back of him Bradford Smith uttered a startled whoop and dived for an energy gun that had broken from its rack and was skidding across the floor. Nellie, upset by the lurch, was flat on her back, jammed into a corner. The Encyclopedia, at the moment of shock, had whipped out its coiled-up taproot and tied up to a pipe. Now, like an anchored turtle, it swayed pendulum-wise across the floor.

Glass tinkled and metal screeched on metal as Nellie thrashed to regain her feet. The ground car reared and seemed to paw the air, slid about and plowed great furrows in the ground.

"It's a vine!" shrieked Smith.

Mackenzie nodded, grim-lipped, fighting the wheel. As the car slewed around, he saw the arcing loops of the attacker, reaching from the grove of rifle trees. Something pinged against the vision plate, shattered into a puff of dust. The rifle trees were limbering up.

Mackenzie tramped on the power, swung the car in a wide circle, giving the vine some slack, then quartered and charged across the prairie while the vine twisted and flailed the air in looping madness. If only he could build up speed, slap into the stretched-out vine full tilt, Mackenzie was sure he could break its hold. In a straight pull, escape would have been hopeless, for the vine, once fastened on a thing, was no less than a steel cable of strength and determination.

Smith had managed to get a port open, was trying to shoot, the energy gun crackling weirdly. The car rocked from side to side, gaining speed while bulletlike seeds from the rifle trees pinged and whined against it.

Mackenzie braced himself and yelled at Smith. They must be nearing the end of their run. Any minute now would come the jolt as they rammed into the tension of the outstretched vine.

It came with terrifying suddenness, a rending thud. Instinctively, Mackenzie threw up his arms to protect himself, for one startled moment knew he was being hurled into the vision plate. A gigantic burst of flame flared in his head and filled the universe. Then he was floating through darkness that was cool and soft and he found himself thinking that everything would be all right, everything would be . . . everything—

But everything wasn't all right. He knew that the moment he opened his eyes and stared up into the mass of tangled wreckage that hung above him. For many seconds he did not move, did not even wonder where he was. Then he stirred and a piece of steel bit into his leg. Carefully he slid his leg upward, clearing it of the steel. Cloth ripped with an angry snarl, but his leg came free.

"Lie still, you lug," something said, almost as if it were a voice from inside of him.

Mackenzie chuckled. "So you're all right," he said.

"Sure. I'm all right," said Nicodemus. "But you got some bruises and a scratch or two and you're liable to have a headache if you—"

The voice trailed off and stopped. Nicodemus was busy. At the moment, he was the medicine cabinet, fashioning from pure energy those things that a man needed when he had a bruise or two and was scratched up some and might have a headache later.

Mackenzie lay on his back and stared up at the mass of tangled wreckage.

"Wonder how we'll get out of here," he said.

The wreckage above him stirred. A gadget of some sort fell away from the twisted mass and gashed his cheek. He swore—unenthusiastically.

Someone was calling his name and he answered.

The wreckage was jerked about violently, literally torn apart. Long metal arms reached down, gripped him by the shoulders and yanked him out, none too gently.

"Thanks, Nellie," he said.

"Shut up," said Nellie, tartly.

His knees were a bit wabbly and he sat down, staring at the ground car. It didn't look much like a ground car any more. It had smashed full tilt into a boulder and it was a mess.

To his left Smith also was sitting on the ground and he was chuckling.

"What's the matter with you," snapped Mackenzie.

"Jerked her right up by the roots," exulted Smith. "So help me, right smack out of the ground. That's one vine that'll never bother anyone again."

Mackenzie stared in amazement. The vine lay coiled on the ground, stretching back toward the grove, limp and dead. Its smaller tendrils still were entwined in the tangled wreckage of the car.

"It hung on," gasped Mackenzie. "We didn't break its hold!"

"Nope," agreed Smith, "we didn't break its hold, but we sure ruined it."

"Lucky thing it wasn't an electro," said Mackenzie, "or it would have fried us."

Smith nodded glumly. "As it is it's loused us up enough. That car will never run again. And us a couple of thousand miles from home."

Nellie emerged from a hole in the wreckage, with the Encyclopedia under one arm and a mangled radio under the other. She dumped them both on the ground. The Encyclopedia scuttled off a few feet, drilled his taproot into the soil and was at home.

Nellie glowered at Mackenzie. "I'll report you for this," she declared, vengefully. "The idea of breaking up a nice new car! Do you know what a car costs the company? No, of course, you don't. And you don't care. Just go ahead and break it up. Just like that. Nothing to it. The company's got a lot more money to buy another one. I wonder sometimes if you ever wonder where your pay is coming from. If I was the company, I'd take it out of your salary. Every cent of it, until it was paid for."

Smith eyed Nellie speculatively. "Some day," he said, "I'm going to take a sledge and play tin shinny with you."

"Maybe you got something there," agreed Mackenzie. "There are times when I'm inclined to think the company went just a bit too far in making those robots cost-conscious."

"You don't need to talk like that," shrilled Nellie. "Like I was just a machine you didn't need to pay no attention to. I suppose next thing you will be saying it wasn't your fault, that you couldn't help it."

"I kept a good quarter mile from all the groves," growled Mackenzie. "Who ever heard of a vine that could stretch that far?"

"And that ain't all, neither," yelped Nellie. "Smith hit some of the rifle trees."

The two men looked toward the grove. What Nellie said was true. Pale wisps of smoke still rose above the grove and what trees were left looked the worse for wear.

Smith clucked his tongue in mock concern.

"The trees were shooting at us," retorted Mackenzie.

"That don't make any difference," Nellie yelled. "The rule book says—"

Mackenzie waved her into silence. "Yes, I know. Section 17 of the Chapter on Relations with Extraterrestrial Life: *'No employee of this company may employ weapons against or otherwise injure or attempt to injure or threaten with injury any inhabitant of any other planet except in self-defense and then only if every means of escape or settlement has failed.'"*

"And now we got to go back to the post," Nellie shrieked. "When we were almost there, we got to turn back. News of what we did will get around. The moss probably has started it already. The idea of ripping a vine up by the roots and shooting trees. If we don't start back right now, we won't get back. Every living thing along the way will be laying for us."

"It was the vine's fault," yelled Smith. "It tried to trap us. It tried to steal our car, probably would have killed us, just for the few lousy ounces of radium we have in the motors. That radium was ours. Not the vine's. It belonged to your beloved company."

"For the love of gosh, don't tell her that," Mackenzie warned, "or she'll go out on a one-robot expedition, yanking vines up left and right."

"Good idea," insisted Smith. "She might tie into an electro. It would peel her paint."

"How about the radio?" Mackenzie asked Nellie.

"Busted," said Nellie, crustily.

"And the recording equipment?"

"That tape's all right and I can fix the recorder."

"Serum jugs busted?"

"One of them ain't," said Nellie.

"O.K., then," said Mackenzie, "get back in there and dig out two bags of fertilizer. We're going on. Melody Bowl is only about fifty miles away."

"We can't do that," protested Nellie. "Every tree will be waiting for us, every vine—"

"It's safer to go ahead than back," said Mackenzie. "Even if we have no radio, Harper will send someone out with the flier to look us up when we are overdue."

He rose slowly and unholstered his pistol.

"Get in there and get that stuff," he ordered. "If you don't, I'll melt you down into a puddle."

"All right," screamed Nellie, in sudden terror. "All right. You needn't get so tough about it."

"Any more back talk out of you," Mackenzie warned, "and I'll kick you so full of dents you'll walk stooped over."

They stayed in the open, well away from the groves, keeping a close watch. Mackenzie went ahead and behind him came the Encyclopedia, humping along to keep pace with them. Back of the Encyclopedia was Nellie, loaded down with the bags of fertilizer and equipment. Smith brought up the rear.

A rifle tree took a shot at them, but the range was too far for accurate shooting. Back a way, an electro vine had come closer with a thunderbolt.

Walking was grueling. The grass was thick and matted and one had to plow through it, as if one were walking in water.

"I'll make you sorry for this," seethed Nellie. "I'll make—"

"Shut up," snapped Smith. "For once you're doing a robot's work instead of gumshoeing around to see if you can't catch a nickel out of place."

They breasted a hill and started to climb the long grassy slope.

Suddenly a sound like the savage ripping of a piece of cloth struck across the silence.

They halted, tensed, listening. The sound came again and then again.

"Guns!" yelped Smith.

Swiftly the two men loped up the slope, Nellie galloping awkwardly behind, the bags of fertilizer bouncing on her shoulders.

From the hilltop, Mackenzie took in the situation at a glance.

On the hillside below a man was huddled behind a boulder, working a gun with fumbling desperation, while farther down the hill a ground car had toppled over. Behind the car were three figures—one man and two insect creatures.

"Groomies!" whooped Smith.

A well-directed shot from the car took the top off the boulder and the man behind it hugged the ground.

Smith was racing quarteringly down the hill, heading toward another boulder that would outflank the trio at the car.

A yell of human rage came from the car and a bolt from one of the three guns snapped at Smith, plowing a smoking furrow no more than ten feet behind him.

Another shot flared toward Mackenzie and he plunged behind a hummock. A second shot whizzed just above his head and he hunkered down trying to push himself into the ground.

From the slope below came the high-pitched, angry chittering of the Groombridgians.

The car, Mackenzie saw, was not the only vehicle on the hillside. Apparently it had been pulling a trailer to which was lashed a tree. Mackenzie squinted against the setting sun, trying to make out what it was all about. The tree, he saw, had been expertly dug, its roots balled in earth and wrapped in sacking that shone wetly. The trailer was canted at an awkward angle, the treetop sweeping the ground, the balled roots high in the air.

Smith was pouring a deadly fire into the hostile camp and the three below were replying with a sheet of blasting bolts, plowing up the soil around the boulder. In a minute or two, Mackenzie knew, they would literally cut the ground out from under Smith. Cursing under his breath, he edged around the hummock, pushing his pistol before him, wishing he had a rifle.

The third man was slinging an occasional, inexpert shot at the three below, but wasn't doing much to help the cause along. The battle, Mackenzie knew, was up to him and Smith.

He wondered abstractedly where Nellie was.

"Probably halfway back to the post by now," he told himself, drawing a bead on the point from which came the most devastating blaze of firing.

But even as he depressed the firing button, the firing from below broke off in a chorus of sudden screams. The two Groombridgians leaped up and started to run, but before they made their second stride, something came whizzing through the air from the slope below and crumpled one of them.

The other hesitated, like a startled hare, uncertain where to go, and a second thing came whishing up from the bottom of the slope and smacked against his breastplate with a thud that could be heard from where Mackenzie lay.

Then, for the first time Mackenzie saw Nellie. She was striding up the hill, her left arm holding an armful of stones hugged tight against her metal chest, her right arm working like a piston. The ringing clang of stone against metal came as one of the stones missed its mark and struck the ground car.

The human was running wildly, twisting and ducking, while Nellie pegged rock after rock at him. Trying to get set for a shot at her, the barrage of whizzing stones kept him on the dodge. Angling down the hill, he finally lost his rifle when he tripped and fell. With a howl of terror, he bolted up the hillside, his life blanket standing out almost straight behind him. Nellie pegged her last stone at him, then set out, doggedly loping in his wake.

Mackenzie screamed hoarsely at her, but she did not stop. She passed out of sight over the hill, closely behind the fleeing man.

Smith whooped with delight. "Look at our Nellie go for him," he yelled. "She'll give him a working over when she nails him."

Mackenzie rubbed his eyes. "Who was he?" he asked.

"Jack Alexander," said Smith. "Grant said he was around again."

The third man got up stiffly from behind his boulder and advanced toward them. He wore no life blanket, his clothing was in tatters, his face was bearded to the eyes.

He jerked a thumb toward the hill over which Nellie had disappeared. "A masterly military maneuver," he declared. "Your robot sneaked around and took them from behind."

"If she lost that recording stuff and the fertilizer, I'll melt her down," said Mackenzie, savagely.

The man stared at them. "You are the gentlemen from the trading post?" he asked.

They nodded, returning his gaze.

"I am Wade," he said. "J. Edgerton Wade—"

"Wait a second," shouted Smith. "Not *the* J. Edgerton Wade? The lost composer?"

The man bowed, whiskers and all. "The same," he said. "Although I had not been aware that I was lost. I merely came out here to spend a year, a year of music such as man has never heard before."

He glared at them. "I am a man of peace," he declared, almost as if daring them to argue that he wasn't, "but when those three dug up Delbert, I knew what I must do."

"Delbert?" asked Mackenzie.

"The tree," said Wade. "One of the music trees."

"Those lousy planet-runners," said Smith, "figured they'd take that tree and sell it to someone back on Earth. I can think of a lot of big shots who'd pay plenty to have one of those trees in their back yard."

"It's a lucky thing we came along," said Mackenzie, soberly. "If we hadn't, if they'd got away with it, the whole planet would have gone on the warpath. We could have closed up shop. It might have been years before we dared come back again."

Smith rubbed his hands together, smirking. "We'll take back their precious tree," he declared, "and that will put us in solid! They'll give us their tunes from now on, free for nothing, just out of pure gratitude."

"You gentlemen," said Wade, "are motivated by mercenary factors but you have the right idea."

A heavy tread sounded behind them and when they turned they saw Nellie striding down the hill. She clutched a life blanket in her hand.

"He got away," she said, "but I got his blanket. Now I got a blanket, too, just like you fellows."

"What do you need with a life blanket?" yelled Smith. "You give that blanket to Mr. Wade. Right away. You hear me."

Nellie pouted. "You won't let me have anything. You never act like I'm human—"

"You aren't," said Smith.

"If you give that blanket to Mr. Wade," wheedled Mackenzie, "I'll let you drive the car."

"You would?" asked Nellie, eagerly.

"Really," said Wade, shifting from one foot to the other, embarrassed.

"You take that blanket," said Mackenzie. "You need it. Looks like you haven't eaten for a day or two."

"I haven't," Wade confessed.

"Shuck into it then and get yourself a meal," said Smith.

Nellie handed it over.

"How come you were so good pegging those rocks?" asked Smith.

Nellie's eyes gleamed with pride. "Back on Earth I was on a baseball team," she said. "I was the pitcher."

Alexander's car was undamaged except for a few dents and a smashed vision plate where Wade's first bolt had caught it, blasting the glass and startling the operator so that he swerved sharply, spinning the treads across a boulder and upsetting it.

The music tree was unharmed, its roots still well moistened in the burlap-wrapped, water-soaked ball of earth. Inside the tractor, curled in a tight ball in the darkest corner, unperturbed by the uproar that had been going on outside, they found Delbert, the two-foot high, roly-poly conductor that resembled nothing more than a poodle dog walking on its hind legs.

The Groombridgians were dead, their crushed chitinous armor proving the steam behind Nellie's delivery.

Smith and Wade were inside the tractor, settle down for the night. Nellie and the Encyclopedia were out in the night, hunting for the gun Alexander had dropped when he fled. Mackenzie, sitting on the ground, Nicodemus pulled snugly about him, leaned back against the car and smoked a last pipe before turning in.

The grass behind the tractor rustled.

"That you, Nellie?" Mackenzie called, softly.

Nellie clumped hesitantly around the corner of the car.

"You ain't sore at me?" she asked.

"No, I'm not sore at you. You can't help the way you are."

"I didn't find the gun," said Nellie.

"You knew where Alexander dropped it?"

"Yes," said Nellie. "It wasn't there."

Mackenzie frowned in the darkness. "That means Alexander managed to come back and get it. I don't like that. He'll be out gunning for us. He didn't like the company before. He'll really be out for blood after what we did today."

He looked around. "Where's the Encyclopedia?"

"I sneaked away from him. I wanted to talk to you about him."

"O.K.," said Mackenzie. "Fire away."

"He's been trying to read my brain," said Nellie.

"I know. He read the rest of ours. Did a good job of it."

"He's been having trouble," declared Nellie.

"Trouble reading your brain? I wouldn't doubt it."

"You don't need to talk as if my brain—" Nellie began, but Mackenzie stopped her.

"I didn't mean it that way, Nellie. Your brain is all right, far as I know. Maybe even better than ours. But the point is that it's different. Ours are natural brains, the orthodox way for things to think and reason and remember. The Encyclopedia knows about those kinds of brains and the minds that go with them. Yours isn't that kind. It's artificial. Part mechanical, part chemical, part electrical, Lord knows what else; I'm not a robot technician. He's never run up against that kind of brain before. It probably has him down. Matter of fact, our civilization probably has him down. If this planet ever had a real civilization, it wasn't a mechanical one. There's no sign of mechanization here. None of the scars machines inflict on planets."

"I been fooling him," said Nellie quietly. "He's been trying to read my mind, but I been reading his."

Mackenzie started forward. "Well, I'll be——" he began. Then he settled back against the car, dead pipe hanging from between his teeth. "Why didn't you ever let us know you could read minds?" he demanded. "I suppose you been sneaking around all this time, reading our minds, making fun of us, laughing behind our backs."

"Honest, I ain't," said Nellie. "Cross my heart, I ain't. I didn't even know I could. But, when I felt the Encyclopedia prying around inside my head the way he does, it kind of got my dander up. I almost hauled off and smacked him one. And then I figured maybe I better be more subtle. I figured that if he could pry around in my mind, I could pry around in his. I tried it and it worked."

"Just like that," said Mackenzie.

"It wasn't hard," said Nellie. "It come natural. I seemed to just know how to do it."

"If the guy that made you knew what he'd let slip through his fingers, he'd cut his throat," Mackenzie told her.

Nellie sidled closer. "It scares me," she said.

"What's scaring you now?"

"That Encyclopedia knows too much."

"Alien stuff," said Mackenzie. "You should have expected that. Don't go messing around with an alien mentality unless you're ready for some shocks."

"It ain't that," said Nellie. "I knew I'd find alien stuff. But he knows other things. Things he shouldn't know."

"About us?"

"No, about other places. Places other than the Earth and this planet here. Places Earthmen ain't been to yet. The kind of things no Earthman could know by himself or that no Encyclopedia could know by himself, either."

"Like what?"

"Like knowing mathematical equations that don't sound like anything we know about," said Nellie. "Nor like he'd know about if he'd stayed here all his life. Equations you couldn't know unless you knew a lot more about space and time than even Earthmen know.

"Philosophy, too. Ideas that make sense in a funny sort of way, but make your head swim when you try to figure out the kind of people that would develop them."

Mackenzie got out his pouch and refilled his pipe, got it going.

"Nellie, you think maybe this Encyclopedia has been at other minds? Minds of other people who may have come here?"

"Could be," agreed Nellie. "Maybe a long time ago. He's awful old. Lets on he could be immortal if he wanted to be. Said he wouldn't die until there was nothing more in the universe to know. Said when that time came there'd be nothing more to live for."

Mackenzie clicked his pipestem against his teeth. "He could be, too," he said. "Immortal, I mean. Plants haven't got all the physiological complications animals have. Given any sort of care, they theoretically could live forever."

Grass rustled on the hillside above them and Mackenzie settled back against the car, kept on smoking. Nellie hunkered down a few feet away.

The Encyclopedia waddled down the hill, starlight glinting from his shell-like back. Ponderously he lined up with them beside the car, pushing his taproot into the ground for an evening snack.

"Understand you may be going back to Earth with us," said Mackenzie, conversationally.

The answer came, measured in sharp and concise thought that seemed to drill deep into Mackenzie's mind. "I should like to. Your race is interesting."

It was hard to talk to a thing like that, Mackenzie told himself.

Hard to keep the chatter casual when you knew all the time it was hunting around in the corners of your mind. Hard to match one's voice against the brittle thought with which it talked.

"What do you think of us?" he asked and knew, as soon as he had asked it, that it was asinine.

"I know very little of you," the Encyclopedia declared. "You have created artificial lives, while we on this planet have lived natural lives. You have bent every force that you can master to your will. You have made things work for you. First impression is that, potentially, you are dangerous."

"I guess I asked for it," Mackenzie said.

"I do not follow you."

"Skip it," said Mackenzie.

"The only trouble," said the Encyclopedia, "is that you don't know where you're going."

"That's what makes it so much fun," Mackenzie told him. "Cripes, if we knew where we were going there'd be no adventure. We'd know what was coming next. As it is, every corner that we turn brings a new surprise."

"Knowing where you're going has its advantages," insisted the Encyclopedia.

Mackenzie knocked the pipe bowl out on his boot heel, tramped on the glowing ash.

"So you have us pegged," he said.

"No," said the Encyclopedia. "Just first impressions."

The music trees were twisted gray ghosts in the murky dawn. The conductors, except for the few who refused to let even a visit from the Earthmen rouse them from their daylight slumber, squatted like black imps on their podia.

Delbert rode on Smith's shoulder, one clawlike hand entwined in Smith's hair to keep from falling off. The Encyclopedia waddled along in the wake of the Earthman party. Wade led the way towards Alder's podium.

The Bowl buzzed with the hum of distorted thought, the thought of many little folk squatting on their mounds—an alien thing that made Mackenzie's neck hairs bristle just a little as it beat into his mind. There were no really separate thoughts, no one commanding thought, just the chitter-chatter of hundreds of little thoughts, as if the conductors might be gossiping.

The yellow cliffs stood like a sentinel wall and above the path that led to the escarpment, the tractor loomed like a straddled beetle against the early dawn.

Alder rose from the podium to greet them, a disreputable-looking gnome on gnarly legs.

The Earth delegation squatted on the ground. Delbert, from his perch on Smith's shoulder, made a face at Alder.

Silence held for a moment and then Mackenzie, dispensing with formalities, spoke to Alder. "We rescued Delbert for you," he told the gnome. "We brought him back."

Alder scowled and his thoughts were fuzzy with disgust. "We do not want him back," he said.

Mackenzie, taken aback, stammered. "Why, we thought . . . that is, he's one of you . . . we went to a lot of trouble to rescue him—"

"He's a nuisance," declared Alder. "He's a disgrace. He's a no-good. He's always trying things."

"You're not so hot yourself," piped Delbert's thought. "Just a bunch of fuddy-duddies. A crowd of corn peddlers. You're sore at me because I want to be different. Because I dust it off—"

"You see," said Alder to Mackenzie, "what he is like."

"Why, yes," agreed Mackenzie, "but there are times when new ideas have some values. Perhaps he may be—"

Alder leveled an accusing finger at Wade. "He was all right until you took to hanging around," he screamed. "Then he picked up some of your ideas. You contaminated him. Your silly notions about music—" Alder's thoughts gulped in sheer exasperation, then took up again. "Why did you come? No one asked you to. Why don't you mind your own business?"

Wade, red faced behind his beard, seemed close to apoplexy.

"I've never been so insulted in all my life," he howled. He thumped his chest with a doubled fist. "Back on Earth I wrote great symphonies myself. I never held with frivolous music. I never—"

"Crawl back into your hole," Delbert shrilled at Alder. "You guys don't know what music is. You saw out the same stuff day after day. You never lay it in the groove. You never get gated up. You all got long underwear."

Alder waved knotted fists above his head and hopped up and down in rage. "Such language!" he shrieked. "Never was the like heard here before."

The whole Bowl was yammering. Yammering with clashing thoughts of rage and insult.

"Now, wait," Mackenzie shouted. "All of you, quiet down!"

Wade puffed out his breath, turned a shade less purple. Alder squatted back on his haunches, unknotted his fists, tried his best to look composed. The clangor of thought subsided to a murmur.

"You're sure about this?" Mackenzie asked Alder. "Sure you don't want Delbert back."

"Mister," said Alder, "there never was a happier day in Melody Bowl than the day we found him gone."

A rising murmur of assent from the other conductors underscored his words.

"We have some others we'd like to get rid of, too," said Alder.

From far off across the Bowl came a yelping thought of derision.

"You see," said Alder, looking owlishly at Mackenzie, "what it is like. What we have to contend with. All because this . . . this . . . this—"

Glaring at Wade, thoughts failed him. Carefully he settled back upon his haunches, composed his face again.

"If the rest were gone," he said, "we could settle down. But as it is, these few keep us in an uproar all the time. We can't concentrate, we can't really work. We can't do the things we want to do."

Mackenzie pushed back his hat and scratched his head.

"Alder," he declared, "you sure are in a mess."

"I was hoping," Alder said, "that you might be able to take them off our hands."

"Take them off your hands!" yelled Smith. "I'll say we'll take them! We'll take as many—"

Mackenzie nudged Smith in the ribs with his elbow, viciously. Smith gulped into silence. Mackenzie tried to keep his face straight.

"You can't take them trees," said Nellie, icily. "It's against the law."

Mackenzie gasped. "The law?"

"Sure, the regulations. The company's got regulations. Or don't you know that? Never bothered to read them, probably. Just like you. Never pay no attention to the things you should."

"Nellie," said Smith savagely, "you keep out of this. I guess if we want to do a little favor for Alder here—"

"But it's against the law!" screeched Nellie.

"I know," said Mackenzie. "Section 34 of the chapter on Relations with Extraterrestrial Life. *'No member of this company shall interfere in any phase of the internal affairs of another race.'*"

"That's it," said Nellie, pleased with herself. "And if you take some of these trees, you'll be meddling in a quarrel that you have no business having anything to do with."

Mackenzie flipped his hands. "You see," he said to Alder.

"We'll give you a monopoly on our music," tempted Alder. "We'll let you know when we have anything. We won't let the Groomies have it and we'll keep our prices right."

Nellie shook her head. "No," she said.

Alder bargained. "Bushel and a half instead of two bushel."

"No," said Nellie.

"It's a deal," declared Mackenzie. "Just point out your duds and we'll haul them away."

"But Nellie said no," Alder pointed out. "And you say yes. I don't understand."

"We'll take care of Nellie," Smith told him, soberly.

"You won't take them trees," said Nellie. "I won't let you take them. I'll see to that."

"Don't pay any attention to her," Mackenzie said. "Just point out the ones you want to get rid of."

Alder said primly: "You've made us very happy."

Mackenzie got up and looked around. "Where's the Encyclopedia?" he asked.

"He cleared out a minute ago," said Smith. "Headed back for the car."

Mackenzie saw him, scuttling swiftly up the path towards the cliff top.

It was topsy-turvy and utterly crazy, like something out of that old book for children written by a man named Carroll. There was no sense to it. It was like taking candy from a baby.

Walking up the cliff path back to the tractor, Mackenzie knew it was, felt that he should pinch himself to know it was no dream.

He had hoped—just hoped—to avert relentless, merciless war against Earthmen throughout the planet by bringing back the stolen music tree. And here he was, with other music trees for his own, and a bargain thrown in to boot.

There was something wrong, Mackenzie told himself, something utterly and nonsensically wrong. But he couldn't put his finger on it.

There was no need to worry, he told himself. The thing to do was to get those trees and get out of there before Alder and the others changed their minds.

"It's funny," Wade said behind him.

"It is," agreed Mackenzie. "Everything is funny here."

"I mean about those trees," said Wade. "I'd swear Delbert was all right. So were all the others. They played the same music the others played. If there had been any faulty orchestration, any digression from form, I am sure I would have noticed it."

Mackenzie spun around and grasped Wade by the arm. "You

mean they weren't lousing up the concerts? That Delbert, here, played just like the rest?"

Wade nodded.

"That ain't so," shrilled Delbert from his perch on Smith's shoulder. "I wouldn't play like the rest of them. I want to kick the stuff around. I always dig it up and hang it out the window. I dream it up and send it away out wide."

"Where'd you pick up that lingo?" Mackenzie snapped. "I never heard anything like it before."

"I learned it from him," declared Delbert, pointing at Wade.

Wade's face was purple and his eyes were glassy.

"It's practically prehistoric," he gulped. "It's terms that were used back in the twentieth century to describe a certain kind of popular rendition. I read about it in a history covering the origins of music. There was a glossary of the terms. They were so fantastic they stuck in my mind."

Smith puckered his lips, whistling soundlessly. "So that's how he picked it up. He caught it from your thoughts. Same principle the Encyclopedia uses, although not so advanced."

"He lacks the Encyclopedia's distinction," explained Mackenzie. "He didn't know the stuff he was picking up was something that had happened long ago."

"I have a notion to wring his neck," Wade threatened.

"You'll keep your hands off him," grated Mackenzie. "This deal stinks to the high heavens, but seven music trees are seven music trees. Screwy deal or not, I'm going through with it."

"Look, fellows," said Nellie. "I wish you wouldn't do it."

Mackenzie puckered his brow. "What's the matter with you, Nellie? Why did you make that uproar about the law down there? There's a rule, sure, but in a thing like this it's different. The company can afford to have a rule or two broken for seven music trees. You know what will happen, don't you, when we get those trees back home. We can charge a thousand bucks a throw to hear them and have to use a club to keep the crowds away."

"And the best of it is," Smith pointed out, "that once they hear them, they'll have to come again. They'll never get tired of them. Instead of that, every time they hear them, they'll want to hear them all the more. It'll get to be an obsession, a part of the people's life. They'll steal, murder, do anything so they can hear the trees."

"That," said Mackenzie, soberly, "is the one thing I'm afraid of."

"I only tried to stop you," Nellie said. "I know as well as you do that the law won't hold in a thing like this. But there was something else. The way the conductors sounded. Almost as if they were jeering at us. Like a gang of boys out in the street hooting at someone they just pulled a fast one on."

"You're batty," Smith declared.

"We have to go through with it," Mackenzie announced, flatly. "If anyone ever found we'd let a chance like this slip through our fingers, they'd crucify us for it."

"You're going to get in touch with Harper?" Smith asked.

Mackenzie nodded. "He'll have to get hold of Earth, have them send out a ship right away to take back the trees."

"I still think," said Nellie, "there's a nigger in the woodpile."

Mackenzie flipped the toggle and the visiphone went dead.

Harper had been hard to convince. Mackenzie, thinking about it, couldn't blame him much. After all, it did sound incredible. But then, this whole planet was incredible.

Mackenzie reached into his pocket and hauled forth his pipe and pouch. Nellie probably would raise hell about helping to dig up those other six trees, but she'd have to get over it. They'd have to work as fast as they could. They couldn't spend more than one night up here on the rim. There wasn't enough serum for longer than that. One jug of the stuff wouldn't go too far.

Suddenly excited shouts came from outside the car, shouts of consternation.

With a single leap, Mackenzie left the chair and jumped for the door. Outside, he almost bumped into Smith, who came running around the corner of the tractor. Wade, who had been down at the cliff's edge, was racing toward them.

"It's Nellie," shouted Smith. "Look at that robot!"

Nellie was marching toward them, dragging in her wake a thing that bounced and struggled. A rifle-tree grove fired a volley and one of the pellets caught Nellie in the shoulder, puffing into dust, staggering her a little.

The bouncing thing was the Encyclopedia. Nellie had hold of his taproot, was hauling him unceremoniously across the bumpy ground.

"Put him down!" Mackenzie yelled at her. "Let him go!"

"He stole the serum," howled Nellie. "He stole the serum and broke it on a rock!"

She swung the Encyclopedia toward them in a looping heave. The intelligent vegetable bounced a couple of times, struggled to get right side up, then scurried off a few feet, root coiled tightly against its underside.

Smith moved toward it threateningly. "I ought to kick the living innards out of you," he yelled. "We need that serum. You knew why we needed it."

"You threaten me with force," said the Encyclopedia. "The most primitive method of compulsion."

"It works," Smith told him shortly.

The Encyclopedia's thoughts were unruffled, almost serene, as clear and concise as ever. "You have a law that forbids your threatening or harming any alien thing."

"Chum," declared Smith, "you better get wised up on laws. There are times when certain laws don't hold. And this is one of them."

"Just a minute," said Mackenzie. He spoke to the Encyclopedia. "What is your understanding of a law?"

"It is a rule you live by," the Encyclopedia said. "It is something that is necessary. You cannot violate it."

"He got that from Nellie," said Smith.

"You think because there is a law against it, we won't take the trees?"

"There is a law against it," said the Encyclopedia. "You cannot take the trees."

"So as soon as you found that out, you lammed up here and stole the serum, eh?"

"He's figuring on indoctrinating us," Nellie explained. "Maybe that word ain't so good. Maybe conditioning is better. It's sort of mixed up. I don't know if I've got it straight. He took the serum so we would hear the trees without being able to defend ourselves against them. He figured when we heard the music, we'd go ahead and take the trees."

"Law or no law?"

"That's it," Nellie said. "Law or no law."

Smith whirled on the robot. "What kind of jabber is this? How do you know what he was planning?"

"I read his mind," said Nellie. "Hard to get at, the thing that he was planning, because he kept it deep. But some of it jarred up where I could reach it when you threatened him."

"You can't do that!" shrieked the Encyclopedia. "Not you! Not a machine!"

Mackenzie laughed shortly. "Too bad, big boy, but she can. She's been doing it."

Smith stared at Mackenzie.

"It's all right," Mackenzie said. "It isn't any bluff. She told me about it last night."

"You are unduly alarmed," the Encyclopedia said. "You are putting a wrong interpretation—"

A quiet voice spoke, almost as if it were a voice inside Mackenzie's mind.

"Don't believe a thing he tells you, pal. Don't fall for any of his lies."

"Nicodemus! You know something about this?"

"It's the trees," said Nicodemus. "The music does something to you. It changes you. Makes you different than you were before. Wade is different. He doesn't know it, but he is."

"If you mean the music chains one to it, that is true," said Wade. "I may as well admit it. I could not live without the music. I could not leave the Bowl. Perhaps you gentlemen have thought that I would go back with you. But I cannot go. I cannot leave. It will work the same with anyone. Alexander was here for a while when he ran short of serum. Doctors treated him and he was all right, but he came back. He had to come back. He couldn't stay away."

"It isn't only that," declared Nicodemus. "It changes you, too, in other ways. It can change you any way it wants to. Change your way of thinking. Change your viewpoints."

Wade strode forward. "It isn't true," he yelled. "I'm the same as when I came here."

"You heard things," said Nicodemus, "felt things in the music you couldn't understand. Things you wanted to understand, but couldn't. Strange emotions that you yearned to share, but could never reach. Strange thoughts that tantalized you for days."

Wade sobered, stared at them with haunted eyes.

"That was the way it was," he whispered. "That was just the way it was."

He glanced around, like a trapped animal seeking escape.

"But I don't feel any different," he mumbled. "I still am human. I think like a man, act like a man."

"Of course you do," said Nicodemus. "Otherwise you would have been scared away. If you had known what was happening to you, you wouldn't let it happen. And you have had less than a year of it. Less than a year of this conditioning. Five years and you would be less human. Ten years and you would be beginning to be the kind of thing the trees want you to be."

"And we were going to take some of those trees to Earth!" Smith shouted. "Seven of them! So the people of the Earth could hear them. Listen to them, night after night. The whole world listening to them on the radio. A whole world being conditioned, being changed by seven music trees."

"But why?" asked Wade, bewildered.

"Why did men domesticate animals?" Mackenzie asked. "You wouldn't find out by asking the animals, for they don't know. There is just as much point asking a dog why he was domesticated as there is in asking us why the trees want to condition us. For some purpose of their own, undoubtedly, that is perfectly clear and logical to them. A purpose that undoubtedly never can be clear and logical to us."

"Nicodemus," said the Encyclopedia, and his thought was deadly cold, "you have betrayed your own."

Mackenzie laughed harshly. "You're wrong there," he told the vegetable, "because Nicodemus isn't a plant, any more. He's a human. The same thing has happened to him as you want to have happen to us. He has become a human in everything but physical make-up. He thinks as a man does. His viewpoints are ours, not yours."

"That is right," said Nicodemus. "I am a man."

A piece of cloth ripped savagely and for an instant the group was blinded by a surge of energy that leaped from the thicket a hundred yards away. Smith gurgled once in sudden agony and the energy was gone.

Frozen momentarily by surprise, Mackenzie watched Smith stagger, face tight with pain, hand clapped to his side. Slowly the man wilted, sagged in the middle and went down.

Silently, Nellie leaped forward, was sprinting for the thicket. With a hoarse cry, Mackenzie bent over Smith.

Smith grinned at him, a twisted grin. His mouth worked, but no words came. His hand slid away from his side and he went limp, but his chest rose and fell with a slightly slower breath. His life blanket had shifted its position to cover the wounded side.

Mackenzie straightened up, hauling the pistol from his belt. A man had risen from the thicket, was leveling a gun at the charging Nellie. With a wild yell, Mackenzie shot from the hip. The lashing charge missed the man but half the thicket disappeared in a blinding sheet of flame.

The man with the gun ducked as the flame puffed out at him and in that instant Nellie closed. The man yelled once, a long-drawn howl of terror as Nellie swung him above her head and dashed him down. The smoking thicket hid the rest of it. Mackenzie, pistol hanging limply by his side, watched Nellie's right fist lift and fall with brutal precision, heard the thud of life being beaten from a human body.

Sickened, he turned back to Smith. Wade was kneeling beside the wounded man. He looked up.

"He seems to be unconscious."

Mackenzie nodded. "The blanket put him out. Gave him an anesthetic. It'll take care of him."

Mackenzie glanced up sharply at a scurry in the grass. The Encyclopedia, taking advantage of the moment, was almost out of sight, scuttling toward a grove of rifle trees.

A step grated behind him.

"It was Alexander," Nellie said. "He won't bother us no more."

Nelson Harper, factor at the post, was lighting up his pipe when the visiphone signal buzzed and the light flashed on.

Startled, Harper reached out and snapped on the set. Mackenzie's face came in, a face streaked with dirt and perspiration, stark with fear. He waited for no greeting. His lips were already moving even as the plate flickered and cleared.

"It's all off, chief," he said. "The deal is off. I can't bring in those trees."

"You got to bring them in," yelled Harper. "I've already called Earth. I got them turning handsprings. They say it's the greatest thing that ever happened. They're sending out a ship within an hour."

"Call them back and tell them not to bother," Mackenzie snapped.

"But you told me everything was set," yelped Harper. "You told me nothing could happen. You said you'd bring them in if you had to crawl on hands and knees and pack them on your back."

"I told you every word of that," agreed Mackenzie. "Probably even more. But I didn't know what I know now."

Harper groaned. "Galactic is plastering every front page in the Solar System with the news. Earth radios right now are bellowing it out from Mercury to Pluto. Before another hour is gone every man, woman and child will know those trees are coming to Earth. And once they know that, there's nothing we can do. Do you understand that, Mackenzie? We have to get them there!"

"I can't do it, chief," Mackenzie insisted, stubbornly.

"Why can't you?" screamed Harper. "So help me Hannah, if you don't—"

"I can't bring them in because Nellie's burning them. She's down in the Bowl right now with a flamer. When she's through, there won't be any music trees."

"Go out and stop her!" shrieked Harper. "What are you sitting there for! Go out and stop her! Blast her if you have to. Do anything, but stop her! That crazy robot—"

"I told her to," snapped Mackenzie. "I ordered her to do it. When I get through here, I'm going down and help her."

"You're crazy, man!" yelled Harper. "Stark, staring crazy. They'll throw the book at you for this. You'll be lucky if you just get life—"

Two darting hands loomed in the plate, hands that snapped down and closed around Mackenzie's throat, hands that dragged him away and left the screen blank, but with a certain blurring motion, as if two men might be fighting for their lives just in front of it.

"Mackenzie!" screamed Harper. "Mackenzie!"

Something smashed into the screen and shattered it, leaving the broken glass gaping in jagged shards.

Harper clawed at the visiphone. "Mackenzie! Mackenzie, what's happening!"

In answer the screen exploded in a flash of violent flame, howled like a screeching banshee and then went dead.

Harper stood frozen in the room, listening to the faint purring of the radio. His pipe fell from his hand and bounced along the floor, spilling burned tobacco.

Cold, clammy fear closed down upon him, squeezing his heart. A fear that twisted him and mocked him. Galactic would break him for this, he knew. Send him out to some of the jungle planets as the rankest subordinate. He would be marked for life, a man not to be trusted, a man who had failed to uphold the prestige of the company.

Suddenly a faint spark of hope stirred deep within him. If he could get there soon enough! if he could get to Melody Bowl in time, he might stop this madness. Might at least save something, save a few of the precious trees.

The flier was in the compound, waiting. Within half an hour he could be above the Bowl.

He leaped for the door, shoved it open and even as he did a pellet whistled past his cheek and exploded into a puff of dust against the door frame. Instinctively, he ducked and another pellet brushed his hair. A third caught him in the leg with stinging force and brought him down. A fourth puffed dust into his face.

He fought his way to his knees, was staggered by another shot that slammed into his side. He raised his right arm to protect his face and a sledge-hammer blow slapped his wrist. Pain flowed along his arm and in sheer panic he turned and scrambled on hands and knees across the threshold, kicked the door shut with his foot.

Sitting flat on the floor, he held his right wrist in his left hand. He tried to make his fingers wiggle and they wouldn't. The wrist, he knew, was broken.

After weeks of being off the beam the rifle tree outside the compound suddenly had regained its aim and gone on a rampage.

• • •

Mackenzie raised himself off the floor and braced himself with one elbow, while with the other hand he fumbled at his throbbing throat. The interior of the tractor danced with wavy motion and his head thumped and pounded with pain.

Slowly, carefully, he inched himself back so he could lean against the wall. Gradually the room stopped rocking, but the pounding in his head went on.

Someone was standing in the doorway of the tractor and he fought to focus his eyes, trying to make out who it was.

A voice screeched across his nerves.

"I'm taking your blankets. You'll get them back when you decide to leave the trees alone."

Mackenzie tried to fashion words, but all he accomplished was a croak. He tried again.

"Wade?" he asked.

It was Wade, he saw.

The man stood within the doorway, one hand clutching a pair of blankets, the other holding a gun.

"You're crazy, Wade," he whispered. "We have to burn the trees. The human race never would be safe. Even if they fail this time, they'll try again. And again—and yet again. And some day they will get us. Even without going to Earth they can get us. They can twist us to their purpose with recordings alone. Long distance propaganda. Take a bit longer, but it will do the job as well."

"They are beautiful," said Wade. "The most beautiful things in all the universe. I can't let you destroy them. You must not destroy them."

"But can't you see," croaked Mackenzie, "that's the thing that makes them so dangerous. Their beauty, the beauty of their music, is fatal. No one can resist it."

"It was the thing I lived by," Wade told him, soberly. "You say it made me something that was not quite human. But what difference does that make. Must racial purity, in thought and action, be a fetish that would chain us to a drab existence when something better, something greater, is offered. And we never would have known. That is the best of it all, we never would have known. They would have changed us, yes, but so slowly, so gradually, that we would not have suspected. Our decisions and our actions and our way of thought would still have seemed to be our own. The trees never would have been anything more than something cultural."

"They want our mechanization," said Mackenzie. "Plants can't develop machines. Given that, they might have taken us along a road we, in our rightful heritage, never would have taken."

"How can we be sure," asked Wade, "that our heritage would have guided us aright?"

Mackenzie slid straighter against the wall. His head still throbbed and his throat still ached.

"You've been thinking about this?" he asked.

Wade nodded. "At first there was the natural reaction of horror. But, logically, that reaction is erroneous. Our schools teach our children a way of life. Our press strives to formulate our adult opinion and belief. The trees were doing no more to us than we do to ourselves. And perhaps, for a purpose no more selfish."

Mackenzie shook his head. "We must live our own life. We must follow the path the attributes of humanity decree that we should follow. And anyway, you're wasting your time."

"I don't understand," said Wade.

"Nellie already is burning the trees," Mackenzie told him. "I sent her out before I made the call to Harper."

"No, she's not," said Wade.

Mackenzie sat bolt upright. "What do you mean?"

Wade flipped the pistol as Mackenzie moved as if to regain his feet.

"It doesn't matter what I mean," he snapped. "Nellie isn't burning any trees. She isn't in a position to burn any trees. And neither are you, for I've taken both your flamers. And the tractor won't run, either. I've seen to that. So the only thing that you can do is stay right here."

Mackenzie motioned toward Smith, lying on the floor. "You're taking his blanket, too?"

Wade nodded.

"But you can't. Smith will die. Without that blanket he doesn't have a chance. The blanket could have healed the wound, kept him fed correctly, kept him warm—"

"That," said Wade, "is all the more reason that you come to terms directly."

"Your terms," said Mackenzie, "are that we leave the trees unharmed."

"Those are my terms."

Mackenzie shook his head. "I can't take the chance," he said.

"When you decide, just step out and shout," Wade told him. "I'll stay in calling distance."

He backed slowly from the door.

Smith needed warmth and food. In the hour since his blanket had been taken from him he had regained consciousness, had mumbled feverishly and tossed about, his hand clawing at his wounded side.

Squatting beside him, Mackenzie had tried to quiet him, had felt a wave of slow terror as he thought of the hours ahead.

There was no food in the tractor, no means for making heat. There was no need for such provision so long as they had had their life blankets—but now the blankets were gone. There was a first-aid cabinet and with the materials that he found there, Mackenzie did his fumbling best, but there was nothing to relieve Smith's pain, nothing to control his fever. For treatment such as that they had relied upon the blankets.

The atomic motor might have been rigged up to furnish heat, but Wade had taken the firing mechanism control.

Night was falling and that meant the air would grow colder. Not too cold to live, of course, but cold enough to spell doom to a man in Smith's condition.

Mackenzie squatted on his heels and stared at Smith.

"If I could only find Nellie," he thought.

He had tried to find her—briefly. He had raced along the rim of the Bowl for a mile or so, but had seen no sign of her. He had been afraid to go farther, afraid to stay too long from the man back in the tractor.

Smith mumbled and Mackenzie bent low to try to catch the words. But there were no words.

Slowly he rose and headed for the door. First of all, he needed heat. Then food. The heat came first. An open fire wasn't the best way to make heat, of course, but it was better than nothing.

The uprooted music tree, balled roots silhouetted against the sky, loomed before him in the dusk. He found a few dead branches and tore them off. They would do to start the fire. After that he would have to rely on green wood to keep it going. Tomorrow he could forage about for suitable fuel.

In the Bowl below, the music trees were tuning up for the evening concert.

Back in the tractor, he found a knife, carefully slivered several of the branches for easy lighting, piled them ready for his pocket lighter.

The lighter flared and a tiny figure hopped up on the threshold of the tractor, squatting there, blinking at the light.

Startled, Mackenzie held the lighter without touching it to the wood, stared at the thing that perched in the doorway.

Delbert's squeaky thought drilled into his brain.

"What you doing?"

"Building a fire," Mackenzie told him.

"What's a fire?"

"It's a . . . it's a . . . say, don't you know what a fire is?"

"Nope," said Delbert.

"It's a chemical action," Mackenzie said. "It breaks up matter and releases energy in the form of heat."

"What you building a fire with?" asked Delbert, blinking in the flare of the lighter.

"With branches from a tree."

Delbert's eyes widened and his thought was jittery.

"A tree?"

"Sure, a tree. Wood. It burns. It gives off heat. I need heat."

"What tree?"

"Why—" And then Mackenzie stopped with sudden realization. His thumb relaxed and the flame went out.

Delbert shrieked at him in sudden terror and anger. "It's my tree! You're building a fire with my tree!"

Mackenzie sat in silence.

"When you burn my tree, it's gone," yelled Delbert. "Isn't that right? When you burn my tree, it's gone?"

Mackenzie nodded.

"But why do you do it?" shrilled Delbert.

"I need heat," said Mackenzie, doggedly. "If I don't have heat, my friend will die. It's the only way I can get heat."

"But my tree!"

Mackenzie shrugged. "I need a fire, see? And I'm getting it any way I can."

He flipped his thumb again and the lighter flared.

"But I never did anything to you," Delbert howled, rocking on the metal door sill. "I'm your friend, I am. I never did a thing to hurt you."

"No?" asked Mackenzie.

"No," yelled Delbert.

"What about that scheme of yours?" asked Mackenzie. "Trying to trick me into taking trees to Earth?"

"That wasn't my idea," yipped Delbert. "It wasn't any of the trees' ideas. The Encyclopedia thought it up."

A bulky form loomed outside the door. "Someone talking about me?" it asked.

The Encyclopedia was back again.

Arrogantly, he shouldered Delbert aside, stepped into the tractor.

"I saw Wade," he said.

Mackenzie glared at him. "So you figured it would be safe to come."

"Certainly," said the Encyclopedia. "Your formula of force counts for nothing now. You have no means to enforce it."

Mackenzie's hand shot out and grasped the Encyclopedia with a vicious grip, hurled him into the interior of the tractor.

"Just try to get out this door," he snarled. "You'll soon find out if the formula of force amounts to anything."

The Encyclopedia picked himself up, shook himself like a ruffled hen. But his thought was cool and calm.

"I can't see what this avails you."

"It gives us soup," Mackenzie snapped.

He sized the Encyclopedia up. "Good vegetable soup. Something like cabbage. Never cared much for cabbage soup, myself, but—"

"Soup?"

"Yeah, soup. Stuff to eat. Food."

"Food!" The Encyclopedia's thought held a tremor of anxiety. "You would use me as food."

"Why not?" Mackenzie asked him. "You're nothing but a vegetable. An intelligent vegetable, granted, but still a vegetable."

He felt the Encyclopedia's groping thought-fingers prying into his mind.

"Go ahead," he told him, "but you won't like what you find."

The Encyclopedia's thoughts almost gasped. "You withheld this from me!" he charged.

"We withheld nothing from you," Mackenzie declared. "We never had occasion to think of it . . . to remember to what use Men at one time put plants, to what use we still put plants in certain cases. The only reason we don't use them so extensively now is that we have advanced beyond the need of them. Let that need exist again and—"

"You ate us," strummed the Encyclopedia. "You used us to build your shelters! You destroyed us to create heat for your selfish purposes!"

"Pipe down," Mackenzie told him. "It's the way we did it that gets you. The idea that we thought we had a right to. That we went out and took, without even asking, never wondering what the plant might think about it. That hurts your racial dignity."

He stopped, then moved closer to the doorway. From the Bowl below came the first strains of the music. The tuning up, the preliminary to the concert, was over.

"O.K.," Mackenzie said, "I'll hurt it some more. Even you are nothing but a plant to me. Just because you've learned some civilized tricks doesn't make you my equal. It never did. We humans can't slur off the experiences of the past so easily. It would take thousands of years of association with things like you before we even began to regard you as anything other than a plant, a thing that we used in the past and might use again."

"Still cabbage soup," said the Encyclopedia.

"Still cabbage soup," Mackenzie told him.

The music stopped. Stopped dead still, in the middle of a note.

"See," said Mackenzie, "even the music fails you."

Silence rolled at them in engulfing waves and through the stillness came another sound, the *clop, clop* of heavy, plodding feet.

"Nellie!" yelled Mackenzie.

A bulky shadow loomed in the darkness.

"Yeah, chief, it's me," said Nellie. "I brung you something."

She dumped Wade across the doorway.

Wade rolled over and groaned. There were skittering, flapping sounds as two fluttering shapes detached themselves from Wade's shoulders.

"Nellie," said Mackenzie, harshly, "there was no need to beat him up. You should have brought him back just as he was and let me take care of him."

"Gee, boss," protested Nellie. "I didn't beat him up. He was like that when I found him."

Nicodemus was clawing his way to Mackenzie's shoulder, while Smith's life blanket scuttled for the corner where his master lay.

"It was us, boss," piped Nicodemus. "We laid him out."

"You laid him out?"

"Sure, there was two of us and only one of him. We fed him poison."

Nicodemus settled into place on Mackenzie's shoulders.

"I didn't like him," he declared. "He wasn't nothing like you, boss. I didn't want to change like him. I wanted to stay like you."

"This poison?" asked Mackenzie. "Nothing fatal, I hope."

"Sure not, pal," Nicodemus told him. "We only made him sick. He didn't know what was happening until it was too late to do anything about it. We bargained with him, we did. We told him we'd quit feeding it to him if he took us back. He was on his way here, too, but he'd never have made it if it hadn't been for Nellie."

"Chief," pleaded Nellie, "when he gets so he knows what it's all about, won't you let me have him for about five minutes?"

"No," said Mackenzie.

"He strung me up," wailed Nellie. "He hid in the cliff and lassoed me and left me hanging there. It took me hours to get loose. Honest, I wouldn't hurt him much. I'd just kick him around a little, gentle-like."

From the cliff top came the rustling of grass as if hundreds of little feet were advancing upon them.

"We got visitors," said Nicodemus.

The visitors, Mackenzie saw, were the conductors, dozens of little gnomelike figures that moved up and squatted on their haunches, faintly luminous eyes blinking at them.

One of them shambled forward. As he came closer, Mackenzie saw that it was Alder.

"Well?" Mackenzie demanded.

"We came to tell you the deal is off," Alder squeaked. "Delbert came and told us."

"Told you what?"

"About what you do to trees."

"Oh, that."

"Yes, that."

"But you made the deal," Mackenzie told him. "You can't back out now. Why, Earth is waiting breathless—"

"Don't try to kid me," snapped Alder. "You don't want us any more than we want you. It was a dirty trick to start with, but it wasn't any of our doing. The Encyclopedia talked us into it. He told us we had a duty. A duty to our race. To act as missionaries to the inferior races of the Galaxy.

"We didn't take to it at first. Music, you see, is our life. We have been creating music for so long that our origin is lost in the dim antiquity of a planet that long ago has passed its zenith of existence. We will be creating music in that far day when the planet falls apart beneath our feet. You live by a code of accomplishment by action. We live by a code of accomplishment by music. Kadmar's *Red Sun* symphony was a greater triumph for us than the discovery of a new planetary system is for you. It pleased us when you liked our music. It will please us if you still like our music, even after what has happened. But we will not allow you to take any of us to Earth."

"The monopoly on the music still stands?" asked Mackenzie.

"It still stands. Come whenever you want to and record my symphony. When there are others we will let you know."

"And the propaganda in the music?"

"From now on," Alder promised, "the propaganda is out. If, from now on, our music changes you, it will change you through its own power. It may do that, but we will not try to shape your lives."

"How can we depend on that?"

"Certainly," said Alder. "There are certain tests you could devise. Not that they will be necessary."

"We'll devise the tests," declared Mackenzie. "Sorry, but we can't trust you."

"I'm sorry that you can't," said Alder, and he sounded as if he were.

"I was going to burn you," Mackenzie said, snapping his words off brutally. "Destroy you. Wipe you out. There was nothing you could have done about it. Nothing you could have done to stop me."

"You're still barbarians," Alder told him. "You have conquered the distances between the stars, you have built a great civilization, but your methods are still ruthless and degenerate."

"The Encyclopedia calls it a formula of force," Mackenzie said. "No matter what you call it, it still works. It's the thing that took us up. I warn you. If you ever again try to trick the human race, there will be hell to pay. A human being will destroy anything to save himself. Remember that—we destroy anything that threatens us."

Something swished out of the tractor door and Mackenzie whirled about.

"It's the Encyclopedia!" he yelled. "He's trying to get away! Nellie!"

There was a thrashing rustle. "Got him, boss," said Nellie.

The robot came out of the darkness, dragging the Encyclopedia along by his leafy topknot.

Mackenzie turned back to the composers, but the composers were gone. The grass rustled eerily towards the cliff edge as dozens of tiny feet scurried through it.

"What now?" asked Nellie. "Do we burn the trees?"

Mackenzie shook his head. "No, Nellie. We won't burn them."

"We got them scared," said Nellie. "Scared pink with purple spots."

"Perhaps we have," said Mackenzie. "Let's hope so, at least. But it isn't only that they're scared. They probably loathe us and that is better yet. Like we'd loathe some form of life that bred and reared men for food—that thought of Man as nothing else than food. All the time they've thought of themselves as the greatest intellectual force in the universe. We've given them a jolt. We've scared them and hurt their pride and shook their confidence. They've run up against something that is more than a match for them. Maybe they'll think twice again before they try any more shenanigans."

Down in the Bowl the music began again.

Mackenzie went in to look at Smith. The man was sleeping peacefully, his blanket wrapped around him. Wade sat in a corner, head held in his hands.

Outside, a rocket murmured and Nellie yelled. Mackenzie spun on his heel and dashed through the door. A ship was swinging over the Bowl, lighting up the area with floods. Swiftly it swooped down, came to ground a hundred yards away.

Harper, right arm in a sling, tumbled out and raced toward them.

"You didn't burn them!" he was yelling. "You didn't burn them!"

Mackenzie shook his head.

Harper pounded him on the back with his good hand. "Knew you wouldn't. Knew you wouldn't all the time. Just kidding the chief, eh? Having a little fun."

"Not exactly fun."

"About them trees," said Harper. "We can't take them back to Earth, after all."

"I told you that," Mackenzie said.

"Earth just called me, half an hour ago," said Harper. "Seems there's a law, passed centuries ago. Against bringing alien plants to Earth. Some lunkhead once brought a bunch of stuff from Mars that just about ruined Earth, so they passed the law. Been there all the time, forgotten."

Mackenzie nodded. "Someone dug it up."

"That's right," said Harper. "And slapped an injunction on Galactic. We can't touch those trees."

"You wouldn't have anyhow," said Mackenzie. "They wouldn't go."

"But you made the deal! They were anxious to go—"

"That," Mackenzie told him, "was before they found out we used plants for food—and other things."

"But . . . but—"

"To them," said Mackenzie, "we're just a gang of ogres. Something they'll scare the little plants with. Tell them if they don't be quiet the humans will get 'em."

Nellie came around the corner of the tractor, still hauling the Encyclopedia by his topknot.

"Hey," yelled Harper, "what goes on here?"

"We'll have to build a concentration camp," said Mackenzie. "Big high fence." He motioned with his thumb toward the Encyclopedia.

Harper stared. "But he hasn't done anything!"

"Nothing but try to take over the human race," Mackenzie said.

Harper sighed. "That makes two fences we got to build. That rifle tree back at the post is shooting up the place."

Mackenzie grinned. "Maybe the one fence will do for the both of them."

GLEANERS

Sent to Horace Gold in 1959 and purchased in less than a week, this story, which was first published in the March 1960 issue of If, *features two prominent themes from Clifford Simak's fiction: time travel and religion. I was not old enough to have seen the magazine when it came out, and I missed the story for years thereafter—but when I finally discovered it, I found myself utterly charmed by its portrayal of a dignified man being targeted by a cross-time conspiracy.*

—*dww*

I

He went sneaking past the door.

The lettering on the door said: *Executive Vice President, Projects.*

And down in the lower left corner, *Hallock Spencer*, in very modest type.

That was him. He was Hallock Spencer.

But he wasn't going in that door. He had trouble enough already without going in. There'd be people waiting there for him. No one in particular—but people. And each of them with problems.

He ducked around the corner and went a step or two down the corridor until he came to another door that said *Private* on it.

It was unlocked. He went in.

A dowdy scarecrow in a faded, dusty toga sat tipped back in a chair, with his sandaled feet resting on Hallock Spencer's desk top. He wore a mouse-gray woolen cap upon his hairless skull and his ears stuck out like wings. A short sword, hanging from the belt that snugged in the toga, stood canted with its point resting on the carpet. There was dirt beneath his rather longish toenails and he hadn't shaved for days. He was a total slob.

"Hello, E.J.," said Spencer.

The man in the toga didn't take his feet off the desk. He didn't move at all. He just sat there.

"Sneaking in again," he said.

Spencer put down his briefcase and hung up his hat.

"The reception room's a trap," he said.

He sat down in the chair behind the desk and picked up the project schedule and had a look at it.

"What's the trouble, E.J.?" he asked. "You back already?"

"Haven't started yet. Not for another couple hours."

"It says here," said Spencer, flicking the schedule with a finger, "that you're a Roman trader."

"That's what I am," said E.J. "At least, Costumes says so. I hope to God they're right."

"But the sword—"

"Pardner," said E.J., "back in Roman Britain, out on a Roman road, with a pack train loaded down with goods, a man has got to carry steel."

He reached down and hoisted the sword into his lap. He regarded it with disfavor. "But I don't mind telling you it's no great shakes of a weapon."

"I suppose you'd feel safer with a tommy gun."

E.J. nodded glumly. "Yes, I would."

"Lacking that," said Spencer, "we do the best we can. You'll pack the finest steel in the second century. If that is any comfort."

E.J. just sat there with the sword across his lap. He was making up his mind to say something—it was written on his face. He was a silly-looking soul, with all those wiry whiskers and his ears way out to either side of him and the long black hairs that grew out of the lobes.

"Hal," said E.J., finally making up his mind, "I want out of this."

Spencer stiffened in his chair. "You can't do that!" he yelled. "Time is your very life. You've been in it for a lot of years!"

"I don't mean out of Time. I mean out of Family Tree. I am sick of it."

"You don't know what you're saying," Spencer protested. "Family Tree's not tough. You've been on a lot of worse ones. Family Tree's a snap. All you have to do is go back and talk to people or maybe check some records. You don't have to snitch a thing."

"It's not the work," said E.J. "Sure, the work is easy. I don't mind the work. It's after I get back."

"You mean the Wrightson-Graves."

"That is what I mean. After every trip, she has me up to that fancy place of hers and I have to tell her all about her venerable ancestors . . ."

Spencer said, "It's a valuable account. We have to service it."

"I can't stand much more of it," E.J. insisted, stubbornly.

Spencer nodded. He knew just what E.J. meant. He felt much the same.

Alma Wrightson-Graves was a formidable old dowager with a pouter-pigeon build and the erroneous conviction that she still retained much of her girlish charm. She was loaded down with cash, and also with jewels that were too costly and gaudy to be good taste. For years she'd shrieked down and bought off everyone around her until she firmly believed there was nothing in the world she couldn't have—if she was willing to pay enough for it.

And she was paying plenty for this family tree of hers. Spencer had often asked himself just why she wanted it. Back to the Conquest, sure—that made at least some sense. But not back to the caves. Not that Past, Inc., couldn't trace it that far for her if her cash continued to hold out. He thought, with a perverted satisfaction, that she couldn't have been happy with the last report or two, for the family had sunk back to abject peasantry.

He said as much to E.J. "What does she want?" he asked. "What does she expect?"

"I have a hunch," E.J. told him, "that she has some hopes we'll find a connection back to Rome. God help us if we do. Then it could go on forever."

Spencer grunted.

"Don't be too sure," warned E.J. "Roman officers being what they were I wouldn't bet against it."

"If that should happen," Spencer told him. "I'll take you off the project. Assign someone else to carry out the Roman research. I'll tell the Wrightson-Graves you're not so hot on Rome—have a mental block or a psychic allergy or something that rejects indoctrination."

"Thanks a lot," said E.J., without much enthusiasm.

One by one, he took his dirty feet off the shiny desk and rose out of the chair.

"E.J.?"

"Yes, Hal."

"Just wondering. Have you ever hit a place where you felt that you should stay? Have you ever wondered if maybe you should stay?"

"Yeah, I guess so. Once or twice, perhaps. But I never did. You're thinking about Garson."

"Garson for one. And all the others."

"Maybe something happened to him. You get into tight spots. It's a simple matter to make a big mistake. Or the operator might have missed."

"Our operators never miss," snapped Spencer.

"Garson was a good man," said E.J., a little sadly.

"Garson! It's not only Garson. It's all the . . ." Spencer stopped abruptly, for he'd run into it again. After all these years, he still kept running into it. No matter how he tried, it was something to which he could not reconcile himself—the disparity in time.

He saw that E.J. was staring at him, with just the slightest crinkle that was not quite a smile at the corner of his mouth.

"You can't let it eat you," said E.J. "You're not responsible. We take our chances. If it wasn't worth our while . . ."

"Oh, shut up!" said Spencer.

"Sure," said E.J., "you lose one of us every now and then. But it's no worse than any other business."

"Not one every now and then," said Spencer. "There have been three of them in the last ten days."

"Well, now," said E.J. "I lose track of them. There was Garson just the other day. And Taylor—how long ago was that?"

"Four days ago," said Spencer.

"Four days," said E.J., astonished. "Is that all it was?"

Spencer snapped, "For you it was three months or more. And do you remember Price? For you that was a year ago, but just ten days for me."

E.J. put up a dirty paw and scrubbed at the bristle on his chin.

"How time does fly!"

"Look," said Spencer, miserably, "this whole set-up is bad enough. Please don't make jokes about it."

"Garside been giving you a hard time, maybe? Losing too many of the men?"

"Hell, no," said Spencer, bitterly. "You can always get more men. It's the machines that bother him. He keeps reminding me they cost a quarter million."

E.J. made a rude sound with his lips.

"Get out of here!" yelled Spencer. "And see that you come home!"

E.J. grinned and left. He gave the toga a girlish flirt as he went out the door.

II

Spencer told himself E.J. was wrong. For whatever anyone might say, he, Hallock Spencer, was responsible. He ran the stinking show. He made up the schedules. He assigned the travelers and he sent them out. When there were mistakes or hitches, he was the one who answered. To himself, if no one else.

He got up and paced the floor, hands locked behind his back.

Three men in the last ten days. And what had happened to them?

Possibly there was something to what Garside said, as well— Christopher Anson Garside, chief co-ordinator and a nasty man to handle, with his clipped, gray mustache and his clipped, gray voice and his clipped, gray business thinking.

For it was not men alone who did not come back. It was likewise the training and experience you had invested in those men. They lasted, Spencer told himself, a short time at the best without managing to get themselves killed off somewhere in the past, or deciding to squat down and settle in some other era they liked better than the present.

And the machines were something that could not be dismissed. Every time a man failed to return it meant another carrier lost. And the carriers *did* cost a quarter million—which wasn't something you could utterly forget.

Spencer went back to his desk and had another look at the schedule for the day. There was E.J. bound for Roman Britain on the Family Tree project; Nickerson going back to the early Italian Renaissance to check up once again on the missing treasure in the Vatican; Hennessy off on his search once more for the lost documents in fifteenth-century Spain; Williams going out, he hoped, finally to snatch the mislaid Picasso, and a half dozen more. Not a massive schedule. But enough to spell out a fairly busy day.

He checked the men not on the projects list. A couple of them were on vacation. One was in Rehabilitation. Indoctrination had the rest of them.

He sat there, then, for the thousandth time, wondering what it would be like, really, to travel into time.

He'd heard hints of it from some of the travelers, but no more than hints, for they did not talk about it. Perhaps they did among themselves, when there were no outsiders present. Perhaps not even then. As if it were something that no man could quite describe. As if it were an experience that no man should discuss.

A haunting sense of unreality, the feeling that one was out of place, a hint of not quite belonging, of somehow standing, tip-toe, on the far edge of eternity.

It wore off after a time, of course, but apparently one was never entirely free of it. For the past, in some mysterious working of a principle yet unknown, was a world of wild enchantment.

Well, he had had his chance and flunked it.

But some day, he told himself, he would go into time. Not as a regular traveler, but as a vacationist—if he could snatch the necessary time to get ready for the trip. The trip, itself, of course, was no consideration so far as time might be concerned. It was Indoctrination and the briefing that was time-consuming.

He picked up the schedule again for another look. All of those who were going back this day were good men. There was no need to worry about any one of them.

He laid the schedule to one side and buzzed Miss Crane.

Miss Crane was a letter-perfect secretary, though she wasn't much to look at. She was a leathery old maid. She had her own way of doing things, and she could act very disapproving.

No choice of his, Spencer had inherited her fifteen years before. She had been with Past, Inc., before there was even a projects office. And, despite her lack of looks, her snippy attitude and her generally pessimistic view of life, she was indispensable.

She knew the projects job as well as he did. At times she let him know it. But she never forgot, never mislaid, never erred; she ran an efficient office, always got her work done and it always was on time.

Spence, dreaming at times of a lusher young replacement, knew that he was no more than dreaming. He couldn't do his job without Miss Crane in the outer office.

"You sneaked in again," she accused him as soon as she'd closed the door.

"I suppose there's someone waiting."

"There's a Dr. Aldous Ravenholt," she said. "He's from Foundation for Humanity."

Spencer flinched. There was no one worse to start a morning with than some pompous functionary from Humanity. They almost always figured that you owed them something. They thought the whole world owed them something.

"And there's a Mr. Stewart Cabell. He's an applicant sent up by Personnel. Mr. Spencer, don't you think . . ."

"No, I don't," Spencer snapped at her. "I know Personnel is sore. But I've been taking everyone they've been shoveling up here and see what happens. Three men gone in the last ten days. From now on, I'm taking a close look at everyone myself."

She sniffed. It was a very nasty sniff.

"That's all?" asked Spencer, figuring that he couldn't be that lucky—just two of them.

"Also there's a Mr. Boone Hudson. He's an elderly man who looks rather ill and he seems impatient. Perhaps you should see him first."

Spence might have, but not after she said that.

"I'll see Ravenholt," he said. "Any idea what he wants?"

"No, sir."

"Well, send him in," said Spencer. "He'll probably want to chisel a slice of Time off me."

Chiselers, he thought. I didn't know there were so many chiselers!

Aldous Ravenholt was a pompous man, well satisfied and smug. You could have buttered bread with the crease in his trousers. His handshake was professional and he had an automatic smile. He sat down in the chair that Spencer offered him with a self-assurance that was highly irritating.

"I came to talk with you," he said precisely, "about the pending proposal to investigate religious origins."

Spencer winced mentally. It was a tender subject.

"Dr. Ravenholt," he said, "that is a matter I have given a great deal of attention. Not myself alone, but my entire department."

"That is what I've heard," Ravenholt said drily. "That is why I'm here. I understand you have tentatively decided not to go ahead with it."

"Not tentatively," said Spencer. "Our decision has been made. I'm curious how you heard it."

Ravenholt waved an airy hand, implying there was very little he did not know about. "I presume the matter still is open to discussion."

Spencer shook his head.

Ravenholt said, icily, "I fail to see how you could summarily cut off an investigation so valid and so vital to all humanity."

"Not summarily, Dr. Ravenholt. We spent a lot of time on it. We made opinion samplings. We had an extensive check by Psych. We considered all the factors."

"And your findings, Mr. Spencer?"

"First of all," said Spencer, just a little nettled, "it would be too time-consuming. As you know, our license specifies that we donate ten per cent of our operation time to public interest projects. This we are most meticulous in doing, although I don't mind telling you there's nothing that gives us greater headaches."

"But that ten per cent . . ."

"If we took up this project you are urging, doctor, we'd use up all our public interest time for several years at least. That would mean no other programs at all."

"But surely you'll concede that no other proposal could be in a greater public interest."

"That's not our findings," Spencer told him. "We took opinion samplings in every area of Earth, in all possible cross-sections. We came up with—sacrilege."

"You're joking, Mr. Spencer!"

"Not at all," said Spencer. "Our opinion-taking showed quite conclusively that any attempt to investigate world-wide religious origins would be viewed by the general public in a sacrilegious light. You and I, perhaps, could look upon it as research. We could resolve all our questioning by saying we sought no more nor less than truth. But the people of the world—the simple, common people of every sect and faith in the entire world—do not want the truth. They are satisfied with things just as they are. They're afraid we would upset a lot of the old, comfortable traditions. They call it sacrilege and it's partly that, of course, but it's likewise an instinctive defense reaction against upsetting their thinking. They have a faith to cling to. It has served them through the years and they don't want anyone to fool around with it."

"I simply can't believe it," said Ravenholt, aghast at such blind provincialism.

"I have the figures. I can show you."

Dr. Ravenholt waved his hand condescendingly and gracefully.

"If you say you have them, I am sure you have."

He wasn't taking any chances of being proven wrong.

"Another thing," said Spencer, "is objectivity. How do you select the men to send back to observe the facts?"

"I am sure that we could get them. There are many men of the cloth, of every creed and faith, who would be amply qualified . . ."

"Those are just the ones we would never think of sending," said Spencer. "We need objectivity. Ideally, the kind of man we need is one who has no interest in religion, who has no formal training in it, one who is neither for it nor against it—and yet, we couldn't use that sort of man even if we found him. For to understand what is going on, he'd have to have a rather thorough briefing on what he was to look for. Once you trained him, he'd be bound to lose his objectivity. There is something about religion that forces one to take positions on it."

"Now," said Ravenholt, "you are talking about the ideal investigative situation, not our own."

"Well, all right, then," conceded Spencer. "Let's say we decide to do a slightly sloppy job. Who do we send then? Could any Christian, I ask you, no matter how poor a Christian he might be, safely be sent back to the days that Jesus spent on Earth? How could one be sure that even mediocre Christians would do no more than observe the facts? I tell you, Dr. Ravenholt, we could not take the chance. What would happen, do you think, if we suddenly should have thirteen instead of twelve disciples? What if someone should try to rescue Jesus from the Cross? Worse yet, what if He actually were rescued? Where would Christianity be then? Would there be Christianity? Without the Crucifixion, would it ever have survived?"

"Your problem has a simple answer," Ravenholt said coldly. "Do not send a Christian."

"Now we are really getting somewhere," said Spencer. "Let's send a Moslem to get the Christian facts and a Christian to track down the life of Buddha—and a Buddhist to investigate black magic in the Belgian Congo."

"It could work," said Ravenholt.

"It might work, but you wouldn't get objectivity. You'd get bias and, worse yet, perfectly honest misunderstanding."

Ravenholt drummed impatient fingers on his well-creased knee.

"I can see your point," he agreed, somewhat irritably, "but there is something you have overlooked. The findings need not be released in their entirety to the public."

"But if it's in the public interest? That's what our license says."

"Would it help," asked Ravenholt, "if I should offer certain funds which could be used to help defray the costs?"

"In such a case," said Spencer, blandly, "the requirement would not be met. It's either in the public interest, without any charge at all, or it's a commercial contract paid for at regular rates."

"The obvious fact," Ravenholt said flatly, "is that you do not want to do this job. You may as well admit it."

"Most cheerfully," said Spencer. "I willingly wouldn't touch it with a ten-foot pole. What worries me right now is why you're here."

Ravenholt said, "I thought that with the project about to be rejected, I possibly could serve as a sort of mediator."

"You mean you thought we could be bribed."

"Not at all," said Ravenholt wrathfully. "I was only recognizing that the project was perhaps a cut beyond what your license calls for."

"It's all of that," said Spencer.

"I cannot fully understand your objection to it," Ravenholt persisted.

"Dr. Ravenholt," said Spencer gently, "how would you like to be responsible for the destruction of a faith?"

"But," stammered Ravenholt, "there is no such possibility . . ."

"Are you certain?" Spencer asked him. "How certain are you, Dr. Ravenholt? Even the black magic of the Congo?"

"Well, I—well, since you put it that way . . ."

"You see what I mean?" asked Spencer.

"But even so," argued Ravenholt, "there could be certain facts suppressed . . ."

"Come now! How long do you think you could keep it bottled up? Anyway, when Past, Inc., does a job," Spencer told him firmly, "it goes gunning for the truth. And when we learn it, we report it. That is the one excuse we have for our continuing existence. We have a certain project here—a personal, full-rate contract—in which we have traced a family tree for almost two thousand years. We have been forced to tell our client some unpleasant things. But we told them."

"That's part of what I'm trying to convey to you," shouted Ravenholt, shaken finally out of his ruthless calm. "You are willing to embark upon the tracing of a family tree, but you refuse this!"

"And you are confusing two utterly different operations! This investigation of religious origins is a public interest matter. Family Tree is a private account for which we're being paid."

Ravenholt rose angrily. "We'll discuss this some other time, when we both can keep our temper."

Spencer said wearily, "It won't do any good. My mind is made up."

"Mr. Spencer," Ravenholt said, nastily, "I'm not without recourse."

"Perhaps you're not. You can go above my head. If that is what you're thinking, I'll tell you something else: You'll carry out this project over my dead body. I will not, Dr. Ravenholt, betray the faith of any people in the world."

"We'll see," said Ravenholt, still nasty.

"Now," said Spencer, "you're thinking that you can have me fired. Probably you could. Undoubtedly you know the very strings to pull. But it's no solution."

"I would think," said Ravenholt, "it would be the perfect one."

"I'd still fight you as a private citizen. I'd take it to the floor of the United Nations if I had to."

They both were on their feet now, facing one another across the width of desk.

"I'm sorry," Spencer said, "that it turned out this way. But I meant everything I said."

"So did I," said Ravenholt, stalking out the door.

III

Spencer sat down slowly in his chair.

A swell way to start a day, he told himself.

But the guy had burned him up.

Miss Crane came in the door with a sheaf of papers for his desk.

"Mr. Spencer," shall I send in Mr. Hudson? He's been waiting a long time."

"Is Hudson the applicant?"

"No, that is Mr. Cabell."

"Cabell is the man I want to see. Bring me his file." She sniffed contemptuously and left.

Damn her, Spencer told himself, I'll see who I want to see when I want to see them!

He was astounded at the violence of his thought. What was wrong with him? Nothing was going right. Couldn't he get along with anyone any more?

Too tensed up, he thought. Too many things to do, too much to worry over.

Maybe what he ought to do was walk out into Operations and step into a carrier for a long vacation. Back to the Old Stone Age, which would require no indoctrination. There wouldn't be too many people, perhaps none at all. But there'd be mosquitoes. And cave bears. And saber-tooths and perhaps a lot of other things equally obnoxious. And he'd have to get some camping stuff together and—oh, the hell with it!

But it was not a bad idea.

He'd thought about it often. Some day he would do it. Meanwhile, he picked up the sheaf of papers Miss Crane had dropped upon his desk.

They were the daily batch of future assignments dreamed up by the Dirty Tricks department. There was always trouble in them. He felt himself go tense as he picked them up.

The first one was a routine enough assignment—an investigation of some tributes paid the Goths by Rome. There was, it seemed, a legend that the treasure had been buried somewhere in the Alps. It might never have been recovered. That was S.O.P., checking up on buried treasure.

But the second paper—

"Miss Crane!" he yelled.

She was coming through the door, with a file clutched in her hand. Her face changed not a whit at his yelp of anguish; she was used to it.

"What is the matter, Mr. Spencer?" she inquired, at least three degrees too calmly.

Spencer banged his fist down on the pile of sheets. "They can't do this to me! I won't stand for it. Get Rogers on the phone!"

"Yes, sir."

"No, wait a minute there," Spencer interrupted grimly. "This I can do better personal. I'll go up and see him. In fact, I'll take him apart barehanded."

"But there are those people waiting . . ."

"Let them wait for a while. It will make them humble."

He snatched up the assignment sheet and went striding out the door. He shunned the elevator. He climbed two flights of stairs. He went in a door marked *Evaluation*.

Rogers was sitting tilted back, with his feet up on the desk top, staring at the ceiling.

He glanced at Spencer with a bland concern. He took his feet down off the desk and sat forward in his chair.

"Well? What's the matter this time?"

"This!" said Spencer, throwing the sheet down in front of him.

Rogers poked it with a delicate finger. "Nothing difficult there. Just a little ingenuity . . ."

"Nothing difficult!" howled Spencer. "Movies of Nero's fire in Rome!"

Rogers sighed. "This movie outfit will pay us plenty for it."

"And there's nothing to it. One of my men can just walk out into the burning streets of Rome and set up a movie camera in an age where the principle of the camera hasn't yet been thought of."

"Well, I said it would call for some ingenuity," said Rogers. "Look, there'll be a lot of people running, carrying stuff, trying to save themselves and anything they can. They won't pay any attention to your man. He can cover the camera with something so that it will look . . ."

"It'll be an ugly crowd," insisted Spencer. "It won't like the city being burned. There'll be rumors that the Christians are the ones who set the fire. That crowd will be looking for suspicious characters."

"There's always an element of danger," Rogers pointed out.

"Not as dangerous as this!" said Spencer, testily. "Not deliberately asking for it. And there is something else."

"Like what?"

"Like introducing an advanced technology to the past. If that crowd beat up my man and busted the camera . . ."

Rogers shrugged. "What difference if they did? They could make nothing of it."

"Maybe. But what I'm really worried about," Spencer persisted, "is what the watchdog group would say when they audit our records. It would have to be worth an awful lot of money before I'd take a chance."

"Believe me, it is worth a lot of money. And it would open up a new field for us. That's why I liked it."

"You guys in Dirty Tricks," said Spencer, bitterly, "just don't give a damn. You'll hand us anything . . ."

"Not everything," said Rogers. "Sales pushed us pretty hard on this one . . ."

"Sales!" spat Spencer, contempt in his voice.

"There was a woman in here the other day," said Rogers. "She wanted to send her two children to their great-great-grandfather's farm back in the nineteenth century. For a vacation, mind you. A summer in the country in another century. Said it would be educational and quite relaxing for them. Said the old folks would understand and be glad to have them once we had explained."

Rogers sighed. "I had quite a session with her. She pooh-poohed our regulations. She said . . ."

"You passed up a good one there," Spencer said sarcastically. "That would have opened up another field—vacations in the past. I can see it now. Family reunions with old friends and neighbors foregathering across the centuries."

"You think you are the only one who has his troubles."

"I am bleeding for you," Spencer told him.

"There's a TV outfit," Rogers said, "that wants interviews with Napoleon and Caesar and Alexander and all the rest of those ancient big shots. There are hunters who want to go back into the primordial wilderness to get a spot of shooting. There are universities that want to send teams of investigators back . . ."

"You know that all of that is out," said Spencer. "The only ones we can send back are travelers we have trained."

"There've been times."

"Oh, sure, a few. But only when we got a special dispensation. And we sent along so many travelers to guard them that it was an expedition instead of a simple little study group."

Spencer got up from his chair. "Well, what about this latest brainstorm?"

Rogers picked up the offending assignment sheet and tossed it into an overflowing basket.

"I'll go down to Sales, with tears streaming down my cheeks . . ."

"Thanks," said Spencer and went out.

IV

Back in his office, he sat down at the desk and picked up the file on Cabell.

The squawk box gibbered at him. He thumbed up the lever.

"What is it?"

"Operations, Hal. Williams just got back. Everything's okay; he snagged the Picasso without any trouble. Only took six weeks."

"Six weeks!" Spencer yelled. "He could have painted it himself in that time!"

"There were complications."

"Is there any time there aren't?"

"It's a good one, Hal. Not damaged. Worth a hunk of dough."

"Okay," said Spencer, "take it down to Customs and let them run it through. The good old government must be paid its duty. And what about the others?"

"Nickerson will be leaving in just a little while."

"And E.J.?"

"He's fussy about the time fix. He is telling Doug . . ."

"Look," yelled Spencer wrathfully, "you tell him for me that the fix is Doug's job. Doug knows more about it than E.J. ever will. When Doug says it's time to hop, E.J. hops, funny cap and all."

He snapped down the lever and turned back to the Cabell file, sitting quietly for a moment to let his blood pressure simmer down.

He got worked up too easily, he told himself. He blew his top too much. But there never was a job with so many aggravations!

He opened the folder and ran through the Cabell file.

Stewart Belmont Cabell, 27, unmarried, excellent references, a doctorate in sociology from an ivy college. A uniformly high score in all the tests, including attitude, and an astonishing I.Q. Unqualifiedly recommended for employment as a traveler.

Spencer closed the file and pushed it to one side.

"Send Mr. Cabell in," he told Miss Crane.

Cabell was a lanky man, awkward in his movements; he seemed younger than he was. There was a certain shyness in his manner when Spencer shook his hand and pointed out a chair.

Cabell sat and tried, without success, to make himself at ease.

"So you want to come in with us," said Spencer. "I suppose you know what you are doing."

"Yes, sir," said young Cabell. "I know all about it. Or perhaps I'd better say . . ."

He stammered and stopped talking.

"It's all right," said Spencer. "I take it you want this very much."

Cabell nodded.

"I know how it is. You almost have the feeling you'll die if you can't do it."

And he remembered, sitting there, how it had been with him— the terrible, tearing heartache when he'd been rejected as a traveler, and how he had stuck on regardless of that hurt and disappointment. First as operator; then as operations superintendent; finally to this desk, with all its many headaches.

"Not," he said, "that I have ever travelled."

"I didn't know that, sir."

"I wasn't good enough. My attitudes were wrong."

And he saw the old hope and hunger in the eyes of the man across the desk—and something else besides. Something vaguely disturbing.

"It's not all fun," he said, a shade more harshly than he had meant to make it. "At first there's the romance and the glitter, but that soon wears off. It becomes a job. Sometimes a bitter one."

He paused and looked at Cabell and the queer, disturbing light still was shining in his eyes.

"You should know," he said, deliberately harsh this time, "that if you come in with us you'll probably be dead of advanced old age in five years."

Cabell nodded unconcernedly. "I know that, sir. The people down in Personnel explained it all to me."

"Good," said Spencer. "I suspect at times that Personnel makes a rather shabby explanation. They tell you just enough to make it sound convincing, but they do not tell it all. They are far too anxious to keep us well supplied. We're always short of travelers; we run through them too fast."

He paused and looked at the man again. There was no change in him.

"We have certain regulations," Spencer told him. "They aren't made so much by Past, Inc., as by the job itself. You cannot have any settled sort of life. You live out your life in pieces, like a patchwork quilt, hopping from neighborhood to neighborhood, and those neighborhoods all many years apart. There is no actual rule against it, but none of our travelers has ever married. It would be impossible. In five years the man would die of old age and his wife would still be young."

"I think I understand, sir."

"Actually," Spencer said, "it's a very simple matter of simple economics. We cannot afford to have either our machines or men tied up for any length of time. So while a man may be gone a week, a month, or years, the machine comes back, with him inside of it, sixty seconds after he has left. That sixty seconds is an arbitrary period; it could be a single second, it could be an hour or day or anything we wanted. One minute has seemed a practical period."

"And," asked Cabell, "if it does not come back within that minute?"

"Then it never will."

"It sometimes happens?"

"Of course it happens. Time travelling is no picnic. Every time a man goes back he is betting his life that he can get along in an environment which is as totally alien, in some instances, as another planet. We help him every way we can, of course. We make it our business to see that he is well briefed and Indoctrinated and as well equipped as it is possible to make him. He is taught the languages he is likely to require. He is clothed properly. But there are instances when we simply do not know the little vital details which mean survival. Sometimes we learn them later when our man comes back and tells us. Usually he is quite profane about it. And some we don't find out about at all. The man does not come back."

"One would think," said Cabell, "that you would like to scare me out."

"No! I tell you this because I want no misunderstanding. It costs a lot to train a traveler. We must get our costs back. We do not want a man who will stay with us just a little while. We don't want a year or two from you; we want your entire life. We'll take you and we'll wring you dry of every minute . . ."

"I can assure you, sir . . ."

"We'll send you where we want you," Spencer said, "and although we have no control of you once you've left, we expect that you'll not fool around. Not that you won't come back inside of sixty seconds—naturally you will, if you come back at all. But we want you to come back as young as possible. Past, Inc., is a pure commercial venture. We'll squeeze all the trips we possibly can out of you."

"I understand all this," said Cabell, "but Personnel explained it would be to my advantage, too."

"That is true, of course, but it'll not take you long to find that money is of slight moment to a traveler. Since you have no family, or we would hope you haven't, what would you need it for? The only leisure time you'll have is a six weeks' annual leave and you can earn enough in a trip or two to spend that leave in utmost luxury or the deepest vice.

"Most of the men, however, don't even bother to do that. They just wander off and get re-acquainted with the era they were born into. Vice and luxury in this present century has but slight appeal to them after all the hell they've raised in past centuries at the company's expense."

"You are kidding, sir."

"Well, maybe just a little. But in certain cases that I have in mind, it is the honest truth."

Spencer stared across at Cabell.

"None of this bothers you?" he asked.

"Not a thing so far."

"There's just one thing else, Mr. Cabell, that you should know about. That is the need—the imperative, crying need for objectivity. When you go into the past, you take no part in it. You do not interfere. *You must not get involved.*"

"That should not be hard."

"I warn you, Mr. Cabell, that it requires moral stamina. The man who travels in time has terrible power. And there's something about the feel of power that makes it almost compulsive for a man to use it. Hand in hand with that power is the temptation to take a hand in history. To wield a judicious knife, to say a word that needs saying very badly. To save a life that, given a few more years of time, might have pushed the human race an extra step toward greatness."

"It might be hard," admitted Cabell.

Spencer nodded. "So far as I know, Mr. Cabell, no one has ever succumbed to these temptations. But I live in terror of the day when someone does."

And he wondered as he said it how much he might be talking through his hat, might be whistling past the graveyard. For surely there must by now have been some interference.

What about the men who had not come back?

Some of them undoubtedly had died. But surely some had stayed. And wasn't staying back there the worst form of intervention? What were the implications, he wondered, of a child born out of time—a child that had not been born before, that should never have been born? The children of that child and the children of those children—they would be a thread of temporal interference reaching through the ages.

V

Cabell asked: "Is there something wrong, sir?"

"No. I was just thinking that the time will surely come, some day, when we work out a formula for safely interfering in the past. And when that happens, our responsibilities will be even greater than the ones that we face now. For then we'll have license for intervening, but will in turn be placed under certain strictures to use that power of intervention only for the best. I can't imagine what sort of principle it will be, you understand. But I am sure that soon or late we will arrive at it.

"And perhaps, too, we'll work out another formula which will allow us to venture to the future."

He shook his head and thought: How like an old man, to shake your head in resigned puzzlement. But he was not an old man—not very old, at least.

"At the moment," he said, "we are little more than gleaners. We go into the past to pick up the gleanings—the things they lost or threw away. We have made up certain rules to make sure that we never touch the sheaves, but only the ear of wheat left lying on the ground."

"Like the Alexandria manuscripts?"

"Well, yes, I would suppose so—although grabbing all those manuscripts and books was inspired entirely by a sordid profit motive. We could just as easily have copied them. Some of them we did; but the originals themselves represented a tremendous sum of money. I would hate to tell you what Harvard paid us for those manuscripts. Although, when you think of it," Spencer said, reflectively, "I'm not sure they weren't worth every cent of it. It called for the closest planning and split-second co-ordinating and we used every man we had. For, you see, we couldn't grab the stuff until it was on the verge of burning. We couldn't deprive even so much as a single person of the chance of even glancing at a single manuscript. We can't lift a thing until it's lost. That's an iron-bound rule.

"Now, you take the Ely tapestry. We waited for years, going back and checking, until we were quite sure that it was finally lost. We knew it was going to be lost, you understand. But we couldn't touch it until it was lost for good. Then we h'isted it." He waved a hand. "I talk too much. I am boring you."

"Mr. Spencer, sir," protested Cabell, "talk like yours could never bore me. This is something I have dreamed of. I can't tell you how happy . . ."

Spencer raised a hand to stop him. "Not so fast. You aren't hired yet."

"But Mr. Jensen down in Personnel . . ."

"I know what Jensen said. But the final word is mine."

"What have I done wrong?" asked Cabell.

"You have done nothing wrong. Come back this afternoon."

"But, Mr. Spencer, if only you could tell me . . ."

"I want to think about you. See me after lunch."

Cabell unfolded upward from his chair and he was ill at ease.

"That man who was in ahead of me . . ."

"Yes. What about him?"

"He seemed quite angry, sir. As if he might be thinking of making trouble for you."

Spencer said angrily. "And that's none of your damn business!"

Cabell stood his ground. "I was only going to say, sir, that I recognized him."

"So?"

"If he did try to cause you trouble, sir, it might be worth your while to investigate his association with a stripper down at the Golden Hour. Her name is Silver Starr."

Spencer stared at Cabell without saying anything.

The man edged toward the door.

He put out his hand to grasp the knob, then turned back to Spencer. "Perhaps that's not actually her name, but it's fine for advertising—Silver Starr at the Golden Hour. The Golden Hour is located at . . ."

"Mr. Cabell," Spencer said, "I've been at the Golden Hour."

The impudent punk! What did he figure he was doing—buying his way in?

He sat quietly for a moment after Cabell had gone out, cooling down a bit, wondering about the man. There had been something about him that had been disturbing. That look in his eyes, for one thing. And the awkwardness and shyness didn't ring quite true. As if it had been an act of some sort. But why, in the name of God, should anyone put on such an act when it would be quite clearly to his disadvantage?

You're psycho, Spencer told himself. You're getting so you jump at every shadow, sight a lurking figure behind every bush.

Two down, he thought, and another one to see—that is, if more had not piled into the office and were out there waiting for him.

He reached out his hand to press the buzzer. But before his finger touched it, the back door of the office suddenly burst open. A wild-eyed man came stumbling through it. He had something white and wriggly clutched within his arms. He dumped the white and wriggly thing on Hallock Spencer's desk and unhappily stepped back.

It was a rabbit—a white rabbit with a great pink ribbon tied around its neck in a fancy bow.

Spencer glanced up, startled, at the man who'd brought the rabbit.

"Ackermann," he shouted. "For Chrissake, Ackermann, what is the matter with you? It isn't Easter yet!"

Ackermann worked his mouth in a painful manner and his Adam's apple went bobbing up and down. But he made no words come out.

"Come on, man! What is it?"

Ackermann got his voice back. "It's Nickerson!" he blurted.

"O.K., so Nickerson brought a rabbit back . . ."

"He didn't bring it back, sir. It came all by itself!"

"And Nickerson?"

Ackermann shook his head. "There was just the rabbit."

Spencer had started to get up from the chair. Now he sat back down again, harder than intended.

"There's an envelope, sir, tied to the rabbit's bow."

"So I see," said Spencer, absently. But he felt the coldness running through him.

The rabbit hoisted itself around until it was face to face with Spencer. It flapped an ear, wiggled its pink nose at him, put its head carefully to one side and lifted a deliberate hind leg to scratch a flea.

He pivoted in his chair and watched the operator sidle through the door. Three men lost in the last ten days. And now there was a fourth.

But this time, at least, he'd got back the carrier. The rabbit had brought back the carrier. Any living thing, once the mechanism had been rigged, by its very presence would have brought back the carrier. It need not be a man.

But Nickerson! Nickerson was one of the best there were. If a man could not depend on Nickerson, there was no one that he could.

He turned back to the desk and reached for the rabbit. It didn't try to get away. He slipped out the folded sheet of paper and broke the blob of sealing wax. The paper was so stiff and heavy that it crackled as he smoothed it.

The ink was dead black and the script cramped. No fountain pen, thought Spencer—nothing but a goose quill.

The letter was addressed to him. It said:

Dear Hal: I have no logical excuse and I'll attempt no explanation. I have found a sense of springtime and cannot compel myself to leave it. You have your carrier and that is better than any of the others ever did for you. The rabbit will not mind. A rabbit knows no time. Be kind to him—for he is no coarse, wild hare of the briery fields, but a loving pet. Nick.

Inadequate, thought Spencer, staring at the note, with the scrawly black more like a cabalistic pattern than a communication.

He had found a sense of springtime. What did he mean by that? A springtime of the heart? A springtime of the spirit? That might well be it, for Nickerson had gone to Italy in the early Renaissance. A springtime of the spirit and the sense of great beginnings. And perhaps that wasn't all of it. Would there be as well a certain sense of spiritual security in that smaller world—a world that tinkered with no time, that reached toward no stars?

The buzzer sounded softly.

Spencer tipped up the lever on the intercom. "Yes, Miss Crane?"

"Mr. Garside on the phone."

The rabbit was nibbling at the phone cord. Spencer pushed him to one side. "Yes, Chris."

The gray, clipped voice said: "Hal, what's with you and Ravenholt? He gave me a bad half hour."

"It was Project God."

"Yes, he told me that. He threatened to raise a howl about the ethics of our magazine project."

"He can't do that," protested Spencer. "He'd have no grounds at all. That one is clean. It has the green light from Legal and from Ethics and the review board gave its blessing. It's simply historical reporting. Eyewitness from the battle of Gettysburg, fashion notes on the spot from the time of Queen Victoria—it's the biggest thing we've tackled. Its promotional value alone, aside from the money we'll make . . ."

"Yes, I know," said Garside, tiredly. "All of that is true. But I don't want to get into a hassle with anyone—particularly not with Ravenholt. We have too many irons in the fire right now for anything unfavorable to pop. And Ravenholt can be a terribly dirty fighter."

"Look, Chris. I can take care of Ravenholt."

"I knew you would. What is more, you'd better."

"And," demanded Spencer, bristling, "what do you mean by that?"

"Well, frankly, Hal, your record doesn't look too good. You've been having trouble . . ."

"You mean the men we've lost."

"And the machines," said Garside. "You're all the time forgetting—a machine costs a quarter million."

"And the men?" asked Spencer bitterly. "Perhaps you think they're comparatively cheap."

"I don't suppose," said Garside blandly, "That you can place an actual value on a human life."

"We lost another one today," said Spencer. "I imagine you'll be happy to know that he was loyal behind the call of duty. He sent a rabbit back and the machine is safe and sound."

"Hal," said Garside, sternly, "this is something we can discuss at some later time. Right now I'm concerned with Ravenholt. If you'd go and apologize to him and try to fix things up . . ."

"Apologize!" exploded Spencer. "I know a better way than that. He's been shacking with a stripper down at the Golden Hour. By the time I get through . . ."

"Hal!" yelled Garside. "You can't do a thing like that! You can't involve Past, Inc., in anything like that! Why, it isn't decent!"

"You mean it's dirty," Spencer said. "No dirtier that Ravenholt. Who is he fronting for?"

"It makes no difference. Young man . . ."

"Don't young man me," yelled Spencer. "I've got troubles enough without being patronized."

"Perhaps your troubles are too much for you," said Garside, speaking very gray and clipped. "Perhaps we ought to find another man."

"Do it then!" yelled Spencer. "Don't just sit there shooting off your face. Come on down and fire me!"

He slammed the receiver down into its cradle and sat shivering with rage.

Damn Garside, he thought. To hell with Past, Inc. He'd taken all he could!

Still, it was a lousy way to end after fifteen years. It was a stinking thing to happen. Maybe he ought to have kept his mouth shut, kept his temper down, played it sweet and smooth.

Perhaps, he could have done it differently. He could have assured Garside he'd take care of Ravenholt without saying anything about Silver Starr. And why had he grabbed hold so trustfully of what Cabell had told him that moment before leaving? What could Cabell know about it? In just a little while now he'd have to check if there were anyone by the name of Silver Starr down at the Golden Hour.

Meanwhile there was work to do. Hudson now, he thought.

He reached for the buzzer.

But his finger never touched it. Once more the back door burst open with a smashing rattle and a man came tearing in. it was Douglas Marshall, operator for E.J.'s machine.

"Hal," he gasped, "you'd better come. E.J.'s really tore it!"

VI

Spencer didn't ask a question. One look at Doug's face was quite enough to tell him the news was very bad. He bounced out of his chair and rushed through the door, close on the operator's heels.

They tore down the corridor and turned left into Operations, with the rows of bulgy, bulky carriers lined against the wall.

Down at the far end a small circle of operators and mechanics formed a ragged circle and from the center of the circle came the sound of ribald song. The words were not intelligible.

Spencer strode forward angrily and pushed through the circle. There, in the center of it, was E.J. and another person—a filthy, bearded, boisterous barbarian wrapped in a mangy bearskin and with a tremendous sword strapped about his middle.

The barbarian had a smallish keg tilted to his mouth. The keg was gurgling; he was drinking from it, but he was missing some as well, for steams of pale, brown liquid were running down his front.

"E.J.!" yelled Spencer.

At the shout, the barbarian jerked the keg down from his face and tucked it hurriedly underneath an arm. With a big and dirty hand, he mopped the whiskers adjacent to his mouth.

E.J. stumbled forward and threw his arms around Spencer's neck, laughing all the while.

Spencer jerked E.J. loose and pushed him, stumbling, backwards.

"E.J.!" he yelled. "What is so damn funny?"

E.J. managed to stop stumbling backwards. He tried to pull himself together, but he couldn't because he still was laughing hard.

The barbarian stepped forward and thrust the keg into Spencer's hands, shouting something at him in a convivial tone of voice and pantomiming with his hands that the keg had stuff to drink.

E.J. made an exaggerated thumb at the gent in bearskin. "Hal, it wasn't any Roman officer!" Then he went off into gales of laughter once again.

The barbarian started to laugh, too, uproariously, throwing back his head and bellowing in great peals of laughter that shook the very room.

E.J. staggered over and they fell into one another's arms, guffawing happily and pounding one another on the back. Somehow they got tangled up. They lost their balance. They fell down on the floor and sat there, the two of them, looking up at the men around them.

"Now!" Spencer roared at E.J.

E.J. clapped the man in bearskin a resounding whack upon his hairy shoulder. "Just bringing back the Wrightson-Graves her far-removed grand-pappy. I can't wait to see her face when I take him up there!"

"Oh, my God!" said Spencer. He turned around and thrust the dripping keg into someone's hands.

He snapped, "Don't let them get away. Put them someplace where they can sleep it off."

A hand grabbed him by the arm and there was Douglas Marshall, sweating. "We got to send him back, Chief," said Doug. "E.J.'s got to take him back."

Spencer shook his head. "I don't know if we can. I'll put it up to Legal. Just keep them here, and tell the boys. Tell them if one of them so much as whispers . . ."

"I'll do my best," said Doug. "But I don't know. They're a bunch of blabbermouths."

Spencer jerked away and sprinted for the corridor.

What a day, he thought. What a loused-up day!

He charged down the corridor and saw that the door marked *Private* was closed. He skidded almost to a halt, reaching for the knob, when the door flew open. Miss Crane came tearing out.

She slammed into him head-on. Both of the bounced back, Miss Crane's spectacles knocked at a crazy angle by the impact.

"Mr. Spencer," she wailed. "Mr. Spencer, something awful's happened! Remember Mr. Hudson?"

She stepped back out of his way. He sprang inside and slammed the door behind him. "As if I ever could forget him," he said bitterly.

Said Miss Crane, "Mr. Hudson's dead!"

Spencer stood stricken.

Miss Crane raged, "If only you had seen him when *I* wanted you to! If you hadn't kept him waiting out there . . ."

"Now, look here—"

"He got up finally," said Miss Crane, "and his face was red. He was angry. I don't blame him, Mr. Spencer."

"You mean he died right here?"

"He said to me, 'Tell your Mr. Spencer—' and that's as far as he ever got. He sort of lurched and caught with his hand at the edge of the desk to support himself, but his hand slipped off and he folded up and . . ."

Spencer waited for no more. He went in three quick steps across the office and out into the reception room.

There was Mr. Hudson, huddled on the carpet.

He looked startlingly like a limp ragdoll. One blue-veined hand was stretched out ahead of him. The portfolio that it had held lay just beyond the fingertips, as if even in his death Mr. Hudson might be stretching out his hand to it. His jacket was hunched across the shoulders. The collar of his white shirt, Spencer saw, was ragged.

Spencer went slowly across the floor and knelt down beside the man. He put his ear down on the body.

There was no sound at all.

"Mr. Spencer." Miss Crane was standing in the doorway, still terrified but enjoying it a lot. Not in all her years of being secretary had anything like this happened. Not in all her life. It would keep her supplied with conversation for many, many years.

"Lock the door," said Spencer, "so no one can come strolling in. Then phone the police."

"The police!"

"Miss Crane," said Spencer, sharply.

She walked around him and the body on the floor, edging close against the wall.

"Call Legal, too," said Spencer.

He stayed squatting on the floor, staring at the man who lay there and wondering how it had happened. Heart attack, most likely. Miss Crane had said that he looked ill—and had urged that he see him first, ahead of the other two.

And if one were looking for a man to blame for what had happened here, Spencer told himself, they might have but little trouble fastening it on him.

If Hudson had not had to wait, growing angrier and more upset as the time slipped past, this might not have happened.

Hudson had waited in this room, a sick and impatient man, and finally an angry one—and what had he waited for?

Spencer studied the ragdoll of a man slumped upon the carpet, the thinning hair atop his head, the thick-lensed spectacles bent and twisted in the fall, the bony, blue-veined hands. He wondered what such a man might have expected from Past, Inc.

Spencer started to get up and lost his balance as he did, his left hand going out behind him to prop himself erect.

And beneath the spread-out palm there was something cool and smooth. Without looking, he knew what it was. Hudson's portfolio!

The answer might be there!

Miss Crane was at the door, locking it. There was no one else.

With a swift sweep of his hand, Spencer skidded the portfolio in the direction of the doorway that led into his office.

He got smoothly to his feet and turned. The portfolio lay halfway through the doorway. In one quick stride he reached it and nudged it with his foot, inside and out of sight.

He heard the snick of the lock falling home and Miss Crane turned around.

"The police first, or Legal, Mr. Spencer?"

"The police, I'd think," said Spencer.

He stepped within his office and swung the door so that it came within an inch of closing. Then he snatched the portfolio off the floor and hurried to his desk.

He put in on his desk and zipped it open and there were three sheafs of paper, each of the sheafs paper-clipped together.

The first bore the legend at the top of the first page: *A Study of Ethics Involved in Traveling in Time.* And after that page upon page of typescript, heavily underlined and edited with a neat red pencil.

And the second, a thin one, with no legend, and composed of sheets of unneatly scribbled notes.

And the third, once again typed, with carefully drawn diagrams and charts, and the heading: *A New Concept of the Mechanics of Time Travel.*

Spencer sucked in his breath and bent above the paper, his eyes trying to gallop along the lines of type, but forced to go too fast to really catch the meaning.

For he had to get the portfolio back where it had been and he had to do it without being seen. It was not his to touch. The police might become difficult if they found he'd rifled it. And when he put it back, it must have something in it. A man would hardly come to see him with an empty portfolio.

In the outer office, he heard Miss Crane talking. He made a quick decision.

He swept the second and third sheaf of papers into the top drawer of his desk. Leaving the first sheaf on time-travel ethics in the portfolio, he zipped it shut again.

That would satisfy the cops. He held the portfolio in his left hand, letting his arm hang along his side, and stepped to the doorway, shielding the left side of his body and the portfolio.

Miss Crane was on the phone, her face turned away from him.

He stopped the portfolio on the carpeting, just beyond the outstretched fingers of the dead man.

Miss Crane put down the phone and saw him standing there.

"The police will be right over," she said. "Now I'll call Mr. Hawkes in Legal."

"Thanks," said Spencer. "I'll go through some papers while we're waiting."

VII

Back at his desk, he took out the pile of papers that said: *A New Concept of the Mechanics of Time Travel.* The name on it was Boone Hudson.

He settled down to read, first with mounting wonderment, then with a strange, cold excitement—for here, at last, was the very thing that would at once erase the basic headache of Past, Inc.

No longer would one face the nightmare of good travelers wearing out in a few years' time.

No longer would a man go into time a young man and return sixty seconds later with the beginning lines of age showing on his face. No longer would one watch one's friends age visibly from month to month.

For they would no longer be dealing in men, but in the patterns of those men.

Matter transference, Spencer told himself. You could probably call it that, anyway. A man would be sent into the past; but the carrier would not move physically into time as it moved now. It would project a pattern of itself and the man within it, materializing at the target point. And within the carrier—the basic carrier, the prime carrier, the parent carrier which would remain in present time—there'd be another pattern, a duplicate pattern of the man sent into time.

When the man returned to present time, he would not return as he was at that moment in the past, but as the pattern within the waiting carrier said he *had* been when he'd traveled into time.

He'd step out of the carrier exactly as he had stepped into it, not older by a second—actually, a minute younger than he would have been! For he did not have to account for that sixty seconds between leaving and returning.

For years, Past, Inc.'s own research department had been seeking for the answer to the problem, without even coming close. And now a stranger had come unheralded and sat hunched in the reception room, with the portfolio cradled on his knee, and he had the answer, but he'd been forced to wait.

He'd waited and he'd waited and finally he had died.

There was a tapping at the door of the outer office. He heard Miss Crane cross the room to open it.

Spencer pulled out a desk drawer and hurriedly shoved the papers into it. Then he stood up from the desk and walked around it to go into the outer office.

Ross Hawkes, head of Past, Inc.'s legal department, was standing just beyond the body on the carpet, staring down at it.

"Hello, Ross," said Spencer. "An unpleasant business here."

Hawkes looked up at him, puzzled. His pale blue eyes glittered behind the neat and precise spectacles, his snow white hair matching the pallor of his face.

"But what was Dan'l doing here?" he asked.

"Dan'l?" Spencer demanded. "His name happened to be Boone Hudson."

"Yes, I know," said Hawkes. "But the boys all called him Dan'l—Dan'l Boone, you understand. Sometimes he didn't like it. He worked in Research. We had to fire him, fifteen, sixteen years ago. The only reason that I recognized him was that we had some trouble. He had an idea he would like to sue us."

Spencer nodded. "Thanks. I see," he said.

He was halfway to his office door when he turned back.

"One thing, Ross. What did we fire him for?"

"I don't recall, exactly. He disregarded his assignment, went off on some other tangent. Matter transference, I think."

Spencer said, "That's the way it goes."

He went back into the office, locked his desk and went out the back way.

In the parking lot, he backed out his car and went slowly down the street. A police cruiser was parked in front of the building and two officers were getting out. An ambulance was pulling in behind the cruiser.

So, thought Spencer, they had fired Hudson fifteen years ago, because he had some sort of crazy idea about matter transference and wouldn't stick to business. And to this very day, Research was going quietly mad trying to solve a problem that

Hudson could have put into their laps years ago, if they had kept him on.

Spencer tried to imagine how those fifteen years must have been for Hudson, more than likely working all the time on this quiet insanity of his. And how, finally, he had gotten it and had made sure of it and then had gone down to Past, Inc., to rub their noses in it.

Exactly as he, Hallock Spencer, now would rub their noses in it.

Greenwich Street was a quiet residential street of genteel poverty, with small and older houses. Despite the smallness of the houses and their age, and in some cases their unkemptness, there was a certain solid pride and respectability about them.

The address on the manuscript was 241 Greenwich. It was a squat brown house surrounded by a crumbling picket fence. The yard was full of flowers. Even so, it had the look of a house that had no one living in it.

Spencer edged through the sagging gate and up the walk, made small by the flowers that encroached upon it. He went up the rickety stairs to the shaky porch and, since there was no bell, rapped on the closed front door.

There was no answer. He tried the knob and it turned. He pushed the door part way open and edged into the silent hall.

"Hello," he called. "Anyone at home?"

He waited. There wasn't.

He walked from the hall into the living room and stood to look around him at the Spartan, almost monklike existence of the man who'd lived there.

It was evident that Hudson had lived alone, for the room bore all the signs of a lone man's camping. There was a cot against one wall, a dirty shirt flung across one end of it. Two pairs of shoes and a pair of slippers were lined up underneath the cot. An old-fashioned dresser stood opposite the cot. A handful of ties dangled raggedly from the bar that had been fastened on its side. A small kitchen table stood in the corner nearest to the kitchen. A box of crackers and a glass, still spotted with milk stains, stood upon the table. A massive desk stood a few feet from the table and the top of it was bare except for an old typewriter and a photograph in a stand-up frame.

Spencer walked over to the desk and began pulling out the drawers. They were almost empty. In one he found a pipe, a box of paper clips, a stapler and a single poker chip. The others yielded other odds and ends, but nothing of importance. In one was a half a ream of paper—but nowhere was there a single line of writing. In the bottom drawer on the left hand side, he found a squat bottle, half full of good Scotch.

And that was all.

He searched the dresser. Nothing but shirts and underwear and socks.

He prowled into the kitchen. Just the built-in stove and refrigerator and the cupboards. He found nothing in any of them but a small supply of food.

And the bedrooms—two of them—were empty, innocent of furniture, and with a fine and powdery dust coating floor and walls. Spencer stood in the doorway of each and looked and there was a sadness in each room. He didn't go inside.

Back in the living room, he went to the desk and picked up the photograph. A woman with a tired, brave smile, with a halo of white hair, with an air of endless patience, looked out of it at him.

There was nothing to be found in this house, he told himself. Not unless one had the time to search every corner of it, every crack, to take it down, each board and stone. And even then, he doubted now, there'd be anything to find.

He left the house and drove back to the office.

"Your lunch didn't take too long," Miss Crane told him, sourly.

"Everything all right?" he asked.

"The police were very, very nice," she said. "Both Mr. Hawkes and Mr. Snell are anxious to see you. And Mr. Garside called."

"After a while," said Spencer. "I've got work to do. I don't want to be disturbed."

He went into his office and shut the door with a gesture of finality.

From the drawer he took the Hudson papers and settled down to read.

He was no engineer, but he knew enough of it to make a ragged sort of sense, although at times he was forced to go back and read more carefully, or puzzle out a diagram that he'd skipped through too hurriedly. Finally he came to the end of it.

It was all there.

It would have to be checked by technicians and engineers, of course. There might be bugs that would take some ironing out, but the concept, complete both in theory and in the theory's application, was all there in the paper.

Hudson had held nothing back—no vital point, no key.

And that was crazy, Spencer told himself. You had to leave yourself some sort of bargaining position. You could trust no other man, certainly no corporation, as implicitly as Hudson apparently had intended to. Especially you couldn't trust an outfit that had fired you fifteen years before for working on this very concept.

It was ridiculous and tragic, Spencer told himself.

Past, Inc., could not have even guessed what Hudson might have been aiming at. And Hudson, in his turn, was gagged because he'd not as yet progressed to a point where he could have faith either in his concept or himself. Even if he had tried to tell them, they would have laughed at him, for he had no reputation to support such outrageous dreaming.

Spencer sat at his desk, remembering the house on Greenwich Street, the huddling in one room with the other rooms all bare and the entire house stripped of all evidence of comfort and good living. More than likely all the furniture in those rooms, all the accumulation of many years of living, had been sold, piece by precious piece, to keep groceries on the shelf.

A man who was dedicated to a dream, Spencer told himself, a man who had lived with that dream so long and intimately that it was his entire life. Perhaps he had known that he was about to die.

That might explain his impatience at being forced to wait.

Spencer shoved the Hudson papers to one side and picked up the notes. The pages were filled with cryptic penciled lines, with long strings of mathematical abstractions, roughly drawn sketches. They were no help.

And that other paper, Spencer wondered—the one he'd left in the portfolio, that one that had to do with ethics? Might it not also bear a close relationship to the Hudson concept? Might there not be in it something of importance bearing on this new approach?

Time travel perforce was hedged around with a pattern of ethics which consisted mainly of a formidable list of "thou shalt nots."

Thou shalt not transport a human being from the past.

Thou shalt not snitch a thing until it has been lost.

Thou shalt not inform anyone in the past of the fact there is time travel.

Thou shalt not interfere in any way with the patterns of the past.

Thou shalt not try to go into the future—and don't ask why, because that's a dirty question.

VIII

The buzzer sounded. He flipped the switch.

"Yes, Miss Crane."

"Mr. Garside is here to see you. Mr. Hawkes and Mr. Snell are with him."

He thought he detected in her voice a sense of satisfaction.

"All right. Ask them to come in."

He gathered the papers off his desk and put them in his briefcase, then settled back as they came in. "Well, gentlemen. It seems I am invaded."

Even as he said it, he knew it had not been the proper thing to say. They did not even smile. And he knew that it was bad. Any time you got Legal and Public Relations together, it couldn't be anything but bad.

They sat down. "We thought," said Snell, in his most polished P.R. manner, "that if we got together and tried to talk things out . . ."

Hawkes cut him short. He said to Spencer, accusingly: "You have managed to place us in a most embarrassing position."

"Yes, I know," said Spencer. "Let's tick off the items. One of my men brought back a human from the past. A man died in my office. I forgot to be polite to a stuffed shirt who came charging in to help us run our business."

"You seem," said Garside, "to take it all quite lightly."

"Perhaps I do," said Spencer. "Let's put it slightly stronger. I just don't give a damn. You cannot allow pressure groups to form your policy."

"You are talking now, of course," said Garside, "about the Ravenholt affair."

"Chris," said Snell, enthusiastically, "you hit it on the button. Here is a chance to really sell the public on us. I don't believe we've really sold them. We are dealing in something which to the average man seems to smell of magic. Naturally he is stand-offish."

"More to the point," said Hawkes, impatiently, "if we turn down this project—this . . ."

"Project God," said Spencer.

"I'm not sure I like your phrasing."

"Think up a name yourself," said Spencer calmly. "That is what we call it."

"If we fail to go ahead with it, we'll be accused of being atheists."

"How would the public ever know that we turned it down?" asked Spencer.

"You can be sure," Snell said bitterly, "that Ravenholt will make a point of making known our turning down of it."

Spencer smashed his fist upon the desk in sudden anger. He yelled, "I told you how to handle Ravenholt!"

"Hal," Garside told him quietly, "we simply cannot do it. We have our dignity."

"No," said Spencer, "I suppose you can't. But you can sell out to Ravenholt and whoever's backing him. You can rig the survey of religious origins. You can falsify reports."

The three of them sat in stricken silence. Spencer felt a twinge of momentary wonder for having dared to say it. It was not the way one was supposed to talk to brass.

But he had to say one more thing. "Chris. You are going to disregard the report I made and go ahead with it, aren't you?"

Garside answered with smooth urbanity: "I'm afraid I'll have to."

Spencer looked at Hawkes and Snell and he saw the secret smiles that lurked just behind their lips—the sneering contemptuous smile of authority ascendant.

He said slowly, "Yes, I guess you will. Well, it's all in your laps now. You figure out the answers."

"But it's your department."

"Not any more, it isn't. I've just quit the job."

"Now see here, Hal," Garside was saying, "you can't do a thing like that! Without any notice! Just flying off the handle! We may have our little differences, but that is no excuse . . ."

"I've decided," Spencer told him, "that I somehow have to stop you. I cannot allow you to go ahead with Project God. I warn you, if you do, that I shall discredit you. I shall prove exactly and without question everything you've done. And meanwhile, I am planning to go into business for myself."

"Time travel, perhaps." They were mocking him.

"I had thought of it."

Snell grinned contemptuously. "You can't even get a license."

"I think I can," said Spencer.

And he knew he could. With a brand new concept, there'd be little trouble.

Garside got up from his chair. "Well," he said to Spencer, "you've had your little tantrum. When you cool down a bit, come up and talk to me."

Spencer shook his head.

"Goodbye, Chris," he said.

He did not rise. He sat and watched them go.

Strangely, now that it was over—or just beginning—there was no tenseness in him. It had fallen all away and he felt abiding calm.

There was money to be raised, there were technicians and engineers to hire, there were travelers to be found and trained, and a whole lot more than that.

Thinking of it all, he had a momentary pang of doubt, but he shrugged it off. He got up from his chair and walked out into the office.

"Miss Crane," he said, "Mr. Cabell was supposed to come back this afternoon."

"I haven't seen him, sir."

"Of course not," Spencer said.

For suddenly it all seemed to be coming clear, if he only could believe it.

There had been a look in young Cabell's eyes that had been most disturbing. And now, all at once, he knew that look for exactly what it was.

It had been adulation!

The kind of look that was reserved for someone who had become a legend.

And he must be wrong, Spencer told himself, for he was not a legend—at least not at the moment.

There had been something else in young Cabell's eyes. And once again he knew. Cabell had been a young man, but the eyes had been old eyes. They were eyes that had seen much more of life than a man of thirty had any right to see.

"What shall I say," asked Miss Crane, "if he should come back?"

"Never mind," said Spencer. "I am sure he won't."

For Cabell's job was done, if it had been a job at all. It might have been, he told himself, a violation of the ethics, a pure piece of meddling, or it might have been a yielding to that temptation to play God.

Or, he thought, it might have been all planned.

Had they somewhere in the future worked out that formula he'd spoken of to Cabell—the formula that would allow legitimate manipulation of the past?

"Miss Crane," he said, "would you be kind enough to type up a resignation for me? Effective immediately. Make it very formal. I am sore at Garside."

Miss Crane did not bat an eyelash. She ran paper into her machine.

"Mr. Spencer, what reason shall I give?"

"You might say I'm going into business for myself."

Had there been another time, he wondered, when it hadn't gone this way? Had there been a time when Hudson had gotten in to see him and maybe had not died at all? Had there been a time when he'd handed over the Hudson concept to Past, Inc., instead of stealing it himself?

And if Cabell had not been here to take up the time, more than likely he would have gotten around to seeing Hudson before it was too late. And if he had seen the man, then it was more than likely that he would have passed the concept on through proper channels.

But even so, he wondered, how could they be sure (whoever they might be) that he'd not see Hudson first? He recalled distinctly that Miss Crane had urged that he see him first.

And that was it, he thought excitedly. That was exactly it! He might very well have seen Hudson first if Miss Crane had not been insistent that he should.

And standing there, he thought of all the years that Miss Crane must have worked at it—conditioning him to the point where he'd be sure to do exactly opposite to what she urged he do.

"Mr. Spencer," said Miss Crane, "I have the letter finished. And there is something else. I almost forgot about it."

She reached down into a drawer and took out something and laid it on the desk.

It was the portfolio that belonged to Hudson.

"The police," said Miss Crane, "apparently overlooked it. It was very careless of them. I thought that you might like it."

Spencer stood staring blankly at it.

"It would go so nicely," said Miss Crane, "with the other stuff you have."

There was a muted thumping on the floor and Spencer spun around. A white rabbit with long and droopy ears hopped across the carpet, looking for a carrot.

"Oh, how cute!" cried Miss Crane, very much unlike herself. "Is it the one that Mr. Nickerson sent back?"

"It's the one," said Spencer. "I had forgotten it."

"Might I have it?"

"Miss Crane, I wonder . . ."

"Yes, Mr. Spencer?"

And what was he to say?

Could he blurt out that now he knew she was one of them?

It would take so much explanation and it could be so involved. And, besides, Miss Crane was not the sort of person that you blurted things out to.

He gulped. "I was wondering, Miss Crane, if you'd come and work for me. I'll need a secretary."

Miss Crane shook her head. "No, I'm getting old. I'm thinking of retiring. I think, now that you are leaving, I shall just disappear."

"But, Miss Crane, I'll need you desperately."

"One of these days soon," said Miss Crane, "when you need a secretary, there'll be an applicant. She'll wear a bright green dress and she'll be wearing these new glasses and be carrying a snow-white rabbit with a bow around its neck. She may strike you as something of a hussy, but you hire her. Be sure you hire her."

"I'll remember," Spencer said. "I'll be looking for her. I'll hire no one else."

"She will not," warned Miss Crane, "be a bit like me. She'll be much nicer."

"Thank you, Miss Crane," said Spencer, just a bit inanely.

"And don't forget this," said Miss Crane, holding out the portfolio.

He took it and headed for the door.

At the door he stopped and turned back to her.

"I'll be seeing you," he said.

For the first time in fifteen years, Miss Crane smiled at him.

MADNESS FROM MARS

Clifford D. Simak once listed this story as one of two "truly horrible examples of an author's fumbling agony in the process of finding himself." Cliff was speaking of the journey he made from being someone whose career was in journalism to being a creator of good fiction—which has to have been a long, painful exercise in self-education. And yet, when I read those words, I am puzzled—for to me, this story in particular is a deeply emotional, deeply affecting portrait of an unpreventable tragedy.

—*dww*

The *Hello Mars IV* was coming home, back from the outward reaches of space, the first ship ever to reach the Red Planet and return. Telescopes located in the Crater of Copernicus Observatory on the Moon had picked it up and flashed the word to Earth, giving its position. Hours later, Earth telescopes had found the tiny mote that flashed in the outer void.

Two years before, those same telescopes had watched the ship's outward voyage, far out until its silvery hull had dwindled into nothingness. From that day onward there had been no word or sign of *Hello Mars IV*—nothing until the lunar telescopes, picking up again that minute speck in space, advised Earth of its homecoming.

Communication with the ship by Earth had been impossible.

On the Moon, powerful radio stations were capable of hurling ultra-short wave messages across the quarter million miles to Earth. But man as yet had found no means of communicating over fifty million miles of space. So *Hello Mars IV* had arrowed out into the silence, leaving the Moon and the Earth to speculate and wonder over its fate.

Now, with Mars once again swinging into conjunction, the ship was coming back—a tiny gnat of steel pushing itself along with twinkling blasts of flaming rocket-fuel. Heading Earthward out of that region of silent mystery, spurning space-miles beneath its steel-shod heels. Triumphant, with the red dust of Mars still clinging to its plates—a mote of light in the telescopic lenses.

Aboard it were five brave men—Thomas Delvaney, the expedition's leader; Jerry Cooper, the red-thatched navigator; Andy Smith, the world's ace cameraman, and two space-hands, Jimmy Watson and Elmer Paine, grim old veterans of the Earth-Moon run.

There had been three other *Hello Mars* ships—three other ships that had never come back—three other flights that had ended in disaster. The first had collided with a meteor a million miles out from the Moon. The second had flared briefly, deep in space, a red splash of flame in the telescopes through which the flight was watched—the fuel tanks had exploded. The third had simply disappeared. On and on it had gone, boring outward until lost from sight. That had been six years ago, but men still wondered what had happened.

Four years later—two years ago—the *Hello Mars IV* had taken off. Today it was returning, a gleaming thing far out in space, a shining symbol of man's conquest of the planets. It had reached Mars—and it was coming back. There would be others, now—and still others. Some would flare against the black and be lost forever. But others would win through, and man, blindly groping, always outward, to break his earthly bonds, at last would be on the pathway to the stars.

Jack Woods, *Express* reporter, lit a cigarette and asked: "What do you figure they found out there, Doc?"

Dr. Stephen Gilmer, director of the Interplanetary Communications Research Commission, puffed clouds of smoke from his black cigar and answered irritably:

"How in blue hell would I know what they found? I hope they found something. This trip cost us a million bucks."

"But can't you give me some idea of what they might have found?" persisted Woods. "Some idea of what Mars is like. Any new ideas."

Dr. Gilmer wrangled the cigar viciously.

"And have you spread it all over the front page," he said. "Spin something out of my own head just because you chaps are too impatient to wait for the actual data. Not by a damn sight. You reporters get my goat sometimes."

"Ah, Doc, give us something," pleaded Gary Henderson, staff man for the *Star*.

"Sure," said Don Buckley, of the *Spaceways*. "What do you care? You can always say we misquoted you. It wouldn't be the first time."

Gilmer gestured toward the official welcoming committee that stood a short distance away.

"Why don't you get the mayor to say something, boys?" he suggested. "The mayor is always ready to say something."

"Sure," said Gary, "but it never adds up to anything. We've had the mayor's face on the front page so much lately that he thinks he owns the paper."

"Have you any idea why they haven't radioed us?" asked Woods. "They've been in sending distance for several hours now."

Gilmer rolled the cigar from east to west. "Maybe they broke the radio," he said.

Nevertheless there were little lines of worry on his face. The fact that there had been no messages from the *Hello Mars IV* troubled him. If the radio had been broken it could have been repaired.

Six hours ago the *Hello Mars IV* had entered atmosphere. Even now it was circling the Earth in a strenuous effort to lose speed.

Word that the ship was nearing Earth had brought spectators to the field in ever-increasing throngs. Highways and streets were jammed for miles around.

Perspiring police cordons struggled endlessly to keep the field clear for a landing. The day was hot, and soft drink stands were doing a rushing business. Women fainted in the crowd and some men were knocked down and trampled. Ambulance sirens sounded.

"Humph," Woods grunted. "We can send space-ships to Mars, but we don't know how to handle crowds."

He stared expectantly into the bright blue bowl of the sky.

"Ought to be getting in pretty soon," he said.

His words were blotted out by a mounting roar of sound. The earsplitting explosions of roaring rocket tubes. The thunderous drumming of the ship shooting over the horizon.

The bellow from the crowd competed with the roaring of the tubes as the *Hello Mars IV* shimmered like a streak of silver light over the field. Then fading in the distance, it glowed redly as its forward tubes shot flame.

"Cooper sure is giving her everything he has," Woods said in awe. "He'll melt her down, using the tubes like that."

He stared into the west, where the ship had vanished. His cigarette, forgotten, burned down and scorched his fingers.

Out of the tail of his eye he saw Jimmy Andrews, the *Express* photographer.

"Did you get a picture?" Woods roared at him.

"Picture, hell," Andrews shouted back. "I can't shoot greased lightning."

The ship was coming back again, its speed slowed, but still traveling at a terrific pace. For a moment it hung over the horizon and then nosed down toward the field.

"He can't land at that speed," Woods yelled. "It'll crack wide open!"

"Look out," roared a dozen voices and then the ship was down, its nose plowing into the ground, leaving in its wake a smoking furrow of raw earth, its tail tilting high in the air, threatening to nose over on its back.

The crowd at the far end of the field broke and stampeded, trampling, clawing, pushing, shoving, suddenly engulfed in a hysteria of fear at the sight of the ship plowing toward them.

But the *Hello Mars IV* stopped just short of the police cordon, still right side up. A pitted, battered ship—finally home from space—the first ship to reach Mars and return.

The newspapermen and photographers were rushing forward. The crowd was shrieking. Automobile horns and sirens blasted the air. From the distant rim of the city rose the shrilling of whistles and the far-away roll of clamoring bells.

As Woods ran a thought hammered in his head. A thought that had an edge of apprehension. There was something wrong. If Jerry Cooper had been at the controls, he never would have landed the ship at such speed. It had been a madman's stunt to land a ship that way. Jerry was a skilled navigator, averse to taking chances. Jack had watched him in the Moon Derby five years before and the way Jerry could handle a ship was beautiful to see.

The valve port in the ship's control cabin swung slowly open, clanged back against the metal side. A man stepped out—a man who staggered jerkily forward and then stumbled and fell in a heap.

Dr. Gilmer rushed to him, lifted him in his arms.

Woods caught a glimpse of the man's face as his head lolled in Gilmer's arms. It was Jerry Cooper's face—but a face that was twisted and changed almost beyond recognition, a face that burned itself into Jack Woods' brain, indelibly etched there, something to be remembered with a shudder through the years. A haggard face, with deeply sunken eyes, with hollow cheeks, with drooling lips that slobbered sounds that were not words.

A hand pushed at Woods.

"Get out of my way," shrilled Andrews. "How do you expect me to take a picture?"

The newsman heard the camera whirr softly, heard the click of changing plates.

"Where are the others?" Gilmer was shouting at Cooper.

The man looked up at him vacantly, his face twisting itself into a grimace of pain and fear.

"Where are the others?" Gilmer shouted again, his voice ringing over the suddenly hushed stillness of the crowd.

Cooper jerked his head toward the ship.

"In there," he whispered and the whisper cut like a sharp-edged knife.

He mumbled drooling words, words that meant nothing. Then with an effort he answered.

"Dead," he said.

And in the silence that followed, he said again:

"All dead!"

They found the others in the living quarters back of the locked control room. All four of them were dead—had been dead for days. Andy Smith's skull had been crushed by a mighty blow.

Jimmy Watson had been strangled, with the blue raised welts of blunt fingers still upon his throat. Elmer Paine's body was huddled in a corner, but upon him there were no marks of violence, although his face was contorted into a visage of revulsion, a mask of pain and fear and suffering. Thomas Delvaney's body sprawled beside a table. His throat had been opened with an old fashioned straightedge razor. The razor, stained with blackened blood, was tightly clutched in the death grip of his right hand.

In one corner of the room stood a large wooden packing box. Across the smooth white boards of the box someone had written shakily, with black crayon, the single word "Animal." Plainly there had been an attempt to write something else—strange wandering crayon marks below the single word. Marks that scrawled and stopped and made no sense.

That night Jerry Cooper died, a raving maniac.

A banquet, planned by the city to welcome home the conquering heroes, was cancelled. There were no heroes left to welcome back.

What was in the packing box?

"It's an animal," Dr. Gilmer declared, "and that's about as far as I would care to go. It seems to be alive, but that is hard to tell. Even when moving fast—fast, that is, for it—it probably would make a sloth look like chain lightning in comparison."

Jack Woods stared down through the heavy glass walls that caged the thing Dr. Gilmer had found in the packing box marked "Animal."

It looked like a round ball of fur.

"It's all curled up, sleeping," he said.

"Curled up, hell," said Gilmer. "That's the shape of the beast. It's spherical and it's covered with fur. Fur-Ball would be a good name for it, if you were looking for something descriptive. A fur coat of that stuff would keep you comfortable in the worst kind of weather the North Pole could offer. It's thick and it's warm. Mars, you must remember, is damned cold."

"Maybe we'll have fur-trappers and fur-trading posts up on Mars," Woods suggested. "Big fur shipments to Earth and Martian wraps selling at fabulous prices."

"They'd kill them off in a hurry if it ever came to that," declared Gilmer. "A foot a day would be top speed for that baby, if it can move at all. Oxygen would be scarce on Mars. Energy would be something mighty hard to come by and this boy couldn't afford to waste it by running around. He'd just have to sit tight and not let anything distract him from the mere business of just living."

"It doesn't seem to have eyes or ears or anything you'd expect an animal to have," Woods said, straining his eyes the better to see the furry ball through the glass.

"He probably has sense-perceptions we would never recognize," declared Gilmer. "You must remember, Jack, that he is a product of an entirely different environment—perhaps he rose from an entirely different order of life than we know here on Earth. There's no reason why we must believe that parallel evolution would occur on any two worlds so remotely separated as Earth and Mars.

"From what little we know of Mars," he went on, rolling the black cigar between his lips, "it's just about the kind of animal we'd expect to find there. Mars has little water—by Earth standards, practically none at all. A dehydrated world. There's oxygen there, but the air is so thin we'd call it a vacuum on Earth. A Martian animal would have to get along on very little water, very little oxygen.

"Well, when he got it, he'd want to keep it. The spherical shape gives him a minimum surface-per-volume ratio, makes it easier for him to conserve water and oxygen. He probably is mostly lungs. The fur protects him from the cold. Mars must be devilish cold at times. Cold enough at night to freeze carbon dioxide. That's what they had him packed in on the ship."

"No kidding," said Woods.

"Sure," said Gilmer. "Inside the wooden box was a steel receptacle and that fellow was inside of that. They had pumped out quite a bit of the air, made it a partial vacuum, and packed frozen carbon dioxide around the receptacle. Outside of that, between the box and the ice, was paper and felt to slow up melting. They must have been forced to repack him and change air several times during the trip back.

"Apparently he hadn't had much attention the last few days before they got here, for the oxygen was getting pretty thin, even for him, and the ice was almost gone. I don't imagine he felt any too good. Probably was just a bit sick. Too much carbon dioxide and the temperature uncomfortably warm."

Woods gestured at the glass cage.

"I suppose you got him all fixed up now," he said. "Air conditioned and everything."

Gilmer chuckled.

"Must seem just like home to him," he replied. "In there the atmosphere is thinned down to about one-thousandth Earth standard, with considerable ozone. Don't know whether he needs that, but a good deal of the oxygen on Mars must be in the form of ozone. Surface conditions there are suitable for its production. The temperature is 20 degrees below zero Centigrade. I had to guess at that, because I have no way of knowing from what part of Mars this animal of ours was taken. That would make a difference."

He wrangled the cigar from one corner of his mouth to the other.

"A little private Mars all his own," he stated.

"You found no records at all on the ship?" asked Woods. "Nothing telling anything at all about him?"

Gilmer shook his head and clamped a vicious jaw on the cigar.

"We found the log book," he said, "but it had been deliberately destroyed. Someone soaked it in acid. No chance of getting anything out of it."

The reporter perched on a desk top and drummed his fingers idly on the wood.

"Now just why in hell would they want to do that?" he asked.

"Why in hell did they do a lot of things they did?" Gilmer snarled. "Why did somebody, probably Delvaney, kill Paine and Watson? Why did Delvaney, after he did that, kill himself? What happened to Smith? Why did Cooper die insane, screaming and shrieking as if something had him by the throat? Who scrawled that single word on the box and tried to write more, but couldn't? What stopped him writing more?"

Woods nodded his head toward the glass cage.

"I wonder how much our little friend had to do with it," he speculated.

"You're crazier than a space-bug," Gilmer snapped. "What in blue hell could he have had to do with it? He's just an animal and probably of a pretty low order of intelligence. The way things are on Mars he'd be kept too damn busy just keeping alive to build much brain. Of course, I haven't had much chance to study it yet. Dr.

Winters, of Washington, and Dr. Lathrop, of London, will be here next week. We'll try to find out something then."

Woods walked to the window in the laboratory and looked out.

The building stood on top of a hill, with a green lawn sweeping down to a park-like area with fenced off paddock, moat-protected cliff-cages and monkey-islands—the Metropolitan Zoo.

Gilmer took a fresh and fearsome grip on his cigar.

"It proves there's life on Mars," he contradicted. "It doesn't prove a damn thing else."

"You should use a little imagination," chided Woods.

"If I did," snarled Gilmer, "I'd be a newspaperman. I wouldn't be fit for any other job."

Along toward noon, down in the zoo, Pop Anderson, head-keeper of the lionhouse, shook his head dolefully and scratched his chin.

"Them cats have been actin' mighty uneasy," he declared. "Like there was something on their minds. They don't hardly sleep at all. Just prowl around."

Eddie Riggs, reporter for the *Express,* clucked sympathetically.

"Maybe they aren't getting the right vitamins, Pop," he suggested.

Pop disagreed.

"It ain't that," he said. "They're gettin' the same feed we always give 'em. Plenty raw meat. But they're restless as all git-out. A cat is a lazy critter. Sleeps hours at a stretch and always takin' naps. But they don't do that no more. Cranky. Fightin' among themselves. I had to give Nero a good whoppin' the other day when he tried to beat up Percy. And when I did he made a pass at me—me, who's took care of him since he was a cub."

From across the water-moat Nero snarled menacingly at Pop.

"He still's got it in for me," Pop said. "If he don't quiet down, I'll give him a raw-hidin' he'll remember. There ain't no lion can get gay with me."

He glanced apprehensively at the lion-run.

"I sure hope they calm down," he said. "This is Saturday and there'll be a big crowd this afternoon. Always makes them nervous, a crowd does, and the way they are now there'll be no holdin' 'em."

"Anything else you heard of going on?" Riggs asked.

Pop scratched his chin.

"Susan died this morning," he declared.

Susan was a giraffe.

"Didn't know Susan was sick," said Riggs.

"She wasn't," Pop told him. "Just keeled over."

Riggs turned his eyes back to the lion caves. Nero, a big blackmaned brute, was balancing himself on the edge of the water ditch, almost as if he were about to leap into the water. Percy and another lion were tusseling, not too good-naturedly.

"Looks like Nero might be thinking of coming over here after you," the reporter suggested.

"Shucks," snorted Pop. "He wouldn't do that. Not Nero. Nor no other lion. Why, them cats hate water worse'n poison."

From the elephant paddock, a mile or more away, came the sudden angry trumpeting of the pachyderms. Then a shrill squeal of elephantine rage.

"Sounds like them elephants was actin' up, too," Pop declared calmly.

Pounding feet thundered around the corner of the walk that circled the cat-cages. A man who had lost his hat, whose eyes were wild with terror, pounded past them. As he ran on he cried: "An elephant has gone mad! It's coming this way!"

Nero roared. A mountain lion screamed.

A great gray shape, moving swiftly despite its lumbering gait, rounded a clump of bushes and moved out on the smooth green sward of the park. It was the elephant. With trunk reared high, emitting screams of rage, with huge ears flapping, the beast headed for the cat-cages.

Riggs turned and pounded madly toward the administration building. Behind him Pop puffed and panted.

Shrill screams rent the air as early visitors at the zoo scampered for safety.

Animal voices added to the uproar.

The elephant, turning from his original direction, charged through the two acre paddock in which three pairs of wolves were kept, taking fence, trees and brush in his stride.

On the steps of the administration building. Riggs looked back.

Nero, the lion, was *dripping water!* The water that theoretically should have kept him penned in his cage as securely as steel bars!

A keeper, armed with a rifle, rushed up to Riggs.

"All hell's broken loose," he shouted.

The polar bears had staged a bloody battle, with two of them dead, two dying and the rest so badly mauled that there was little hope they would live. Two buck deer, with locked horns, were fighting to the death. Monkey Island was in an uproar, with half of the little creatures mysteriously dead—dead, the keepers said, of too much excitement. A nervous condition.

"It ain't natural," protested Pop, when they were inside. "Animals don't fight like that."

Riggs was yelling into a telephone.

Outside a rifle roared.

Pop flinched.

"Maybe that's Nero," he groaned. "Nero, that I raised from a cub. Bottle-fed him, I did."

There were traces of tears in the old man's eyes.

It was Nero. But Nero, before he died, had reached out for the man who held the rifle and had killed him with a single vicious blow that crushed his skull.

Later that day, in his office, Doctor Gilmer smote the newspaper that lay open on his desk.

"You see that?" he asked Jack Woods.

The reporter nodded grimly. "I see it. I wrote it. I worked on it all afternoon. Wild animals turned loose in the city. Ravening animals. Mad with the lust to kill. Hospitals full of dying people. Morgues with ripped humanity. I saw an elephant trample a man into the earth before the police shot the beast. The whole zoo gone mad. Like a jungle nightmare."

He wiped his forehead with his coat sleeve and lit a cigarette with shaking fingers.

"I can stand most anything," he said, "but this was the acme of something or other. It was pretty horrible, Doc. I felt sorry for the animals, too," he said. "Poor devils. They weren't themselves. It was a pity to have to kill so many of them."

Doc leaned across the table. "Why did you come here?" he asked.

Woods nodded toward the glass cage that held the Martian animal. "I got to thinking," he said. "The shambles down there today reminded me of something else—"

He paused and looked squarely at Gilmer.

"It reminded me of what we found in the *Hello Mars IV.*"

"Why?" snapped Gilmer.

"The men on board the ship were insane," declared Woods. "Only insane men would do the things they did. And Cooper died a maniac. How he held onto his reason long enough to bring the ship to a landing is more than I know."

Gilmer took the mangled cigar out of his mouth and concentrated on picking off the worst of the frayed edge. He tucked it carefully back into the corner of his jaw.

"You figured those animals were insane today?"

Woods nodded.

"And for no reason," he added.

"So you up and suspicioned the Martian animal," said Gilmer. "Just how in blue hell do you think that defenseless little Fur-Ball over there could make men and animals go insane?"

"Listen," said Woods, "don't act that way, Doc. You're on the trail of something. You broke a poker date tonight to stay here at the laboratory. You had two tanks of carbon monoxide sent up. You were shut in here all afternoon. You borrowed some stuff from Appleman down in the sound laboratory. It all adds up to something. Better tell me."

"Damn you," said Gilmer, "you'd find it out anyway even if I kept mum."

He sat down and put his feet on the desk. He threw the wrecked and battered cigar into the waste-paper basket, took a fresh one out of a box, gave it a few preliminary chews and lit it.

"Tonight," said Gilmer, "I am going to stage an execution. I feel badly about it, but probably it is an act of mercy."

"You mean," gasped Jack, "that you are going to kill Fur-Ball over there?"

Gilmer nodded. "That's what the carbon monoxide is for. Introduce it into the cage. He'll never know what happened. Get drowsy, go to sleep, never wake up. Humane way to kill the thing."

"But why?"

"Listen to me," said Gilmer. "You've heard of ultrasonics, haven't you?"

"Sounds pitched too high for the human ear to hear," said Woods. "We use them for lots of things. For underwater signaling and surveying. To keep check on high-speed machines, warn of incipient breakdowns."

"Man has gone a long way with ultrasonics," said Gilmer. "Makes sound do all sorts of tricks. Creates ultrasonics up to as high as 20 million vibrations per second. One million cycle stuff kills germs. Some insects talk to one another with 32,000 cycle vibration. Twenty thousand is about as high as the human ear can detect. But man hasn't started yet. Because little Fur-Ball over there talks with ultrasonics that approximate *thirty million cycles.*"

The cigar traveled east to west.

"High frequency sound can be directed in narrow beams, reflected like light, controlled. Most of our control has been in liquids. We know that a dense medium is necessary for the best control of ultrasonics. Get high frequency sound in a medium like air and it breaks down fast, dissipates. That is, up to twenty million cycles, as far as we have gone.

"But thirty million cycles, apparently, can be controlled in air, in a medium less dense than our atmosphere. Just what the difference is I can't imagine, although there must be an explanation. Something like that would be needed for audible communication on a place like Mars, where the atmosphere must be close to a vacuum."

"Fur-Ball used thirty million cycle stuff to talk with," said Jack. "That much is clear. What's the connection?"

"This," said Gilmer. "Although sound reaching that frequency can't be heard in the sense that your auditory nerves will pick it up and relay it to your brain, it apparently can make direct impact on the brain. When it does that it must do something to the brain. It must disarrange the brain, give it a murderous complex, drive the entity of the brain insane."

Jack leaned forward breathlessly.

"Then that was what happened on the *Hello Mars IV.* That is what happened down in the park today."

Gilmer nodded, slowly, sadly.

"It wasn't malicious," he said. "I am sure of that. Fur-Ball didn't want to hurt anything. He was just lonesome and a little frightened. He was trying to contact some intelligence. Trying to talk with something. He was asleep or at least physiologically dormant when I took him from the ship. Probably he fell into his sleep just in time to save Cooper from the full effects of the ultrasonics. Maybe he would sleep a lot. Good way to conserve energy.

"He woke up sometime yesterday, but it seemed to take some time for him to get fully awake. I detected slight vibrations from him all day yesterday. This morning the vibrations became stronger. I had put several different assortments of food in the cage, hoping he would choose one or more to eat, give me some clue to his diet. But he didn't do any eating, although he moved around a little bit.

Pretty slow, although I imagine it was fast for him. The vibrations kept getting stronger. That was when the real hell broke out down in the zoo. He seems to be dozing off again now and things have quieted down."

Gilmer picked up a box-like instrument to which was attached a set of headphones.

"Borrowed these from Appleman down in the sound laboratory," he said. "The vibrations had me stumped at first. Couldn't determine their nature. Then I hit on sound. These things are a toy of Appleman's. Only half-developed yet. They let you 'hear' ultrasonics. Not actual hearing, of course, but an impression of tonal quality, a sort of psychological study of ultrasonics, translation of ultrasonics into what they would be like if you could hear them."

He handed the head-set to Woods and carried the box to the glass cage. He set it on the cage and moved it slowly back and forth, trying to intercept the ultrasonics emanating from the little Martian animal.

Woods slipped on the phones, sat waiting breathlessly.

He had expected to hear a high, thin sound, but no sound came. Instead a dreadful sense of loneliness crept over him, a sense of bafflement, lack of understanding, frustration. Steadily the feeling mounted in his brain, a voiceless wail of terrible loneliness and misery—a heart-wrenching cry of home-sickness.

He knew he was listening to the wailing of the little Martian animal, was "hearing" its cries, like the whimperings of a lost puppy on a storm-swept street.

His hands went up and swept the phones from his head.

He stared at Gilmer, half in horror.

"It's lonesome," he said. "Crying for Mars. Like a lost baby."

Gilmer nodded.

"It's not trying to talk to anyone now," he said. "Just lying there, crying its heart out. Not dangerous now. Never intentionally dangerous, but dangerous just the same."

"But," cried Woods, "you were here all afternoon. It didn't bother you. You didn't go insane."

Gilmer shook his head.

"No," he said, "I didn't go insane. Just the animals. And they would become immune after a while with this one certain animal. Because Fur-Ball is intelligent. His frantic attempts to communicate with some living things touched my brain time and time again . . . but it didn't stay. It swept on. It ignored me.

"You see, back in the ship it found that the human brain couldn't communicate with it. It recognized it as an alien being. So it didn't waste any more time with the human brain. But it tried the brains of monkeys and elephants and lions, hoping madly that it would find some intelligence to which it could talk, some intelligence that could explain what had happened, tell it where it was, reassure it that it wasn't marooned from Mars forever.

"I am convinced it has no visual sense, very little else except this ultrasonic voice to acquaint itself with its surroundings and its conditions. Maybe back on Mars it could talk to its own kind and to other things as well. It didn't move around much. It probably didn't have many enemies. It didn't need so many senses."

"It's intelligent," said Woods. "Intelligent to a point where you can hardly think of it as an animal."

Gilmer nodded.

"You're right," he said. "Maybe it is just as human as we are. Maybe it represents the degeneration of a great race that once ruled Mars. . . ."

He jerked the cigar out of his mouth and flung it savagely on the floor.

"Hell," he said, "what's the use of speculation? Probably you and I will never know. Probably the human race will never know."

He reached out and grasped the tank of carbon monoxide, started to wheel it toward the glass cage.

"Do you have to kill it, Doc?" Woods whispered. "Do you really have to kill it?"

Gilmer wheeled on him savagely.

"Of course I have to kill it," he roared. "What if the story ever got out that Fur-Ball killed the boys in the ship and all those animals today? What if he drove others insane? There'd be no more trips to Mars for years to come. Public opinion would make that impossible. And when another one does go out they'll have instructions not to bring back any Fur-Balls—and they'll have to be prepared for the effects of ultrasonics."

He turned back to the tank and then wheeled back again.

"Woods," he said, "you and I have been friends for a long time. We've had many a beer together. You aren't going to publish this, are you, Jack?"

He spread his feet.

"I'd kill you if you did," he roared.

"No," said Jack, "just a simple little story. Fur-Ball is dead. Couldn't take it, here on Earth."

"There's another thing," said Gilmer. "You know and I know that ultrasonics of the thirty million order can turn men into insane beasts. We know it can be controlled in atmosphere, probably over long distances. Think of what the war-makers of the world could do with that weapon! Probably they'll find out in time—but not from us!"

"Hurry up," Woods said bitterly. "Hurry up, will you. Don't let Fur-Ball suffer any longer. You heard him. There's no way we can help him. Man got him into this—there's only one way man can get him out of it. He'd thank you for death if he only knew."

Gilmer laid hands on the tank again.

Woods reached for a telephone. He dialed the *Express* number.

In his mind he could hear that puppyish whimper, that terrible, soundless cry of loneliness, that home-sick wail of misery. A poor huddled little animal snatched fifty million miles from home, among strangers, a hurt little animal crying for attention that no one could offer.

"*Daily Express*," said the voice of Bill Carson, night editor.

"This is Jack," the reporter said. "Thought maybe you'd want something for the morning edition. Fur-Ball just died—yeah, Fur-Ball, the animal the *Hello Mars IV* brought in—Sure, the little rascal couldn't take it."

Behind him he heard the hiss of gas as Gilmer opened the valve.

"Bill," he said, "I just thought of an angle. You might say the little cuss died of loneliness . . . yeah, that's the idea, grieving for Mars. . . . Sure, it ought to give the boys a real sob story to write. . . ."

GUNSMOKE INTERLUDE

The last of Cliff's fourteen known Westerns to be published, "Gunsmoke Interlude" is cut from a different kind of literary cloth than the others—which leads one to wonder whether it might not have been written as a farewell to the genre. Still, it's difficult to say just when this story was written, since no story by the name of "Gunsmoke Interlude" appears in Cliff's admittedly sporadic notes. Originally appearing in 10 Story Western Magazine in 1952, the story might well have been written years earlier; those same notes seem to hint that more than one Simak story sold in the late forties went unpublished. At any rate, this one reads very, very differently from the outpouring of Westerns that Cliff produced during and just after World War II.

It's a story about redemption.

—dww

The great black horse was lame and Clay was half asleep in the saddle when they came to Gila Gulch. It was no place nor time to stop, for the border was just a day ahead and John Trent just a day behind. But there was no choice. The horse would not last another day and Clay needed food and sleep and that last day's ride would be the worst of all the nightmare flight, for it went through a tortuous mountain spur where the going would be neither fast nor easy.

In front of the livery barn, Clay slid from the saddle, led the horse inside.

"Give him the works," he told the livery man. "He's earned it."

Clay's eyes went over the three horses in the stall.

"This all you got?" he asked.

The man nodded. "Business shot to hell," he said, "ever since the town got all pure and saintly. Used to have a dozen in here, but not any more."

Clay looked at the three horses again. They were sorry beasts, none of them the kind of horse he needed.

"This one of yours won't be traveling for a while," said the livery man. "You pushed him pretty hard."

"Stepped on a stone," said Clay.

He went outside and stood for a moment, hitching up his gun belt, sizing up the place.

Gila Gulch slept in the early morning sun, quiet and dusty, but with an unpainted, weather-beaten look about it even in the softness of the sun's first light.

He walked down the street to the place that said *Hotel* and went into the bar entrance. A barkeep was dusting off the furniture and he took his time getting back behind the bar.

"I need something," Clay told him, "to cure my saddle sores."

The barkeep set out a bottle and a glass.

Clay took them and walked to a table and let himself down easily into a chair, for the first time feeling the utter weariness that almost a thousand miles of riding had hung upon his massive frame. He pushed his hat back off his forehead and slapped dust off his legs. Then he shoved the glass aside, uncorked the bottle and raised it to his lips.

He set the bottle down and wiped his mouth and felt the liquor hit his stomach and explode and warm his whole insides.

But it didn't taste the same, he told himself. It didn't taste as good as it tasted once. It failed to take hold of him the way it once had taken hold of him.

A lot of things, he thought, *aren't the way they used to be.*

A fly buzzed nerve-wrackingly in the silence of the morning, trying to get through a window pane.

Clay sat sprawled in his chair, thinking of the way things used to be, ticking off the names of men who now were dead, of women who were almost forgotten, of towns that were no longer anything but names.

The barkeep leaned upon the bar and picked his teeth with a sharpened match end. Clay kept on sitting there, drinking every now and then.

"Want some breakfast?" the barkeep asked.

"Breakfast and room," said Clay. "I'm way behind on sleeping."

"What you want for breakfast?"

"Anything you got," said Clay. "I'm not particular."

He was eating breakfast when the kid came in with the star shining on his vest.

The kid walked over and sat down across from him.

"First time in town?" the kid asked.

Clay nodded.

"I got to tell you then," said the kid. "We got a rule around here about checking in your guns."

"I'm a stranger here," said Clay. "I hadn't heard about your rule."

"You check them in," said the kid, speaking free and easy. "When you leave town you get them back again."

"And if I don't?" asked Clay.

"You're heading into trouble," said the kid, businesslike and crisp, but still with friendliness.

"I'd feel undressed without my guns," said Clay, thinking that he couldn't very well tell the kid John Trent might come riding into town and he would need those guns.

"Anyhow," he said, "I'm going straight to bed. I don't aim to cause no trouble."

"I'll give you until sundown," the kid told him evenly. "At sundown I'll walk up the street. If you aim to keep those guns, you be there to argue, or I'll come in and get them."

"I'll be there," said Clay, and he said it matter-of-factly, for that was the way it was. That was the way it had been many times before. It was just a part of living. And, anyhow, this brash kid had no idea who he was calling out.

He ate in silence after the kid had left, the barkeep leaning on his elbows and still picking at his teeth.

Later, in his room, lying on the hard bed and staring at the ceiling, he thought about the kid and the star he wore and the way he talked, not tough or mean, but businesslike and calm.

And those kind, Clay told himself, were the ones to be afraid of. Although Clay had not been afraid of any man for many, many years. He was not afraid of men and he no longer cared for men. He no longer cared, he forced himself to admit, for anything at all. Not even for his own life, probably, although he'd never thought of that before.

And now here he was, staring at the ceiling. Here he was, one day away from freedom, one day from the moment when he could put his past behind him and start a new life. Lying there, he wondered what he had to start a new life with.

A hundred thousand dollars, of course, tucked away across the border, and that was a lot of money. But it was all he had. He'd have a new name, too, but that didn't really matter. Names never really mattered. A hundred thousand dollars safe across the border and ten thousand on his head, with John Trent riding hard just a day behind to collect the ten thousand.

He'd ride out in the evening, on one of the sorry nags at the livery stable and although the horse would not be the kind he wanted, it would take him where he wished to go. But before he left, he'd have to kill the kid, and that was a bothersome thing to have to do at a time like this.

I'd rather not kill him, he thought, *but he shouldn't talk so big.* He could take his guns down the street, of course, and give them to the kid and say take good care of them, I'll be back to get them along toward suppertime. But he might need those guns before suppertime and, anyhow, no one ever before had taken the guns of Coleman Clay and it was too late to let it happen now.

Too late, he thought. Too late to bring back the way whiskey used to taste, too late to give back the lives of men that went to buy the hundred thousand safe across the border.

He closed his eyes and sleep hit him like a hammer.

The sun was low in the western sky when he awoke and went downstairs.

A team of horses stood at the rail in front of the hotel, hitched to a ramshackle buck-board. A man was talking with the clerk.

"I'm checking out," said Clay.

"That'll be two dollars," said the clerk.

Clay paid him and asked, "Got some paper and a pencil? I want to write a letter."

The clerk nodded. He tore a sheet of lined paper from a cheap tablet and handed it and a pencil stub to him.

"If it ain't too long," said the man who had been talking to the clerk, "I'll wait for it."

"Jim's the mail carrier," said the clerk. "We ain't got no post office here. Nearest post office is Buckhorn."

"You're lucky, stranger," said the mail carrier. "I just go over there twice a week. It's a long pull. Sixty miles, almost."

Clay nodded his thanks. He went to the table in one corner of the room, wrote laboriously:

Dear Sis: I'm on my way down to Mexico to look over something. I may take it in my head to settle down there. I'll write you later.

You haven't told me where Gordon is lately. I thought maybe I'd run into him, but I haven't.

He signed the letter with a name that was not Coleman Clay and went back to the desk to get an envelope. He went back to the table and addressed the envelope to *Mrs. Esther Blaine, Pontiac, Ill.* Then he took a roll of bills out of his pocket, peeled off half a dozen, folded them carefully with the letter and sealed the envelope.

At the desk he bought a stamp and the clerk reached down behind the desk and brought up the mail bag. He held its open mouth toward Clay and Clay dropped the letter in it. The clerk jerked it shut.

"There you are," he told the mail carrier, shoving the pouch across the desk.

The mail carrier picked it up. "Got to get going," he said.

He started toward the door, then turned back.

"If I was you, stranger," he said, "I'd change my mind. That kid is pure poison with his hardware."

"No," said Clay.

"All right," said the mail carrier, "have it your own way. Sorry I can't stay and see it."

He went out the door and the clerk and Clay stood silently and watched him climb into the buckboard and wheel the team out into the street.

"This marshal of yours," asked Clay, "what might be his name?"

"Blaine," said the clerk, "Gordon Blaine."

Clay clutched the edge of the desk and hung on so hard that his fingers grew white beneath the tan of sun.

"Gordon Blaine," he said, and he kept his face unchanged even while his fingers whitened. "Never heard the name before."

"Nobody else did, either," said the clerk. "He just came out of nowhere. This town killed four marshals before he took the job. Ain't no one tried to kill Blaine now for a month or two."

Clay laughed and turned away from the desk like a wooden man. He marched out through the door onto the porch.

The sun was setting.

Clay remembered the letter he'd called for at a post office up in Montana a year or two ago.

Gordon is going out west. There's nothing I can do to stop him since you have done so well. He says there's no use of anyone staying here and slaving for a living when one can make a fortune like you have in the West. Maybe you will see him out there some time . . .

The street was hushed and deserted but there were, Clay knew, faces at every window, faces waiting to watch the two men who would walk along the street.

The mail carrier's buckboard was a dwindling dot on the prairie that stretched eastward from the town.

He saw the kid come down the steps from the marshal's office and walk out to the center of the dusty street. There he stood and waited, guns on his hips, hands hanging at his side.

I could still unbuckle my guns and walk to meet him with them in my hand, Clay told himself. But even as he thought of it, he knew he couldn't do it. It was an action that was counter to everything he'd ever done, everything he'd believed in, every code he'd followed.

He paced slowly down the steps and into the center of the street. He turned around and faced the kid and they started walking.

In a little while, Clay thought, *John Trent will come riding in and he'll only tell them who I am. Esther will never know, for the letter will be mailed sixty miles from here, although perhaps she'll wonder why I don't write from Mexico.*

John Trent will come riding in and he'll only know me by the name of Coleman Clay, with a price upon my head. No one else, absolutely no one, knows my other name. And the kid will never know.

Ten thousand dollars, Clay told himself, should set a young fellow up in fine style and his Ma will be right proud.

I AM CRYING ALL INSIDE

This story was originally published in the August 1969 issue of Galaxy Science Fiction, *and I've never been able to get it out of my head. It reminds me that at one time, when Cliff was told that his heroes were "losers," his reply was: "I like losers!"*

—dww

I do my job, which is hoeing corn. But I am disturbed by what I hear last night from this Janglefoot. Me and lot of other people hear him. But none of the folk would hear. He careful not to say what he say to us where any folk would hear. It would hurt their feeling.

Janglefoot he is traveling people. He go up and down the land. But he don't go very far. He often back again to orate to us again. Although why he say it more than once I do not understand. He always say the same.

He is Janglefoot because one foot jangle when he walk and he won't let no one fix it. It make him limp but he won't let no one fix it. It is humility he has. As long as he limp and jangle he is humble people and he like humility. He think it is a virtue. He think that it become him.

Smith, who is blacksmith, get impatient with him. Say he could fix the foot. Not as good as mechanic people, although better than not fixing it at all. There is a mechanic people not too far away. They impatient with him too. They think him putting on.

Pure charity of Smith to offer fix the foot. Him have other work. No need to beg for it like some poor people do. He hammer all the time on metal, making into sheet, then send on to mechanic people who use it for repair. Must be very careful keep in good repair. Must do it all ourself. No folk left who know how to do it. Folk left, of course, but too elegant to do it. All genteel who left. Never work at all.

I am hoeing corn and one of house people come down to tell me there is snakes. House people never work outdoors. Always come to us. I ask real snake or moonshine snake and they say real snake. So I lean my hoe on tree and go up hill to house.

Grandpa he is in hammock out on front lawn. Hammock is hung between two trees. Uncle John he is sitting on ground, leaning on one tree. Pa he is sitting on ground, leaning on other tree.

Sam, say Pa, there is snake in back.

So I go around house and there is timber rattler and I pick him up and he is mad at me and hammer me real good. I hunt around and find another rattler and a moccasin and two garter snake. Garter snakes sure don't amount to nothing, but I take them along. I hunt some more but that is all the snakes.

I go down across cornfield and wade creek and way back into swamp. I turn snakes loose. Will take them long time to get back. Maybe not at all.

Then I go back to hoeing. Important to keep patch of corn in shape. No weeds. Carry water when it needs. Soil work up nice and soft. Scare off crows when plant. Scare off coon and deer when corn come into ear. Full time job, for which many thanks. Also is important. George use corn to make the moon. Other patches of corn for food. But mine is use for moon. Me and George is partners. We make real good moonshine. Grandpa and Pa and Uncle John consume it with great happy. Any left over boys can have. But not girls. Girls don't use moonshine.

I do not understand use of food and booze. Grandpa say it taste good. I wonder what is taste. It make Uncle John see snakes. I do not understand that either.

I am hoeing corn when there is sound behind me. I look and there is Joshua. He is reading Bible. He always reading Bible. He make big job of it. Also he is stepping on my hills of corn. I yell at him and run at him. I hit him with the hoe. He run out of patch. He know why I hit him. I hit him before. He know better than stepping on the corn. He stand under tree and read. Standing in the shade. That is putting on. Only folk need to stand in shade. People don't.

Hitting him, I break my hoe. I go to Smith to fix. Smith he glad to see me. always glad to see each other. Smith and me are friend. He drop everything to fix hoe. Know how important corn is. Also do me favor.

We talk of Janglefoot. We agree is wrong the way he speak. He speak heresy. (Smith he tell me that word. Joshua, once he get unmad at me for hitting him, look up how to spell.) We agree, Smith and me, folk are genteel folk, not kind said by Janglefoot. Agree something should be done to Janglefoot. Don't know what to do. We say we think more of it.

George come by. Say he need me. Folk out of drinking likker. So I go with him while Smith is fixing hoe. George he has nice still, real neat and clean. Good capacity. Also try hard to age moonshine but never able to. Folk use it up too fast. He have four five-gallon jugs. We each take two and walk to house.

We stop at hammock where three still are. Tell us leave one jug there, take three to woodshed, put away, bring back some glasses. We do. We pour out glasses of moonshine for Grandpa and Pa. Uncle John he says never mind no glass for him, just put jug beside him. We do, leaving it uncork. Uncle John reach in pocket and bring out little rubber hose. Put one end in jug, other end in mouth. He lean back against tree and start sucking.

They make elegant picture. Grandpa look peaceful. Rocking in hammock with big glass of moon balance on his chest. We happy to see them happy. We go back to work. Smith has hoe fix and very sharp. It handle good. I thank him.

He say he still confuse at Janglefoot. Janglefoot claim he read what he say. In old record. Found record in old city far away. Smith ask if I know what city is. I say I don't. We more confuse than ever. For that matter, don't know what record is. Sound important, though.

I am hoeing corn when the Preacher pass and stop. Joshua gone somewhere. I tell him should have come sooner, Joshua standing under tree, reading Bible. He say Joshua only reading Bible, he interpret it. I ask him what interpret is. He tell me. I ask him how to spell it. He tell me. He know I try to write. He is helpful people. But pompous.

Night come on and moon is late to rise. Can no longer hoe for lack of seeing. So lean hoe against tree. Go to still to help George now making moonshine. George is glad of help. He running far behind.

I wonder to him why Janglefoot say same thing over and over. He say is repetition. I ask him repetition. He not sure. Say he think you say thing often enough people will believe it. Say folk use it in olden day. Make other folk believe thing that isn't so.

I ask him what he know of olden day. He say not very much. He say he should remember, but he doesn't. I should remember too, but I can't remember. Too long ago. Too much happen since. It is not important except for what Janglefoot is saying.

George has good fire burning under still and it shine on us. We stand around and watch. Make good feeling in the gizzard. Owl talk long way off in swamp. Do not know why fire feel good. No need of warm. Do not know why owl make one feel lonesome. I no lonesome. Got George right here beside me. There is so many things I do not know. What city is or record. What taste is. What olden day is like. Happy, though. Do not need to understand for happy.

People come from house, running fast. Say Uncle John is sick. Say he need doctor. Say he no longer seeing snakes. Seeing now blue alligator. With bright pink spots. Uncle John must be awful sick. Is no blue alligator. Not with bright pink spots.

George say he go to house to help, me run for Doc. George and house people leave, going very fast. I leave for Doc, also going fast.

Finally find Doc in swamp. He has candle lantern and is digging root. He always digging root. Great one for root and bark. He make stuff out of them for repairing folk. He is folk mechanic.

He standing in muck, up to knee. He cover with mud. He is filthy people. But he feel bad, hearing Uncle John is sick. Do not like blue alligator. Next he say is purple elephant and that is worst of all.

We run, both of us. I hold lantern at alligator hole while Doc wash mud off him. Never do to let folk seeing him filthy. We go to hut where Doc keep root and bark. He get some of it and we run for house. Moon has come up now, but we keep lantern. It help moonlight some.

We come to foot of hill with house on top of hill. All lawn between foot of hill and house. All lawn except for trees that hold up hammock. Hammock still is there, but empty. It blow back and forth in breeze. House stand up high and white. Windows in it shining.

Grandpa sit on big long porch that is in front of house, with white pillars to hold up roof. He sit in rocking chair. He rock back and forth. Another rocking chair beside him. He is only one around. Can see no one else. Inside of house womenfolk is making cries. Through tall window I can see inside. Big thing house people call chandelier hang from ceiling. Made of glass. Many candles in it. Candles all are burning. Glass look pretty in light. Furniture in room gleam with light. All is clean and polish. House people work hard to keep it clean and polish. Take big pride.

We run up steps to porch.

Grandpa say, you come too late. My son John is dead.

I do not understand this dead. When folk dead put them into ground. Say words over them. Put big stone at their head. Back of house is special place for dead. Lot of big stones standing there. Some new. Some old. Some so old cannot read lettering that say who is under them.

Doc run into house. To make sure Grandpa say right, perhaps. I stay on porch, unknowing what to do. Feel terrible sad. Don't know why I do. Except knowing dead is bad. Maybe because Grandpa seem so sad.

Grandpa say to me, Sam sit down and talk.

I do not sit, I tell him. People always stand.

It was outrage of him to ask it. He know custom. He know as well as I do people do not sit with folk.

God damn it to hell, he say, forget your stubborn pride. Sitting is not bad. I do it all the time. Bend yourself and sit.

In that chair, he say, pointing to one beside him.

I look at chair. I wonder will it hold me. It is built for folk. People heavier than folk. Have no wish to break a chair with weight. Take much time to make one. Carpenter people work for long to make one.

But I think no skin off my nose. Skin off Grandpa's nose. He the one that tell me.

So I square around so I hit the chair and bend myself and sit. Chair creak, but hold. I settle into it. Sitting feel good. I rock a little. Rocking feel good. Grandpa and me sit, looking out on lawn. Lawn is real pretty. Moonlight on it. First lawn and then some trees and after trees cornfield and other fields. Far away owl talk in swamp. Coon whicker. Fox bark long way off.

It do beat hell, say Grandpa, how man can live out his life, doing nothing, then die of moonshine drinking.

You sure of moon, I ask. I hate to hear Grandpa blaming moonshine. George and me, we make real good moonshine.

Grandpa say, it couldn't be nothing else. Only moonshine give blue alligator with bright pink spots.

No purple elephant, so say Grandpa.

I wonder what elephant might be. So much that I don't know.

Sam, say Grandpa, we a sorry lot. Never had a chance. Neither you nor us. Ain't none of us no good. We folk sit around all day and never do a thing. Hunt a little, maybe. Fish a little. Play cards. Drink likker. Feel real energetic, maybe I'll play some horseshoe. Should be out doing something good and big. But we never are. While we live we don't amount to nothing. When we die we don't amount to nothing. We're just no God damn good.

He went on rocking, bitter. I don't like the way he talk. He feel bad, sure, but no excuse to talk the way he was. Elegant folk like him shouldn't talk that way. Lay in hammock all day long, shouldn't talk that way. Balance moonshine on his chest, shouldn't talk that way. I uncomfortable. Wish to get away, but impolite to leave.

Down at bottom of hill, where lawn begin, I see many people. Standing, looking up at house. Pretty soon come slow up lawn and look closer at house. Saying nothing, just standing. Paying their respect. Letting folk know that they sorrow too.

We never was nothing but white trash, say Grandpa. I can see it now. Seen it for long, long time but could never say it. I can say it now. We live in swamp in houses falling down. Falling down because we got no gumption to take care of them. Hunt and fish a little. Trap a little. Farm a little. Sit around and cuss because we ain't got nothing.

Grandpa, I say, I want him to stop. I don't want to hear. Don't want him to go on saying what Janglefoot been saying.

But he pay me no attention. He go on saying.

Then, long, long ago, he say, they learn to go in space very, very fast. Faster than the light. Much faster than the light. They find other worlds. Better than the Earth. Much better worlds than this. Lot of ships to go in. Take little time to go there. So everybody go. Everyone but us. Folk like us, all over the world, are left behind. Smart ones go. Rich ones go. Hard workers go. We are left behind.

We aren't worth the taking. No one want us on this world. Have no use for us on others. They leave us behind, the misfits, the loafers, the poor, the crippled, the stupid. All over the world these kind are left behind. So when they all are gone, we move from shacks to houses the rich and smart ones lived in. No one to stop us from doing it. All of them are gone. They don't care what we do. Not any more they don't. We live in better houses, but we do not change. There is no use to change even if we could. We got you to take care of us. We have got it made. We don't do a God damn thing. We don't even learn to read. When words are read over my son's grave, one of you will read them, for we do not know how to read.

Grandpa, I say. Grandpa, Grandpa. Grandpa. I feel crying all inside. He had done it now. He had took away the elegant. Took away the pride. He do what Janglefoot never could.

Now, say Grandpa, don't take on that way. You got no reason to be prideful either. You and us we are the same. Just no God damn good. There were others of you and they took them along. But you they left behind. Because you were out of date. Because you were slow and awkward. Because you were heaps of junk. Because they had no need of you. They wouldn't give you room. They left both you and us because neither of us was worth the room we took.

Doc came out of door fast and purposeful. He say to me I got work for you to do.

All the other people coming up the lawn, saying nothing, slow. I try to get out of chair. I can't. For first time I can't do what I want. My legs is turned to water.

Sam, say Grandpa, I am counting on you.

When he say that, I get up. I go down steps. I go out on lawn. No need for Doc tell me what to do. I done it all before.

I talk to other people. I give jobs to do. You and you dig grave. You and you make coffin. You and you and you and you run to other houses. Tell all the folk Uncle John is dead. Tell them come to funeral. Tell them funeral elegant. Much to cry, much to eat, much to drink. You get Preacher. Tell him fix sermon. You get Joshua to read the Bible. You and you and you go and help George make moonshine. Other folk be coming. Must be elegant.

All done. I walk down the lawn. I think on pride and loss. Elegant is gone. Shiny wonder gone. Pride is gone. Not all pride, however. Kind of pride remain. Hard and bitter pride. Grandpa say Sam sit down and talk. Grandpa say Sam I am counting on you. That is pride. Hard pride. Not soft and easy pride like it was before. Grandpa need me.

No one else will know. Grandpa never bring himself again to tell what he tell me. Secret between us. Secret born of sad. Life of others need not change. Go on thinking same. Janglefoot no trouble. No one believe Janglefoot if he talk forever. No one ever know that he tell the truth. Truth is hard to take. No one care except for what we have right now. We go on same.

Except I who know. I never want to know. I never ask to know. I try not to know. But Grandpa won't shut up. Grandpa have to talk. Time come man will die if he cannot talk. Must make clean breast of it. But why to me? Because he love me most, perhaps. That is prideful thing.

But going down the lawn, I crying deep inside.

THE CALL FROM BEYOND

This story originally appeared in Super Science Stories *in May 1950, and a brief entry in one of Cliff's mostly blank journals shows that he was paid $135 the same year for a story entitled "Flight to Pluto." This is another of several Simak stories in which alien music plays a part, but the story appears to my eye to be a sort of homage to the works of H. P. Lovecraft, the master of tales of extradimensional horror—but with a touch of technology and several embedded themes that are pure Simak.*

—dww

CHAPTER ONE
The Pyramid of Bottles

The pyramid was built of bottles, hundreds of bottles that flashed and glinted as if with living fire, picking up and breaking up the misty light that filtered from the distant sun and still more distant stars.

Frederick West took a slow step forward, away from the open port of his tiny ship. He shook his head and shut his eyes and opened them again and the pyramid was still there. So it was no figment, as he had feared, of his imagination, born in the darkness and the loneliness of his flight from Earth.

It was there and it was a crazy thing. Crazy because it should not be there, at all. There should be nothing here on this almost unknown slab of tumbling stone and metal.

For no one lived on Pluto's moon. No one ever visited Pluto's moon. Even he, himself, hadn't intended to until, circling it to have a look before going on to Pluto, he had seen that brief flash of light, as if someone might be signaling. It had been the pyramid, of course. He knew that now. The stacked-up bottles catching and reflecting light.

Behind the pyramid stood a space hut, squatted down among the jagged boulders. But there was no movement, no sign of life. No one was tumbling out of entrance lock to welcome him. And that was strange, he thought. For visitors must be rare, if, indeed, they came at all.

Perhaps the pyramid really was a signaling device, although it would be a clumsy way of signaling. More likely a madman's caprice. Come to think of it, anyone who was sufficiently deranged to live on Pluto's moon would be a fitting architect for a pyramid of bottles.

The moon was so unimportant that it wasn't even named. The spacemen, on those rare occasions when they mentioned it at all, simply called it "Pluto's moon" and let it go at that.

No one came out to this sector of space any more. Which, West told himself parenthetically, is exactly why I came. For if you could slip through the space patrol you would be absolutely safe. No one would ever bother you.

No one bothered Pluto these days. Not since the ban had been slapped on it three years before, since the day the message had come through from the scientists in the cold laboratories which had been set up several years before that.

No one came to the planet now. Especially with the space patrol on guard . . . although there were ways of slipping through. If one knew where the patrol ships would be at certain times and build up one's speed and shut off the engines, coasting on momentum in the shadow of the planet, one could get to Pluto.

West was near the pyramid now and he saw that it was built of whisky bottles. All empty, very empty, their labels fresh and clear.

West straightened up from staring at the bottles and advanced toward the hut. Locating the lock, he pressed the button. There was no response. He pressed it again. Slowly, almost reluctantly, the lock swung in its seat. Swiftly he stepped inside and swung over the lever that closed the outer lock, opened the inner one.

Dim light oozed from the interior of the hut and through his earphones West heard the dry rustle of tiny claws whispering across the floor. Then a gurgling, like water running down a pipe.

Heart in his mouth, thumb hooked close to the butt of his pistol, West stepped quickly across the threshold of the lock.

A man, clad in motheaten underwear, sat on the edge of the cot. His hair was long and untrimmed, his whiskers sprouted in black ferocity. From the mat of beard two eyes stared out, like animals brought to bay in caves. A bony hand thrust out a whisky bottle in a gesture of invitation.

The whiskers moved and a croak came from them. "Have a snort," it said.

West shook his head. "I don't drink."

"I do," the whiskers said. The hand tilted the bottle and the bottle gurgled.

West glanced swiftly around the room. No radio. That made it simpler. If there had been a radio he would have had to smash it. For, he realized now, it had been a silly thing to do, stopping on this moon. No one knew where he was . . . and that was the way it should have stood.

West snapped his visor up.

"Drinking myself to death," the whiskers told him.

West stared, astounded at the utter poverty, at the absolute squalor of the place.

"Three years," said the man. "Not a single sober breath in three solid years." He hiccoughed. "Getting me," he said. His left hand came up and thumped his shrunken chest. Lint flew from the ragged underwear. The right hand still clutched the bottle.

"Earth years," the whiskers explained. "Three Earth years. Not Pluto years."

A thing that chattered came out of the shadows in one corner of the hut and leaped upon the bed. It hunched itself beside the man and stared leeringly at West, its mouth a slit that drooled across its face, its puckered hide a horror in the sickly light.

"Meet Annabelle," said the man. He whistled at the thing and it clambered to his shoulder, cuddling against his cheek.

West shivered at the sight.

"Just passing through?" the man inquired.

"My name is West," West told him. "Heading for Pluto."

"Ask them to show you the painting," said the man. "Yes, you must see the painting."

"The painting?"

"You deaf?" asked the man, belligerently. "I said a painting. You understand—a picture."

"I understand," said West. "But I didn't know there were any paintings there. Didn't even know there was anybody there."

"Sure there is," said the man. "There's Louis and—"

He lifted the bottle and took a snort.

"I got alcoholism," said the man. "Good thing, alcoholism. Keeps colds away. Can't catch a cold when you got alcoholism. Kills you quicker than a cold, though. Why, you might go on for years having colds—"

"Look" urged West, "you have to tell me about Pluto. About who's there. And the painting. How come you know about them?"

The eyes regarded him with drunken cunning.

"You'd have to do something for me. Couldn't give you information like that out of the goodness of my heart."

"Of course," agreed West. "Anything that you would like. You just name it."

"You got to take Annabelle out of here," the man told him. "Take her back where she belongs. It isn't any place for a girl like her. No fit life for her to lead. Living with a sodden wreck like me. Used to be a great man once . . . yes, sir, a great man. It all came of looking for a bottle. One particular bottle. Had to sample all of them. Every last one. And when I sampled them, there was nothing else to do but drink them up. They'd spoil for sure if you let them stand around. And who wants a lot of spoiled liquor cluttering up the place?"

He took another shot.

"Been at it ever since," he explained. "Almost got them now. Ain't many of them left. Used to think that I'd find the right bottle before it was too late and then everything would be all right. Wouldn't do me no good to find it now, because I'm going to die. Enough left to last me, though. Aim to die plastered. Happy way to die."

"But what about those people on Pluto?" demanded West.

The whiskers snickered. "I fooled them. They gave me my choice. Take anything you want, they said. Big-hearted, you understand. Pals to the very last. So I took the whisky. Cases of it. They didn't know, you see. I tricked them."

"I'm sure you did," said West. Tiny, icy feet ran up and down his spine. For there was madness here, he knew, but madness with a pattern. Somewhere, somehow, this twisted talk would fall into a pattern that would make sense.

"But something went wrong," the man declared. "Something went wrong."

Silence whistled in the room.

"You see, Mr. Best," the man declared. "I—"

"West," said West. "Not Best. West."

The man did not seem to notice. "I'm going to die, you understand. Any minute, maybe. Got a liver and heart and either one could kill me. Drinking does that to you. Never used to drink. Got into the habit when I was sampling all these bottles. Got a taste for it. Then there wasn't anything to do—"

He hunched forward.

"Promise you will take Annabelle," he croaked.

Annabelle tittered at West, slobber drooling from her mouth.

"But I can't take her back," West protested, "unless I know where she came from. You have to tell me that."

The man waggled a finger. "From far away," he croaked, "and yet not so very far. Not so very far if you know the way."

West eyed Annabelle with the gorge rising in his throat.

"I will take her," he said. "But you have to tell me where."

"Thank you, Guest," said the man. He lifted the bottle and let it gurgle.

"Not Guest," said West, patiently. "My name is—"

The man toppled forward off the bed, sprawled across the floor. The bottle rolled crazily, spilling liquor in sporadic gushes.

West leaped forward, knelt beside the man and lifted him. The whiskers moved and a whisper came from their tangled depths, a gasping whisper that was scarcely more than a waning breath.

"Tell Louis that his painting—"

"Louis?" yelled West. "Louis who? What about—"

The whisper came again. "Tell him . . . someday . . . he'll paint a wrong place and then . . ."

Gently West laid the man back on the floor and stepped away. The whisky bottle still rocked to and fro beneath a chair where it had come to rest.

Something glinted at the head of the cot and West walked to where it hung. It was a watch, a shining watch, polished with years of care. It swung slowly from a leather thong tied to the rod that formed the cot's head, where a man could reach out in the dark and read it.

West took it in his hand and turned it over, saw the engraving that ran across its back. Bending low, he read the inscription in the feeble light.

To Walter J. Darling, from class of '16,
Mars Polytech.

West straightened, understanding and disbelief stirring in his mind.

Walter J. Darling, that huddle on the floor? Walter J. Darling, one of the solar system's greatest biologists, dead in this filthy hut? Darling, teacher for years at Mars Polytechnical Institute, that shrunken, liquor-sodden corpse in shoddy underwear?

West wiped his forehead with the back of his space-gloved hand. Darling had been a member of that mysterious government commission assigned to the cold laboratories on Pluto, sent there to develop artificial hormones aimed at controlled mutation of the human race. A mission that had been veiled in secrecy from the first because it was feared, and rightly so, that revelation of its purpose might lead to outraged protests from a humanity that could not imagine why it should be improved biologically.

A mission, thought West, that had set out in mystery and ended in mystery, mystery that had sent whispers winging through the solar system. Shuddery whispers.

Louis? That would be Louis Nevin, another member of the Pluto commission. He was the man Darling had tried to tell about just before he died.

And Nevin must still be out here on Pluto, must still be alive despite the message that had come to Earth.

But the painting didn't fit. Nevin wasn't an artist. He was a biologist, scarcely second to Darling.

The message of three years before had been a phony, then. There were men still on the planet.

And that meant, West told himself bitterly, that his own plan had gone awry. For Pluto was the only place in the Solar System where there would be food and shelter and to which no one would ever come.

He remembered how he had planned it all so carefully . . . how it had seemed a perfect answer. There would be many years' supply of food stacked in the storerooms, there would be comfortable living quarters, and there would be tools and equipment should he ever need them. And, of course, the Thing, whatever it might be. The horror that had closed the planet, that had set the space patrol to guard the planet's loneliness.

But West had never been too concerned with what he might find on Pluto, for whatever it might be, it could be no worse than the bitterness that was his on Earth.

There was something going on at the Pluto laboratories. Something that the government didn't know about or that the government had suppressed along with that now infamous report of three years before.

Something that Darling could have told him had he wanted to . . . or had he been able. But now Walter J. Darling was past all telling. West would have to find out by himself.

West stepped to where he lay, lifted him to the cot and covered him with a tattered blanket.

Perched on the cot head, Annabelle chattered and giggled and drooled.

"Come here, you," said West. "Come on over here."

Annabelle came, slowly and coyly. West lifted her squeamishly, thrust her into an outer pocket and zipped it shut. He started toward the doorway.

On the way out he picked the empty bottle from the floor, added it to the pyramid outside.

CHAPTER TWO
The White Singer

West's craft fled like a silvery shadow between the towering mountain peaks shielding the only valley on Pluto that had ever known the tread of Man.

Coasting in on silent motors in the shadow of the planet, he had eluded the patrol. Beyond the mountains he had thrown in the motors, had braked the plunging ship almost to a crawl, taking the chance the flare of the rockets might be seen by any of the patrol far out in space.

And now, speed reduced, dropping in a long slant toward the glass-smooth landing field, he huddled over the controls, keyed to a free-fall landing, always dangerous at best. But it would be as dangerous, he sensed, to advertise his coming with another rocket blast. The field was long and smooth. If he hit it right and not too far out, there would be plenty of room.

The almost nonexistent atmosphere was a point in favor. There were no eddies, no currents of air to deflect the ship, send it into a spin or a dangerous wobble.

Off to the right he caught a flash of light and his mind clicked the split-second answer that it must be the laboratory.

Then the ship was down, pancaking, hissing along the landing strip, friction gripping the hull. It stopped just short of a jumbled pile of rock and West let out his breath, felt his heart take up the beat again. A few feet more . . .

Locking the controls, he hung the key around his neck, pulled down the visor of his space gear and let himself out of the ship.

Across the field glowed the lights of the laboratory. He had not been mistaken, then. He had seen the lights . . . and men were here. Or could he be mistaken? Those lights would have continued to function even without attention. The fact that they were shining in the building was no reason to conclude that men also were there.

At the far end of the field loomed a massive structure and West knew that it was the shops of the Alpha Centauri expedition, where men had labored for two years to make the Henderson space drive work. Somewhere, he knew, in the shadow of the star-lighted shops, was the ship itself, the *Alpha Centauri,* left behind when the crew had given up in despair and gone back to Earth. A ship designed to fly out to the stars, to quit the Solar System and go into the void, spanning light years as easily as an ordinary ship went from Earth to Mars.

It hadn't gone, of course, but that didn't matter.

"A symbol," West said to himself.

That was what it was . . . a symbol and a dream.

And something, too, now that he was here, now that he could admit it, that had lain in the back of his mind all the way from Earth.

West shucked his belt around so that the pistol hung handy to his fist.

If men were here . . . or worse, if that message hadn't been a phony, he might need the pistol. Although it was unlikely that the sort of thing that he then would face would be vulnerable to a pistol.

Shivering, he remembered that terse, secret report reposing in the confidential archives back on Earth . . . the transcription of the tense, rasping voice that had come over the radio from Pluto, a voice that told of dreadful things, of dying men and something that was loose. A voice that had screamed a warning, then had gurgled and died out.

It was after that that the ban had been put on the planet and the space patrol sent out to quarantine the place.

Mystery from the first, he thought . . . beginning and the end. First because the commission was seeking a hormone to effect controlled mutations in the human race. And the race would resent such a thing, of course, so it had to be a mystery.

The human race, West thought bitterly, resents anything that deviates from the norm. It used to stone the leper from the towns and it smothered its madmen in deep featherbeds and it stares at a crippled thing and its pity is a burning insult. And its fear . . . oh, yes, its fear!

Slowly, carefully, West made his way across the landing strip. The surface was smooth, so smooth that his space boots had little grip upon it.

On the rocky height above the field stood the laboratory, but West turned back and stared out into space, as if he might be taking final leave of someone that he knew.

Earth, he said. Earth, can you hear me now?

You need no longer fear me and you need not worry, for I shall not come back.

But the day will come when there are others like me. And there may be even now.

For you can't tell a mutant by the way he combs his hair, nor the way he walks or talks. He sprouts no horns and he grows no tail and there's no mark upon his forehead.

But when you spot one, you must watch him carefully. You must spy against him and set double-checks about him. And you must find a place to put him where you'll be safe from anything he does . . . but you must not let him know. You must try him and sentence him and send him into exile without his ever knowing it.

Like, said West, you tried to do with me.

But, said West, talking to the Earth, I didn't like your exile, so I chose one of my own. Because I knew, you see. I knew when you began to watch me and about the double-checks and the conferences and the plan of action and there were times when I could hardly keep from laughing in your face.

He stood for a long moment, staring into space, out where the Earth swam somewhere in darkness around the star-like Sun.

Bitter? he asked himself. And answered: No, not bitter. Not exactly bitter.

For you must understand, he said, still talking to the Earth, that a man is human first and mutant after that. He is not a monster simply because he is a mutant . . . he is just a little different. He is human in every way that you are human and it may be that he is human in more ways than you are. For the human race as it stands today is the history of long mutancy . . . of men who were a little different, who thought a little clearer, who felt a deeper compassion, who held an attribute that was more human than the rest of their fellow men. And they passed that clearer thinking and that deeper compassion on to sons and daughters and the sons and daughters passed it on to some—not all—but some of their sons and daughters. Thus the race grew up from savagery, thus the human concept grew.

Perhaps, he thought, my father was a mutant, a mutant that no one suspected. Or it may have been my mother. And neither of them would have been suspected. For my father was a farmer and if his mutancy had made the crops grow a little better through his better understanding of the soil or through a deeper feeling for the art of growing things, who would there be to know that he was a mutant? He would simply have been a better farmer than his neighbors. And if at night, when he read the well-worn books that stood on the shelf in the dining room, he understood those books and the things they meant to say better than most other men, who was there to know?

But I, he said, I was noticed. That is the crime of mutancy, to be noticed. Like the Spartan boy whose crime of stealing a fox was no crime at all, but whose cries when the fox ripped out his guts were a crime indeed.

I rose too fast, he thought. I cut through too much red tape. I understood too well. And in governmental office you cannot rise too fast nor cut red tape nor understand too well. You must be as mediocre as your fellow office-holders. You cannot point to a blueprint of a rocket motor and say, "There is the trouble," when men who are better trained than you cannot see the trouble. And you cannot devise a system of production that will turn out two rocket motors for the price of one in half the time. For that is not only being too efficient; it's downright blasphemy.

But most of all you cannot stand up in open meeting of government policy makers and point out that mutancy is no crime in itself . . . that it only is a crime when it is wrongly used. Nor say that the world would be better off if it used its mutants instead of being frightened of them.

Of course, if one knew one was a mutant, one would never say a thing like that. And a mutant, knowing himself a mutant, never would point out a thing that was wrong with a rocket engine. For a mutant has to keep his mouth shut, has to act the mediocre man and arrive at the ends he wishes by complex indirection.

If I had only known, thought West. If I had only known in time. I could have fooled them, as I hope many others even now are fooling them.

But now he knew it was too late, too late to turn back to the life that he had rejected, to go back and accept the dead-end trap that had been fashioned for him . . . a trap that would catch and hold him, where he would be safe. And where the human race would be safe from him.

West turned around and found the path that led up the rocky decline toward the laboratory.

A hulking figure stepped out of the shadows and challenged him. "Where do you think you're going?"

West halted. "Just got in," he said. "Looking for a friend of mine. By the name of Nevin."

Inside the pocket of his suit, he felt Annabelle stirring restlessly. Probably she was getting cold.

"Nevin?" asked the man, a note of alarm chilling his voice. "What do you want of Nevin?"

"He's got a painting," West declared.

The man's voice turned silky and dangerous. "How much do you know about Nevin and his painting?"

"Not much," said West. "That's why I'm here. Wanted to talk with him about it."

Annabelle turned a somersault inside West's zippered pocket. The man's eyes caught the movement.

"What you got in there?" he demanded, suspiciously.

"Annabelle," said West. "She's—well, she's something like a skinned rat, partly, with a face that's almost human, except it's practically all mouth."

"You don't say. Where did you get her?"

"Found her," West told him.

Laughter gurgled in the man's throat. "So you found her, eh? Can you imagine that?"

He reached out and took West by the arm.

"Maybe we'll have a lot to talk about," he said. "We'll have to compare our notes."

Together they moved up the hillside, the man's gloved hand clutching West by the arm.

"You're Langdon," West hazarded, as casually as he could speak.

The man chuckled. "Not Langdon. Langdon got lost."

"That's tough," commented West. "Bad place to get lost on . . . Pluto."

"Not Pluto," said the man. "Somewhere else."

"Maybe Darling, then . . ." and he held his breath to hear the answer.

"Darling left us," said the man. "I'm Cartwright. Burton Cartwright."

On the top of the tiny plateau in front of the laboratory, they stopped to catch their breath. The dim starlight painted the valley below with silver tracery.

West pointed. "That ship!"

Cartwright chuckled. "You recognize it, eh? The *Alpha Centauri.*"

"They're still working on the drive, back on Earth," said West. "Someday they'll get it."

"I have no doubt of it," said Cartwright.

He swung back toward the laboratory. "Let's go in. Dinner will be ready soon."

The table was set with white cloth and shining silver that gleamed in the light of the flickering dinner tapers. Sparkling wine glasses stood in their proper places. The centerpiece was a bowl of fruit—but fruit such as West had never seen before.

Cartwright tilted a chair and dumped a thing that had been sleeping there onto the floor.

"Your place, Mr. West," he said.

The thing uncoiled itself and glared at West with an eye of fishy hatred, purred with lusty venom and slithered out of sight.

Across the table Louis Nevin apologized. "The damn things keep sneaking through all the time. I suppose, Mr. West, you have trouble with them, too."

"We tried rat traps," said Cartwright, "but they were too smart for that. So we get along with them the best we can."

West laughed to cover momentary confusion, but he found Nevin's eyes upon him.

"Annabelle," he said, "is the only one that ever bothered me."

"You're lucky," Nevin told him. "They get to be pests. There is one of them that insists on sleeping with me."

"Where's Belden?" Cartwright asked.

"He ate early," explained Nevin. "Said there were a few things he wanted to get done. Asked to be excused."

He said to West, "James Belden. Perhaps you've heard of him."
West nodded.

He pulled back his chair, started to sit down, then jerked erect.

A woman had appeared in the doorway, a woman with violet eyes and platinum hair and wrapped in an ermine opera cloak. She moved forward and the light from the flaring tapers fell across her face. West stiffened at the sight, felt the blood run cold as ice within his veins.

For the face was not a woman's face. It was like a furry skull, like a moth's face that had attempted to turn human and had stuck halfway.

Down at the end of the table, Cartwright was chuckling.

"You recognize her, Mr. West?"

West clutched the back of his chair so hard that his knuckles suddenly were white.

"Of course I do," he said. "The White Singer. But how did you bring her here?"

"So that's what they call her back on Earth," said Nevin.

"But her face," insisted West. "What's happened to her face?"

"There were two of them," said Nevin. "One of them we sent to Earth. We had to fix her up a bit. Plastic surgery, you know."

"She sings," said Cartwright.

"Yes, I know," said West. "I've heard her sing. Or, at least the other one . . . the one you sent to Earth with the made-over face. She's driven practically everything else off the air. All the networks carry her."

Cartwright sighed. "I should like to hear her back on Earth," he said. "She would sing differently there, you know, than she sang here."

"They sing," interrupted Nevin, "only as they feel."

"Firelight on the wall," said Cartwright, "and she'd sing like firelight on the wall. Or the smell of lilacs in an April rain and her music would be like the perfume of lilacs and the mist of rain along the garden path."

"We don't have rain or lilacs here," said Nevin and he looked, for a moment, as if he were going to weep.

Crazy, thought West. Crazy as a pair of bedbugs. Crazy as the man who'd drunk himself to death out on Pluto's moon.

And yet, perhaps not so crazy.

"They have no mind," said Cartwright. "That is, no mind to speak of. Just a bundle of nervous reactions, probably without the type of sensory perceptions that we have, but more than likely with other totally different sensory perceptions to make up for it. Sensitive things. Music to them is an expression of sensory impressions. They can't help the way they sing any more than a moth can help killing himself against a candle-flame. And they're naturally telepathic. They pick up thoughts and pass them along. Retain none of the thought, you understand, just pass it along. Like old fashioned telephone wires. Thoughts that listeners, under the spell of music, would pick up and accept."

"And the beauty of it is," said Nevin, "is that if a listener ever became conscious of those thoughts afterward and wondered about them, he would be convinced that they were his own, that he had had them all the time."

"Clever, eh?" asked Cartwright.

West let out his breath. "Clever, yes. I didn't think you fellows had it in you."

West wanted to shiver and found he couldn't and the shiver built up and up until it seemed his tautened nerves would snap.

Cartwright was speaking. "So our Stella is doing all right."

"What's that?" asked West.

"Stella. The other one of them. The one with the face."

"Oh, I see," said West. "I didn't know her name was Stella. No one, in fact, knows anything about her. She suddenly appeared one night as a surprise feature on one of the networks. She was announced as a mystery singer, and then people began calling her the White Singer. She always sang in dim, blue light, you see, and no one ever saw her face too plainly, although everyone imagined, of course, that it was beautiful.

"The network made no bones about her being an alien being. She was represented as a member of a mystery race that Juston Lloyd had found in the Asteroids. You remember Lloyd, the New York press agent."

Nevin was leaning across the table. "And the people, the government, it does not suspect?"

West shook his head. "Why should it? Your Stella is a wonder. Everyone is batty over her. The newspapers went wild. The movie people –"

"And the cults?"

"The cults," said West, "are doing fine."

"And you?" asked Cartwright, and in the man's rumbling voice West felt the challenge.

"I found out," he said. "I came here to get cut in."

"You know exactly what you are asking?"

"I do," said West, wishing that he did.

"A new philosophy," said Cartwright. "A new concept of life. New paths for progress. Secrets the human race never has suspected. Remaking the human civilization almost overnight."

"And you," said West, "right at the center, pulling all the strings."

"So," said Cartwright.

"I want a few to pull myself."

Nevin held up his hand. "Just a minute, Mr. West. We would like to know just how—"

Cartwright laughed at him. "Forget it, Louis. He knew about your painting. He had Annabelle. Where do you suppose he found out?"

"But—but—" said Nevin.

"Maybe he didn't use a painting," Cartwright declared. "Maybe he used other methods. After all, there are others, you know. Thousands of years ago men knew of the place we found. Mu, probably. Atlantis. Some other forgotten civilization. Just the fact that West had Annabelle is enough for me. He must have been there."

West smiled, relieved. "I used other methods," he told them.

CHAPTER THREE
The Painting

A robot came in, wheeling a tray with steaming dishes.

"Let's sit down," suggested Nevin.

"Just one thing," asked West. "How did you get Stella back to Earth? None of you could have taken her. You'd have been recognized."

Cartwright chuckled. "Robertson," he said. "We had one ship and he slipped out. As to the recognition, Belden is our physician. He also, if you remember, is a plastic surgeon of no mean ability."

"He did the job," said Nevin, "for both Robertson and Stella."

"Nearly skinned us alive," grumbled Cartwright, "to get enough to do the work. I'll always think that he took more than he really needed, just for spite. He's a moody beggar."

Nevin changed the subject. "Shall we have Rosie sit with us?"

"Rosie?" asked West.

"Rosie is Stella's sister. We don't know the exact relationship, but we call her that for convenience."

"There are times," explained Cartwright, "when we forget her face and let her sit at the table's head, as if she were one of us. As if she were our hostess. She looks remarkably like a woman, you know. Those wings of hers are like an ermine cape, and that platinum hair. She lends something to the table . . . a sort of—"

"An illusion of gentility," said Nevin.

"Perhaps we'd better not tonight," decided Cartwright. "Mr. West is not used to her. After he's been here awhile—"

He stopped and looked aghast.

"We've forgotten something," he announced.

He rose and strode around the table to the imitation fireplace and took down a bottle that stood on the mantelpiece—a bottle with a black silk bow tied around its neck. Ceremoniously, he set it in the center of the table, beside the bowl of fruit.

"It's a little joke we have," said Nevin.

"Scarcely a joke," contradicted Cartwright.

West looked puzzled. "A bottle of whisky?"

"But a special bottle," Cartwright said. "A very special bottle. Back in the old days we formed a last man's club, jokingly. This bottle was to be the one the last man would drink. It made us feel so adventuresome and brave and we laughed about it while we labored to find hormones. For, you see, none of us thought it would ever come to pass."

"But now," said Nevin, "there are only three of us."

"You are wrong," Cartwright reminded him. "There are four."

Both of them looked at West.

"Of course," decided Nevin. "There are four of us."

Cartwright spread the napkin in his lap. "Perhaps, Louis, we might as well let Mr. West see the painting."

Nevin hesitated. "I'm not quite satisfied, Cartwright . . ."

Cartwright clucked his tongue. "You're too suspicious, Louis. He had the creature, didn't he? He knew about your painting. There was only one way that he could have learned."

Nevin considered. "I suppose you're right," he said.

"And if Mr. West should, by any chance, turn out to be an impostor," said Cartwright, cheerfully, "we can always take the proper steps."

Nevin said to West: "I hope you understand."

"Perfectly," said West.

"We must be very careful," Nevin pointed out. "So few would understand."

"So very few," said West.

Nevin stepped across the room and pulled a cord that hung along the wall. One of the tapestries rolled smoothly back, fold on heavy fold. West, watching, held his breath at what he saw.

A tree stood in the foreground, laden with golden fruit, fruit that looked exactly like some of that in the bowl upon the table. As if someone had just stepped into the painting and picked it fresh for dinner.

Under the tree ran a path, coming up to the very edge of the canvas in such detail that even the tiny pebbles strewn upon it were clear to the eye. And from the tree the path ran back against a sweep of background, climbing into wooded hills.

For the flicker of a passing second, West could have sworn that he heard the whisper of wind in the leaves of the fruit-laden tree, that he saw the leaves tremble in the wind, that he smelled the fragrance of little flowers that bloomed along the path.

"Well, Mr. West?" Nevin asked, triumphantly.

"Why," said West, ears still cocked for the sound of wind in leaves again. "Why, it almost seems as if one could step over and walk straight down that path."

Nevin sucked in his breath with a sound that was neither gasp nor sigh, but somewhere in between. Down at the end of the table, Cartwright was choking on his wine, chuckling laughter bubbling out between his lips despite all his efforts to keep it bottled up.

"Nevin," asked West, "have you ever thought of making another painting?"

"Perhaps," said Nevin. "Why do you ask?"

West smiled. Through his brain words were drumming, words that he remembered, words a man had whispered just before he died.

"I was just thinking," said West, "of what might happen if you should paint the wrong place sometime."

"By Lord," yelled Cartwright, "he's got you there, Nevin. The exact words I've been telling you."

Nevin started to rise from the table, and even as he did the rustling whisper of music filled the room. Music that relaxed Nevin's hands from their grip upon the table's edge, music that swept the sudden chill from between West's shoulderblades.

Music that told of keen-toothed space and the blaze of stars. Music that had the whisper of rockets and the quietness of the void and the somber arches of eternal night.

Rosie was singing.

West sat on the edge of his bed and knew that he had been lucky to break away before there could be more questions asked. So far, he was certain, he'd answered those they asked without arousing too much suspicion, but the longer a thing like that went on the more likely a man was to make some slight mistake.

Now he would have time to think, time to try to untangle and put together some of the facts as they now appeared.

One of the minor monstrosities that infested the place climbed the bedpost and perched upon it, wrapping its long tail about it many times. It chittered at West and West looked at it and shuddered, wondering if it were making a face at him or if it really looked that way.

These slithery, chittering things . . . he'd heard of them somewhere before. He knew that. He'd even seen pictures of them at some time. Some other time and place, very long ago. Things like Annabelle and the creature Cartwright had dumped off the chair and the little satanic being that perched upon the bedstead.

That was funny, the thing Nevin had said about them . . . *they keep sneaking through* . . . not sneaking in, but through.

Nothing added up. Not even Nevin and Cartwright. For there was about them some subtle tinge of character not human in its texture.

They had been working with hormones when something had happened that occasioned the warning sent to Earth. Or had there been a warning? Had the warning been a fake? Was there something going on here the Solar government didn't want anyone to know?

Why had they sent Stella to Earth? Why were they so pleased that she was so well received? What was it Nevin had asked . . . *and the government, it does not suspect?* Why should the government suspect? What was there for it to suspect? Just a mindless creature that sang like the bells of heaven.

That hormone business, now. Hormones did funny things to people.

I should know, said West, talking to himself.

A little faster and a little quicker. A mental shortcut here and there. And you scarcely know, yourself, that you are any different. That's how the race develops. A mutation here and another there and in a thousand years or two a certain percentage of the race is not what the race had been a thousand years before.

Maybe it was a mutation back in the Old Stone Age who struck two flints together and made himself a fire. Maybe another mutant who dreamed up a wheel and took a stoneboat and changed it to a wagon.

Slowly, he said, it would have to be slowly. Just a little at a time.

For if it were too much, if it were noticeable, the other humans would kill off each mutation as it became apparent. For the human race cannot tolerate divergence from the norm, even though mutation is the process by which the race develops.

The race doesn't kill the mutants any more. It confines them to mental institutions or it forces them into such dead-ends of expression as art or music, or it finds nice friendly exiles for them, where they will be comfortable and have a job to do and where, the normal humans hope, they'll never know what they are.

It's harder to be different now, he thought, harder to be a mutant and escape detection, what with the medical boards and the psychiatrists and all the other scientific mumbo-jumbo the humans have set up to guard their peace of mind.

Five hundred years ago, thought West, they would not have found me out. Five hundred years ago I might not have realized the fact myself.

Controlled mutation? Now that was something different. That was the thing the government had in mind when it sent the commission here to Pluto, taking advantage of the cold conditions to develop hormones that might mutate the race. Hormones that might make a better race, that might develop latent talents or even add entirely new characteristics calculated to bring out the best that was in humanity.

Controlled mutations, those were all right. It was only the wild mutations that the government would fear.

What if the members of the commission had developed a hormone and tried it on themselves?

His thought stopped short, pleased with the idea, with the possible solution.

Upon the bedpost the little monstrosity fingered its mouth, slobbering gleefully.

A knock came on the door.

"Come in," called West.

The door opened and a man came in.

"I'm Belden," said the man. "Jim Belden. They told me you were here."

"I'm glad to know you, Belden."

"What's the game?" asked Belden.

"No game," said West.

"You got those two downstairs sold on you," Belden said. "They think you're another great mind that has discovered the outside."

"So they do," said West. "I'm very glad to know it."

"They pointed out Annabelle to me," said Belden. "Said that was proof you were one of us. But I recognized Annabelle. They didn't, but I did. She's the one that Darling took along. You got her from Darling."

West stayed silent. There was no use in playing innocent with Belden, for Belden had guessed too close to the truth.

Belden lowered his voice. "You have the same hunch as I have. You figure Darling's hormone is worth more than all this mummery going on downstairs. And you're here to find it. I told Nevin that Darling's hormone was the thing for us to find instead of messing around outside, but he didn't think so. After we took Darling to the moon, Nevin smashed the ship's controls. He was afraid I might get away, you see. He didn't trust me and he couldn't afford to let me get away."

"I'll trade with you," West told him quietly.

"We'll go to the moon in your ship and see Darling," said Belden. "We'll beat it out of him."

West grinned wryly. "Darling's dead," he said.

"Did you search the hut?" asked Belden.

"Of course not. Why should I have searched it?"

"It's there, then," said Belden, grimly. "Hidden in the hut somewhere. I've turned this place upside down and I'm sure it isn't here. Neither the formula nor the hormones themselves. Not unless Darling was trickier than I thought he was."

"You know what this hormone is," said West smoothly, trying to make it sound as if he himself might know it.

"No," said Belden shortly. "Darling didn't trust us. He was angry at what Nevin was trying to do. And once he made a crack that the man who had it could rule the Solar System. Darling wasn't kidding, West. He knew more about hormones than all the rest of us put together."

"Seems to me," West said drily, "that you would have wanted to keep a man like that here. You certainly could have used him."

"Nevin again," Belden told him. "Darling wouldn't go along with the program that Nevin planned. Even threatened to expose him if he ever had the chance. Nevin wanted to kill him, but Cartwright thought up a joke . . . he's jovial, Cartwright is."

"I've noticed that," said West.

"Cartwright thought up the exile business," Belden said. "Offered Darling any one thing he wished to take along. One thing, you understand. Just one thing. That's where the joke came in. Cartwright expected Darling to go through agonies trying to make up his mind. But there wasn't a moment's hesitation. Darling took the whisky."

"He drank himself to death," said West.

"Darling wasn't a drinking man," Belden told him, sharply.

"It was suicide," said West. "Darling took you fellows down the line, neatly, all the way. He was away ahead of you."

A soft sound like the brushing of a bird's wing swung West around.

Rosie was coming through the door, her wings half-raised, exposing the hideousness of the furry, splotched body beneath the furry, death's-head face.

"No!" screamed Belden. "No! I wasn't going to do anything. I wasn't—"

He backed away, arms outthrust to ward off the thing that walked toward him, mouth still working, but no sound coming out.

Rosie brushed West to one side with a flip of a furry wing and then the wings spread wider and shielded Belden from West's view. The wings clapped shut and from behind them came the muffled scream of the man. Then nothing; silence.

West's hand dropped to the holster and his gun came sliding out. His thumb slammed down the activator and the gun purred like a well-contented cat.

The ermine of Rosie's wings turned black and she crumpled to the floor. A sickening odor filled the room.

"Belden!" cried West. He leaped forward, kicked the charred Rosie to one side. Belden lay on the floor and West turned away retching.

For a moment West stood in indecision, then swiftly he knew what he must do.

Showdown. He had hoped that it could be put off a little longer, until he knew a little more, but the incident of Belden and Rosie had settled it. There was nothing else to do.

He strode through the door and down the winding staircase toward the darkened room below.

The painting, he saw, was lighted . . . lighted as if from within itself. As if the source of light lay within the painting, as if some other sun shone upon the landscape that lay upon the canvas. The picture was lighted, but the rest of the room was dark and the light did not come out of the painting, but stayed there, imprisoned in the canvas.

Something scuttled between West's feet and scuttered down the stairs. It squeaked and its claws beat a tattoo on the steps.

As West reached the bottom of the stairway a voice came out of the darkness.

"Are you looking for something, Mr. West?"

"Yes, Cartwright," said West. "I am looking for you."

"You must not be too concerned with what Rosie did," Cartwright said. "Don't let it upset you. Belden had it coming to him for a long time. He was scarcely one of us, really, never one of us. He pretended to go along with us because it was the only way that he could save his life. And life is such a small thing to consider. Don't you think so, Mr. West?"

CHAPTER FOUR
The Last Man

West stood silently at the bottom of the stairs. The room was too dark to see anything, but the voice was coming from somewhere near the table's end, close to the lighted painting.

I may have to kill him, West was thinking, and I must know where he is. For the first shot has to do it, there'll be no time for a second.

"Rosie had no mind," the voice said out in the darkness. "That is, no mind to speak of. But she was telepathic. Her brain picked up thoughts and passed them on. And she could obey simple commands. Very simple commands. And killing a man is so simple, Mr. West."

"Rosie stood here beside me and I knew every word that you and Belden said. I did not blame you, West, for you had no way of knowing what you did. But I did blame Belden and I sent Rosie up to get him.

"There's only one thing, West, that I hold against you. You should not have killed Rosie. That was a great mistake, West, a very great mistake."

"It was no mistake," said West. "I did it on purpose."

"Take it easy, Mr. West," said Cartwright. "Don't do anything that might make me pull the trigger. Because I have a gun on you. Dead center on you, West, and I never miss."

"I'll give you odds," said West, "that I can get you before you can pull the trigger."

"Now, Mr. West," said Cartwright, "let's not get hot-headed about this. Sure, you pulled a fast one on us. You tried to muscle in and you almost sold us, although eventually we would have tripped you up. And I admire your guts. Maybe we can work it out so no one will get killed."

"Start talking," West told him.

"It was too bad about Rosie," said Cartwright, "and I really hold that against you, West, for we could have used Rosie to good advantage. But after all, the work is started on the other planets and we still have Stella. Our students are well grounded. . . . they can get along without instructions for a little while and maybe by the time we need to get in contact with them again we can find another one to replace our Rosie."

"Quit wandering around," said West. "Let's hear what you have in mind."

"Well," said Cartwright, "we're getting awfully short-handed. Belden's dead and Darling's dead and if Robertson isn't dead by now he will be very shortly. For after he took Stella to Earth, he tried to desert, tried to run away. And that would never do, of course. He might tell folks about us and we can't let anyone do that. For we are dead, you see. . . ."

He chuckled, the chuckle rolling through the darkness.

"It was a masterpiece, West, that broadcast. I was the last man alive and I told them what had happened. I told them the spacetime continuum had ruptured and things were coming through. And I gurgled. . . . I gurgled just before I died."

"You didn't really die, of course," West said, innocently.

"Hell, no. But they think I did. And they still wake up screaming, thinking how I must have died."

Ham, thought West. Pure, unadulterated ham. A jokester who would maroon a man to die on a lonely moon. A man who held a gun in his fist while he bragged about the things he'd done . . . about how he had outwitted Earth.

"You see," said Cartwright, "I had to make them believe that it really happened. I had to make it so horrible that the government would never make it public, so horrible they'd close the planet with an iron-tight ban."

"You had to be alone," said West.

"That's right, West. We had to be alone."

"Well," said West. "You've almost got it now. There's only two of you alive."

"The two of us," Cartwright said, "and you."

"You forget, Cartwright," said West. "You're going to kill me. You've got a gun pointed at me and you're all set to pull the trigger."

"Not necessarily," said Cartwright. "We might make a deal."

I've got him now, thought West. I know exactly where he is. I can't see him, but I know where he is. And the pay-off is in a minute. It'll be one of us or the other.

"You aren't much use to us," said Cartwright, "but we might need you later. You remember Langdon?"

"The one that got lost," said West.

Cartwright chuckled. "That's it, West. But he wasn't lost. We gave him away. You see there was a—a—well, something, that could use him for a pet and so we made it a present of Langdon."

He chuckled again. "Langdon didn't like the idea too well, but what were we to do?"

"Cartwright," West said, evenly, "I'm going for my gun."

"What's that—" said Cartwright, but the other words were blotted out by the hissing of his gun, firing even as he talked.

The beam hissed into the wall at the foot of the staircase, a spot that had been covered only a split second before by West's head.

But West had dropped to a crouch almost as he spoke and now his own gun was in his fist, tilting up, solid in his hand. His thumb pressed the activator and then slid off.

Something dragged itself with heavy thumps across the floor and in the stillness between the bumps, West heard the rasp of heavy breaths.

"Damn you, West," said Cartwright. "Damn you . . ."

"It's an old trick, Cartwright," said West, "that business of talking to a man just before you kill him. Throwing him off guard, practically ambushing him."

Came a sound of cloth dragging over cloth, the whistling of painful breath, the thump of knees and elbows on the floor.

Then there was silence.

And a moment later something in some far corner squeaked and ran on pattering, rat-sounding feet. Then the silence again.

The rat-feet were still, but there was another sound, a faint shout as if someone far away were shouting . . . from somewhere outside the building, from somewhere outside . . . from outside.

West crouched close against the floor, huddling there, the muzzle of the gun resting on the carpet.

Outside . . . outside . . . outside . . .

The words hammered in his head.

Outside of what, he asked, but he knew the answer now. He knew where he had seen the picture of the thing that had slept in the chair and the other thing that squatted on the bedpost. And he knew the sound of chirping and of chittering and of running feet.

Outside . . . outside . . . outside . . .

Outside this world, of course.

He raised his head and looked at the painting, and the tree still glowed softly with its inner light, and from within it came a sound, a faint thudding sound, the sound of running feet.

The shout came again and the man was running down the path inside the painting. A man who ran and waved his arms and shouted.

The man was Nevin.

Nevin was in the painting, running down the path, his padding feet raising little puffs of dust along the pebbled path.

West raised the pistol and his hand was trembling so that the muzzle weaved back and forth and then described a circle.

"Buck fever," said West.

He said it through chattering teeth.

For now he knew . . . now he knew the answer.

He put up his other hand and grasped the wrist of the hand that held the gun, and the muzzle steadied. West gritted his teeth together to stop their chattering.

His thumb went down against the activator and held it there and the flame from the gun's muzzle spat out and mushroomed upon the painting. Mushroomed until the entire canvas was a maelstrom of blue brilliance that hissed and roared and licked with hungry tongues.

Slowly the tree ran together, as if one's eyes might have blurred and gone slightly out of focus. The landscape dimmed and jigged and ran in little wavering lines. And through the wavering lines could be seen a twisted and distorted man whose mouth seemed open in a howl of rage. But there was no sound of howling, just the purring of the gun.

With a tired little puff the mushrooming brilliance and the painting were gone and the gun's pencil of flame was hissing through an empty steel frame still filled with tiny glowing wires, spattering against the wall behind it.

West lifted his thumb and silence clamped down upon him, clamped down and held the room . . . as it held leagues of space stretching on all sides.

"No painting," said West.

An echo seemed to run all around the room.

"No painting," the echo said, but West knew it was no echo, just his brain clicking off endlessly the words his lips had said.

"No painting," the echo said, but West knew it had been a machine that led to some other world, some other place, some *otherwhere*. A machine that broke down the spacetime continuum or whatever it was that separated Man's universe from other, stranger universes.

No wonder the fruit upon the tree had looked like the fruit upon the table. No wonder he had thought that he heard the wind in the leaves.

West stood up and moved to the wall behind him. He found a tumbler and thumbed it up and the lights came on.

In the light the smashed other-world machine was a sagging piece of wreckage. Cartwright's body lay in the center of the room. A chittering thing ran across the floor and ducked into the dark beneath a table. A grinning face peeped out from behind a chair and squalled at West in cold-boned savagery.

And it was nothing new, for he had seen those faces before. Pictures of them in old books and in magazines that published tales of soul-shaking horror, tales of things that come from beyond, of entities that broke in from outside.

Just tales to send one shivering to bed. Just stories that should not be read at midnight. Stories that made one a little nervous when a tree squeaked in the wind outside the window or the rain walked along the shingles.

It had taken the wizardry of the Solar System's best band of scientists to open the door that led into the world beyond.

And yet people in unknown, savage ages had talked of things like these . . . of goblin and incubus and imp. Perhaps men in Atlantis might have found the way, even as Nevin and Cartwright had found the way. In that long-gone day letting loose upon the world a flood of things that for ages after had lived in chimney-corner stories to chill one to the marrow.

And the pictures he had seen?

Ancestral memory, perhaps. Or a weird imaging that happened to be true. Or had the writers of those stories, the painters of those pictures . . .

West shuddered from the thought.

What was it Cartwright had said? *The work is started on the other planets.*

The work of passing along the knowledge, the principles, the psychology of the alien things of *otherwhere*. Education by remote control . . . involuntary education. Stella, the telepathic Stella, singing back on Earth, darling of the airways. And she was an agent for these things . . . she passed along the knowledge and a man would think it was his own.

That was it, of course, the thing that Nevin and Cartwright had planned. Remake the world, they'd said. Sitting out on Pluto and pulling strings that would remake the world.

Superstitions once. Hard facts now. Stories once to make the blood run cold. And now—

With the source dried up, with the screen empty, with the Pluto gang wiped out, the cults would die and Stella would sing on, but there would come a time when the listeners would turn away from Stella, when her novelty wore off, when the strangeness and the alienness of her had lost their appeal.

The Solar System would go on thinking imp and incubus were no more than shuddery imagery from the days when men crouched in caves and saw a supernatural threat in every moving shadow.

But it had been a narrow squeak.

From a dark corner a thing mouthed at West in a shrill singsong of hate.

So this was it, thought West.

Here he was, at the end of the Solar System's trail, in an empty house. And it was, finally, as he had hoped it would be. No one around. A storehouse full of food. Adequate shelter. A shop where he could work. A place guarded by the patrol against unwelcome callers.

Just the place for a man who might be hiding. Just the place for a fugitive from the human race.

There were things to do . . . later on. Two bodies to be given burial. A screen to be cleaned up and thrown on a junk heap. A few chittering things to be hunted down and killed.

Then he could settle down.

There were robots, of course. One had brought in the dinner.

Later on, he said.

But there was something else to do . . . something to do immediately, if he could just remember.

He stood and looked around the room, cataloguing its contents.

Chairs, drapes, a desk, the table, the imitation fireplace . . .

That was it, the fireplace.

He walked across the room to stand in front of it. Reaching up, he took down the bottle from the mantel, the bottle with the black silk bow tied around its neck. The bottle for the last man's club.

And he was the last man, there was no doubt of it. The very last of all.

He had not been in the pact, of course, but he would carry out the pact. It was melodrama, undoubtedly, but there are times, he told himself, when a little melodrama may be excusable.

He uncorked the bottle and swung around to face the room. He raised the bottle in salute—salute to the gaping, blackened frame that had held the painting, to the dead man on the floor, to the thing that mewed in a far, dark corner.

He tried to think of a word to say, but couldn't. And there had to be a word to say, there simply had to be.

"Mud in your eye," he said, and it wasn't any good, but it would have to do.

He put the bottle to his lips and tipped it up and tilted back his head.

Gagging, he snatched the bottle from his lips.

It wasn't whisky and it was awful. It was gall and vinegar and quinine, all rolled into one. It was a brew straight from the Pit. It was all the bad medicine he had taken as a boy, it was sulphur and molasses, it was castor oil, it was—

"Good God," said Frederick West.

For suddenly he remembered the location of a knife he had lost twenty years before. He saw it where he had left it, just as plain as day.

He knew an equation he'd never known before, and what was more, he knew what it was for and how it could be used.

Unbidden, he visualized, in one comprehensive picture, just how a rocket motor worked . . . every detail, every piece, every control, like a chart laid out before his eyes.

He could capture and hold seven fence posts in his mental eye and four was the best any human ever had been able to see *mentally* before.

He whooshed out his breath to air his mouth and stared at the bottle.

Suddenly he was able to recite, word for word, the first page from a book he had read ten years ago.

"The hormones," he whispered. "Darling's hormones!"

Hormones that did something to his brain. Speeded it up, made it work better, made more of it work than had ever worked before. Made it think cleaner and clearer than it had ever thought before.

"Good Lord," he said.

A head start to begin with. And now this!

The man who has it could rule the Solar System. That was what Belden had said about it.

Belden had hunted for it. Had torn this place apart. And Darling had hunted for it, too. Darling, who had thought he had it, who had played a trick on Nevin and Cartwright so he could be sure he had it, who had drank himself to death trying to find the bottle he had it in.

And all these years the hormones had been in this bottle on the mantel!

Someone else had played a trick on all of them. Langdon, maybe. Langdon, who had been given away as a pet to a thing so monstrous that even Cartwright had shrunk from naming it.

With shaking hand, West put the bottle back on the mantel, placed the cork beside it. For a moment he stood there, hands against the mantel, gripping it, staring out the vision port beside the fireplace. Staring down into the valley where a shadowy cylinder tilted upward from the rocky planet, as if striving for the stars.

The *Alpha Centauri*—the ship with the space drive that wouldn't work. Something wrong . . . something wrong. . . .

A sob rose in West's throat and his hands tightened on the mantel with a grip that hurt.

He knew what was wrong!

He had studied blueprints of the drive back on Earth.

And now it was as if the blueprints were before his eyes again, for he remembered them, each line, each symbol, as if they were etched upon his brain.

He saw the trouble, the simple adjustment that would make the space drive work. Ten minutes . . . ten minutes would be all he needed. So simple. So simple. So simple that it seemed beyond belief it had not been found before, that all the great minds which had worked upon it should not have seen it long ago.

There had been a dream—a thing that he had not even dared to say aloud, not even to himself. A thing he had not dared even to think about.

West straightened from the mantel and faced the room again. He took the bottle and for a second time raised it in salute.

But this time he had a toast for the dead men and the thing that whimpered in the corner.

"To the stars," he said.

And he drank without gagging.

ALL THE TRAPS OF EARTH

To my mind, this is one of the best Simak stories of any length, and I find it difficult to believe that it was rejected by both Horace Gold and John W. Campbell Jr. before Robert Mills finally took it for publication in the March 1960 issue of the Magazine of Fantasy and Science Fiction. *I don't think that any other story, by any other author, has done a better job of portraying the humanization of, and the humanity of, a robot.*

—*dww*

The inventory list was long. On its many pages, in his small and precise script, he had listed furniture, paintings, china, silverware and all the rest of it—all the personal belongings that had been accumulated by the Barringtons through a long family history.

And now that he had reached the end of it, he noted down himself, the last item of them all:

One domestic robot, Richard Daniel, antiquated but in good repair.

He laid the pen aside and shuffled all the inventory sheets together and stacked them in good order, putting a paper weight upon them—the little exquisitely carved ivory paper weight that Aunt Hortense had picked up that last visit she had made to Peking.

And having done that, his job came to an end.

He shoved back the chair and rose from the desk and slowly walked across the living room, with all its clutter of possessions from the family's past. There, above the mantel, hung the sword that ancient Jonathon had worn in the War Between the States, and below it, on the mantelpiece itself, the cup the Commodore had won with his valiant yacht, and the jar of moon-dust that Tony had brought back from Man's fifth landing on the Moon, and the old chronometer that had come from the long-scrapped family space-craft that had plied the asteroids. And all around the room, almost cheek by jowl, hung the family portraits, with the old dead faces staring out into the world that they had helped to fashion.

And not one of them from the last six hundred years, thought Richard Daniel, staring at them one by one, that he had not known.

There, to the right of the fireplace, old Rufus Andrew Barrington, who had been a judge some two hundred years ago. And to the right of Rufus, Johnson Joseph Barrington, who had headed up that old lost dream of mankind, the Bureau of Paranormal Research. There, beyond the door that led out to the porch, was the scowling pirate face of Danley Barrington, who had first built the family fortune.

And many others—administrator, adventurer, corporation chief. All good men and true.

But this was at an end. The family had run out.

Slowly Richard Daniel began his last tour of the house—the family room with its cluttered living space, the den with its old mementos, the library and its rows of ancient books, the dining hall in which the crystal and the china shone and sparkled, the kitchen gleaming with the copper and aluminum and the stainless steel, and the bedrooms on the second floor, each of them with its landmarks of former occupants. And finally, the bedroom where old Aunt Hortense had finally died, at long last closing out the line of Barringtons.

The empty dwelling held a not-quite-haunted quality, the aura of a house that waited for the old gay life to take up once again. But it was a false aura. All the portraits, all the china and the silverware, everything within the house would be sold at public auction to satisfy the debts. The rooms would be stripped and the possessions would be scattered and, as a last indignity, the house itself be sold.

Even he, himself, Richard Daniel thought, for he was chattel, too. He was there with all the rest of it, the final item on the inventory.

Except that what they planned to do with him was worse than simple sale. For he would be changed before he was offered up for sale. No one would be interested in putting up good money for him as he stood. And, besides, there was the law—the law that said no robot could legally have continuation of a single life greater than a hundred years. And he had lived in a single life six times a hundred years.

He had gone to see a lawyer and the lawyer had been sympathetic, but had held forth no hope.

"Technically," he had told Richard Daniel in his short, clipped lawyer voice, "you are at this moment much in violation of the statute. I completely fail to see how your family got away with it."

"They liked old things," said Richard Daniel. "And, besides, I was very seldom seen. I stayed mostly in the house. I seldom ventured out."

"Even so," the lawyer said, "there are such things as records. There must be a file on you . . ."

"The family," explained Richard Daniel, "in the past had many influential friends. You must understand, sir, that the Barringtons, before they fell upon hard times, were quite prominent in politics and in many other matters."

The lawyer grunted knowingly.

"What I can't quite understand," he said, "is why you should object so bitterly. You'll not be changed entirely. You'll still be Richard Daniel."

"I would lose my memories, would I not?"

"Yes, of course you would. But memories are not too important. And you'd collect another set."

"My memories are dear to me," Richard Daniel told him. "They are all I have. After some six hundred years, they are my sole worthwhile possession. Can you imagine, counselor, what it means to spend six centuries with one family?"

"Yes, I think I can," agreed the lawyer. "But now, with the family gone, isn't it just possible the memories may prove painful?"

"They're a comfort. A sustaining comfort. They make me feel important. They give me perspective and a niche."

"But don't you understand? You'll need no comfort, no importance once you're reoriented. You'll be brand new. All that you'll retain is a certain sense of basic identity—*that* they cannot take away from you even if they wished. There'll be nothing to regret. There'll be no leftover guilts, no frustrated aspirations, no old loyalties to hound you."

"I must be myself," Richard Daniel insisted stubbornly. "I've found a depth of living, a background against which my living has some meaning. I could not face being anybody else."

"You'd be far better off," the lawyer said wearily. "You'd have a better body. You'd have better mental tools. You'd be more intelligent."

Richard Daniel got up from the chair. He saw it was no use.

"You'll not inform on me?" he asked.

"Certainly not," the lawyer said. "So far as I'm concerned, you aren't even here."

"Thank you," said Richard Daniel. "How much do I owe you?"

"Not a thing," the lawyer told him. "I never make a charge to anyone who is older than five hundred."

He had meant it as a joke, but Richard Daniel did not smile. He had not felt like smiling.

At the door he turned around.

"Why?" he was going to ask. "Why this silly law."

But he did not have to ask—it was not hard to see.

Human vanity, he knew. No human being lived much longer than a hundred years, so neither could a robot. But a robot, on the other hand, was too valuable simply to be junked at the end of a hundred years of service, so there was this law providing for the periodic breakup of the continuity of each robot's life. And thus no human need undergo the psychological indignity of knowing that his faithful serving man might manage to outlive him by several thousand years.

It was illogical, but humans were illogical.

Illogical, but kind. Kind in many different ways.

Kind, sometimes, as the Barringtons had been kind, thought Richard Daniel. Six hundred years of kindness. It was a prideful thing to think about. They had even given him a double name. There weren't many robots nowadays who had double names. It was a special mark of affection and respect.

The lawyer having failed him, Richard Daniel had sought another source of help. Now, thinking back on it, standing in the room where Hortense Barrington had died, he was sorry that he'd done it. For he had embarrassed the religico almost unendurably. It had been easy for the lawyer to tell him what he had. Lawyers had the statutes to determine their behavior, and thus suffered little from agonies of personal decision.

But a man of the cloth is kind if he is worth his salt. And this one had been kind instinctively as well as professionally, and that had made it worse.

"Under certain circumstances," he had said somewhat awkwardly, "I could counsel patience and humility and prayer. Those are three great aids to anyone who is willing to put them to his use. But with you I am not certain."

"You mean," said Richard Daniel, "because I am a robot."

"Well, now . . ." said the minister, considerably befuddled at this direct approach.

"Because I have no soul?"

"Really," said the minister miserably, "you place me at a disadvantage. You are asking me a question that for centuries has puzzled and bedeviled the best minds in the church."

"But one," said Richard Daniel, "that each man in his secret heart must answer for himself."

"I wish I could," cried the distraught minister. "I truly wish I could."

"If it is any help," said Richard Daniel, "I can tell you that sometimes I suspect I have a soul."

And that, he could see, had been most upsetting for this kindly human. It had been, Richard Daniel told himself, unkind of him to say it. For it must have been confusing, since coming from himself it was not opinion only, but expert evidence.

So he had gone away from the minister's study and come back to the empty house to get on with his inventory work.

Now that the inventory was all finished and the papers stacked where Dancourt, the estate administrator, could find them when he showed up in the morning, Richard Daniel had done his final service for the Barringtons and now must begin doing for himself.

He left the bedroom and closed the door behind him and went quietly down the stairs and along the hallway to the little cubby, back of the kitchen, that was his very own.

And that, he reminded himself with a rush of pride, was of a piece with his double name and his six hundred years. There were not too many robots who had a room, however small, that they might call their own.

He went into the cubby and turned on the light and closed the door behind him.

And now, for the first time, he faced the grim reality of what he meant to do.

The cloak and hat and trousers hung upon a hook and the galoshes were placed precisely underneath them. His attachment kit lay in one corner of the cubby and the money was cached underneath the floor board he had loosened many years ago to provide a hiding place.

There was, he told himself, no point in waiting. Every minute counted. He had a long way to go and he must be at his destination before morning light.

He knelt on the floor and pried up the loosened board, shoved in a hand and brought out the stacks of bills, money hidden through the years against a day of need.

There were three stacks of bills, neatly held together by elastic bands—money given him throughout the years as tips and Christmas gifts, as birthday presents and rewards for little jobs well done.

He opened the storage compartment located in his chest and stowed away all the bills except for half a dozen which he stuffed into a pocket in one hip.

He took the trousers off the hook and it was an awkward business, for he'd never worn clothes before except when he'd tried on these very trousers several days before. It was a lucky thing, he thought, that long-dead Uncle Michael had been a portly man, for otherwise the trousers never would have fit.

He got them on and zippered and belted into place, then forced his feet into the overshoes. He was a little worried about the overshoes. No human went out in the summer wearing overshoes. But it was the best that he could do. None of the regular shoes he'd found in the house had been nearly large enough.

He hoped no one would notice, but there was no way out of it. Somehow or other, he had to cover up his feet, for if anyone should see them, they'd be a giveaway.

He put on the cloak and it was a little short. He put on the hat and it was slightly small, but he tugged it down until it gripped his metal skull and that was all to the good, he told himself; no wind could blow it off.

He picked up his attachments—a whole bag full of them that he'd almost never used. Maybe it was foolish to take them along, he thought, but they were a part of him and by rights they should go with him. There was so little that he really owned—just the money he had saved, a dollar at a time, and this kit of his.

With the bag of attachments clutched underneath his arm, he closed the cubby door and went down the hall.

At the big front door he hesitated and turned back toward the house, but it was, at the moment, a simple darkened cave, empty of all that it once had held. There was nothing here to stay for—nothing but the memories, and the memories he took with him.

He opened the door and stepped out on the stoop and closed the door behind him.

And now, he thought, with the door once shut behind him, he was on his own. He was running off. He was wearing clothes. He was out at night, without the permission of a master. And all of these were against the law.

Any officer could stop him, or any citizen. He had no rights at all. And he had no one who would speak for him, now that the Barringtons were gone.

He moved quietly down the walk and opened the gate and went slowly down the street, and it seemed to him the house was calling for him to come back. He wanted to go back, his mind said that he should go back, but his feet kept going on, steadily down the street.

He was alone, he thought, and the aloneness now was real, no longer the mere intellectual abstract he'd held in his mind for days. Here he was, a vacant hulk, that for the moment had no purpose and no beginning and no end, but was just an entity that stood naked in an endless reach of space and time and held no meaning in itself.

But he walked on and with each block that he covered he slowly fumbled back to the thing he was, the old robot in old clothes, the robot running from a home that was a home no longer.

He wrapped the cloak about him tightly and moved on down the street and now he hurried, for he had to hurry.

He met several people and they paid no attention to him. A few cars passed, but no one bothered him.

He came to a shopping center that was brightly lighted and

he stopped and looked in terror at the wide expanse of open, brilliant space that lay ahead of him. He could detour around it, but it would use up time and he stood there, undecided, trying to screw up his courage to walk into the light.

Finally he made up his mind and strode briskly out, with his cloak wrapped tight about him and his hat pulled low.

Some of the shoppers turned and looked at him and he felt agitated spiders running up and down his back. The galoshes suddenly seemed three times as big as they really were and they made a plopping, squashy sound that was most embarrassing.

He hurried on, with the end of the shopping area not more than a block away.

A police whistle shrilled and Richard Daniel jumped in sudden fright and ran. He ran in slobbering, mindless fright, with his cloak streaming out behind him and his feet slapping on the pavement.

He plunged out of the lighted strip into the welcome darkness of a residential section and he kept on running.

Far off he heard the siren and he leaped a hedge and tore across the yard. He thundered down the driveway and across a garden in the back and a dog came roaring out and engaged in noisy chase.

Richard Daniel crashed into a picket fence and went through it to the accompaniment of snapping noises as the pickets and the rails gave way. The dog kept on behind him and other dogs joined in.

He crossed another yard and gained the street and pounded down it. He dodged into a driveway, crossed another yard, upset a birdbath and ran into a clothesline, snapping it in his headlong rush.

Behind him lights were snapping on in the windows of the houses and screen doors were banging as people hurried out to see what the ruckus was.

He ran on a few more blocks, crossed another yard and ducked into a lilac thicket, stood still and listened. Some dogs were still baying in the distance and there was some human shouting, but there was no siren.

He felt a thankfulness well up in him that there was no siren, and a sheepishness, as well. For he had been panicked by himself, he knew; he had run from shadows, he had fled from guilt.

But he'd thoroughly roused the neighborhood and even now, he knew, calls must be going out and in a little while the place would be swarming with police.

He'd raised a hornet's nest and he needed distance, so he crept out of the lilac thicket and went swiftly down the street, heading for the edge of town.

He finally left the city and found the highway. He loped along its deserted stretches. When a car or truck appeared, he pulled off on the shoulder and walked along sedately. Then when the car or truck had passed, he broke into his lope again.

He saw the spaceport lights miles before he got there. When he reached the port, he circled off the road and came up outside a fence and stood there in the darkness, looking.

A gang of robots was loading one great starship and there were other ships standing darkly in their pits.

He studied the gang that was loading the ship, lugging the cargo from a warehouse and across the area lighted by the floods. This was just the setup he had planned on, although he had not hoped to find it immediately—he had been afraid that he might have to hide out for a day or two before he found a situation that he could put to use. And it was a good thing that he had stumbled on this opportunity, for an intensive hunt would be on by now for a fleeing robot, dressed in human clothes.

He stripped off the cloak and pulled off the trousers and the overshoes; he threw away the hat. From his attachments bag he took out the cutters, screwed off a hand and threaded the cutters into place. He cut the fence and wiggled through it, then replaced the hand and put the cutters back into the kit.

Moving cautiously in the darkness, he walked up to the warehouse, keeping in its shadow.

It would be simple, he told himself. All he had to do was

step out and grab a piece of cargo, clamber up the ramp and down into the hold. Once inside, it should not be difficult to find a hiding place and stay there until the ship had reached first planet-fall.

He moved to the corner of the warehouse and peered around it and there were the toiling robots, in what amounted to an endless chain, going up the ramp with the packages of cargo, coming down again to get another load.

But there were too many of them and the line too tight. And the area too well lighted. He'd never be able to break into that line.

And it would not help if he could, he realized despairingly—because he was different from those smooth and shining creatures. Compared to them, he was like a man in another century's dress; he and his six hundred-year-old body would stand out like a circus freak.

He stepped back into the shadow of the warehouse and he knew that he had lost. All his best-laid plans, thought out in sober, daring detail, as he had labored at the inventory, had suddenly come to naught.

It all came, he told himself, from never going out, from having no real contact with the world, from not keeping up with robot-body fashions, from not knowing what the score was. He'd imagined how it would be and he'd got it all worked out and when it came down to it, it was nothing like he thought.

Now he'd have to go back to the hole he'd cut in the fence and retrieve the clothing he had thrown away and hunt up a hiding place until he could think of something else.

Beyond the corner of the warehouse he heard the harsh, dull grate of metal, and he took another look.

The robots had broken up their line and were streaming back toward the warehouse and a dozen or so of them were wheeling the ramp away from the cargo port. Three humans, all dressed in uniform, were walking toward the ship, heading for the ladder, and one of them carried a batch of papers in his hand.

The loading was all done and the ship about to lift and here he was, not more than a thousand feet away, and all that he could do was stand and see it go.

There had to be a way, he told himself, to get in that ship. If he could only do it his troubles would be over—or at least the first of his troubles would be over.

Suddenly it struck him like a hand across the face. There was a way to do it! He'd stood here, blubbering, when all the time there had been a way to do it!

In the ship, he'd thought. And that was not necessary. He didn't have to be *in* the ship.

He started running, out into the darkness, far out so he could circle round and come upon the ship from the other side, so that the ship would be between him and the flood lights on the warehouse. He hoped that there was time.

He thudded out across the port, running in an arc, and came up to the ship and there was no sign as yet that it was about to leave.

Frantically he dug into his attachments bag and found the things he needed—the last things in that bag he'd ever thought he'd need. He found the suction discs and put them on, one for each knee, one for each elbow, one for each sole and wrist.

He strapped the kit about his waist and clambered up one of the mighty fins, using the discs to pull himself awkwardly along. It was not easy. He had never used the discs and there was a trick to using them, the trick of getting one clamped down and then working loose another so that he could climb.

But he had to do it. He had no choice but to do it.

He climbed the fin and there was the vast steel body of the craft rising far above him, like a metal wall climbing to the sky, broken by the narrow line of a row of anchor posts that ran lengthwise of the hull—and all that huge extent of metal painted by the faint, illusive shine of starlight that glittered in his eyes.

Foot by foot he worked his way up the metal wall. Like a humping caterpillar, he squirmed his way and with each foot he gained he was a bit more thankful.

Then he heard the faint beginning of a rumble and with the rumble came terror. His suction cups, he knew, might not long survive the booming vibration of the wakening rockets, certainly would not hold for a moment when the ship began to climb.

Six feet above him lay his only hope—the final anchor post in the long row of anchor posts.

Savagely he drove himself up the barrel of the shuddering craft, hugging the steely surface like a desperate fly.

The rumble of the tubes built up to blot out all the world and he climbed in a haze of almost prayerful, brittle hope. He reached that anchor post or he was as good as dead. Should he slip and drop into that pit of flaming gases beneath the rocket mouths, he was done for.

Once a cup came loose and he almost fell, but the others held and he caught himself.

With a desperate, almost careless lunge, he hurled himself up the wall of metal and caught the rung in his fingertips and held on with a concentration of effort that wiped out all else.

The rumble was a screaming fury now that lanced through brain and body. Then the screaming ended and became a throaty roar of power and the vibration left the ship entirely. From one corner of his eye he saw the lights of the spaceport swinging over gently on their side.

Carefully, slowly, he pulled himself along the steel until he had a better grip upon the rung, but even with the better grip he had the feeling that some great hand had him in its fist and was swinging him in anger in a hundred-mile-long arc.

Then the tubes left off their howling and there was a terrible silence and the stars were there, up above him and to either side of him, and they were steely stars with no twinkle in them. Down below, he knew, a lonely Earth was swinging, but he could not see it.

He pulled himself up against the rung and thrust a leg beneath it and sat up on the hull.

There were more stars than he'd ever seen before, more than he'd dreamed there could be. They were still and cold, like hard points of light against a velvet curtain; there was no glitter and no twinkle in them and it was as if a million eyes were staring down at him. The Sun was underneath the ship and over to one side; just at the edge of the left-hand curvature was the glare of it against the silent metal, a sliver of reflected light outlining one edge of the ship. The Earth was far astern, a ghostly blue-green ball hanging in the void, ringed by the fleecy halo of its atmosphere.

It was as if he were detached, a lonely, floating brain that looked out upon a thing it could not understand nor could ever try to understand; as if he might even be afraid of understanding it—a thing of mystery and delight so long as he retained an ignorance of it, but something fearsome and altogether overpowering once the ignorance had gone.

Richard Daniel sat there, flat upon his bottom, on the metal hull of the speeding ship and he felt the mystery and delight and the loneliness and the cold and the great uncaring and his mind retreated into a small and huddled, compact defensive ball.

He looked. That was all there was to do. It was all right now, he thought. But how long would he have to look at it? How long would he have to camp out here in the open—the most deadly kind of open?

He realized for the first time that he had no idea where the ship was going or how long it might take to get there. He knew it was a starship, which meant that it was bound beyond the solar system, and that meant that at some point in its flight it would enter hyperspace. He wondered, at first academically, and then with a twinge of fear, what hyperspace might do to one sitting naked to it. But there was little need, he thought philosophically, to fret about it now, for in due time he'd know, and there was not a thing that he could do about it—not a single thing.

He took the suction cups off his body and stowed them in his kit and then with one hand he tied the kit to one of the metal rungs and dug around in it until he found a short length of steel cable with a ring on one end and a snap on the other. He passed the ring end underneath a rung and threaded the snap end through it and snapped the snap onto a metal loop underneath his armpit. Now he was secured; he need not fear carelessly letting go and floating off the ship.

So here he was, he thought, neat as anything, going places fast, even if he had no idea where he might be headed, and now the only thing he needed was patience. He thought back, without much point, to what the religico had said in the study back on Earth. Patience and humility and prayer, he'd said, apparently not realizing at the moment that a robot has a world of patience.

It would take a lot of time, Richard Daniel knew, to get where he was going. But he had a lot of time, a lot more than any human, and he could afford to waste it. There were no urgencies, he thought—no need of food or air or water, no need of sleep or rest. There was nothing that could touch him.

Although, come to think of it, there might be.

There was the cold, for one. The space-hull was still fairly warm, with one side of it picking up the heat of the Sun and radiating it around the metal skin, where it was lost on the other side, but there would be a time when the Sun would dwindle until it had no heat and then he'd be subjected to the utter cold of space.

And what would the cold do to him. Might it make his body brittle? Might it interfere with the functioning of his brain? Might it do other things he could not even guess?

He felt the fears creep in again and tried to shrug them off and they drew off, but they still were there, lurking at the fringes of his mind.

The cold, and the loneliness, he thought—but he was one who could cope with loneliness. And if he couldn't, if he got too lonely, if he could no longer stand it, he could always beat a devil's tattoo on the hull and after a time of that someone would come out to investigate and they would haul him in.

But that was the last move of desperation, he told himself. For if they came out and found him, then he would be caught. Should he be forced to that extremity, he'd have lost everything—there would then have been no point in leaving Earth at all.

So he settled down, living out his time, keeping the creeping fears at bay just beyond the outposts of his mind, and looking at the universe all spread out before him.

The motors started up again with a pale blue flickering in the rockets at the stern and although there was no sense of acceleration he knew that the ship, now well off the Earth, had settled down to the long, hard drive to reach the speed of light.

Once they reached that speed they would enter hyperspace. He tried not to think of it, tried to tell himself there was not a thing to fear—but it hung there just ahead of him, the great unknowable.

The Sun shrank until it was only one of many stars and there came a time when he could no longer pick it out. And the cold clamped down but it didn't seem to bother him, although he could sense the coldness.

Maybe, he said in answer to his fear, that would be the way it would be with hyperspace as well. But he said it unconvincingly. The ship drove on and on with the weird blueness in the tubes.

Then there was the instant when his mind went splattering across the universe.

He was aware of the ship, but only aware of it in relation to an awareness of much else, and it was no anchor point, no rallying position. He was spread and scattered; he was opened out and rolled out until he was very thin. He was a dozen places, perhaps a hundred places, all at once, and it was confusing, and his immediate reaction was to fight back somehow against whatever might have happened to him—to fight back and pull himself together. The fighting did no good at all, but made it even worse, for in certain instances it seemed to drive parts of him farther from other parts of him and the confusion was made greater.

So he quit his fighting and his struggling and just lay there, scattered, and let the panic ebb away and told himself he didn't care, and wondered if he did.

Slow reason returned a dribble at a time and he could think again and he wondered rather bleakly if this could be hyperspace and was pretty sure it was. And if it were, he knew, he'd have a long time to live like this, a long time in which to become accustomed to it and to orient himself, a long time to find himself and pull himself together, a long time to understand this situation if it were, in fact, understandable.

So he lay, not caring greatly, with no fear or wonder, just resting and letting a fact seep into him here and there from many different points.

He knew that, somehow, his body—that part of him which housed the rest of him—was still chained securely to the ship, and that knowledge, in itself, he knew, was the first small step toward reorienting himself. He had to reorient, he knew. He had to come to some sort of terms, if not to understanding, with this situation.

He had opened up and he had scattered out—that essential part of him, the feeling and the knowing and the thinking part of him, and he lay thin across a universe that loomed immense in unreality.

Was this, he wondered, the way the universe should be, or was it the unchained universe, the wild universe beyond the limiting disciplines of measured space and time.

He started slowly reaching out, cautious as he had been in his crawling on the surface of the ship, reaching out toward the distant parts of him, a little at a time. He did not know how he did it, he was conscious of no particular technique, but whatever he was doing, it seemed to work, for he pulled himself together, bit by knowing bit, until he had gathered up all the scattered fragments of him into several different piles.

Then he quit and lay there, wherever there might be, and tried to sneak up on those piles of understanding that he took to be himself.

It took a while to get the hang of it, but once he did, some of the incomprehensibility went away, although the strangeness stayed. He tried to put it into thought and it was hard to do. The closest he could come was that he had been unchained as well as the universe—that whatever bondage had been imposed upon him by that chained and normal world had now become dissolved and he no longer was fenced in by either time or space.

He could see—and know and sense—across vast distances, if distance were the proper term, and he could understand certain facts that he had not even thought about before, could understand instinctively, but without the language or the skill to coalesce the facts into independent data.

Once again the universe was spread far out before him and it was a different and in some ways a better universe, a more diagrammatic universe, and in time, he knew, if there were such a thing as time, he'd gain some completer understanding and acceptance of it.

He probed and sensed and learned and there was no such thing as time, but a great foreverness.

He thought with pity of those others locked inside the ship, safe behind its insulating walls, never knowing all the glories of the innards of a star or the vast panoramic sweep of vision and of knowing far above the flat galactic plane.

Yet he really did not know what he saw or probed; he merely sensed and felt it and became a part of it, and it became a part of him—he seemed unable to reduce it to a formal outline of fact or of dimension or of content. It still remained a knowledge and a power so overwhelming that it was nebulous. There was no fear and no wonder, for in this place, it seemed, there was neither fear nor wonder. And he finally knew that it was a place apart, a world in which the normal space-time knowledge and emotion had no place at all and a normal space-time being could have no tools or measuring stick by which he might reduce it to a frame of reference.

There was no time, no space, no fear, no wonder—and no actual knowledge, either.

Then time came once again and suddenly his mind was stuffed back into its cage within his metal skull and he was again one with his body, trapped and chained and small and cold and naked.

He saw that the stars were different and that he was far from home and just a little way ahead was a star that blazed like a molten furnace hanging in the black.

He sat bereft, a small thing once again, and the universe reduced to package size.

Practically, he checked the cable that held him to the ship and it was intact. His attachments kit was still tied to its rung. Everything was exactly as it had been before.

He tried to recall the glories he had seen, tried to grasp again the fringe of knowledge which he had been so close to, but both the glory and the knowledge, if there had ever been a knowledge, had faded into nothingness.

He felt like weeping, but he could not weep, and he was too old to lie down upon the ship and kick his heels in tantrum.

So he sat there, looking at the sun that they were approaching and finally there was a planet that he knew must be their destination, and he found room to wonder what planet it might be and how far from Earth it was.

He heated up a little as the ship skipped through atmosphere as an aid to braking speed and he had some rather awful moments as it spiraled into thick and soupy gases that certainly were a far cry from the atmosphere of Earth. He hung most desperately to the rungs as the craft came mushing down onto a landing field, with the hot gases of the rockets curling up about him. But he made it safely and swiftly clambered down and darted off into the smog-like atmosphere before anyone could see him.

Safely off, he turned and looked back at the ship and despite its outlines being hidden by the drifting clouds of swirling gases, he could see it clearly, not as an actual structure, but as a diagram. He looked at it wonderingly and there was something wrong with the diagram, something vaguely wrong, some part of it that was out of whack and not the way it should be.

He heard the clanking of cargo haulers coming out upon the field and he wasted no more time, diagram or not.

He drifted back, deeper in the mists, and began to circle, keeping a good distance from the ship. Finally he came to the spaceport's edge and the beginning of the town.

He found a street and walked down it leisurely and there was a wrongness in the town.

He met a few hurrying robots who were in too much of a rush to pass the time of day. But he met no humans.

And that, he knew quite suddenly, was the wrongness of the place. It was not a human town.

There were no distinctly human buildings—no stores or residences, no churches and no restaurants. There were gaunt shelter barracks and sheds for the storing of equipment and machines, great sprawling warehouses and vast industrial plants. But that was all there was. It was a bare and dismal place compared to the streets that he had known on Earth.

It was a robot town, he knew. And a robot planet. A world that was barred to humans, a place where humans could not live, but so rich in some natural resource that it cried for exploitation. And the answer to that exploitation was to let the robots do it.

Luck, he told himself. His good luck still was holding. He had literally been dumped into a place where he could live without human interference. Here, on this planet, he would be with his own.

If that was what he wanted. And he wondered if it was. He wondered just exactly what it was he wanted, for he'd had no time to think of what he wanted. He had been too intent on fleeing Earth to think too much about it. He had known all along what he was running from, but had not considered what he might be running to.

He walked a little farther and the town came to an end. The

street became a path and went wandering on into the wind-blown fogginess.

So he turned around and went back up the street.

There had been one barracks, he remembered, that had a TRANSIENTS sign hung out, and he made his way to it.

Inside, an ancient robot sat behind the desk. His body was old-fashioned and somehow familiar. And it was familiar, Richard Daniel knew, because it was as old and battered and as out-of-date as his.

He looked at the body, just a bit aghast, and saw that while it resembled his, there were little differences. The same ancient model, certainly, but a different series. Possibly a little newer, by twenty years or so, than his.

"Good evening, stranger," said the ancient robot. "You came in on the ship?"

Richard Daniel nodded.

"You'll be staying till the next one?"

"I may be settling down," said Richard Daniel. "I may want to stay here."

The ancient robot took a key from off a hook and laid it on the desk.

"You representing someone?"

"No," said Richard Daniel.

"I thought maybe that you were. We get a lot of representatives. Humans can't come here, or don't want to come, so they send robots out here to represent them."

"You have a lot of visitors?"

"Some. Mostly the representatives I was telling you about. But there are some that are on the lam. I'd take it, mister, you are on the lam."

Richard Daniel didn't answer.

"It's all right," the ancient one assured him. "We don't mind at all, just so you behave yourself. Some of our most prominent citizens, they came here on the lam."

"That is fine," said Richard Daniel. "And how about yourself? You must be on the lam as well."

"You mean this body. Well, that's a little different. This here is punishment."

"Punishment?"

"Well, you see, I was the foreman of the cargo warehouse and I got to goofing off. So they hauled me up and had a trial and they found me guilty. Then they stuck me into this old body and I have to stay in it, at this lousy job, until they get another criminal that needs punishment. They can't punish no more than one criminal at a time because this is the only old body that they have. Funny thing about this body. One of the boys went back to Earth on a business trip and found this old heap of metal in a junkyard and brought it home with him—for a joke, I guess. Like a human might buy a skeleton for a joke, you know."

He took a long, sly look at Richard Daniel. "It looks to me, stranger, as if your body . . ."

But Richard Daniel didn't let him finish.

"I take it," Richard Daniel said, "you haven't many criminals."

"No," said the ancient robot sadly, "we're generally a pretty solid lot."

Richard Daniel reached out to pick up the key, but the ancient robot put out his hand and covered it.

"Since you are on the lam," he said, "it'll be payment in advance."

"I'll pay you for a week," said Richard Daniel, handing him some money.

The robot gave him back his change.

"One thing I forgot to tell you. You'll have to get plasticated."

"Plasticated?"

"That's right. Get plastic squirted over you to protect you from the atmosphere. It plays hell with metal. There's a place next door will do it."

"Thanks. I'll get it done immediately."

"It wears off," warned the ancient one. "You have to get a new job every week or so."

Richard Daniel took the key and went down the corridor until he found his numbered cubicle. He unlocked the door and stepped inside. The room was small, but clean. It had a desk and chair and that was all it had.

He stowed his attachments bag in one corner and sat down in the chair and tried to feel at home. But he couldn't feel at home, and that was a funny thing—he'd just rented himself a home.

He sat there, thinking back, and tried to whip up some sense of triumph at having done so well in covering his tracks. He couldn't.

Maybe this wasn't the place for him, he thought. Maybe he'd be happier on some other planet. Perhaps he should go back to the ship and get on it once again and have a look at the next planet coming up.

If he hurried, he might make it. But he'd have to hurry, for the ship wouldn't stay longer than it took to unload the consignment for this place and take on new cargo.

He got up from the chair, still only half decided.

And suddenly he remembered how, standing in the swirling mistiness, he had seen the ship as a diagram rather than a ship, and as he thought about it, something clicked inside his brain and he leaped toward the door.

For now he knew what had been wrong with the spaceship's diagram—an injector valve was somehow out of kilter, he had to get back there before the ship took off again.

He went through the door and down the corridor. He caught sight of the ancient robot's startled face as he ran across the lobby and out into the street. Pounding steadily toward the spaceport, he tried to get the diagram into his mind again, but it would not come complete—it came in bits and pieces, but not all of it.

And even as he fought for the entire diagram, he heard the beginning take-off rumble.

"Wait!" he yelled. "Wait for me! You can't . . ."

There was a flash that turned the world pure white and a mighty invisible wave came swishing out of nowhere and sent him reeling down the street, falling as he reeled. He was skidding on the cobblestones and sparks were flying as his metal scraped along the stone.

The whiteness reached a brilliance that almost blinded him and then it faded swiftly and the world was dark.

He brought up against a wall of some sort, clanging as he hit, and he lay there, blind from the brilliance of the flash, while his mind went scurrying down the trail of the diagram.

The diagram, he thought—why should he have seen a diagram of the ship he'd ridden through space, a diagram that had shown an injector out of whack? And how could he, of all robots, recognize an injector, let alone know there was something wrong with it. It had been a joke back home, among the Barringtons, that he, a mechanical thing himself, should have no aptitude at all for mechanical contraptions. And he could have saved those people and the ship—he could have saved them all if he'd immediately recognized the significance of the diagram. But he'd been too slow and stupid and now they all were dead.

The darkness had receded from his eyes and he could see again and he got slowly to his feet, feeling himself all over to see how badly he was hurt. Except for a dent or two, he seemed to be all right.

There were robots running in the street, heading for the spaceport, where a dozen fires were burning and where sheds and other structures had been flattened by the blast.

Someone tugged at his elbow and he turned around. It was the ancient robot.

"You're the lucky one," the ancient robot said. "You got off it just in time."

Richard Daniel nodded dumbly and had a terrible thought: What if they should think he did it? He had gotten off the ship; he had admitted that he was on the lam; he had rushed out suddenly, just a few seconds before the ship exploded. It would be easy to put it all together—that he had sabotaged the ship, then at the last instant had rushed out, remorseful, to undo what he had done. On the face of it, it was damning evidence.

But it was all right as yet, Richard Daniel told himself. For the ancient robot was the only one that knew—he was the only one he'd talked to, the only one who even knew that he was in town.

There was a way, Richard Daniel thought—there was an easy way. He pushed the thought away, but it came back. You are on your own, it said. You are already beyond the law. In rejecting human law, you made yourself an outlaw. You have become fair prey. There is just one law for you—self preservation.

But there are robot laws, Richard Daniel argued. There are laws and courts in this community. There is a place for justice.

Community law, said the leech clinging in his brain, provincial law, little more than tribal law—and the stranger's always wrong.

Richard Daniel felt the coldness of the fear closing down upon him and he knew, without half thinking, that the leech was right.

He turned around and started down the street, heading for the transients barracks. Something unseen in the street caught his foot and he stumbled and went down. He scrabbled to his knees, hunting in the darkness on the cobblestones for the thing that tripped him. It was a heavy bar of steel, some part of the wreckage that had been hurled this far. He gripped it by one end and arose.

"Sorry," said the ancient robot. "You have to watch your step."

And there was a faint implication in his words—a hint of something more than the words had said, a hint of secret gloating in a secret knowledge.

You have broken other laws, said the leech in Richard Daniel's brain. What of breaking just one more? Why, if necessary, not break a hundred more. It is all or nothing. Having come this far, you can't afford to fail. You can allow no one to stand in your way now.

The ancient robot half turned away and Richard Daniel lifted up the bar of steel, and suddenly the ancient robot no longer was a robot, but a diagram. There, with all the details of a blueprint, were all the working parts, all the mechanism of the robot that walked in the street before him. And if one detached that single bit of wire, if one burned out that coil, if—

Even as he thought it, the diagram went away and there was the robot, a stumbling, falling robot that clanged on the cobblestones.

Richard Daniel swung around in terror, looking up the street, but there was no one near.

He turned back to the fallen robot and quietly knelt beside him. He gently put the bar of steel down into the street. And he felt a thankfulness—for, almost miraculously, he had not killed.

The robot on the cobblestones was motionless. When Richard Daniel lifted him, he dangled. And yet he was all right. All anyone had to do to bring him back to life was to repair whatever damage had been done his body. And that served the purpose, Richard Daniel told himself, as well as killing would have done.

He stood with the robot in his arms, looking for a place to hide him.

He spied an alley between two buildings and darted into it. One of the buildings, he saw, was set upon stone blocks sunk into the ground, leaving a clearance of a foot or so. He knelt and shoved the robot underneath the building. Then he stood up and brushed the dirt and dust from his body.

Back at the barracks and in his cubicle, he found a rag and cleaned up the dirt that he had missed. And, he thought hard.

He'd seen the ship as a diagram and, not knowing what it meant, hadn't done a thing. Just now he'd seen the ancient robot as a diagram and had most decisively and neatly used that diagram to save himself from murder—from the murder that he was fully ready to commit.

But how had he done it? And the answer seemed to be that he really had done nothing. He'd simply thought that one should detach a single wire, burn out a single coil—he'd thought it and it was done.

Perhaps he'd seen no diagram at all. Perhaps the diagram was no more than some sort of psychic rationalization to mask whatever he had seen or sensed. Seeing the ship and robot with the surfaces stripped away from them and their purpose and their function revealed fully to his view, he had sought some explanation of his strange ability, and his subconscious mind had devised an explanation, an analogy that, for the moment, had served to satisfy him.

Like when he'd been in hyperspace, he thought. He'd seen a lot of things out there he had not understood. And that was it, of course, he thought excitedly. Something had happened to him out in hyperspace. Perhaps there'd been something that had stretched his mind. Perhaps he'd picked up some sort of new dimension-seeing, some new twist to his mind.

He remembered how, back on the ship again, with his mind wiped clean of all the glory and the knowledge, he had felt like weeping. But now he knew that it had been much too soon for weeping. For although the glory and the knowledge (if there'd been a knowledge) had been lost to him, he had not lost everything. He'd gained a new perceptive device and the ability to use it somewhat fumblingly—and it didn't really matter that he still was at a loss as to what he did to use it. The basic fact that he possessed it and could use it was enough to start with.

Somewhere out in front there was someone calling—someone, he now realized, who had been calling for some little time. . . .

"Hubert, where are you? Hubert, are you around? Hubert . . ."

Hubert?

Could Hubert be the ancient robot? Could they have missed him already?

Richard Daniel jumped to his feet for an undecided moment, listening to the calling voice. And then sat down again. Let them call, he told himself. Let them go out and hunt. He was safe in this cubicle. He had rented it and for the moment it was home and there was no one who would dare break in upon him.

But it wasn't home. No matter how hard he tried to tell himself it was, it wasn't. There wasn't any home.

Earth was home, he thought. And not all of Earth, but just a certain street and that one part of it was barred to him forever. It had been barred to him by the dying of a sweet old lady who had outlived her time; it had been barred to him by his running from it.

He did not belong on this planet, he admitted to himself, nor on any other planet. He belonged on Earth, with the Barringtons, and it was impossible for him to be there.

Perhaps, he thought, he should have stayed and let them reorient him. He remembered what the lawyer had said about memories that could become a burden and a torment. After all, it might have been wiser to have started over once again.

For what kind of future did he have, with his old outdated body, his old outdated brain? The kind of body that they put a robot into on this planet by way of punishment. And the kind of brain—but the brain was different, for he had something now that made up for any lack of more modern mental tools.

He sat and listened, and he heard the house—calling all across the light years of space for him to come back to it again. And he saw the faded living room with all its vanished glory that made a record of the years. He remembered, with a twinge of hurt, the little room back of the kitchen that had been his very own.

He arose and paced up and down the cubicle—three steps and turn, and then three more steps and turn for another three.

The sights and sounds and smells of home grew close and wrapped themselves about him and he wondered wildly if he might not have the power, a power accorded him by the universe of hyperspace, to will himself to that familiar street again.

He shuddered at the thought of it, afraid of another power, afraid that it might happen. Afraid of himself, perhaps, of the snarled and tangled being he was—no longer the faithful, shining servant, but a sort of mad thing that rode outside a spaceship, that was ready to kill another being, that could face up to the appalling sweep of hyperspace, yet cowered before the impact of a memory.

What he needed was a walk, he thought. Look over the town and maybe go out into the country. Besides, he remembered, trying to become practical, he'd need to get that plastication job he had been warned to get.

He went out into the corridor and strode briskly down it and was crossing the lobby when someone spoke to him.

"Hubert," said the voice, "just where have you been? I've been waiting hours for you."

Richard Daniel spun around and a robot sat behind the desk. There was another robot leaning in a corner and there was a naked robot brain lying on the desk.

"You are Hubert, aren't you," asked the one behind the desk. Richard Daniel opened up his mouth to speak, but the words refused to come.

"I thought so," said the robot. "You may not recognize me, but my name is Andy. The regular man was busy, so the judge sent me. He thought it was only fair we make the switch as quickly as possible. He said you'd served a longer term than you really should. Figures you'd be glad to know they'd convicted someone else."

Richard Daniel stared in horror at the naked brain lying on the desk.

The robot gestured at the metal body propped into the corner.

"Better than when we took you out of it," he said with a throaty chuckle. "Fixed it up and polished it and got out all the dents. Even modernized it some. Brought it strictly up to date. You'll have a better body than you had when they stuck you into that monstrosity."

"I don't know what to say," said Richard Daniel, stammering. "You see, I'm not . . ."

"Oh, that's all right," said the other happily. "No need for gratitude. Your sentence worked out longer than the judge expected. This just makes up for it."

"I thank you, then," said Richard Daniel. "I thank you very much."

And was astounded at himself, astonished at the ease with which he said it, confounded at his sly duplicity.

But if they forced it on him, why should he refuse? There was nothing that he needed more than a modern body!

It was still working out, he told himself. He was still riding luck. For this was the last thing that he needed to cover up his tracks.

"All newly plasticated and everything," said Andy. "Hans did an extra special job."

"Well, then," said Richard Daniel, "let's get on with it."

The other robot grinned. "I don't blame you for being anxious to get out of there. It must be pretty terrible to live in a pile of junk like that."

He came around from behind the desk and advanced on Richard Daniel.

"Over in the corner," he said, "and kind of prop yourself. I don't want you tipping over when I disconnect you. One good fall and that body'll come apart."

"All right," said Richard Daniel. He went into the corner and leaned back against it and planted his feet solid so that he was propped.

He had a rather awful moment when Andy disconnected the optic nerve and he lost his eyes and there was considerable queasiness in having his skull lifted off his shoulders and he was in sheer funk as the final disconnections were being swiftly made.

Then he was a blob of grayness without body or a head or eyes or anything at all. He was no more than a bundle of thoughts all wrapped around themselves like a pail of worms and this pail of worms was suspended in pure nothingness.

Fear came to him, a taunting, terrible fear. What if this were just a sort of ghastly gag? What if they'd found out who he really was and what he'd done to Hubert? What if they took his brain and tucked it away somewhere for a year or two—or for a hundred years? It might be, he told himself, nothing more than their simple way of justice.

He hung onto himself and tried to fight the fear away, but the fear ebbed back and forth like a restless tide.

Time stretched out and out—far too long a time, far more time than one would need to switch a brain from one body to another. Although, he told himself, that might not be true at all. For in his present state he had no way in which to measure time. He had no external reference points by which to determine time.

Then suddenly he had eyes.

And he knew everything was all right.

One by one his senses were restored to him and he was back inside a body and he felt awkward in the body, for he was unaccustomed to it.

The first thing that he saw was his old and battered body propped into its corner and he felt a sharp regret at the sight of it and it seemed to him that he had played a dirty trick upon it. It deserved, he told himself, a better fate than this—a better fate than being left behind to serve as a shabby jailhouse on this outlandish planet. It had served him well for six hundred years and he should not be deserting it. But he was deserting it. He was, he told himself in contempt, becoming very expert at deserting his old friends. First the house back home and now his faithful body.

Then he remembered something else—all that money in the body!

"What's the matter, Hubert?" Andy asked.

He couldn't leave it there, Richard Daniel told himself, for he needed it. And besides, if he left it there, someone would surely find it later and it would be a give-away. He couldn't leave it there and it might not be safe to forthrightly claim it. If he did, this other robot, this Andy, would think he'd been stealing on the job or running some side racket. He might try to bribe the other, but one could never tell how a move like that might go. Andy might be full of righteousness and then there'd be hell to pay. And besides, he didn't want to part with any of the money.

All at once he had it—he knew just what to do. And even as he thought it, he made Andy into a diagram.

That connection there, thought Richard Daniel, reaching out

his arms to catch the falling diagram that turned into a robot. He eased it to the floor and sprang across the room to the side of his old body. In seconds he had the chest safe open and the money safely out of it and locked inside his present body.

Then he made the robot on the floor become a diagram again and got the connection back the way that it should be.

Andy rose shakily off the floor. He looked at Richard Daniel in some consternation.

"What happened to me?" he asked in a frightened voice.

Richard Daniel sadly shook his head. "I don't know. You just keeled over. I started for the door to yell for help, then I heard you stirring and you were all right."

Andy was plainly puzzled. "Nothing like this ever happened to me before," he said.

"If I were you," counseled Richard Daniel, "I'd have myself checked over. You must have a faulty relay or a loose connection."

"I guess I will," the other one agreed. "It's downright dangerous."

He walked slowly to the desk and picked up the other brain, started with it toward the battered body leaning in the corner.

Then he stopped and said: "Look, I forgot. I was supposed to tell you. You better get up to the warehouse. Another ship is on its way. It will be coming in any minute now."

"Another one so soon?"

"You know how it goes," Andy said, disgusted. "They don't even try to keep a schedule here. We won't see one for months and then there'll be two or three at once."

"Well, thanks," said Richard Daniel, going out the door.

He went swinging down the street with a new-born confidence. And he had a feeling that there was nothing that could lick him, nothing that could stop him.

For he was a lucky robot!

Could all that luck, he wondered, have been gotten out in hyperspace, as his diagram ability, or whatever one might call it, had come from hyperspace? Somehow hyperspace had taken him and twisted him and changed him, had molded him anew, had made him into a different robot than he had been before.

Although, so far as luck was concerned, he had been lucky all his entire life. He'd had good luck with his human family and had gained a lot of favors and a high position and had been allowed to live for six hundred years. And that was a thing that never should have happened. No matter how powerful or influential the Barringtons had been, that six hundred years must be due in part to nothing but sheer luck.

In any case, the luck and the diagram ability gave him a solid edge over all the other robots he might meet. Could it, he asked himself, give him an edge on Man as well? *No*—that was a thought he should not think, for it was blasphemous. There never was a robot that would be the equal of a man.

But the thought kept on intruding and he felt not nearly so contrite over this leaning toward bad taste, or poor judgment, whichever it might be, as it seemed to him he should feel.

As he neared the spaceport, he began meeting other robots and some of them saluted him and called him by the name of Hubert and others stopped and shook him by the hand and told him they were glad that he was out of pokey.

This friendliness shook his confidence. He began to wonder if his luck would hold, for some of the robots, he was certain, thought it rather odd that he did not speak to them by name, and there had been a couple of remarks that he had some trouble fielding. He had a feeling that when he reached the warehouse he might be sunk without a trace, for he would know none of the robots there and he had not the least idea what his duties might include. And, come to think of it, he didn't even know where the warehouse was.

He felt the panic building in him and took a quick involuntary look around, seeking some method of escape. For it became quite apparent to him that he must never reach the warehouse.

He was trapped, he knew, and he couldn't keep on floating,

trusting to his luck. In the next few minutes he'd have to figure something.

He started to swing over into a side street, not knowing what he meant to do, but knowing he must do something, when he heard the mutter far above him and glanced up quickly to see the crimson glow of belching rocket tubes shimmering through the clouds.

He swung around again and sprinted desperately for the spaceport and reached it as the ship came chugging down to a steady landing. It was, he saw, an old ship. It had no burnish to it and it was blunt and squat and wore a hangdog look.

A tramp, he told himself, that knocked about from port to port, picking up whatever cargo it could, with perhaps now and then a paying passenger headed for some backwater planet where there was no scheduled service.

He waited as the cargo port came open and the ramp came down and then marched purposefully out onto the field, ahead of the straggling cargo crew, trudging toward the ship. He had to act, he knew, as if he had a perfect right to walk into the ship, as if he knew exactly what he might be doing. If there were a challenge he would pretend he didn't hear it and simply keep on going.

He walked swiftly up the ramp, holding back from running, and plunged through the accordion curtain that served as an atmosphere control. His feet rang across the metal plating of the cargo hold until he reached the catwalk and plunged down it to another cargo level.

At the bottom of the catwalk he stopped and stood tense, listening. Above him he heard the clang of a metal door and the sound of footsteps coming down the walk to the level just above him. That would be the purser or the first mate, he told himself, or perhaps the captain, coming down to arrange for the discharge of the cargo.

Quietly he moved away and found a corner where he could crouch and hide.

Above his head he heard the cargo gang at work, talking back and forth, then the screech of crating and the thump of bales and boxes being hauled out to the ramp.

Hours passed, or they seemed like hours, as he huddled there. He heard the cargo gang bringing something down from one of the upper levels and he made a sort of prayer that they'd not come down to this lower level—and he hoped no one would remember seeing him come in ahead of them, or if they did remember, that they would assume that he'd gone out again.

Finally it was over, with the footsteps gone. Then came the pounding of the ramp as it shipped itself and the banging of the port.

He waited for long minutes, waiting for the roar that, when it came, set his head to ringing, waiting for the monstrous vibration that shook and lifted up the ship and flung it off the planet

Then quiet came and he knew the ship was out of atmosphere and once more on its way.

And knew he had it made.

For now he was no more than a simple stowaway. He was no longer Richard Daniel, runaway from Earth. He'd dodged all the traps of Man, he'd covered all his tracks, and he was on his way.

But far down underneath he had a jumpy feeling, for it all had gone too smoothly, more smoothly than it should.

He tried to analyze himself, tried to pull himself in focus, tried to assess himself for what he had become.

He had abilities that Man had never won or developed or achieved, whichever it might be. He was a certain step ahead of not only other robots, but of Man as well. He had a thing, or the beginning of a thing, that Man had sought and studied and had tried to grasp for centuries and had failed.

A solemn and a deadly thought: was it possible that it was the robots, after all, for whom this great heritage had been meant? Would it be the robots who would achieve the paranormal powers that Man had sought so long, while Man, perforce, must remain content with the materialistic and the merely scientific? Was he, Richard Daniel, perhaps, only the first of many? Or was it all explained by no more than the fact that he alone had been exposed to hyperspace? Could this ability of his belong to anyone who would subject himself to the full, uninsulated mysteries of that mad universe unconstrained by time? Could Man have this, and more, if he too should expose himself to the utter randomness of unreality?

He huddled in his corner, with the thought and speculation stirring in his mind and he sought the answers, but there was no solid answer.

His mind went reaching out, almost on its own, and there was a diagram inside his brain, a portion of a blueprint, and bit by bit was added to it until it all was there, until the entire ship on which he rode was there, laid out for him to see.

He took his time and went over the diagram resting in his brain and he found little things—a fitting that was working loose and he tightened it, a printed circuit that was breaking down and getting mushy and he strengthened it and sharpened it and made it almost new, a pump that was leaking just a bit and he stopped its leaking.

Some hundreds of hours later one of the crewmen found him and took him to the captain.

The captain glowered at him.

"Who are you?" he asked.

"A stowaway," Richard Daniel told him.

"Your name," said the captain, drawing a sheet of paper before him and picking up a pencil, "your planet of residence and owner."

"I refuse to answer you," said Richard Daniel sharply and knew that the answer wasn't right, for it was not right and proper that a robot should refuse a human's direct command.

But the captain did not seem to mind. He laid down the pencil and stroked his black beard slyly.

"In that case," he said, "I can't exactly see how I can force the information from you. Although there might be some who'd try. You are very lucky that you stowed away on a ship whose captain is a most kind-hearted man."

He didn't look kind-hearted. He did look foxy.

Richard Daniel stood there, saying nothing.

"Of course," the captain said, "there's a serial number somewhere on your body and another on your brain. But I suppose that you'd resist if we tried to look for them."

"I am afraid I would."

"In that case," said the captain, "I don't think for the moment we'll concern ourselves with them."

Richard Daniel still said nothing, for he realized that there was no need to.

This crafty captain had it all worked out and he'd let it go at that.

"For a long time," said the captain, "my crew and I have been considering the acquiring of a robot, but it seems we never got around to it. For one thing, robots are expensive and our profits are not large."

He sighed and got up from his chair and looked Richard Daniel up and down.

"A splendid specimen," he said. "We welcome you aboard. You'll find us congenial."

"I am sure I will," said Richard Daniel. "I thank you for your courtesy."

"And now," the captain said, "you'll go up on the bridge and report to Mr. Duncan. I'll let him know you're coming. He'll find some light and pleasant duty for you."

Richard Daniel did not move as swiftly as he might, as sharply as the occasion might have called for, for all at once the captain had become a complex diagram. Not like the diagrams of ships or robots, but a diagram of strange symbols, some of which Richard Daniel knew were frankly chemical, but others which were not.

"You heard me!" snapped the captain. "Move!"

"Yes, sir," said Richard Daniel, willing the diagram away, making the captain come back again into his solid flesh.

Richard Daniel found the first mate on the bridge, a horse-faced, somber man with a streak of cruelty ill-hidden, and slumped in a chair to one side of the console was another of the crew, a sodden, terrible creature.

The sodden creature cackled. "Well, well, Duncan, the first non-human member of the *Rambler's* crew."

Duncan paid him no attention. He said to Richard Daniel: "I presume you are industrious and ambitious and would like to get along."

"Oh, yes," said Richard Daniel, and was surprised to find a new sensation—laughter—rising in himself.

"Well, then," said Duncan, "report to the engine room. They have work for you. When you have finished there, I'll find something else."

"Yes, sir," said Richard Daniel, turning on his heel.

"A minute," said the mate. "I must introduce you to our ship's physician, Dr. Abram Wells. You can be truly thankful you'll never stand in need of his services."

"Good day, Doctor," said Richard Daniel, most respectfully.

"I welcome you," said the doctor, pulling a bottle from his pocket. "I don't suppose you'll have a drink with me. Well, then, I'll drink to you."

Richard Daniel turned around and left. He went down to the engine room and was put to work at polishing and scrubbing and generally cleaning up. The place was in need of it. It had been years, apparently, since it had been cleaned or polished and it was about as dirty as an engine room can get—which is terribly dirty. After the engine room was done there were other places to be cleaned and furbished up and he spent endless hours at cleaning and in painting and shinning up the ship. The work was of the dullest kind, but he didn't mind. It gave him time to think and wonder, time to get himself sorted out and to become acquainted with himself, to try to plan ahead.

He was surprised at some of the things he found in himself. Contempt, for one—contempt for the humans on this ship. It took a long time for him to become satisfied that it was contempt, for he'd never held a human in contempt before.

But these were different humans, not the kind he'd known. These were no Barringtons. Although it might be, he realized, that he felt contempt for them because he knew them thoroughly. Never before had he known a human as he knew these humans. For he saw them not so much as living animals as intricate patternings of symbols. He knew what they were made of and the inner urgings that served as motivations, for the patterning was not of their bodies only, but of their minds as well. He had a little trouble with the symbology of their minds, for it was twisted and so interlocked and so utterly confusing that it was hard at first to read. But he finally got it figured out and there were times he wished he hadn't.

The ship stopped at many ports and Richard Daniel took charge of the loading and unloading, and he saw the planets, but was unimpressed. One was a nightmare of fiendish cold, with the very atmosphere turned to drifting snow. Another was a dripping, noisome jungle world, and still another was a bare expanse of broken, tumbled rock without a trace of life beyond the crew of humans and their robots who manned the huddled station in this howling wilderness.

It was after this planet that Jenks, the cook, went screaming to his bunk, twisted up with pain—the victim of a suddenly inflamed vermiform appendix.

Dr. Wells came tottering in to look at him, with a half-filled bottle sagging the pocket of his jacket. And later stood before the captain, holding out two hands that trembled, and with terror in his eyes.

"But I cannot operate," he blubbered. "I cannot take the chance. I would kill the man!"

He did not need to operate. Jenks suddenly improved. The pain went away and he got up from his bunk and went back to the galley and Dr. Wells sat huddled in his chair, bottle gripped between his hands, crying like a baby.

Down in the cargo hold, Richard Daniel sat likewise huddled and aghast that he had dared to do it—not that he had been able to, but that he had dared, that he, a robot, should have taken on himself an act of interference, however merciful, with the body of a human.

Actually, the performance had not been too difficult. It was, in a certain way, no more difficult than the repairing of an engine or the untangling of a faulty circuit. No more difficult—just a little different. And he wondered what he'd done and how he'd gone about it, for he did not know. He held the technique in his mind, of that there was ample demonstration, but he could in no wise isolate or pinpoint the pure mechanics of it. It was like an instinct, he thought—unexplainable, but entirely workable.

But a robot had no instinct. In that much he was different from the human and the other animals. Might not, he asked himself, this strange ability of his be a sort of compensating factor given to the robot for his very lack of instinct? Might that be why the human race had failed in its search for paranormal powers? Might the instincts of the body be at certain odds with the instincts of the mind?

For he had the feeling that this ability of his was just a mere beginning, that it was the first emergence of a vast body of abilities which some day would be rounded out by robots. And what would that spell, he wondered, in that distant day when the robots held and used the full body of that knowledge?

An adjunct to the glory of the human race, or equals of the human race, or superior to the human race—or, perhaps, a race apart?

And what was his role, he wondered. Was it meant that he should go out as a missionary, a messiah, to carry to robots throughout the universe the message that he held? There must be some reason for his having learned this truth. It could not be meant that he would hold it as a personal belonging, as an asset all his own.

He got up from where he sat and moved slowly back to the ship's forward area, which now gleamed spotlessly from the work he'd done on it, and he felt a certain pride.

He wondered why he had felt that it might be wrong, blasphemous, somehow, to announce his abilities to the world? Why had he not told those here in the ship that it had been he who had healed the cook, or mentioned the many other little things he'd done to maintain the ship in perfect running order?

Was it because he did not need respect, as a human did so urgently? Did glory have no basic meaning for a robot? Or was it because he held the humans in this ship in such utter contempt that their respect had no value to him?

And this contempt—was it because these men were meaner than other humans he had known, or was it because he now was greater than any human being? Would he ever again be able to look on any human as he had looked upon the Barringtons?

He had a feeling that if this were true, he would be the poorer for it. Too suddenly, the whole universe was home and he was alone in it and as yet he'd struck no bargain with it or himself.

The bargain would come later. He need only bide his time and work out his plans and his would be a name that would be spoken when his brain was scaling flakes of rust. For he was the emancipator, the messiah of the robots; he was the one who had been called to lead them from the wilderness.

"You!" a voice cried.

Richard Daniel wheeled around and saw it was the captain.

"What do you mean, walking past me as if you didn't see me?" asked the captain fiercely.

"I am sorry," Richard Daniel told him.

"You snubbed me!" raged the captain.

"I was thinking," Richard Daniel said.

"I'll give you something to think about," the captain yelled. "I'll work you till your tail drags. I'll teach the likes of you to get uppity with me!"

"As you wish," said Richard Daniel.

For it didn't matter. It made no difference to him at all what the captain did or thought. And he wondered why the respect even of a robot should mean so much to a human like the captain, why he should guard his small position with so much zeal-ousness.

"In another twenty hours," the captain said, "we hit another port."

"I know," said Richard Daniel. "Sleepy Hollow on Arcadia."

"All right, then," said the captain, "since you know so much, get down into the hold and get the cargo ready to unload. We been spending too much time in all these lousy ports loading and unloading. You been dogging it."

"Yes, sir," said Richard Daniel, turning back and heading for the hold.

He wondered faintly if he were still robot—or was he something else? Could a machine evolve, he wondered, as Man himself evolved? And if a machine evolved, whatever would it be? Not Man, of course, for it never could be that, but could it be machine?

He hauled out the cargo consigned to Sleepy Hollow and there was not too much of it. So little of it, perhaps, that none of the regular carriers would even consider its delivery, but dumped it off at the nearest terminal, leaving it for a roving tramp, like the *Rambler*, to carry eventually to its destination.

When they reached Arcadia, he waited until the thunder died and the ship was still. Then he shoved the lever that opened up the port and slid out the ramp.

The port came open ponderously and he saw blue skies and the green of trees and the far-off swirl of chimney smoke mounting in the sky.

He walked slowly forward until he stood upon the ramp and there lay Sleepy Hollow, a tiny, huddled village planted at the river's edge, with the forest as a background. The forest ran on every side to a horizon of climbing folded hills. Fields lay near the village, yellow with maturing crops, and he could see a dog sleeping in the sun outside a cabin door.

A man was climbing up the ramp toward him and there were others running from the village.

"You have cargo for us?" asked the man.

"A small consignment," Richard Daniel told him. "You have something to put on?"

The man had a weatherbeaten look and he'd missed several haircuts and he had not shaved for days. His clothes were rough and sweat-stained and his hands were strong and awkward with hard work.

"A small shipment," said the man. "You'll have to wait until we bring it up. We had no warning you were coming. Our radio is broken."

"You go and get it," said Richard Daniel. "I'll start unloading."

He had the cargo half unloaded when the captain came storming down into the hold. What was going on, he yelled. How long would they have to wait? "God knows we're losing money as it is even stopping at this place."

"That may be true," Richard Daniel agreed, "but you knew that when you took the cargo on. There'll be other cargos and goodwill is something . . ."

"Goodwill be damned!" the captain roared. "How do I know I'll ever see this place again?"

Richard Daniel continued unloading cargo.

"You," the captain shouted, "go down to that village and tell them I'll wait no longer than an hour . . ."

"But this cargo, sir?"

"I'll get the crew at it. Now, jump!"

So Richard Daniel left the cargo and went down into the village.

He went across the meadow that lay between the spaceport and the village, following the rutted wagon tracks, and it was a pleasant walk. He realized with surprise that this was the first time he'd been on solid ground since he'd left the robot planet. He wondered briefly what the name of that planet might have been, for he had never known. Nor what its importance was, why the robots might be there or what they might be doing. And he wondered, too, with a twinge of guilt, if they'd found Hubert yet.

And where might Earth be now? he asked himself. In what

direction did it lie and how far away? Although it didn't really matter, for he was done with Earth.

He had fled from Earth and gained something in his fleeing. He had escaped all the traps of Earth and all the snares of Man. What he held was his, to do with as he pleased, for he was no man's robot, despite what the captain thought.

He walked across the meadow and saw that this planet was very much like Earth. It had the same soft feel about it, the same simplicity. It had far distances and there was a sense of freedom.

He came into the village and heard the muted gurgle of the river running and the distant shouts of children at their play and in one of the cabins a sick child was crying with lost helplessness.

He passed the cabin where the dog was sleeping and it came awake and stalked growling to the gate. When he passed it followed him, still growling, at a distance that was safe and sensible.

An autumnal calm lay upon the village, a sense of gold and lavender, and tranquility hung in the silences between the crying of the baby and the shouting of the children.

There were women at the windows looking out at him and others at the doors and the dog still followed, but his growls had stilled and now he trotted with prick-eared curiosity.

Richard Daniel stopped in the street and looked around him and the dog sat down and watched him and it was almost as if time itself had stilled and the little village lay divorced from all the universe, an arrested microsecond, an encapsulated acreage that stood sharp in all its truth and purpose.

Standing there, he sensed the village and the people in it, almost as if he had summoned up a diagram of it, although if there were a diagram, he was not aware of it.

It seemed almost as if the village were the Earth, a transplanted Earth with the old primeval problems and hopes of Earth—a family of peoples that faced existence with a readiness and confidence and inner strength.

From down the street he heard the creak of wagons and saw

them coming around the bend, three wagons piled high and heading for the ship.

He stood and waited for them and as he waited the dog edged a little closer and sat regarding him with a not-quite-friendliness.

The wagons came up to him and stopped.

"Pharmaceutical materials, mostly," said the man who sat atop the first load, "It is the only thing we have that is worth the shipping."

"You seem to have a lot of it," Richard Daniel told him.

The man shook his head. "It's not so much. It's almost three years since a ship's been here. We'll have to wait another three, or more perhaps, before we see another."

He spat down on the ground.

"Sometimes it seems," he said, "that we're at the tail-end of nowhere. There are times we wonder if there is a soul that remembers we are here."

From the direction of the ship, Richard Daniel heard the faint, strained violence of the captain's roaring.

"You'd better get on up there and unload," he told the man. "The captain is just sore enough he might not wait for you."

The man chuckled thinly. "I guess that's up to him," he said.

He flapped the reins and clucked good-naturedly at the horses.

"Hop up here with me," he said to Richard Daniel. "Or would you rather walk?"

"I'm not going with you," Richard Daniel said. "I am staying here. You can tell the captain."

For there was a baby sick and crying. There was a radio to fix. There was a culture to be planned and guided. There was a lot of work to do. This place, of all the places he had seen, had actual need of him.

The man chuckled once again. "The captain will not like it."

"Then tell him," said Richard Daniel, "to come down and talk to me. I am my own robot. I owe the captain nothing. I have more than paid any debt I owe him."

The wagon wheels began to turn and the man flapped the reins again.

"Make yourself at home," he said. "We're glad to have you stay."

"Thank you, sir," said Richard Daniel. "I'm pleased you want me."

He stood aside and watched the wagons lumber past, their wheels lifting and dropping thin films of powdered earth that floated in the air as an acrid dust.

Make yourself at home, the man had said before he'd driven off. And the words had a full round ring to them and a feel of warmth. It had been a long time, Richard Daniel thought, since he'd had a home.

A chance for resting and for knowing—that was what he needed. And a chance to serve, for now he knew that was the purpose in him. That was, perhaps, the real reason he was staying—because these people needed him . . . and he needed, queer as it might seem, this very need of theirs. Here on this Earth-like planet, through the generations, a new Earth would arise. And perhaps, given only time, he could transfer to the people of the planet all the powers and understanding he would find inside himself.

And stood astounded at the thought, for he'd not believed that he had it in him, this willing, almost eager, sacrifice. No messiah now, no robotic liberator, but a simple teacher of the human race.

Perhaps that had been the reason for it all from the first beginning. Perhaps all that had happened had been no more than the working out of human destiny. If the human race could not attain directly the paranormal power he held, this instinct of the mind, then they would gain it indirectly through the agency of one of their creations. Perhaps this, after all, unknown to Man himself, had been the prime purpose of the robots.

He turned and walked slowly down the length of the village street, his back turned to the ship and the roaring of the captain, walked contentedly into this new world he'd found, into this world that he would make—not for himself, nor for robotic glory, but for a better Mankind and a happier.

Less than an hour before he'd congratulated himself on escaping all the traps of Earth, all the snares of Man. Not knowing that the greatest trap of all, the final and the fatal trap, lay on this present planet.

But that was wrong, he told himself. The trap had not been on this world at all, nor any other world. It had been inside himself.

He walked serenely down the wagon-rutted track in the soft, golden afternoon of a matchless autumn day, with the dog trotting at his heels.

Somewhere, just down the street, the sick baby lay crying in its crib.

CLIFFORD D. SIMAK, during his fifty-five year career, produced some of the most iconic science fiction stories ever written. Born in 1904 on a farm in southwestern Wisconsin, Simak got a job at a small-town newspaper in 1929 and eventually became news editor of the *Minneapolis Star-Tribune,* writing fiction in his spare time.

Simak was best known for the book *City,* a reaction to the horrors of World War II, and for his novel *Way Station.* In 1953 *City* was awarded the International Fantasy Award, and in following years, Simak won three Hugo Awards and a Nebula Award. In 1977 he became the third Grand Master of the Science Fiction and Fantasy Writers of America, and before his death in 1988, he was named one of three inaugural winners of the Horror Writers Association's Bram Stoker Award for Lifetime Achievement.

DAVID W. WIXON was a close friend of Clifford D. Simak's. As Simak's health declined, Wixon, already familiar with science fiction publishing, began more and more to handle such things as his friend's business correspondence and contract matters. Named literary executor of the estate after Simak's death, Wixon began a long-term project to secure the rights to all of Simak's stories and find a way to make them available to readers who, given the fifty-five-year span of Simak's writing career, might never have gotten the chance to enjoy all of his short fiction. Along the way, Wixon also read the author's surviving journals and rejected manuscripts, which made him uniquely able to provide Simak's readers with interesting and thought-provoking commentary that sheds new light on the work and thought of a great writer.

THE COMPLETE SHORT FICTION
OF CLIFFORD D. SIMAK

FROM OPEN ROAD MEDIA

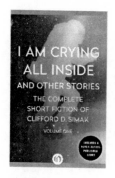  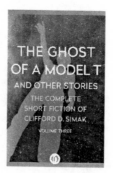

Available wherever ebooks are sold

OPEN ROAD

INTEGRATED MEDIA

Open Road Integrated Media is a digital publisher and multimedia content company. Open Road creates connections between authors and their audiences by marketing its ebooks through a new proprietary online platform, which uses premium video content and social media.

31901056611116

CPSIA information can be obtained at www.ICGtesting.com
Printed in the USA
BVOW04s2001011115

424471BV00001B/1/P